M000315556

BURYING THE LEDE

BURYING
THE LEDE

JOSEPH LEVALLEY

BookPress®
publishing

www.bookpresspublishing.com

Copyright © 2019 by Joseph LeValley. All rights reserved.

No portion of this book may be reproduced, stored in a retrieval system, or transmitted in any form or by any means—electronic, mechanical, photocopy, recording, scanning, or other—except for brief quotations in critical reviews or articles, without prior written permission of the publisher. Requests to the publisher for permission or information should be submitted via email at info@bookpresspublishing.com.

Any requests or questions for the author should be submitted to him directly at levalleyjoseph@gmail.com.

This is a work of fiction. Names, characters, businesses, places, events, locales, and incidents are either the products of the author's imagination or used in a fictitious manner. Any resemblance to actual persons, living or dead, or actual events is purely coincidental.

Published in Des Moines, Iowa, by:

Bookpress Publishing
P.O. Box 71532
Des Moines, IA 50325
www.BookpressPublishing.com

Publisher's Cataloging-in-Publication Data

Names: LeValley, Joseph Darl, author.
Title: Burying the Lede / Joseph LeValley.
Description: Des Moines, IA: Bookpress Publishing, 2019.
Identifiers: ISBN 978-0-9967616-7-3 | LCCN 2018955047
Subjects: LCSH: Governors--Election--Fiction. | Murder--Fiction. | Journalism--Fiction. | Iowa--Fiction. | BISAC: FICTION / Mystery & Detective / General
Classification: LCC PS3612.E92311 B87 2019 | DDC 813.6-- dc23

First Edition
Printed in the United States of America
10 9 8 7 6 5 4 3 2 1

"The truth is rarely pure and never simple."

— *Oscar Wilde*

bury the lede

To "bury the lede" is to begin the article with background information or details of secondary importance to the readers, forcing them to read more deeply into an article than they should have to in order to discover the essential point(s).

Cotter, C. (2010). *News talk: Investigating the language of journalism.* Cambridge University Press. p. 167

Chapter 1

It was simple. The couple had to die. The killer didn't know why and didn't care. He got the call with all the information he needed: who, where, when, and in this case, how. It was just before midnight when he drove the stolen 1993 Chevy Malibu to the couple's farmstead. Snow was falling steadily, but the near-zero temperature prevented the flakes from sticking to the windshield. Even with the wipers off, they just blew past. However, the wind-driven snow in the headlights made it difficult to see the gravel road. The man behind the wheel was pleased. He knew the way to the farmhouse, but the snow would lessen the chances of him being seen.

At the bottom of a long hill, the metal rails of an old bridge passed the car windows as the hollow sounds of the wooden bridge planks resounded through the floor of the car. After a brief *ka-lump*, *ka-lump*, he was back on gravel, climbing out of the valley. He peered into the snow, knowing the farmhouse lay at the top of the hill. As the car reached the crest, the road curved around a grove of trees to the right. The man slowed and turned off the headlights, creeping past the mailbox to the entrance of the lane. He turned, moving slowly to ensure the snow had not drifted too deeply across the lane. Halfway to the house, under the bare, looming branches of a huge tree, he stopped.

He shut off the engine and opened the driver's door. No interior light came on. The bulb lay on the passenger seat beside him. He turned and pulled himself out of the open door, standing to his full six feet, three inches. The brown work shoes felt cold and uncomfortable as they compacted the thin layer of snow. He stepped briskly to the rear of the car and opened the trunk. A light popped on. A mistake. "Shit," he said softly through clenched teeth. Anger flashed through him, and he instantly pushed the trunk lid down again. He quickly told himself to stay in control. Forgetting to remove the trunk light was a minor error. The rear of the car faced away from the house, so it was unlikely to be noticed from inside. He glanced over his shoulder through the snow to the road. No cars could be seen in either direction, so no harm was done. Besides, even if he was seen from a passing car, at this distance it almost certainly would aid in the deception. It occurred to the killer this would be especially true if he was wearing the kid's jacket. Not putting it on sooner might be considered mistake number two. The man wanted to curse again but held his tongue. It wasn't easy to control his frustration. These were blunders, and he had vowed there would be no blunders.

Slowly his calm returned. He re-lifted the trunk lid a few inches, reached through with his gloved hand, and twisted the bulb from its socket. He raised the lid to its full height, and in the relative safety of darkness and blowing snow, slipped out of his leather jacket. The wind blew right through his shirt and he quickly grabbed the yellow NAPA windbreaker from the trunk. The nylon material, stiff from the cold, did little to warm him, but he pulled it on and snapped it to the neck. He reached back into the trunk and removed a long, narrow case made of cheap vinyl. Corroded metal and the cold made the zipper difficult to maneuver, but he managed to open the end far enough to extract the rifle.

He shook his head in disgust. No self-respecting sportsman... hell, no man he had ever known would fail to provide at least basic care for his weapon. It was an old Remington .22 caliber single shot rifle – the kind fathers had been buying for their 12-year-old sons for generations of Christmases. It looked like it hadn't been cleaned since the first of those generations. He pulled a pen light from his pocket and knelt in the snow behind the car. A quick but close inspection of the rifle convinced him it would fire but reinforced his opinion of the loser who owned it and the piece of shit car from which he took it. *Pathetic*, he thought as he loaded a cartridge in the chamber and dropped another handful into the right pocket of the yellow jacket. He raised one eyebrow in mild surprise when the bolt opened easily and slid forward smoothly as he pushed the cartridge home. *It will do,* he thought, as he pushed the trunk lid softly down onto its latch and trudged through the snow toward the house.

A wooden porch wrapped around two sides of the house, serving the front door on the east and the back door on the south. A single light fixture hung by a wire stretched between the house and a small outbuilding. Its soft yellow light brought the snowflakes to life, dancing to the rhythm of the gusts of wind. The lane turned and widened on the south side. It was obvious the east door was seldom used. He walked past it and turned right, not hesitating as he moved into the light flickering across the south side of the porch. A quick examination of the stairs convinced him to sidle past them. Instead, he raised one leg high, found firm footing, and lightly pulled himself up onto the oak flooring of the porch. The boards creaked, but no more loudly than the shed or barn boards protesting the relentless wind. He paused only an instant to peer through the porch door, and then he turned the knob.

It was no surprise the door was unlocked. People living in rural Iowa never lock their doors. Even those with enemies feel isolated and safe, with miles of cornfields between them and the nearest town. The door was old and far from silent. As he pulled it open, the wood creaked and a long metal spring squeaked as it stretched. Quickly stepping through, never taking his hand from the knob, he turned and inched the door shut. A shuffle step to the left put him in a deep shadow where he waited, slowed his breathing, and listened. He was in an unheated mudroom with pegs on the inside wall and an old wooden barrel holding a broom and a snow shovel. On the pegs hung coveralls, sweatshirts, a seedcorn cap, and a couple of baseball gloves. There was no sign of pet supplies. *Good.* He had not expected any, and a dog would have been a very unwelcome surprise. A doorway led into the kitchen, beyond which was a wide archway. Through it, he could see the living room. As he stepped through the opening, the aroma changed immediately from farm animals to fresh cream and cinnamon.

He looked for the two young girls he knew were there and could just make them out through the darkness, asleep on the pullout couch in the living room. He tried to step lightly, cursing the work shoes and the old linoleum that crackled with each step. When he reached the archway, he could see clearly the small bodies wrapped in sleeping bags. An old TV set at the foot of the bed was off, but the picture tube emitted just the slightest glow in the darkness. The intruder looked left. The door to the stairway was precisely where he expected it. It was closed. He grasped the knob and turned it slowly. The door swung open silently. He contemplated two strategies from here. Climb as slowly and quietly as possible, risking the certain creaks and squeaks of the worn stairs, or bound up the stairs and end this quickly. He decided on the former and took one step up the narrow stairway and pulled the door shut behind him.

The upstairs was a single room with slanted ceilings and dormer windows, common in the upper half stories of the old farmhouses that still stood at the centers of some farmsteads. From the stairs, he could look straight up to the ceiling and see the glowing light fixture he had seen through the north window. He silently raised the rifle and gripped it with both hands. The thin, tight-fitting gloves added to his sense of control as he checked to be sure the safety was off and slid his trigger finger into place. As he tensed to resume his climb, he realized the couple upstairs was not asleep. He strained to hear, debating whether to abort. Then a wide grin spread across his face as he realized he was listening to the sounds of lovemaking. This provided a perfect distraction from any other noise in the house. The intruder climbed the rest of the stairs rapidly and confidently. He looked over his right shoulder into the room as he ascended past the edge of the stairway opening. The bed was at the far end of the dormer. He saw the woman first, from the back, and the sight of her nearly took his breath away. She was moving back and forth, riding her husband with an intensity that could have aroused a corpse. Beads of sweat inched down her back. She was so beautiful and so filled with passion. She was so *alive*.

Well, not anymore.

These thoughts came and went without slowing the killer's stride. He knew his only chance of failure would come from hesitating. He didn't.

When he pulled the trigger, slamming a bullet into the blonde woman's brain, he felt a pang of regret. It was not a familiar feeling. The man had killed before. Not often, but enough to know it never bothered him. He assumed it was why his boss always called him first. He could be relied on to do the job, do it right, and not think about it again. No spilling the beans to some babe during pillow talk or to the boys at the Iron Range Tap during a night of hard drinking. Once the job was done, he simply forgot about it and moved on. He supposed his lack of remorse defined him as some sort of sociopath. Yeah, he knew about sociopaths. He was smart. He read books. He knew he wasn't normal. But then, being a sociopath, he didn't let that bother him. This irony often brought a smile to his face. It was funny when he thought about it. But not tonight. Tonight he had a job to do.

"It's nothing personal," he said quietly as the blonde's head lurched forward and her body was thrown down onto her husband's chest. The man with the rifle moved right along with her, shoving another shell into the .22 as he stepped up onto the footboard of the bed.

The husband had just enough time to squeak out, "Oh my God...what? No! Please..." He clawed at his wife's lifeless body, trying to move. As he thrashed at her, he may have been trying to scream, but the noises from his mouth were muffled, terror seizing his vocal cords. Then even those stopped abruptly as he watched the man drop the gun toward his face. "Oh no, please," his voice rasped.

The killer calmly fired once more, directly into the husband's left eye. The second victim instantly fell silent. The killer reloaded twice more, firing a second shot into the head of each victim. As he headed down the stairs, he caught himself looking at the rifle almost in admiration. The .22 might be a child's rifle, but it was a perfect assassin's tool at close range. It left very little mess, and made little noise. He hoped it had made just enough to wake the girls downstairs. This thought reminded him to pull a ski mask from his back pocket and stretch it over his face. He adjusted the eyes and stepped through the door into the living room.

"Dad?" a small voice called out.

The killer said nothing but walked slowly past the pullout bed, turned right, and continued into the kitchen. He stopped in front of the kitchen counter and pried open the lid on the flour tin. He reached in his pocket, pulled out a plastic baggie, and pushed it down into the flour. After replacing the lid, he stepped quickly to the porch door, flipped up the switch next to the door turning on the kitchen light, and waited a beat, two beats. He could feel eyes on his back. Smiling inside the mask, he stepped out through the mudroom and into the cold wind. The weather hadn't changed since he had made the drive out to the farmhouse. Snow was still falling. It had the cold, icy feel of a January storm. One last task. With his back to the door, the killer punched hard backwards with his elbow, breaking out a pane of the door. *Best to have it look like the door had been locked,* he thought.

He glanced at his watch. He had been on the farmstead less than 12 minutes. Probably not long enough for anyone to have noticed the car parked in the middle of the lane, but if someone did, all the better. The car wasn't his. It belonged to that lazy-ass kid who was about to become the third victim of this little assignment.

When the killer reached the car, he turned and looked back at the house. The lone ceiling light in the bedroom shone from the upstairs window, the same as when he had arrived. It was an older, small house, probably built during World War II, when building supplies were scarce and expensive. Shadows in the farmyard jumped left then right, as the wind bullied the yard light on its wire. The killer appreciated the light. It had provided enough illumination to guide him, but not so much that he had worried about being seen. The car was parked nearly forty yards from the house, still in the shadows of the grove, but closer than he would have parked if the wind had not been carrying away the sound of his approach.

As he started the car he wondered if the girls had gone back to sleep, or if one of them was climbing the stairs to the parents' bedroom now. No matter. Even if they called 9-1-1 right now, the nearest deputy sheriff was more than twenty minutes away. The killer knew this to be a fact. He had planned very carefully.

***

As he drove down Main Street of Orney, Iowa, he saw the empty parking space on the side street next to the bowling alley – right where it had been when he had taken the maroon Chevy. There were perhaps a dozen cars and pickup trucks parked in the entire business district. He quickly turned the car into its space, shut off the engine, climbed out, and shut the door just firmly enough to make sure the latches caught. As soon as he reached the sidewalk, his stride slowed. He knew that now he was free of suspicion unless he created it by the way he behaved.

After taking care of one last piece of business in the back room at the Iron Range, the killer walked the last block to his own car. As he pushed the key into the lock, he could feel the cold tumblers resist turning. He slid into the seat and started the engine. As it warmed, he ran through the list in his mind one last time. The shoes, rifle, and NAPA jacket were back in the trunk of the Chevy; the light bulbs were back in their sockets in the trunk and in the passenger compartment; the ski mask and key were in his pocket but would soon be at the bottom of the well on his aunt's farm. The kid who owned the car was tucked away in the back room of the bar where he would wake up later. Nothing had been left in the borrowed car and nothing else had been touched. He wasn't really surprised to find he felt good. *Why the hell not?* he asked himself, thinking that, like all good soldiers, he had done what he had been told to do. He had done it well and without any unexpected complications. He didn't relish killing, but he was man enough to do the job that needed to be done, pleasant or not. It was no different than Iraq, he thought, except the face of the commanding officer had changed, the pay was better, and it was a hell of a lot colder.

He backed out of the parking space and drove the twenty-five blocks to the edge of town without even seeing another person. *God, how I love a small town,* he thought, smiling and shaking his head. As the glow of the streetlights disappeared in the blowing snow behind him, he turned on the radio. KIOA in Des Moines had a new overnight jock, a woman with a husky voice who was trying too hard to broadcast her sensuality across central Iowa. Her selection of classic rock, however, was just fine. As Roger Daltrey sang "Behind Blue Eyes," the killer leaned back into his seat and relaxed. It would be a leisurely drive out to his aunt's farm and then back home. He knew he would sleep soundly, at least until the call came, rousting him out of bed to tell him two young girls had found their parents dead in their home. *Well, won't I be surprised?* he thought sarcastically, and then let his mind go blank as he drove into the snowy winter night.

Town Crier

Couple Found Shot to Death in Rural Orney Home

Motive, Circumstances Are Mysteries

Tony Harrington, Staff Writer

ORNEY, Iowa – Jerry and Anne Ennis were found dead in the second-floor bedroom of their rural Orney home early Saturday morning, according to Quincy County Deputy Sheriff Daniel Bodke. The couple was discovered by one of their two young daughters, who had been asleep on the main floor of the home prior to the killings, Bodke said. Names and ages of the children were not released.

Bodke, who is the chief deputy in charge of criminal investigations, said it appeared the couple died of gunshot wounds to their heads, but the official cause of death would not be known until after examination by the county medical examiner.

When asked if the killings were a murder-suicide, Bodke said no further details would be released until after officials had a chance to conduct at least a preliminary investigation.

"However," Bodke said, "I discourage any speculation at this point regarding any aspect of the incident.

I also encourage the news media and the public to remember that two young girls have lost their parents. We should focus our attention on supporting and praying for them, and not on speculation about what might or might not have happened last night."

The Iowa Division of Criminal Investigation has been called to assist in the investigation. When asked, Bodke acknowledged the DCI mobile crime lab was already at the scene where the bodies were found.

He declined to comment about the condition or location of the two daughters, except to say they had been taken out of the county and would be staying with relatives.

No further information will be released until the next press conference, currently scheduled for 11 a.m. Monday, Bodke said.

The apparent murders are the first in Quincy County since 2013, when Barbara...

Chapter 2

Tony Harrington gazed out the large plate glass window of Willie's Bar onto the town square. It was an overcast September day, warm and threatening rain. Almost no one in Iowa wanted rain now. A five-ton John Deere tractor mired in the mud of an Iowa cornfield was not conducive to getting the harvest done. The trees on the square were still green. It would be another month before their leaves exploded in color, making everyone who had endured the long, hot summer feel like Dorothy stepping out of the black and white Kansas farmhouse into the spectacular scenery of Munchkinland. *It may be September,* Tony thought, *but today is a summer day.*

As Tony watched, a handful of young people with long hair, tattoos, and various forms of metal protruding from their facial features were playing Frisbee by the fountain on the square. He found it remarkable that whenever the weather was nice there were Goth kids hanging in the square. It was remarkable because he rarely saw kids like these, with their brightly colored spiked hair, tats, and piercings, anywhere else in town. He never saw them with parents

or in stores or at school events. He supposed that was why they were
called alternative lifestyles. They didn't socialize at the same times
or in the same places as the majority of Iowans. Tony decided he
would walk over to the square one day soon and get to know them.
I'll bet there's more than one good story there, Tony thought. *But
not today.*

Tony would spend this day in the Quincy County Courthouse.
He, his media peers from across the state, and 200 or so other interested spectators would cram themselves into the old, ornate courtroom, to see Ralph Adam Wells go on trial for the double murder of
Jerry and Anne Ennis eight months ago. Although Tony was more
than an interested spectator, he felt the same morbid curiosity as the
retirees, store clerks, and professionals who crowded into the courtroom. He also felt a familiar stress, a tightness at the back of his neck
and shoulders that came from covering a major trial. As a writer for
Orney's *Town Crier,* Tony was the eyes and ears for all those people
who couldn't leave work for the day to watch or who were turned
away at the courthouse door. Tony took his responsibility seriously,
and as he thought about the murder case, he rolled his head on his
shoulders to try to shake the stiffness. At least he didn't have to fight
the crowd. As a member of the press, he would have the privilege of
sharing one of the two front benches. It was a spot from which he
would easily be able to see the subtleties of the trial's progress and
all the visual cues for which he had learned to watch: the posture of
the defendant, the eyes of the jurors, the expressions of the attorneys
as they performed for the judge and jury...and the media. Tony smiled
grimly, as he acknowledged to himself for the hundredth time that
his birds-eye view and his self-proclaimed insights into the process
added nothing to his work. In the end, all he could do was report
what was said and done in the courtroom and let the readers and the
jury draw their own conclusions.

***

Tony knew he had to guard against his own high opinion of himself – his writing as well as his so-called insights. His ego was a direct result of his upbringing, but he knew not to let it get in the way of his work. Fortunately or unfortunately, Tony had been told since he was six years old what a wonderful writer he was. The person doing the telling, Charles Anthony Harrington, was someone who should know. Charles was his dad. He was also the man known to millions of readers as C.A. Harker. Writing as Harker, his dad was the author of more than twenty novels, seven of which had made the *New York Times* best seller list and three of which had been converted to movie scripts for Hollywood.

Charles and his wife, Carla, lived in Chicago for years as Charles published one successful book after another. It was there that Tony and his sister Rita were born and raised through the early years of their lives. They lived in a nice home in Highland Park, north of downtown, and grew up enjoying all the wonders the city had to offer: the lake, the zoo and aquarium, the museums and festivals, the sports teams and music. His mother, especially, loved music. From the time Tony was old enough to sit up in a chair or a theater seat, he had been to every conceivable type of music venue. He had heard the Chicago Symphony, the Lyric Opera, traveling Broadway musicals, concert bands, jazz groups, and even marching bands. His mother loved them all, and her enthusiasm was infectious. She also made each of the musical excursions special for her children, taking the time before each performance to explain to them the background of what they were about to see, telling them what to watch for, and explaining why they should be excited to hear a particular performer or piece of music.

From this, both Tony and Rita grew up appreciating music and,

inevitably, studying music in varying degrees. Tony took the obligatory piano lessons. While he had a good ear and learned quickly, it
never competed with his love of writing.

Rita, however, found her soul among the notes and time signa-
tures of musical scores. In absolute terms, she may not have been a
prodigy, but she was enormously talented. By the time she entered
middle school, she was taking lessons in cello, flute, voice, and
piano. Tony often envied her enthusiasm and clear understanding of
where her life was headed. He also envied her ability to reach into
her soul, and everyone else's, with whatever instrument she held.

The event that most changed both their lives occurred one
evening during Tony's sophomore in high school. As he, his mother,
and his sister were eating pasta and salads at the kitchen table, his
dad arrived home. After the typical greetings and hair tousling, his
dad announced they were moving to Iowa. His shocked children listened as Charles explained he was tired of traveling. A successful
writer spends a lot of time on the road conducting book tours, speaking at events, and meeting with industry professionals. Tony's dad
had decided the toll it was taking was too great. So, he said, he had
accepted a position as a writer-in-residence at the University of Iowa
in Iowa City, and as director of the Iowa Writers' Workshop.

It was, of course, the worst possible time for a move from
Tony's perspective. He was in high school. He had great friends and
was involved in many activities. In just a couple more years, some
of Chicago's best attributes, such as the live music bars and comedy
clubs, would be accessible to him. *Iowa, Dad? Really? Iowa?* Tony
must have asked himself a thousand times.

Carla assured her children they would return to Chicago frequently. It was an easy drive from Iowa City and they wouldn't let
the distance keep them from enjoying the city. Tony found it small
comfort. However, because he loved and respected his father, he tried

to be a good soldier. He promised his dad he would do all he could to make it work and, for the most part, lived up to his promise. Because Rita was younger, it was less of an issue for her. She and her friends cried, but once Rita had been assured there were excellent music teachers available to her in Iowa City, she was fine.

Once they arrived and settled in, Tony quickly realized he actually liked Iowa City. This was a revelation almost as shocking as the announcement of the move. The city of 76,000 people, including 33,000 college students, had more to offer than he had imagined. As host to a Big Ten university, the community had a lot of the attractions of the big city: music, culture, beautiful girls, and of course, Big Ten sports. It didn't have Lake Michigan, but the Iowa River was a prominent feature flowing through the center of town, and one of Iowa's biggest recreational lakes wasn't far away. Looking back on them now, Tony knew his years in Iowa City were nearly perfect; certainly far better than he dreamed possible when he first learned he was leaving the city. He benefitted from a great education, terrific friends, a close-knit family, and the security that comes from feeling like your home is, well, *home.* The old stone and hardwood house his father had purchased on a bluff above the Iowa River wasn't exactly a mansion, but it would have cost more than a million dollars in Chicago. Tony didn't know what his dad had paid, but whatever the cost, it was worth it. He and Rita each had a bedroom on the second floor. Large and comfortable, the rooms overlooked a big back yard.

In fact, Tony had enjoyed Iowa City so much that after graduating from Regina Catholic High School, he decided to stay and attend the University of Iowa.

During his time in Iowa City, Tony could only remember ever having two complaints. The first was autumn, when he and Rita were expected to rake and bag the leaves from more than thirty big oak and maple trees scattered throughout the family's five-acre property. Their first fall, they filled five dozen Hefty lawn bags. They learned their lesson and in all subsequent years did not bag the leaves at all. They realized it was easier to remove a couple of rails from the fence at the back of the property and push the leaves over the edge and down the bluff toward the river. Their mother was in a constant state of panic whenever they were outside the fence at the top of the bluff, but as always, she bit back her urge to make them stop.

The other complaint was the predictable weirdness of being a celebrity's son. Because his dad was a famous author, and now ran the nationally-renowned writers' workshop, Tony learned that nearly everyone he met brought some pre-conceived ideas to the encounter. Some people resented the family's money and social status. Some people liked or disliked him based on their opinions of his father's novels, or even worse, a character in one of the novels. Nearly everyone made assumptions about Tony's intentions and likelihood of success when he began telling people he wanted to be a writer.

Fortunately, his dad was as unassuming as a successful man can be. He was also good at giving advice and guiding his children through their various tribulations, usually by simply encouraging them to ignore the pettiness of strangers and focus on the support of family and friends. As a result, the problems were minimized and kept in perspective.

Tony encountered one more very big surprise while in Iowa City. He had agonized for weeks, early in his college career, about how to tell his dad he wanted to write for newspapers. When he finally worked up the courage to announce he would be majoring in journalism, and not in English, he said it almost apologetically, assuming his dad would want him to do something more creative or meatier and would want him in the department of English, where he taught, rather than in journalism.

To Tony's surprise and relief, however, his dad thought it was a wonderful career choice. He sat and talked with Tony at length about the impact some of the great reporters and columnists at the *Chicago Tribune* and the *Sun-Times* had on him as a young man.

Then his dad surprised him further by offering to help him financially. Charles was careful how he offered, not wanting to offend his son, and Tony was careful how he accepted, not wanting to be too beholden to, or a burden for, his parents. However, both Tony and his dad knew newspaper work would pay very little, and Tony would benefit greatly from some financial security early in his career. In the end, his dad set it up as a trust, which paid Tony an annual supplement to his salary. Tony could use the money for travel or a home or a hobby or whatever he pleased. Tony only accepted after his dad assured him Rita would receive the same accommodation when she graduated two years later.

This arrangement had allowed Tony to accept the position at the Orney *Town Crier* for a modest salary plus an even more modest benefit plan. Tony hadn't believed he could enjoy living in a town even smaller than Iowa City, but after five years in Orney, he had to admit he couldn't be happier.

***

Tony glanced once more around the square and considered what was really remarkable about the scene. Everything looked so normal: mothers ducking into Drugs and Things with small children in tow; Harold taking advantage of the clear fall weather and washing the windows of his appliance and television store; Betty stealing a quick smoke in the doorway of her beauty shop; and the mystery kids playing Frisbee in the square.

Similarly, here in Willie's Bar, farmers, bankers, mechanics, car salesmen, and retirees crowded in to have their morning coffee with Erma's homemade cinnamon rolls or a Hostess powdered donut. The trial was a topic of conversation, but not the only topic. As Tony turned his attention inside the bar and grill, he could hear discussions of the weather, the soybeans, the corn prices, the latest threat of an interest rate hike, and the damn Cubs. Nobody ever said just the "Cubs" or the "Chicago Cubs." Always it was the "damn Cubs." Despite the fact the team wore the mantle of World Champions not so long ago, neither their fans nor their critics had changed their banter one bit. This morning the fans were grumbling about last night's loss, ending a three-game series with the archrival St. Louis Cardinals without a win. The playoffs just might be out of reach again this year.

"Hey, Earth to Harrington." The voice was Doug Tenny's, his best friend in Orney and his most frequent partner for coffee or a meal at Willie's. Doug was a reporter for KKAR, the local AM radio station. In a town like Orney, competition between the only two news media outlets was almost nonexistent, at least at the staff reporter level. Tony often thought he and Doug kept a small remnant of competition alive only so they would have something to joke about when their conversations dragged.

"This is Harrington," Tony smiled as he spoke into his cupped hand. "I read you loud and clear. Houston, we have a problem."

Doug laughed and dropped into the nearest vinyl-covered booth. "You've got a problem all right. And it ain't a broken space capsule."

"Yeah, yeah, give it a rest," Tony said as he followed Doug to the booth and slid into the opposite seat. "I was just thinking about how normal everything and everyone seems while this extraordinary murder trial is about to begin in their courthouse."

"Well, what did you expect?" Doug asked. "Most folks in town can't drop everything to stand in line at the courthouse door, even for a murder trial. That's why they need us."

"No, that's not all," Tony quickly replied. "As I was wondering why people weren't more focused on the trial, I ended up thinking about the Chicago Cubs."

"The Cubs?" Doug's eyes narrowed. Then he smiled and said, "Well, yeah, I guess I can understand how thinking about a murder could remind you of Garcia's error in the eighth last night. If he hadn't had his head up his butt, the Cubs actually might have salvaged one in that series with the Cardinals. Now *everyone* wants to kill him."

Tony smiled again. "My point," he said, "is that while I was wondering how everybody else could think about everyday stuff, I ended up doing the same thing. Don't you find that ironic?"

"My friend the psychologist," Doug sighed. "You should try just thinking sometime, without thinking about why you're thinking what you're thinking."

"Hmm, sounds kinda dull, but maybe I'll give it a try," Tony grinned and finally turned his attention to the coffee Doug set in front of him. Steam rose from the cup like smoke from a tiny volcano. Tony knew from experience it was about the same temperature as molten lava. It remained untouched as he let it cool.

"Speaking of normal things," Doug said, "would you like to grab a date for Friday night and join me and Ellen for some steaks in the backyard? ...Tony?"

"Huh? Sorry. What was that?"

"What is it now, more murder trial, or contemplating the likelihood the Bears will make the Super Bowl? I said steaks, Friday night."

"Well, it sounds great, but there's no way this trial is going to wrap up by Friday, and I wouldn't put it past old Schroeder to make them work on Saturday, which means I gotta get out of bed that morning. Either way, there's a 90% chance I'll be working Friday night, writing the latest for the Saturday paper."

"You know your job is putting a serious damper on your social life, and as your best friend, it's not doing mine any good either," Doug replied, trying to sound put out. "If you keep working nights, how are you going to meet any decent women?"

"In the first place, Mr. Love Connection, please consider the possibility I don't want to meet *decent* women. Secondly, as you well know, Lisa is all the woman I need right now. Not to mention she is both faster and stronger than me. If she caught me cheating on her, I'm pretty sure I would regret it, in more ways than one. And by the way, I only work two nights a week."

"Wrong!" Doug called out as he slapped at an imaginary buzzer on the table. "Bzzzz. Go directly to jail. Do not pass 'Go!' You're only scheduled to work two nights a week, but you're in that newsroom practically every night."

"That's because I spend my days in the courthouse, spying on all the cute chicks in the jail." Tony smiled.

Doug laughed out loud. "You're a sick man, Tony Harrington."

"Well, that's what gives my writing its unique perspective." He drained his cup and looked at his watch. "Speaking of which, I need to get to the courthouse. Schroeder has a cow when reporters walk in after the proceedings have begun and, the last I heard, it was not a good idea to get a district court judge pissed at you."

"Hold on, I'm coming too."

"You're kidding. You're actually going to attend a news event you're covering? What happened to simply reading it out of the paper? Your listeners might be disappointed if you cheat them out of my prose tomorrow morning."

"Very funny, Mr. Pulitzer. I figured I'd better start coming, you know, just to give you a hand. I want to make sure you know the definitions of all those fancy words you're using."

"Yeah, there'll be some tough ones in this case, like 'sequester,'" Tony deadpanned.

"Oh, and don't forget 'guilty sonofabitch.' You'll need that one," Doug shot back with a grin.

"Don't be so sure," Tony wasn't grinning in return as he paused and lifted his face to stare at his friend. He wanted to continue, but stopped himself.

"What?" Doug asked. But Tony stood up, dropped his tip on the Formica tabletop, and walked across the room to the bar where Willie was punching numbers and making change at an old brass cash register. As Doug slid out of the booth and pried his wallet from his rear pocket, he glanced at Tony's back, wondering what was bothering his friend.

Chapter 3

W. Rodney Nelson shook his head at the bathroom mirror, pulled the knot from his tie, and started again.

"Rod?" It was Lillian's voice from the main portion of their small motel room. "Give it a rest. It would be infinitely worse to be late than to have your tie hang a quarter inch too short."

"Sorry honey, but I'll only be a moment." As Nelson spoke, he pulled the tie through its final gyration and slid the knot up to his Adam's apple. He stepped back and examined...no, *admired* his image in the mirror. Tall and fit, his sculpted features were clean-shaven and capped by thick wavy hair, with just a hint of gray at the edges. Small, wire-framed glasses completed the look of intelligence, competence, and strength. Nelson couldn't contain a smile as he slipped on his suit coat, smoothed the lapels, and took one last look at the total package.

People often told Nelson how lucky he was or how good Mother Nature had been to him, and it irritated the hell out of him. It wasn't Mother Nature who worked her butt off to get into law school or to graduate number three in the class. It wasn't Mother Nature who worked seventy-plus hours a week doing grunt work as a staff lawyer in the Attorney General's office, or orchestrated his promotion to assistant attorney general, or campaigned for two years to get elected to lead the office. For that matter, it wasn't Mother Nature who climbed on the treadmill at sunrise every morning to keep in shape. In short, W. Rodney Nelson was proud of everything he was and everything he had accomplished. And he wasn't about to give anyone, including Mother Nature or his beautiful wife in the next room, credit for his hard work.

"Yes, Rod, you look great," said Lillian as she sidled up beside him, being careful not to get her makeup on the sleeve of his Armani suit coat. "Now let's *go*."

He glanced at his watch and smiled. "We'll be right on time." His confidence filled the room like the aroma of warm bread. "Remember, honey, this is Orney. It can't take over ten minutes to get to the farthest point in town, and that's with a flat tire and a dead battery."

"Well, you don't have to worry about the latter," Lillian smiled, as Nelson turned with a quizzical look. "I already started the car so it would have a chance to cool down. Can't have you showing up in court all sweaty now, can we?"

"You are something," Nelson smiled as he pulled her close and planted a kiss on her neck. "What would I do without you?"

"You'd find some other smart, personable, and devoted woman to make first lady of Iowa when you get elected governor."

Nelson chuckled but quickly turned serious as they walked out of the motel into the warm August sunshine. "Let's be careful not to joke about the future, even among ourselves. One mistake..."

"One mistake can sink the ship," she finished for him. "Don't worry dear. I'll be careful, as always."

"Of course, you know I trust you completely," Nelson replied, and felt almost as sincere as he sounded. He opened her car door and held it while she gracefully slid into the seat. "But remember, I'm not even going to formally announce until after this trial. When we have Mr. Wells locked up for good and all of Iowa is praising me for getting another heartless killer behind bars, then we'll kick things off publicly."

Nelson shut her door firmly and walked around to the driver's side. As he settled in behind the wheel, Lillian spoke softly, almost tentatively. "Honey, what if you...well, you know, what if you don't win?"

Nelson smiled broadly and brushed the side of her face with the back of his fingers. "Are you doubting your husband is the wizard he thinks he is?" His wife chuckled and shook her head as he added, "Seriously honey, I won't lose. This hillbilly killed two people in cold blood, and then practically handed us all the evidence we need to put him away for life. They say he's slow, but I call him just plain dumb."

Nelson continued, stating with confidence that the whole trial wouldn't last much over a week, two at the most. "My God, the guy has no alibi. In fact, he has no defense of any kind that we've been able to discern."

Nelson noted the defense was not claiming temporary insanity, which he believed would have been their only chance of gaining an acquittal on the first-degree murder charge. He had to assume Wells was maintaining his story that he didn't do it, even to his own attorney. This was more evidence of stupidity, not of innocence. Or perhaps the defense was hoping to elicit some sympathy from the jury because of Wells' limited mental capacity. Nelson was certain that would not be enough for Wells to escape justice. He said, "Wells' I.Q. is below average, but he's far from incompetent. You and I both know that no jury is going to have sympathy for a guy who kills an innocent couple in their own home, particularly when two small children had to find their parents' bodies."

Nelson realized he was testing threads of his potential opening arguments on his wife. After so many years together, he still worked hard to impress her with his oratory. And of course, to convince her he was right. As he described it, there was no question Wells was guilty and on his way to prison for life. He could see in Lillian's smile that she was proud to be his wife. He smiled in return.

As Nelson turned the car into the courthouse parking lot, he saw a crowd on the front steps. It was the crowd he had dreamed of seeing, complete with cameras, microphones, and questions. He pulled to a stop in one of the stalls marked "Reserved" and turned to his wife of 22 years. "Lillian, I'm telling you, this is the perfect case from which to launch our campaign. You know I don't like to attribute much to luck, but this is like manna from heaven. I couldn't have created a better case if I had done the crime myself."

A boyish excitement filled his face as he stepped out of the car. By the time he stepped quickly around the car and opened her door, he was grim-faced and ready to face the media. For the next week or two, no one besides her would see W. Rodney Nelson look anything but concerned, serious, and very professional.

As they walked up the curving sidewalk, the reporters surrounded them before they even reached the wide marble steps. "Mr. Nelson! Could you answer a few questions?" One of the television reporters thrust a microphone forward.

"Well, I'll try," Nelson said. "But of course you understand I will refuse to make any comments that might jeopardize this trial. We're going to make sure that every aspect of this case is handled appropriately so we can successfully send a cold-blooded murderer to prison and deliver to the people of Quincy County the justice they deserve."

***

Behind the crowd, Tony Harrington stood on the courthouse steps, leaning against the handrail, and flipped open his note pad. He hadn't followed his peers down to greet the attorney general, and even though he could hear everything from where he stood, he hadn't written anything down. The little he knew of W. Rodney Nelson was confirmed by the opening remarks. Another politician looking to score points with the voters. That would explain why the high-profile Iowa Attorney General was in Orney to handle a murder case that normally would be prosecuted by the local county attorney. It might even confirm the talk around the state that Nelson was considering a run for governor. A conviction in a double murder case would generate plenty of positive publicity, and not just in Quincy County.

In fact, Tony had never seen media representatives in the county from so many places. He had spotted TV crews from Des Moines, Waterloo, Mason City, and Ames. *The Des Moines Register* reporter was here, which he expected, but so were reporters from four or five other dailies and several of the area weekly papers. The guy in the tan blazer might even be from the Associated Press. This many reporters hadn't shown up even when a natural gas leak had ignited inside Smithers' Greenhouse. The resulting explosion had leveled the building and burned down two neighboring houses, killing three people. It was the biggest news story in Orney's 125-year history, until today apparently.

For some reason he couldn't begin to understand, Tony found this irritating. He listened to a few more of Nelson's answers, and determined they were more meaningless fluff, perfect for the sound bites the television and radio reporters needed for their noon broadcasts but with no meaningful insights into the trial. He turned and walked up the steps, deciding it was more important to get a front row seat in the courtroom.

I don't care who you are or even are how determined you are, Tony thought. *I want to see you in action, and I want to know the facts of this case. Now let's get on with it.*

Chapter 4

It was day six of the proceedings. The first two days had been devoted to jury selection, not an easy task when trying to find fourteen people – twelve jurors and two alternates – who hadn't heard about and formed opinions on a case as sensational as this one. Day three was confined to opening statements by the lead attorneys representing the prosecution and the defense, W. Rodney Nelson and Lawrence Pike respectively. Days four and five had been filled with testimony from the Division of Criminal Investigation agents and sheriff's deputies regarding the events surrounding the murder – the response to the 9-1-1 call, the preservation of the crime scene, the processes used to collect and gather evidence, and the routine investigation that had led them to Ralph Wells.

Wells had not been a suspect. In fact, his name had not come up in any context as investigators looked deep into the lives of the two victims. However, when all the usual steps had been exhausted, and fears were growing that the case would go "cold," investigators decided they needed to expand their interviews to a broader range of people. "Any ideas?" Daniel Bodke, the deputy sheriff in charge of the investigation, had asked the team one morning during the daily briefing in the sheriff's conference room. One deputy then volunteered that he had known a lot of guys in high school with .22 rifles. In fact, the deputy had noted, some of those guys still lived in the area.

"Maybe we should start gathering up .22s and doing ballistics tests on as many as we can find." The suggestion had drawn groans from the deputies and state DCI agents gathered in the room. They knew this would be an enormous amount of work and would draw the ire of the ballistics team in the State Crime Laboratory. It also had almost no chance of producing a meaningful lead.

However, Bodke had surprised them. "Hang on folks. Unless someone has a better idea, I think we might want to give this a try." He held his hands out to quell the protests, "We'll keep this reasonable. We'll only go to people who lived within a twenty-mile radius of the Ennis house, and only those in the age range of, say, 18 to 45. No kids and no elderly guys. That should keep the rifles we ask for at a reasonable number."

One of the deputies asked, "What if someone refuses to hand over his rifle?"

"That's his right," Bodke said. "You simply thank him and leave. And then you call me immediately so we can put him under the microscope."

This simple suggestion had led two DCI agents to the trailer house of young Ralph Wells and his even younger wife. The state's witnesses had described how and why Wells had quickly become a suspect and eventually why they decided to arrest him and charge him with two counts of first-degree murder.

Throughout it all, Lawrence Pike had asked very few questions. He made sure to get each witness on the record noting that Wells had never said anything incriminating and had never admitted to knowing or harming the Ennises. Each witness acknowledged Wells had stead-fastly maintained his innocence, although at least two had managed to make the point that this was to be expected, as it was common for all criminals to do likewise. Pike was careful to object during the state's direct examination only when a witness began to stray beyond the facts into supposition or opinion. But all in all, Pike seemed con-tent to let the state lay out all the evidence it had assembled.

For this, Tony was grateful. It meant the trial was moving quickly.

***

"The state calls Dr. Lance Torgeson."

Tony had to refrain from rolling his eyes as he heard Nelson call out the coroner's name. Torgeson's only role could be to present the forensic evidence, and Tony had covered just enough trials to know how incredibly boring he would almost certainly be. A fastid-ious little man with wire rim glasses and curly gray hair, Torgeson looked the part of a pathologist, more comfortable with corpses and lab specimens than with people. He had spent plenty of time on the stand over the years, usually testifying about blood alcohol levels in OWI and accident cases and physical evidence in the occasional rape case. This afternoon he looked especially uneasy. Clearly, a double murder was outside the scope of his normal practice.

As Nelson launched into his questions about the blood on the sheets and the headboard, Tony knew he should pay attention. Guilt or innocence could be hiding in the details of a splatter pat-tern or the position of an exit wound. Despite understanding this, Tony found his mind wandering. It was irritating to listen to the self-aggrandizing Nelson, and tedious to listen to Torgeson's long, meticulous responses.

Tony found himself staring at the defendant. From where he sat, Tony could see the back of his head and upper torso. If Wells turned toward the judge, Tony could catch just a glimpse of his left profile, part of a bushy eyebrow and fleshy nose. What kind of guy was he, really? Examining Wells' thick and somewhat disheveled hair and the suit coat that didn't quite fit, Tony realized he knew almost nothing about him. He had reported the basic facts about Wells; a farm laborer, husband, and native of nearby Oak Grove. However, he had never really looked into the person. Tony's heart sank to his gut and settled there as he realized he had dropped the ball. One of the first lessons that Ben Smalley, the editor of the *Town Crier,* had taught him was that if he found himself wondering something, then other people undoubtedly had the same questions. In this case, everyone he knew was curious about the quiet guy who had been charged with this horrible crime. *I should have written the profile,* Tony almost said aloud, amazed that he hadn't taken the initiative in the months leading up to the trial. Just as quickly, Tony vowed that he would do the in-depth personality piece, even if he had to travel to the State Penitentiary at Fort Madison to do it. He flipped to the last page of his reporter's spiral notebook and started jotting notes about what he knew about Wells so far. Starting at the beginning, Tony's mind went back to the night of Wells' arrest the previous spring.

***

The phone by the bed clanged like a fire bell. Tony kept the setting all the way to "loud" because he knew nothing less could wake him in the middle of the night. When the calls came at 2 or 3 a.m., Tony didn't mind. The obnoxious ring tone usually meant a banner headline the next day: "Pinchet Mansion Burns," or "Explosion Levels

Smithers' Greenhouse," or "Couple Found Shot to Death in Rural Orney Home."

As Tony forced himself awake, he rolled onto his side and grabbed the phone. It bothered him that the sound of it triggered memories of the double murder, even from a deep sleep. *My God, it's been three months. Am I obsessed with this case?* he wondered, even as he forced his dry throat to respond, "Harrington."

"We're going for the collar," a familiar voice said with a tinge of excitement. "You interested?"

"That depends," Tony said, sitting upright and looking at a glowing 2:37 on the face of his clock radio. "I mean, it depends on what collar. It would have to be darn good to get me out at this hour." Tony knew the voice on the other end belonged to Rich Davis, a bright young investigator with the State DCI. Davis was officed at the Sheriff's Department in Quincy County, and often assisted local officials in their work. Considering the hour, and the respect he held for Davis, Tony knew he should be getting excited at whatever was coming.

"You dumb shit," Davis said, with uncharacteristic bluntness. "I'm talking about *the* collar. We're on our way to grab the man who killed Jerry and Anne Ennis."

"Holy Jeeez-sus!" Tony squawked, trying to contain himself and failing. "Why didn't you... of course, of course. Where? Where and when should I be where...?" Tony rarely got flustered by such things, but then he rarely got called to witness an arrest in a double murder case. In fact, he never got called to witness an arrest. He knew he had to calm down. Friendly or not, Davis would not want a blubbering idiot to accompany him.

"Relax, Tony," Davis responded evenly. "I'll stop in front of your house in ten minutes to pick you up. Can you make it?"

"Are you kidding? I'm already on the porch waiting for you," Tony felt an urge to giggle, but held it back. "And Rich, thanks."

Davis didn't respond except to end the call.

Precisely ten minutes later, with the taste of toothpaste still in his mouth, Tony was sitting in the front seat of Davis' state car, repeating his thank-you and taking big gulps from a 16-ounce Diet Dr. Pepper. He was wearing blue jeans and a sweatshirt under his down-filled winter coat and hunter's boots, all to ward off the cold. It was early March, and the ground was still covered with snow. Tony glanced at the dashboard of Davis' sedan and learned it was twenty-six degrees outside. Not horrible, but too cold to enjoy working outside for very long.

"This really is great of you, Rich. I don't know why you guys decided to include me on this, but I really appreciate the opportunity."

"Enough said. You're here because we know we can trust you, and because we expect this to be simple," Davis replied.

And, Tony wanted to say, *because it's an election year next year and Sheriff George Mackey can use the extra publicity.* The DCI was always looking for ways to strengthen its relationships with the locals. Tony choked back the comment out of fear he would offend Davis, at whom the cynical thought wasn't even aimed. And besides, Tony didn't mind being used a little, as long as he was smart enough to see it and control it, and as long as it meant he had access to a great story. Putting these thoughts into words made the whole affair seem more sordid, so Tony put it out of his mind.

"So where are we going? Who is this guy?" Tony asked.

Davis replied, "His name is Wells, Ralph Adam Wells. Beyond that I can't tell you much. Not because I don't want to, but because there isn't much to tell."

"Ralph Wells?" Tony was more than a little taken aback. "The young guy who practically lives at the Iron Range?" He was thinking of a rather chubby kid who couldn't be more than 21 or 22 years old.

He was a quiet guy who liked to play pool and drink beer. Tony had seen him in the pub on numerous occasions, but couldn't remember ever talking to him. He was pretty sure Wells had never been in trouble, at least nothing serious enough to make the paper. He wasn't even sure where the guy worked or lived.

"I don't know about his social life, or lack of it," Davis responded. "All I can tell you is what's in the official trial information."

Tony knew grand juries were used rarely in Iowa. The trial information was the document employed by most prosecutors to file charges against a suspect. It included the facts of the case, as believed to be true by law enforcement at the time. It was the basis for the arrest warrant and for a judge to order a suspect held until a plea could be entered, and in some cases, a preliminary hearing held. The fact that a prosecutor had completed a trial information and had already taken it before a judge made Tony very anxious to get to their destination. They were likely about to encounter a man responsible for the brutal murders of two people.

"At this point, it's pretty straightforward," Davis said as he turned the cruiser east on the highway, then quickly turned south on a gravel road that ran past the Farmers' Cooperative grain elevator, and then led them out of town. "So far we know Wells was in town drinking the night of the murders, and we know he can't account for his whereabouts for hours. We also know he owns clothing matching what was seen by the girls who were in the house when their parents were killed. But I'm sure the main reason we're here, and this is an editorial comment not for print, is the gun."

"The murder weapon?" Tony was almost embarrassed to ask the obvious.

"Yes. Wells owned the .22 caliber rifle that killed the Ennises."

"Wow," is all Tony said, but question after question was racing through his mind. The statement that Wells couldn't account for hours of his time implied that investigators had already talked to him at least once. What else had they learned? Could he assume Wells had denied any involvement? Even if he had, if the authorities had his rifle and had proved it was the murder weapon, would Wells already be on the run? Or at home waiting for them?

"You expecting any trouble?" Tony asked aloud. "You said this would be simple."

Davis smiled. "Getting nervous? Just because we brought you along as a shield?"

Tony returned a grin, but held his tongue awaiting an answer.

"No, seriously, and off the record, our perception is that Wells is a little slow, both physically and mentally. We expect to surprise him and have him in custody before he knows what hit him."

Tony was comforted somewhat, but could still envision all kinds of problems, from embarrassing glitches to deadly catastrophes, as men with loaded guns tried to conduct business in the dark.

"How many of us...uh, you...are there tonight?" Tony asked, trying to assess the risk.

"Seven," Davis said casually, missing the implication in Tony's question. "Sheriff Mackey, two deputies, two state troopers, Dan, and myself."

Tony knew that "Dan" meant Dan Rooney, Davis' DCI partner stationed in Quincy County.

Davis continued, "We're the trigger car. Relax. It's not trigger in the sense of a trigger on a weapon. We, in effect, trigger the operation. Everyone else should be in place by now. When they see my car approach on the road, they'll enter the house and secure Wells. By the time we drive up, he should be in cuffs."

Despite his earlier thoughts about the risk, Tony was disappointed that he was likely to see only the tail end of the operation.

The gravel road they traveled on in the dark generally followed the path of what had been the Rock Island Railroad tracks. The tracks had been pulled up years ago. Today the land was used primarily by hikers and dirt bike riders, who begrudgingly shared the wide path through the countryside and into the woods along the Raccoon River. Tony wasn't sure but assumed the State of Iowa owned the land now and would pave it eventually as part of the state's bicycle trail system. Years ago, Tony knew, the rail line had been vital to farmers in the area, carrying grain to major distribution centers in Chicago, Minneapolis, and Kansas City. Because freight trains don't make very appealing neighbors, most of the path's miles were bordered by farm fields or roads. Where the contour of the land, the thickness of the trees, or other features prevented farming, the land often held the lowest income families living in old farmhouses, converted farm buildings, or trailer homes.

As Davis slowed, Tony realized they were headed for the latter. It was an older trailer home – the type with the wheels still underneath – partly visible behind a botched attempt at skirting the home with trellis and of a width that was legal to pull down most highways. Rust at the seams and under the windows revealed the home's age and poor condition. The yard was uncut and cluttered with debris, including an old Frigidaire refrigerator missing the door handle and a rusty gas stove missing pretty much everything. The long gravel drive didn't really end as it reached the home, but dissipated into the weeds and snow. In short, the home revealed not only the residents' economic status, but their lack of ambition and pride. *Hang on Tony,* he thought to himself. *Don't be so judgmental. You have no idea what the circumstances or issues are with this family.* Tony's face began to visibly curl in disgust, but he stopped himself. He found the conditions distasteful, but he knew he had to keep an open mind.

Suddenly – so suddenly Tony almost missed it – two darkly clothed deputies with guns drawn were on the front step. A crowbar popped the door open and in an instant they were inside, followed almost as quickly by two uniformed troopers.

Davis stopped his cruiser about halfway up the drive, the only visible law enforcement vehicle. He shut off the engine but left the lights shining on the trailer. Tony was out the door before Davis could tell him not to. He walked briskly along the side of the drive, staying close to the trees for cover, but moving toward the trailer. He didn't want to miss any more of this than he had to.

Tony wasn't more than a dozen feet from the front step of the trailer, with Davis right behind him, when the two deputies brought Ralph Adam Wells out the door. Wells looked frightened and completely submissive. He was whining his objections, almost in whispers, as the officers dragged his bare feet down the three metal stairs to the ground. Wearing boxer shorts and an old high school baseball jersey, he looked like absolutely anything but a killer. The word *pathetic* formed in Tony's mind. It was the best description of the scene, but he had no idea how he would work it into the newspaper story.

"Guys!" Davis called from behind Tony's left shoulder, almost sending him out of his khaki slacks. "Watch his feet."

The officers pulling Wells down the driveway slowed and provided more support to keep his feet from dragging on the rocks protruding from the packed snow. Tony wondered how much of that extra care was for his benefit, rather than the suspect's, and then wondered if he was being too cynical. As Wells was tossed into the back seat of the sheriff's squad car, Davis tugged at Tony's coat, holding him back as Davis passed him and approached the car. Tony got the hint and stepped back, but not so far that he couldn't hear. Before Davis uttered a word, both he and Tony were surprised by a small voice from behind them.

"Ralph?" Tony turned and saw a small, dark-haired, and not

entirely unattractive girl. She may have been in her early twenties, but the word *woman* never entered his mind as his eyes moved down her pixie-like frame, dwarfed further by a faded Tweety Bird nightshirt and by the two deputies standing just behind her, inside the door of the trailer. "What's going on? Are they hurting you?"

"I'm okay. I don't know," Ralph called in a high-pitched voice from the back seat. Tony was struck by the sound of it. This was no arrogant punk like in a made-for-TV movie, claiming his innocence while rubbing his guilt in the faces of the cops. This was a tired, frightened voice filled with questions. "It'll be all right. Just hang on and I'll get this square. Why don't you get some clothes on and call your sister to come wait with you?"

Tony was struck by the naivety. Wells sounded like he expected to be back home in an hour or two. Just a chat with the boys in town and then back home for breakfast. Was he ignorant...or innocent?

Four of the officers stayed behind to begin the search of Wells' trailer, property, car, and every other possession he owned, borrowed, or rented. Two were in the car with Wells, and Davis was back in the car with Tony.

"Did he strike you as a cold-blooded murderer?" Tony couldn't help but ask.

"Hey, pal, don't be fooled. John Gacy was a Boy Scout leader and Jeffrey Dahmer was a charming guy with a girlfriend. You're smart enough to know that appearances don't mean squat when it comes to what someone may have done in the heat of a moment or as a result of a carefully calculated plan."

Tony knew Davis was right, but he also knew Wells looked about as guilty as Lumpy on *Leave It to Beaver*. He struggled to reconcile his intellectual and emotional reactions to what he saw. Almost as if he could read his mind, Davis said, "My advice is to wait until you have all the facts and see what they tell you, or more importantly, what they tell the jury."

***

The thought of the jury pulled Tony back to reality. Or had it been something Lawrence Pike just asked in cross examination? Something about the angle of the bullets.

"So it's your expert opinion that three of the bullets were fired while the shooter was standing on the bed, aiming down at the couple?" Pike asked.

"That's my opinion," the doctor answered.

"Let's talk about that fourth bullet," Pike said. "From where was it fired?"

"I believe all the evidence is consistent with the fourth bullet being fired from the floor behind the bed. It seems obvious to me this actually was the first shot. The killer fired into the back of the female victim's skull, and then stepped up on the bed, firing three more shots, killing both the husband and the wife before they had any chance to react."

Tony glanced over and noticed the prosecutor squirming in his chair, probably wanting to object, as the doctor had gone beyond the facts and into the realm of speculation, but not wanting to object and risk alienating his own witness.

"So in your expert opinion," Pike was asking, "the female victim was on her knees, on top of Mr. Ennis, engaged in sexual intercourse at the time the bullet entered the back of her skull?"

"That's correct," Torgeson answered, "but of course no one..."

Pike cut him off. "And based on the spatters on the wall and the exit wound from the female victim's face, she apparently was upright, and not bent over her husband at the time of the shot?"

"That's correct," the doctor said again.

"So, based on all these facts, the apparent position of the couple, the placement of the bullet wounds, and the resulting human tissue splattered on the wall at the head of the bed, would you say the rifle would have been pointed straight ahead, in other words, positioned roughly parallel to the floor?"

"That's right," Torgeson said more slowly, clearly wondering where Pike was headed.

"So then doctor, knowing all of this, and knowing the height of the bed and size of the bodies, did you calculate an approximate height of the murderer?" Pike asked.

"Objection!" Nelson was on his feet. "Your Honor, Dr. Torgeson is a fine pathologist, but there's no way he could know all he needs to know, such as the way in which the gun was being held in order to estimate the height of the killer."

"Sustained," Schroeder said.

"I withdraw the question, Your Honor," Pike said, unruffled.

Tony smiled, understanding immediately that Pike had made his point. If the gun was against the killer's shoulder, which any reasonable person might assume, then the gun had to be positioned at a particular height for the bullet to travel the line it did from the back of the skull through the middle of the brain and into the wall.

Tony began sketching the picture in his mind: the old-fashioned bed several feet off the floor, the man on top the bed, the woman on top the man, the gunman behind them by at least a few feet...

Damn, I should have been paying attention, Tony chastised himself. The woman upright, the gun pointed at her skull. *Holy shit!* He almost said it out loud. It wasn't too hard to envision the butt of the rifle nearly six feet above the floor. Tony glanced over at Ralph Wells, five-foot, five-inch Ralph Wells, and wondered again just what was going on.

***

The state's second witness on day six was a ballistics expert from the DCI. Everett Anderson described in excruciating detail the chain of custody that ensured the rifle he tested was that received from Ralph Wells, and then in equally great detail, the process used to fire the weapon in the lab and compare both the lead bullets and the brass shell casings with those found at the murder scene. The testimony was as compelling as it was detailed. There was no doubt the rifle that killed Jerry and Anne Ennis was the one Ralph Wells had pulled from the trunk of his older model Chevy Malibu and had handed to DCI investigators months earlier. As the prosecutor took his seat, looking very pleased with the testimony as well as with his own performance, the judge turned to the defense table. "Any cross examination, Mr. Pike?" he asked.

Pike rose slowly. He was wearing a light tan suit that needed pressed with a striped tie that didn't quite match and was 20 years too wide. His sparse white hair appeared to be uncombed since his morning shower. In short, he looked like someone's grandfather rising slowly from his favorite chair to answer the family's call to dinner, which was, Tony understood, exactly how he wanted to look.

"Just a moment, Your Honor," Pike said quietly as he picked up his legal pad and examined his notes. He seemed to be talking to himself, but just loud enough for the jury to hear, as he ticked through the lines. "Hmm, no, no, no, well... no, no," he said. Then, looking up and in a normal tone of voice, "No, your honor, I don't think I have anything to add to Mr. Anderson's fine testimony." Pike appeared to be turning to sit when he stopped in his tracks, turned, and said, "Well actually, Mr. Anderson, I do have one or two very quick questions."

"You may proceed," Schroeder said.

"You already have described for the jury your outstanding qualifications, so I won't ask you to repeat them," Pike began. "If I summarized your experience by saying you've been doing this a really long time and you're really good at your job, would that be a fair assessment?"

"I'd like to think so," Anderson replied, just a little wary of this too-nice approach from the opposition's counsel.

"So, in all those years, how many murder cases have you assisted the state in prosecuting? Would it be dozens? Hundreds?"

"Well, I don't know. I guess I would say somewhere in between. More than a few dozen but fewer than hundreds. Perhaps a hundred cases or more in total."

"Just one more question, Mr. Anderson," Pike turned to face the jury. "In all that time...in all those one hundred cases...have you ever heard of a murderer volunteering to investigators that he had the murder weapon in his trunk and voluntarily turning it over to them?"

"Objection!" Nelson was on his feet like a jack-in-the-box.

Pike responded before Schroeder could rule. "Never mind, Your Honor. I withdraw the question," he said, still looking at the jurors.

Again, Tony couldn't help but smile. Nelson had succeeded in making sure one of the most troubling facts of the case was firmly in the forefront of the jurors' minds. Why *had* Ralph Wells offered up his rifle so easily?

Back on that spring day, when DCI agents stopped by his residence, one of the routine questions they asked was, "Do you own a .22 caliber rifle?" Wells had immediately responded yes, but said he hadn't used it in years. In answer to follow-up questions from the agents, Wells said he had received it as a gift from his father when he was twelve or thirteen years old, the same as other boys he knew on nearby farms. He used it during his teen years to shoot possums and raccoons that were trying to make the barn their home. Otherwise, he said, he'd never had much interest in hunting and had never owned a weapon beyond the original rifle his dad had given him.

When the agents asked Wells if they could see the rifle, he had said sure, and offered that he kept it in the trunk of the car, not because he used it but because the trailer house was so small and his wife needed the limited storage space for other things. Wells had walked the agents to his car, opened the trunk, and dug the rifle out from below a mass of other junk.

The agents quickly noted it was the type of rifle likely used in the killings and asked Wells if they could test it. Wells had said, "Well, sure, but I don't know why you'd wanna. Don't those tests cost money? I didn't know these people you're asking about, and I can guarantee you that rifle hasn't been fired in three years or more."

The agents assured Wells it was just routine and said very politely that if he really didn't mind, it would be nice to rule it out, just for the record. So, Wells had signed the necessary paperwork without further comment and had accepted the agents' cards with the promise to call if he saw or heard anything that would be helpful to the investigation. Hands were then shaken all around and Wells went back into his trailer, presumably to watch the last round of *Wheel of Fortune* playing on the TV set opposite the trailer's door.

Of course, now everyone, including the jury, knew that Wells' rifle had indeed been the weapon that killed the young couple as they were making love in their home. And almost everyone assumed Wells was the dumbest murderer in the history of violent crime. At this point in the proceedings it was obvious Wells would not be on trial for murder, and in fact never would have been a serious suspect, had he simply taken the rifle and pitched it into the bottom of a lake or cut it into pieces and buried it in the woods somewhere. He could have told investigators he lost it or threw it away years before, and that would have been the end of it.

During the previous day's testimony, the agents had been asked the same question Tony had asked them months ago, when Wells was arrested: "How can you think a guilty man would volunteer that he owned the rifle and then turn it over to you without any resistance?" Each agent had answered Pike the same way he had answered Tony, with a variation on, "There's no way to know why criminals act as they do. We often see criminals do astoundingly stupid things that lead to their capture." One agent even referenced Jay Leno's long-standing "stupid criminals" bits, which had aired frequently on *The Tonight Show.*

Still, the issue nagged at Tony. Was Wells that dumb? At the risk of being unkind, Tony had to admit the man was a couple of octaves short of a full keyboard. So it was possible he just didn't understand the magnitude of trouble that the rifle would rain down on him. *Possible, but damn unlikely,* was Tony's final thought as the judge's gavel announced a lunch break.

Chapter 5

Tony was back at Willie's digging through meatloaf and mashed potatoes with a side of green beans and warm apple pie. It was the kind of comfort food he loved, and now that Lisa was in his life, he had to eat it at lunch or not at all...not that Lisa would have demanded he change his eating habits. Tony doubted such a thought would ever occur to her. But she was the type who ate a grilled chicken salad for dinner and might skip lunch altogether if someone didn't remind her to eat. Tony simply couldn't bring himself to stuff his face in the manner common to Willie's patrons when he was with her. He would have been embarrassed, and worse, would have worried about her thinking less of him.

He still marveled at their relationship. Lisa was the type of drop-dead beautiful blonde Tony never dared even dream about. More importantly, she was smart, funny, honest, and hardworking. Lisa had grown up with money. Her father was the founding partner of Orney's largest law firm. Despite this, she didn't talk or act like the rich girls he had known in college. She didn't flaunt either her privileged life or her looks, but didn't deny them either. Tony found it remarkable how Lisa just accepted her beauty and her bank account as parts of who she was and hoped people wouldn't use them as a basis to assume too much. In this, Lisa and Tony understood each other perfectly.

In everything else, Tony felt completely inadequate. His ego about his writing did not extend to his relationships with women. He knew he was a decent-looking, if average, guy. Five feet, ten inches, and slender, he was fortunate to not have any serious physical short-comings. He was healthy, but he was a bookworm, a term he preferred over "wimp" or "nerd." The dark hair and eyes he inherited from his mother's Italian blood seemed to attract some girls and had allowed him to enjoy some of the seedier perks of college life. But when it came to building a meaningful relationship with a girl, he just didn't seem to have the right stuff. Tony had been hurt badly a couple of times, which gave him a healthy perspective on who he was and what he could expect. In short, he was no great catch and he knew it.

All of this served to make Lisa's interest in him all the more baffling. From the moment they met, he felt as if he was being buried under a tsunami of emotions. Wonderful, positive emotions. Could this apparently perfect woman really be as crazy about him as she seemed? Or was she actually some kind of mental case, obsessed with writers? Or had she made a bet with a friend, like in one of those bad romantic comedies? Or was he simply an idiot for looking a gift horse from heaven in the mouth? "Yes" was the simple answer to the last question.

He allowed his mind to wander back to the night they had met at a political fundraising dinner at the local Marriott Hotel ballroom. Tony hated covering politics, and Ben normally was kind enough to avoid giving him those assignments. However, on that evening, the paper was particularly short-staffed and Tony had accepted the task without much grumbling. As soon as he spotted Lisa, Tony had completely forgotten his objections to attending. She was wearing a dark dress with a high collar and no sleeves. It was just short enough to show off her perfect legs, and it was just tight enough to show off everything else. She wore her blonde hair up, accenting her long neck and her sculpted nose and cheekbones. Tony was entranced.

As he was contemplating how to maneuver an introduction, Lisa had simply walked up to him and put out her hand saying, "You're Tony Harrison, right?" As Tony managed a mute, wide-eyed nod, she had continued, "I'm Lisa Freed. I've been wanting to meet you. I've read your work in the paper, especially your 'My Turn' columns, and you seem like a person I would enjoy knowing."

And just like that, it had started. They grabbed a couple of drinks from the bar and wandered out onto the patio by the pool behind the Marriott. They sat close together on a teak bench and talked for a very long time. Tony found himself staring a lot at the water, the dark sky, the bushes, or anything but Lisa. He didn't want to be impolite, but he was afraid if he looked into those eyes from six inches away, he would drool or faint. Worse, he would do or say something incredibly stupid and break the spell. So he listened as Lisa explained she had finished dual degrees in economics and political science from Northwestern University in Chicago and had come home for the summer to be with her dad. Her mother had passed away when she was nine and, as a result, she and her father were especially close. Rather than get a job right away, Lisa had begun volunteering at the party's county headquarters in Orney, content to have a summer of relative ease after five years of school.

Tony, of course, was well aware of her dad, Nathan Freed. Everyone in Orney was aware of Nathan Freed. Tony had even seen him in action in the courtroom a few times. He knew Lisa's dad to be a smart and capable lawyer, but he hadn't seen him in any really big or controversial cases. Freed was obviously at a point in his career when he could pick and choose the work he did, and he chose not to get in the middle of the worst legal battles. He undoubtedly had paid his dues for many years before achieving his current emeritus status.

When Tony finally did talk, he related his history as well, interspersing the facts with two or three carefully selected amusing stories from his college days and from his experience as a reporter. When he mentioned his love of music, Lisa asked if he played an instrument. Tony confessed to his years of piano lessons.

"Do you still play?" she asked.

"Well, I don't have a piano in my rental house, so I rarely get the chance. Sometimes I go over to the high school and use one of the pianos in the music department. And a couple of times, people have talked me into playing at a party or even at one of the bars downtown."

Lisa smiled broadly.

"What?" Tony asked.

"Talked you into it?" She was still smiling.

"Okay, okay," Tony said, returning the smile. "You're right. It doesn't take much talking. I have to admit I like playing for people. Without sheet music, my repertoire is a little slim, but I usually can last longer than anyone wants to hear me."

"So play for me," Lisa said quietly, taking his hand, standing up, and pulling Tony to his feet.

Tony nodded, swallowed hard, and followed her back into the hotel. She led him down a hallway through the conference center and turned into a darkened meeting room. At the back of the room was a Yamaha baby grand. Light from the doorway gleamed off its polished surface. Tony turned to look for a light switch, but Lisa held him back.

"Do you need more light to play?"

"No, I guess not," Tony replied.

"Then leave it dark."

Tony pulled out the bench from beneath the keyboard and they both sat. He raised the cover from the keys and began playing "New York State of Mind" by Billy Joel. A tiny gasp of air slipped from between Lisa's lips.

"How did you know I love this song?" she whispered. Tony didn't reply, but simply kept playing. Lisa leaned in closer and put her head on his shoulder. Tony wondered if she could feel his goose bumps through the fabric of his shirt.

Thirty minutes later, they left together in Tony's Ford Explorer. Tony almost fainted at her response to his innocent question: "Where to?"

"Let's park," Lisa replied with a smile that could have melted a steel I-beam.

"You want to come to my place?" Tony squeaked out.

"No, I want to *park*," she whispered into his ear and started to nibble.

Tony wasn't inclined to argue, and quickly pulled the floor shifter into gear, stomped on the gas, and headed for the country. After he wasted considerable time searching for an appropriate spot, Lisa surprised him again by directing him to "Harvey's."

Harvey's was the site where Lisa's Uncle Harvey had once lived. At the intersection of two gravel roads, the acreage no longer included the house or barn from which Uncle Harvey had operated his 280-acre farm. However, still standing were a couple dozen big trees and a few outbuildings, including a large wooden corncrib. The crib had been designed for a tractor and wagons to drive through. It looked like a giant car wash, but was made of old wood instead of concrete block. When the farm had been active, the crib had provided a convenient way to unload and store the harvest. Now the acreage was vacant and the crib was an ideal hiding place for two lovers.

Once parked inside, the Explorer was invisible from the road. Tony and Lisa wasted no time in taking advantage of the privacy. It was one of the most memorable nights of his life. Much later, as he drove back out onto the gravel road, Tony muttered, "Thank you, Uncle Harvey," and Lisa laughed.

***

Tony smiled at the memory but then frowned as he looked down at the table full of food. He realized he didn't want to do anything that would make Lisa think less of him, whether she was watching or not. He pushed away the plate with the remaining meat and potatoes, took one bite of apple pie – he was human after all – and headed for the cash register.

Chapter 6

Tony barely had time to admire the stained glass panels in the ceiling of the spectacular old courthouse before the bailiff announced, "All rise," and the afternoon was underway. Once everyone was seated again, the judge asked Nelson if he was prepared to proceed.

"We are, Your Honor," he responded as he rose once more. "The state calls Quincy County Sheriff George Mackey."

Tony settled in for a long and most likely boring afternoon as the sheriff took the stand. The sheriff was well known as a soft-spoken man, unless he was angry. After the tedium of establishing the sheriff's credentials and role as the coordinator of the investigation, Nelson asked the sheriff about the arrest and initial questioning of Wells. A few minutes into the testimony, Tony began to speculate that the primary purpose of the sheriff's appearance at the trial was to make the point that Wells had no alibi for the night of the murders.

Nelson pressed him hard on the point. "In your multiple interviews of Ralph Wells did he ever offer any explanation as to his whereabouts?"

"Well, I think during our third interrogat...uh interview...with him, Mr. Wells said he had been drinking at the Iron Range Tap, a local bar, that night and had fallen asleep in a booth in the back room of the establishment."

"Did you attempt to verify his story?" Nelson asked.

"Of course," the sheriff replied. "We talked to the people working there as well as some of the regulars who play pool in the place. Some of them remember Wells being there that night, but none saw him asleep in a booth. I have all their names if you need to bring them here to tell you directly."

At that, Lawrence Pike rose and said, "Your Honor, the defense is willing to stipulate that no one interviewed by the investigating team saw my client asleep in the bar that night."

Tony was surprised at this, but not as surprised as some in the courtroom. He knew Pike was willing to stipulate to this simply to avoid a roster of God knows how many people being paraded through the courtroom, all saying, in effect, that Wells was lying about his alibi. Nelson agreed to the stipulation, and the judge allowed him to move on.

The bigger surprise soon followed when Nelson asked the sheriff if the Ennis' home had been searched following the murder. The sheriff said yes, and carefully described the team and methodology used. Tony wondered why the search of the victims' home was garnering this careful foundation-laying, but soon understood.

"Sheriff Mackey, did you find anything in the residence that you believe has relevance to the case?" Nelson asked.

"We did. Or I should say I did. In searching the kitchen, I found a plastic bag containing what I believed to be illegal drugs hidden in the flour canister on the counter."

Tony stared at Mackey open-mouthed. It was the first he had

heard any confirmation of drugs being found in this case. He was immediately excited to have something new to report, but equally miffed that it came as a surprise. Davis had to have known about this. Why was this fact kept secret until the trial?

Nelson produced the plastic bag, sealed inside another clear plastic evidence bag, and Mackey confirmed it was the substance found at the Ennis home.

"Your Honor," Nelson said, carrying the bag to the bench, "the prosecution would like to enter this into evidence. We believe later testimony will show this to contain methamphetamines, a class one prohibited substance under Iowa law."

Once again Pike surprised the courtroom when he rose and said additional testimony regarding the chain of evidence and testing of the substance would not be necessary. "I have reviewed the reports from the state, Your Honor, and the defense is willing to stipulate that the substance found in the Ennis home is what Sheriff Mackey and Mr. Nelson state it to be."

This time Tony struggled harder to understand Pike's logic. He knew it was a judgment call. On the one hand, forcing the prosecution to parade more witnesses through the trial to establish proper chain of custody and testing procedures might reveal a mistake that could be exploited by the defense. However, adding witnesses to this issue also would serve to elevate the importance of the find in the mind of the jurors. If Pike was going to argue the drugs were irrelevant, then it made sense to swallow hard and move on as quickly as possible.

Because the sheriff was central to the investigation and his involvement touched virtually every piece of evidence or process undertaken in some way, his testimony was long. The judge ordered a break when he was finished at nearly 4 p.m. Before pounding the gavel, the judge asked Nelson, "Do you have a witness you can fit into the final hour or so of our day?"

"Yes, Your Honor. The state has one more witness it would like to call. While we can't speculate about what questions the defense counsel will have, we're very confident we'll be done with our direct in less than thirty minutes."

"Very well," the judge replied. "This proceeding is in recess for twenty minutes." With a bang, he turned and stepped down into the judge's chambers behind the courtroom.

Tony had barely heard Nelson's comment and didn't give it a thought. He soon learned he should have.

***

"The state calls to the stand Francie Wells."

This was a surprise. Tony didn't know who Francie Wells was, but it seemed obvious she was related to the defendant. A murmur went through the room as a thirtyish, slightly overweight but attractive woman stepped out of a spectator seat and walked to the witness box. She was dressed in a simple charcoal-colored dress with buttons to the collar. She wore no jewelry except what appeared to be an inexpensive copper bracelet and matching combs pinning back her auburn hair. Perfect witness attire, Tony thought with more than a touch of cynicism.

Nelson quickly established that Francie was the older sister of the accused. When finished with the preliminaries, he asked, "Miss Wells, do you know why you're here?"

"Yes," she said quietly. "To testify in my brother's trial."

"Do you want to be here?"

"Not really. You told me I had to come."

Nelson smiled. "Miss Wells, just so everyone understands what the state did or didn't do, let's take a moment to clarify what you just said. Did I say you had to come, or did I encourage you to come in order to do the right thing?"

"Well, you said it was up to me, but after talking to you I felt like this was what I had to do."

"As long as we're on the subject, let's be even more clear, shall we? Did I or anyone representing the state threaten you in any way, or promise you anything in return for your testimony today?"

"Well, you said I would sleep better at night."

At that, the spectators, jurors, and even the judge released a quick chuckle.

Tony admired Nelson's skillful setting of the stage. With a few apparently harmless questions, he had firmly established Francie as the reluctant witness, only here to do her civic duty. Tony knew whatever was coming was not going to be good for Ralph Wells. He was right.

***

Francie's direct testimony was, indeed, short and simple. She told the court she heard her brother threaten to kill Jerry Ennis. She said Ralph Wells had said it while visiting Francie's Viscount, Iowa, home two months before the killings. Francie said Ralph was angry with Ennis for cheating him out of his share of the cash in a methamphetamine sale. Ralph Wells, his sister testified, became increasingly upset as he talked about Ennis. When Francie urged him to calm down, she said, her brother told her, "I will calm down after I kill that SOB."

Nelson asked other questions but kept it within his promised thirty minutes. None of it mattered. Tony knew the prosecution now had presented the jury with the crucial missing piece – a motive.

Defense counsel Lawrence Pike clearly understood the

devastating nature of Francie Wells' words, and did all he could to mitigate their effect. Cross-examination lasted longer than the direct. At one point, he pressed her about her brother's character. "So are you saying your brother was a dealer of illegal drugs?" he asked.

Wells replied, "Yes. Not a big one, but I knew he sold some drugs from time to time, mostly to his friends."

"Are you aware that selling drugs is a crime in Iowa, in some cases a serious crime?"

"Yes."

"Did you ever report to anyone, particularly to law enforcement such as the county sheriff, that your brother was involved in illegal activities?"

"No."

"So can you explain to the court, Miss Wells, why your sense of civic duty brought you here today, but seemed to be absent previously?"

At that, prosecutor Nelson objected. The judge sustained the objection, so no answer was given.

Near the end of his cross-examination, Pike turned to the topic of the alleged threat. "Miss Wells, if this conversation with your brother really occurred, would you please tell the court to whom you reported it?"

"Excuse me?"

"Well, Miss Wells, if you heard your brother threaten to kill someone, as you claim, you must have reported it to the authorities, did you not?"

"Well... no, I guess I didn't."

"You guess you didn't?"

She stiffened, looked Pike in the eye and said more firmly, "No, I didn't."

"I assume you can explain to the court why you kept this

astonishing, perhaps I should say unbelievable, revelation to yourself."

"Objection!" Nelson had yelled loudly enough that Tony actually jumped in his seat in the gallery. "Your Honor..."

"I apologize, Your Honor," Pike was quick to interject. "I retract the editorial comment, but the question still stands…Miss Wells, why did you not report this alleged conversation?"

"I, well, I just didn't think he meant it. After all, he's my brother and I just didn't assume he would really do such a thing."

Pike was quiet for several seconds before turning to the jury, but addressing another question to Wells. "You just said your brother isn't the type of person to commit a heinous crime such as the one we're discussing today. Is that right?"

"Well...uh, no, I mean I'm not sure," Francie Wells stared down at the wooden railing in front of the witness stand.

"You're *not sure* he's the type to kill two people in cold blood?" Pike turned back to face the witness.

"I don't know. I already told you I didn't think so."

At that, Pike had no further questions and Francie Wells was dismissed from the witness stand.

The exchange left Tony an even greater appreciation for Lawrence Pike. He had taken a gamble, but not as big a gamble as it appeared. If the sister had been ready to paint her brother as having the personality of a heartless killer, Pike undoubtedly was prepared to counter that with facts, such as the fact Ralph Wells had never been in trouble for anything and such as the fact Wells didn't like to hunt. In his reporting of the case, Tony had encountered several of Wells' friends willing to tell him that Wells was squeamish about killing animals, so he assumed Pike had the same information.

But Francie Wells had backed down, unwilling to push the issue further. Pike had gotten into the trial record a key prosecution witness saying she didn't believe Ralph Wells was the type of person to commit the crime. Despite this, however, Tony knew the testimony for the prosecution had been far more powerful. He left the courthouse that day thinking it had been a very bad day for Ralph Adam Wells. For some reason, it filled him with a nearly suffocating sense of gloom. He didn't know why, but he had to admit that deep inside he was pulling for the defendant.   The only saving grace regarding today, he thought, was that things couldn't get any worse. He had no idea how wrong he was.

Chapter 7

Tony walked out the glass doors to the top of the courthouse stairs. He broke into a wide smile as he saw Lisa sitting on the bottom step in the late afternoon sun, reading a copy of Bill Bryson's *Thunderbolt Kid*. Lisa recently had confessed to Tony that she'd never read it, and Tony had immediately insisted they go to Walker's Books on the square and buy a copy. "I can just get it from the library," Lisa protested, but Tony insisted.

"Once you read it, you're going to want to keep it, or at least pass it along to someone else," he had assured her.

He was happy to see her reading it now, giggling out loud as she turned a page. He was even happier just to see her. He paused on the stairs just to feast on the sight. She was wearing white capris with a simple navy V-neck sweater. One hand toyed absently with the gold chain around her neck and the other held the book on her lap. Tony reminded himself to breathe and then skipped down the steps to greet her.

"Hey, gorgeous, what brings you to the halls of justice?" he asked as she turned and rose to give him a quick hug.

"Well, I heard some hotshot reporter was here covering a murder trial, so I thought I would ambush him as he left the building. Then I thought I would offer to buy him an early dinner before he headed to the newsroom to write his story."

"Hmmm," Tony nodded thoughtfully, and pulled her to him for a second, longer embrace. "If I see a hotshot reporter anywhere, I'll be sure to let him know. In the meantime, how about dinner with me?"

Lisa laughed. "Well, I don't like to settle, but I guess I could handle it this one time. How about Panucci's for a large sausage and mushroom?"

"Sounds great, but what will you eat?" Tony shot back, only half kidding. He knew Lisa would have one piece to complement her trip to the salad bar while he fought the urge to eat all that remained. Regardless, it was a great idea. Panucci's was his favorite pizza place. Not just his favorite in Orney, but his favorite anywhere, and that was saying something for a kid from Chicago. It was owned by second-generation Italian immigrants and featured a thin crust pizza he craved. In fact, he craved almost everything Mama Panucci cooked. He gladly would have paid money to stand in the doorway and just inhale the aroma of the place.

Located in one of the oldest buildings on the square, Panucci's was modest in every respect except flavor. The seating consisted of six booths along one wall and six small tables scattered in the open dining area. Along the wall at the back of the room was one counter where food was ordered and tabs were paid. Mama didn't wait on you. She stayed in the kitchen, which was just fine with everyone who had tasted her cooking. Her nephew, a young man who was developmentally disabled, worked behind the counter. He could take orders correctly, make change, and run the credit card machine, and that was all Mama needed. Everyone loved Burt who, as far as Tony knew, held the world record for going the most consecutive days with an unbroken smile on his face.

One large plate glass window faced the sidewalk, parking meters, and street. Tony and Lisa sat in the booth nearest the window. Lisa knew it was Tony's favorite spot and knew he preferred to sit facing the window. She assumed it was the reporter in him – always wanting to know what was going on outside. Tony suspected it had more to do with a scene from one of his dad's novels in which a man was shot in the back by a bad guy bursting through the front door of a restaurant. Tony had read the novel when he was young, probably too young. The scene had touched something in him that he couldn't shake. From that point on, whenever the family went to dinner, Tony had insisted on sitting in the seat facing the door. Today, many years later, it was more habit than phobia, but still...

Once settled in, Lisa asked about the trial and Tony related the facts of the day. He confided in her his disappointment at how damaging the testimony had been for Wells.

Lisa listened without interrupting. When Tony finished, she was quiet for a long moment before saying, "Obviously I've been able to tell this case is wearing on you, but I have to admit I'm not sure why. The evidence seems clear, and I don't get the sense that you typically have a lot of sympathy for someone who kills two people in cold blood."

"Of course not. You're right. I'm not sure I understand it myself. I can tell you this, though. I keep thinking back to the night of Wells' arrest. I can see him in my mind like it was yesterday. He seemed so confused, so naive about what was happening, so *innocent*." Tony had a pained look. "I just can't reconcile that scared, dumb kid with my idea of the kind of person who commits premeditated murder."

"Don't all criminals proclaim their innocence, and aren't a lot of them really good actors?"

"Sure, but I was there, six feet away as they dragged him to the squad car. I saw his face. I would bet my house he wasn't acting. And, at the risk of being truly unkind, I don't believe Wells is smart enough to know how to act, let alone pull off an Academy Award performance. Something in this case is out of whack. I can feel it."

"Well, first of all, you don't own a house." Lisa smiled. "I wasn't there so I'm sure not going to disagree with you about what you saw. My only advice is don't let it drive you crazy. Let the justice system do its job, and you concentrate on putting great prose in the local newspaper."

"Good advice," Tony sighed. He didn't sound like he meant it.

Lisa wasn't really worried about Tony. She knew he was a good reporter who could manage his emotions and personal biases. He had covered tough stories before, including stories that affected him deeply. Somehow he managed to set it aside when it was done and move on. However, her angst did rise a little when, after nearly an hour of chatting, Tony excused himself to pay the bill. Lisa glanced at the pizza pan and noticed Tony had eaten only a portion of one piece.

***

Tony parked his SUV in the small lot off the alley behind the *Town Crier* building, actually called the Sanderson Building if you read the etched granite cornerstone, and walked in the back door to the newsroom. He never failed to notice, or appreciate, the scent that greeted him. One hundred years of ink, glue, paper, chemicals, and most likely sweat combined to create a unique smell that lingered in the background of all old newspaper buildings, never letting you forget you were someplace special.

Tony pulled the small spiral reporter's pad from his sport coat pocket, dropped it on his desk, and plopped into his chair, letting out a sigh. After a few moments of staring at the florescent lights in the ceiling, he spun a half turn, glanced at his mail slot to see how much had accumulated, and then turned back to his computer.

"You've got great stuff for tomorrow morning I trust?" Benjamin "Ben" Smalley had sidled up next to his desk. Tony hadn't seen him coming, so he must have been up front at the reception/ad sales desk, or perhaps in the darkroom.

"Actually, I do," Tony said, always pleased to give his boss good news. "Wells' sister testified against him. It was pretty damning stuff."

"His sister... really? Well, I'll be interested to see it." Ben was a good boss and a great editor, which meant he was smart enough not to ask any more questions. He didn't want his reporters relating the news verbally and losing enthusiasm for the story. He knew an article always flowed from the reporters' fingers faster and read with more intensity when the written version was its first telling.

Ben Smalley was the reason Tony was here. Ben had worked in major newspapers for nearly two decades, first in Detroit and later in Baltimore. He had won two Pulitzer Prizes as an investigative journalist and was one of the most respected print journalists on the East Coast. Then about ten years ago, without warning, he quit. Five months later, he bought the *Town Crier* in Orney, Iowa. His colleagues in Baltimore were surprised. The residents of Orney were shocked.

While Iowans pride themselves on being nice and rarely hesitate to welcome a stranger into their communities or even their homes, control of a local newspaper was a serious matter. Some people feared that the "hot shot reporter from New York" – they couldn't seem to get the city right – would try to use the paper for daily exposés of whatever private business they had. In Orney, of course, this was close to laughable. Others feared Ben would trivialize life in Orney, and in effect use the paper to perpetuate outdated stereotypes of farmers or outright make fun of the people and events it covered. Some hoped Ben *would* use the newspaper to shake things up and change whatever they had been griping about for years. No one expected what actually happened.

Ben Smalley loved Orney, Iowa. He found the people surprisingly well educated and deeply interested in all kinds of news and information. He found them willing to discuss, debate, and even argue about issues, but then stand side-by-side to serve pancakes at the fire department's annual fundraiser or harvest a neighbor's crops when misfortune kept the neighbor out of the fields. He found them to be intensely passionate about preserving and improving their community as they fought to stem the natural shrinkage in population. Ben knew they were up against an irreversible trend. The simple truth was that fewer people were needed to work the ever-larger farms. Fewer farm families meant fewer shoppers in town and fewer kids in the schools. Struggling businesses and consolidating schools had become the norm in rural Iowa.

Ben also found Iowans to be an odd mix of conservative and liberal. Regardless of party affiliation, most Iowa conservatives were relatively progressive on social issues, and most Iowa liberals were relatively strong on the need for individual responsibility and well-controlled government spending.

What many people didn't know about Ben was that he had first become intrigued by Iowa twenty years earlier, when he came to the state as a journalist to cover the first-in-the-nation presidential caucuses. The whole process fascinated him. The campaigning in coffee shops and town squares, the debates in local colleges featuring six or eight different candidates from one party, and the caucuses themselves were like nothing else in American politics. The caucus night process was remarkably informal. The word "quaint" might have described it if it didn't have such incredible impact on the future of the nation, and therefore the world. People gathered in church basements, school gymnasiums, and even people's homes. They didn't use secret ballots. They "voted" by a variety of means, but often by visibly and literally standing in their preferred candidate's corner of the room. Even the head counts, which formed the basis for the rise or fall of potential future leaders of the free world, were relatively informal. After spending most of two winter months – December and January – in Iowa that year, Ben had come to appreciate and respect Iowans. However, it wasn't until he actually moved to Orney that he realized how much he loved them.

Ben had done a lot of things right. From the first day in town, he spent every morning at Willie's or one of the other local establishments drinking coffee with the local farmers and others. Each morning he would ask a table of strangers if he could join them. He would assure them he wasn't gathering news, and would proceed to simply get to know them and to help them know him. Word quickly spread that the new guy in town was "darn nice" and simply interested in producing a good newspaper. Within months, there were no longer tables of strangers to join. He was greeted by name and urged to join whatever tables had empty seats.

Of course the owner/editor of a small town paper can't be friends with everyone all the time. Regrettably, sometimes the difficult article had to be published; the friend from the coffee shop had to be told, "I'm sorry, but I have to run the article about your son's arrest." The small size of the paper, which limited the funds available and the size of the staff, also prevented the paper from covering every little league game, every school concert, and every blue ribbon at the county fair. These sins of omission often raised the most ire. But Ben had thick skin, and regardless of what scathing phone call or letter he received, he was always back in the coffee shop the next morning, trading fish tales with the natives.

Ben was careful to tell plenty of stories as well as ask questions. He didn't want to appear aloof in any way. He talked about growing up in Michigan, shooting archery competitively, going to Michigan State on a scholarship, lucking into an internship that later became a job at the *Free Press*, and his experiences there and in Baltimore. He told endless stories about police raids, five-alarm fires, riots, embezzlements, and at least one prison escape. He did it all with a writer's flair for storytelling and a dry sense of humor fueled by his natural cynicism.

The one topic, however, that Ben consistently dismissed with a casual brush off, was why he left the East Coast. He would simply say, "It was time for a change of pace," or something equally unpersuasive, and then change the subject and move on. His new Iowa friends were perceptive enough to know there was something more he wasn't sharing. They also were polite enough to not push it.

Most journalism students at the colleges and universities in Iowa knew Ben Smalley was in Orney. It was like having Eric Clapton playing guitar for a house band in a small town bar. For this reason, Ben received dozens, sometimes hundreds, of résumés every year from students seeking internships or employment. For any student wishing to remain in Iowa, the *Town Crier* seemed the perfect place to begin a journalism career.

Five-and-a-half years earlier, when Tony was nearing college graduation, Orney was high on his list as well. He decided to make a run at Ben Smalley, and he decided he would go all out in the effort. He had driven to Orney one Tuesday afternoon, and sat in a courtroom to watch the trial of a thirty-something schoolteacher who was fighting a charge of operating a vehicle while intoxicated. Tony hadn't known if he would find a trial in session or what the trial might be if he did. It would have been easy to be disappointed that it was something as trivial as an OWI, but Tony was glad to see it was a schoolteacher fighting the charge. It didn't take a genius to understand that if the teacher was convicted, it could cost him his job. Even if he kept his job, it would severely curtail his future opportunities in education. Tony found the testimony more emotional and compelling than he expected.

After leaving the trial and getting some dinner, Tony had gone to City Hall and sat through the semi-weekly meeting of the Orney City Council. Most of the business was routine. Most exciting was a dispute over a request for a zoning variance from a man who wanted to repair cars for money in his residential garage.

When Tony left that meeting, he rushed back to his motel room, pulled out his laptop, and wrote both stories – the trial and the council meeting. He saved them on a thumb drive and carried it to the motel office, asking the clerk to print the two documents. Tony then put the two stories, along with the thumb drive and his résumé, in a manila envelope and drove to the *Town Crier*.

At 10 p.m. only the newsroom door in the back of the building was open. When Tony walked in, two pairs of eyes had looked up from computer terminals. A dark-haired woman with a streak of gray on one side of her short bangs was at the terminal closest to Tony. Smalley was at a desk in the far corner.

"Can I help you?" the woman asked.

"I have something for Mr. Smalley, if he wouldn't mind being bothered for just a minute," Tony said.

"If that's a résumé, you can leave it with me." The woman had eyed the envelope, trying to sound firm. "We have a well-established process for reviewing résumés and deciding who gets invited for interviews. I'm sure you understand we can't take time out for that when we're on deadline."

"Actually, it's more than a résumé. I noticed no one was at the trial today in the courthouse. So I took the liberty of writing it up."

"You took the..."

Ben interrupted the woman, calling from where he sat, "It's alright, Eve. Come on back here, young man."

Tony thanked the woman as he scooted to the back of the room.

"Thank you, Mr. Smalley," Tony said in a rush. "I readily admit I'm one more graduating journalism student who would love to work for you. So, I took the liberty of writing two stories for you today, one about the trial in the courthouse and one about the city council meeting tonight. I figured even if you had them covered, you might like to see how my reporting abilities compare. And if you didn't..." He was trying to get it all out in one breath, but Ben stopped him by simply holding up the palm of his hand.

"Okay, I get it," Ben said. "Very ambitious of you. You accomplished your goal of convincing me you're willing to take a risk and you work fast. Now, two things. One, I trust you don't mean 'stories.' I trust these are articles, written to reflect the facts. And two, please get the hell out of here and let me get my newspaper put to bed."

Tony had mumbled a thank you and slunk away, red-faced. As he drove back to his hotel, he was heartsick. It wasn't exactly the level of admiration or even appreciation he had been seeking. He couldn't be sure Smalley would even read his stuff, let alone offer him a job. He agonized and debated over what he could have done better or differently as he finally fell asleep on the too-stiff mattress of the Iowa Motor Inn next to U.S. Highway 26 south of town.

The next morning Tony had taken advantage of the free coffee and donuts in the lobby of the motel. As he sat at a small Formica table sipping the surprisingly good, strong coffee, he pulled the *Town Crier* from a newspaper rack and scanned the front page. There was a story, *article*, about the city council meeting. "By Eve Cramer, Staff Writer," it said. There next to it, wrapped around a file photo of the schoolteacher, was the article: "Teacher Disputes Results of Alcohol Test in OWI Trial, by Tony Harrington, Special to the *Town Crier*." His hands were shaking as he ran to his SUV to find a convenience store that sold papers.

A week later Tony had received his manila envelope back via the U.S. Postal Service. In it was a copy of his article, as if he hadn't purchased ten of them before leaving town, a check for $100, and a job offer.

***

Nearly six years later, Tony was still churning articles for Ben. He loved the work. The variety of experiences, the opportunity to learn something new every day, and the freedom to be creative in how he told a story – all kept him energized. His admiration of Ben and his affection for the characters with whom he shared the newsroom kept him devoted to the *Town Crier*.

The people who worked in small town newspapers, Tony observed, usually fell into one of two categories: the very young and the very old. The very young were there because the paper primarily hired new graduates. Once they honed their skills, they usually sought, and found, career opportunities at larger newspapers or in other businesses seeking good writers. The *Town Crier* could not compete with the salaries or the glamour of jobs in larger cities.

The very old were those rare exceptions who stayed in Orney because of longstanding family ties or a spouse's job or, occasionally, a general lack of interest in climbing the career ladder.

As a result, Tony's co-workers ranged from the newest reporter, a woman younger than Tony who had just graduated from Coe College in Cedar Rapids, to the 78-year-old sports editor, who still trudged out night and day to cover everything from high school sports to Little League tournaments to the Chamber of Commerce-sponsored half marathon. The young graduate, Madeline, was cute, talented, and not at all interested in small talk. Tony was still trying hard to get a read on her. He doubted she would be in Orney for long. The sports editor, Jim, had a voice loud enough to announce sports events without a public address system and cussed continuously. Tony had found his ranting distracting at first, but he grew accustomed to it over time. Now, when Tony sat at his keyboard in the newsroom to write, he didn't even hear the hubbub around him. Well, the occasional holler from the sports desk of "Well fuck me!" could still break his concentration. But it only caused him to smile. The fact was, Jim could make a game come to life on a newspaper page. He still worked as hard as any twenty-something, and he almost never made mistakes. Any editor would put up with a lot to keep those qualities on his staff.

As Tony surveyed the room over the top of his computer screen, he took a deep breath and basked in the aromas and sounds of the room. Like a great stew, the final taste relied on an array of different ingredients. Tony was deeply happy to be one of them. But he couldn't bring himself to be very happy about the article he had just finished writing about the Wells trial.

Town Crier

Sister Testifies Wells Threatened to Kill Shooting Victim

Methamphetamines Found in Victims' Home

Tony Harrington, Staff Writer

ORNEY, Iowa - Francie Wells, sister of accused murderer Ralph Adam Wells, 29, of rural Orney, testified on Wednesday that she heard her brother threaten to kill Jerry Ennis, one of the victims of a double homicide in a rural Quincy County farmhouse in January.

In a second development, Quincy County Sheriff George Mackey testified he found a bag of what later proved to be methamphetamines in the kitchen of the Ennis home during a routine search after Jerry and Anne Ennis were found shot to death in the bedroom of the house.

The information provided by the two witnesses Wednesday appeared to relate to a potential motive for the crime.

Francie Wells said her brother came to visit her in neighboring Viscount, Iowa, two months before the killings, expressing his anger at Ennis for cheating him out of his share of the cash in a drug deal involving a large amount of methamphetamines. Ralph Wells, his sister testified Wednesday, "...became more and more upset as he talked about it. I kept asking him to calm down but then he said, 'I will calm down after I kill that SOB.'"

Prosecuting attorney W. Rodney Nelson asked Francie Wells to repeat for the jury…

Chapter 8

Tony slept an extra half hour the next morning, enjoying the much-needed rest, but not enjoying the required rush that followed. He skipped breakfast and got a donut and coffee to go from Willie's, leaving his SUV at the parking meter as he hurried down the street to the courthouse. He knew it would cost him at least one ticket by the time the trial broke for lunch, but he preferred the fine over Judge Schroeder's wrath. After pushing through the doors into the courthouse, he paused to take one more gulp of coffee, then dropped the cup and its remaining contents into the shiny aluminum trash bin in the hallway before nodding to the deputy at the door to the courtroom and pulling on the big iron handle.

Nick of time, he thought, as everyone was just rising to respect the judge's entry. Tony scooted to the front and slid into the wooden seat reserved for the press just as the judge said, "Please be seated."

After the preliminaries, the judge once more called on the prosecutor, who rose to announce, "The state calls Alissa Ennis."

The doors at the back of the room opened as necks craned to

see a tall man, perhaps retirement age, in a simple gray suit enter the room. At his side, and holding his hand, was a little girl with short blonde hair and surprisingly dark eyes. She wore a simple white and green print dress, brown shoes, and a dark green plastic hairband.

As the man and the girl reached the front, the man dropped to one knee and looked the girl in the eyes. "Are you okay?" he asked gently. The girl nodded, and the man stood holding open the gate in the bar, allowing her to approach the witness stand.

Tony swallowed hard and began writing furiously. He knew Alissa was the older of the two girls left orphaned by the murders. She would be about ten now. He assumed the elderly escort was the girls' grandfather.

The girl seemed remarkably well-composed, considering all she had been through and considering all eyes in the room were focused on her.

When Judge Schroeder spoke, Tony couldn't help looking up quickly from his notepad. The judge's voice had changed completely. He sounded kind...almost human.

"Alissa," the judge said. "I need you to swear to me and to God that you will tell the truth today. Do you swear that?"

"Yes sir," the girl said without hesitation.

"That's great, Alissa. Now I want you to do one other thing for me, okay?" The girl nodded. "I want you to pretend there's no one here in this room but you, me, Mr. Nelson, and Mr. Pike. Can you try to do that for me?"

"I'll try," the girl responded.

"Good. Just answer the gentlemen's questions clearly and honestly, and then we'll get you back to school lickety-split."

Lickety-split? Tony thought. *Good grief. Who are you and what have you done with the judge?*

Then it began. With Nelson's help, the girl described that

terrible night. Waking in the dark, not sure what had interrupted her sleep. Seeing a man emerge from the stairway to the upstairs and watching him walk to the kitchen and out the door into the winter night. Calling after him and not getting an answer. Then calling for her parents, and still not getting an answer. Then climbing out of the bed, walking up the stairs, and discovering what no child should ever have to see.

By that point in her testimony, Alissa had tears running down her face. So did every other person in the room, including the judge, the attorneys, and Tony. Tony understood all too well it didn't matter what evidence the girl had to share or not share. After seeing this, there was no way a jury was going to acquit anyone.

Tony tuned back in to the proceedings as Nelson asked the girl, "Can you describe the man you saw walk through the house that night?"

Alissa said, "Not really. His face looked really dark, even when the light was on it. I think he was wearing one of those caps like we wear when we do chores on a really cold day."

"You mean a ski mask?" Nelson prompted.

"Yeah, like that."

"Can you tell us what clothes the man was wearing?"

"Yeah. That was easy to see because his coat was bright yellow."

Nelson interjected, "By coat, do you mean a long coat, like a rain coat, or more of a jacket?"

"It was a jacket."

"And did it have writing on the back?"

At this point, the prosecutor was clearly leading the witness, and Tony knew that Pike must be coming out of his skin, wanting to object. Tony also knew there was no way in hell Pike was going to say a word. If he interrupted this, the jury would despise him for it.

Alissa responded to Nelson's question, "Yes. Big letters. I couldn't see it all, but it started with an 'N.' "

"You're sure about the first letter being an 'N'," Nelson asked.

"Yes sir. I'm positive. He had a yellow jacket with big letters, starting with an 'N'."

Tony started to sense this testimony was a little too rehearsed. Nelson must have sensed it too, because he quickly moved on.

"Anything else you remember?" he asked.

"Yes. He had on big brown boots, like the work boots we wear outside in the barnyard. I remember seeing his boots as he went into the kitchen because my mom doesn't...uh...didn't let us wear boots in the house. I thought I should warn him that Mom would be mad if she caught him in the house with boots on."

At this several spectators began weeping openly, and two elderly women sitting near the back actually got up and quietly left the room.

The judge stepped in and asked in a soft voice, "Are you nearly finished, counselor, or do I need to gavel a quick break here?"

Nelson gave a wan smile and said, "Actually, Your Honor, I'm completely finished. I have no further questions of this fine young woman." He mouthed a "good job" to Alissa and then turned and took his seat.

The judge turned to Pike. "Does the defense have any questions of the witness?"

Pike rose. "No questions, Your Honor. Thank you."

No shit, thought Tony, and then joined the throng headed for the doors to get some air.

***

Tony wondered if Nelson would rest at this point, but wasn't overly surprised that he spent the rest of the morning extracting small snippets of testimony from DCI agents and sheriff's deputies regarding the physical evidence and other details, closing any loopholes and ensuring everything tied together nicely.

Right before lunchtime, Nelson called Denny Peters to the stand. Peters was a redheaded, middle-aged deputy whom Tony barely knew. Peters had been a deputy long enough that he rarely worked the night shifts, when most of the newsworthy incidents occurred. Tony's cynicism reared its head again as he thought of Peters as one of those public servants who is essentially "retired in place." He didn't actually know if this was fair or not. He did know the deputy had grown a bit of a stomach as he aged. While he wore the weight well on his six-foot, three-inch frame, he clearly needed to invest in a new uniform at least one size bigger than the one currently stretched tightly across his middle.

Peters testified he had been in charge of the search of the defendant's home, property, and car. He painted in great detail, and all too accurately, the poor condition of all three. By the time he was finished, jurors were shaking their heads. Tony could imagine these Iowa farmers, teachers, bankers, and nurses saying to themselves, "What kind of man lives like that?"

And then, the punch line.

"Deputy Peters, in searching the trunk of Mr. Wells' car, did you find anything of relevance to this case?" Nelson asked. "In addition to the rifle, I mean, which testimony has already established was previously turned in to authorities."

"Yes sir."

"And what did you find that you believed to be relevant?"

"I found a jacket and a pair of boots."

Nelson lifted two clear plastic bags from the floor and asked, "Are these the items you found in Mr. Wells' car trunk? You may examine them if you like."

Peters turned the bags over in his hands, peering through the plastic of each one and reading the labels affixed to them. He then said, "Yes sir, these are the items."

"Your Honor, the state offers into evidence three items – two work boots and a jacket," Nelson said with just a hint of smugness.

Judge Schroeder responded, "Very well. Bailiff, you will mark these items exhibits uh, let me see, Exhibits 'T' and 'U.' You may proceed, Mr. Nelson."

The prosecutor held the bags in front of the witness once more and said, "Deputy Peters, before I turn these over to the bailiff, and just to ensure we have it in the oral record, would you describe for the court these items."

"Yes sir. The two boots appear to be ordinary work boots such as worn by many people living or working on farms, brown in color. The jacket is a bright yellow jacket with large navy-colored letters on the back that spell the word 'NAPA.'"

"I have no further questions, Your Honor, " Nelson said and returned to his seat.

Pike once again had no questions and the judge turned back to the prosecutor. "Mr. Nelson?"

"Your Honor," Nelson said loudly as he stood. "The prosecution rests."

***

Tony and Doug met for lunch back at Willie's. This time it was burgers and fries for both. Doug had the apple pie and Tony added a side salad.

"Salad. Really?" Doug remarked. "I'm starting to think you're in love with this girl."

"Yeah, me too," Tony smiled, but then waved his hand to cut off the barrage of follow-up questions he could sense were coming. It was a futile effort.

"Love, really? Well, well," Doug's voice trailed off.

"Let it go," Tony practically pleaded, but again to no avail.

"Have you told her?" His friend avoided Tony's eyes and pretended to focus on the slice of an onion protruding from his hamburger bun.

"No."

"And why not, pray tell?"

"Do we really have to talk about this?"

"Of course we do. What could be more important?"

Tony was primed to reply with some witty response about the trial, or the weather, or the baseball playoffs, or even the latest conflict in the Middle East, but then suddenly caved. "Well, nothing, I suppose."

"There you go!" Doug smiled and swiped a drop of ketchup from the corner of his mouth with his napkin. "So why haven't you told her?"

"I'm not sure," Tony said. "I guess I don't want to spoil it."

His friend's face scrunched into a tight portrait of skepticism to which Tony responded, "No, really. Everything is so perfect, I'm terrified I'll do or say something to mess it up."

Doug shook his head but was uncertain what to say. Tony filled the awkward silence. "When I was a senior at Iowa, one of my friends was in a terrible relationship with a girl who walked all over him like he was a hotel bath mat."

Doug had to be wondering what this had to do with anything, but to his credit he held his tongue. Tony continued, "When they finally broke up, Tru – that was his name, Tru – was devastated. He knew he was better off without her, but he still was inconsolable. He said something to me at the time that sounds corny but has a grain of truth at its core."

Tony paused to dip a trio of fries in ketchup and wolf them down.

"I'm waiting," Doug reminded him.

"Tru said, 'The greatest day of your life is when you realize you're in love, and the worst day of your life is when *she* realizes it.' He said his relationship with Jennifer was never the same after she knew she had him wrapped around her finger."

Doug was shaking his head again. "Do you really think that's what Lisa would do if she knew you loved her?"

"No!" Tony was horrified at the thought he had implied something so awful about Lisa. "Of course not, but..."

"But nothing. Tell the girl how you feel. She deserves to know and you deserve to find out if she feels the same way."

Tony nodded, "I would love to believe that's how it would go, but what if it doesn't? Maybe I'm just a coward. Maybe I just don't want to know the truth."

"Maybe you're an idiot," Doug leaned back in the booth and stretched his arms across the back.

Tony smiled. Determined to change the subject, he suddenly asked his friend, "How much of the trial did you see today? I didn't see you in there until after the break."

"Yeah, I skipped out this morning. Slept in and had a big breakfast," Doug pushed his fork through the apple pie to take his first bite. "From what I've heard, it sounds like I was smart to miss it."

"You're absolutely right." Tony nodded, pointing his fork at his friend's face. "It was horrifying to hear such a young kid describe that night."

"So what do you think?" Doug asked. "I mean about the whole thing. Does Wells have any chance at all?"

"Despite the fact this whole thing stinks, I think the evidence is overwhelming; the prosecution's witnesses are unimpeachable; and the emotions are so high they could bring down a GPS satellite. Let me put it this way...if this was a football game, I would say the prosecution is leading 45 to 3, late in the fourth quarter. Mr. Wells and Mr. Pike need a miracle to win. And I mean a literal miracle, like angels floating down from Heaven proclaiming Wells to be innocent."

Doug chuckled. Football and angels? It might be an awkward way to say it, but it made the point. Doug also wondered, of course, about Tony's comment that the "whole thing stinks." He wanted to ask but decided it should wait until they had more time and fewer ears nearby. He was sure that by the time the town heard about today's testimony, nearly everyone would hate Ralph Adam Wells. He didn't want that hate to spill over onto someone foolish enough to question the evidence against him, especially when that someone was his best friend.

Chapter 9

As Tony and Doug walked across the square to the courthouse, Tony suddenly offered, "There's only one thing that bothers me about the state resting its case." Doug looked up in anticipation and waited for him to continue. "Why didn't Nelson use the room?"

Doug nodded knowingly and said, "Who knows? Probably they felt they didn't need it." Doug was the only person Tony had told about the room.

Tony knew Doug was probably right. Nelson had the case won. *Hell,* Tony thought. *The verdict was practically chiseled on the foreheads of the jurors before the defense even began its case. Why risk the state's case with unnecessary testimony?*

On the other hand, Tony also knew that W. Rodney Nelson loved to grandstand, as much for the press as for the jury. He hadn't expected Nelson to rest his case without a visit to, or at least a mention of, the room.

As they walked, Tony irresistibly gazed past the courthouse in the direction of the county maintenance garage, eight or ten blocks away. Not many people knew what was there, but Tony had seen it. A good reporter had friends in many places. Barry Allen was the union steward for the local maintenance workers, and he appreciated what he considered to be Tony's balanced coverage of union activities and labor disputes. So Barry had called Tony at home late one night two months previously and had invited him to come to the garage to "see something interesting."

Tony's curiosity never would have allowed him to say no, and besides, the call already had caused him to miss the opening monologue on *The Late Show.* So Tony had hopped in his Explorer and ten minutes later greeted Barry in the large gravel parking lot that surrounded the garage on all sides. Barry was still wearing his coveralls, steel-toed boots, and a pale green cotton shirt with the union logo over the pocket. Barry was a big man, perhaps six feet, two inches or more, with a pocked face from teenage acne decades before. That night, however, Barry's grin made him look about twelve. He was as giddy as a kid who couldn't wait to show his pals his new skateboard.

Tony had expected to see some document. The union guys were always accusing the county officials of acting improperly or in bad faith in their dealings with employees. The "evidence" assembled by the union guys had come to him before in a late-night rendezvous like this. However, he had been astonished when he entered the garage.

"What'd ya think?" Barry had chuckled, spitting a chew into the drainage grate in the garage floor. "I bet y'all and Miss Freed could live in a room like this."

At one end of the huge building was a mock-up of a bedroom. It looked completely real, except for one missing wall. Tony had never seen a Hollywood movie set, but he was pretty sure this was what it would look like.

Tony also had not been in the Ennis house. In this case, his friends in the DCI had stopped short of allowing him inside. It had irritated him at the time, but he had understood their caution. A double murder in rural Iowa was very rare, and statewide attention was focused on the case. He backed down, on the condition that the restriction apply to everyone. His actual words to agent Davis had been, "If I open *The Des Moines Register* and find a photograph of the murder scene, I swear I'll put your eighth grade yearbook picture on the *Crier's* website." Davis had laughed, but had gotten the point.

On that night two months ago, however, standing inside the maintenance garage, there had been no question in Tony's mind about what he was seeing. It was an exact replica of the inside of the Ennis bedroom.

"My God," he said as he approached it slowly, almost with reverence. "This is unbelievable. Who did this? Not you guys surely?"

"Nah," Barry laughed, and spit. "This was some smart-ass suits from Des Moines. You haven't lived 'til ya seen guys in button down collars swingin' hammers and paint brushes. They take off their suit coats and they think they've dressed for real work."

"Can I get my camera?" Tony had practically pleaded. But Barry had declined. He could get in enough trouble for just showing it to him. But he allowed Tony to stay more than an hour there, going over the room, imagining how the murders had occurred, and imagining how the prosecution would use this mock-up in the trial.

"Is this the actual furniture?" he asked.

"That's what they tell me, right down to the sheets on the bed and curtains on the window."

"Obviously they can't move this to the courthouse," Tony pressed. "They must be planning to bring the jury here."

"Yep," Barry said. "Me 'n Charlie have been given the task of cleaning up the rest of the building. I guess them county supervisors don't want the outside world seein' how we peons usually live."

Tony had covered murder trials and other sensational crimes in his nearly six years as a reporter, but he had never seen anything like this. He knew Nelson wanted a conviction in this case. Staring at this movie set, he realized just how desperately Nelson wanted to win.

***

Back in the courtroom, Tony found himself staring at the lead prosecutor. It must have killed Nelson to leave the mock bedroom in the county shed, unused. Tony smiled as he imagined the scene down the hall in the county attorney's office, where Nelson and his team had set up temporary offices. He could see Nelson fuming as his underlings, and perhaps the county attorney, convinced him it would be a mistake to disrupt a trial going this well, to haul everyone eight blocks down the street for an unnecessary 3-D look at the crime scene, and perhaps a demonstration of the crime.

Judge Schroeder turned to Wells' attorney, Lawrence Pike. Tony thought of Pike as a has-been. On the verge of retirement, with a relatively quiet career in small-town law to his credit, Pike was certainly not the type of attorney Tony would have selected if his life was on the line. "Is the defense prepared to proceed, Mr. Pike?"

"To be honest, Your Honor, the brevity of the state's case has surprised us. I respectfully request a recess to give us an opportunity to contact and schedule our witnesses."

"Very well, Mr. Pike," Schroeder replied. "This court stands adjourned until 9 a.m. tomorrow morning, at which time the defense will begin presenting its case. Any other issues or motions for the court at this time?"

This was the point in the trial at which, in some cases, the defense attorney would make a motion to dismiss the case, claiming the state failed to present adequate evidence. In covering three previous murder trials, Tony had never seen a judge rule on the motion in the defendant's favor. He knew attorneys only used it as a way to plant doubt in the jurors' minds that they had seen convincing evidence. Tony was not surprised that Pike didn't attempt it. In this case, the jury could only have thought Pike was crazy if he tried to claim there wasn't enough evidence to require a defense. Besides, if Pike made the motion, the jury would hear the judge deny it, which would only lend credibility to the state's case. So no motion was made.

Hearing no response to his offer, Schroeder began his routine admonishing of the jury not to discuss the case and not to read, view, or listen to any media during the course of the trial. Tony wasn't listening. He was already preparing to bolt from the courtroom as soon as the judge was off the bench. As a matter of habit, he was writing the next morning's story in his head. It was predictably straightforward.

Because he had the afternoon free to write, Tony was able to get away from the newsroom early. It was just after 4 p.m. when he drove down the alley behind his rented bungalow and turned into the small detached garage. He was spent, but not too spent to appreciate seeing Lisa's classic 1967 Mustang parked in the yard beside the garage. The relationship with Lisa was still new enough that his heart beat just a little faster at the thought of her, and even faster at the realization that, before the night was out, it was likely they would be in his bed resuming their exploration of the physical side of their romance. *Hell,* Tony thought, *I've been exploring so much lately I feel like Christopher Columbus.*

He was smiling broadly as he walked through the back door, dropped his keys on the kitchen counter, and slowly stepped around the corner into the living room. His expression changed to a different kind of pleasure when he discovered he was not going to be disappointed. Sitting cross-legged on top of the old RCA console television cabinet, which now served primarily as a pedestal for his real TV, was Lisa. She was wearing his blue and white striped bathrobe. The robe was open to her navel, where it was tied. Much of her chest was exposed, with just her nipples hidden by the soft terrycloth. Her blonde hair lay loosely on her shoulders, and her hands rested lightly in her lap. Tony was certain she wore nothing underneath.

Lisa was smiling but her face was slightly flushed. At the sight of her, Tony was instantly hard and at a complete loss for words.

"I thought I would fix your problem," Lisa said, her voice low and raspy.

"What...?"

"You know, you always complain that by the time you get home, there's nothing on TV."

It was an old, tired joke, but it was perfect. Tony practically raced across the room and wrapped his arms around her. As their lips met, she opened her legs and locked her ankles behind his back. Tony was consumed by her – her looks, her smell, the feel of her skin, her silliness, her passion. Almost before he realized it, they were on the floor, her hands under his shirt, tugging at his belt. As quickly as he was free, she was on him and he was in her. He wanted her so much. They rolled over, then rolled again, never slowing their furious pace. He couldn't contain himself and it was over quickly, but before either of them uttered a word, he picked her up and lay her gently on the couch. He was all over her again, using his lips and tongue until he was ready to enter her again. The third time was in his bed, where they had room to stretch and twist and explore.

"My, oh my," Tony gasped as the quivering finally subsided. Lisa snuggled up next to him, head on his chest.

"I agree," Lisa said quietly. "That was wonderful." She closed her eyes and began humming softly. It was a melody Tony recognized but he couldn't quite place it.

He looked down at the top of her head and followed the lines of her body all the way to her toes. She was simply beautiful, inside and out. Tony wasn't sure how true love was supposed to feel, but he knew this had to be close.

***

After pulling on shorts and T-shirts, Tony and Lisa fixed a late dinner of BLTs and chips. They boiled a couple of ears of sweet corn, making it feel like a real meal, and ate in front of the TV. Lisa volunteered to "do the dishes" which primarily meant throwing paper plates in the trash and putting two pans and two glasses into the dishwasher. When she returned, she was carrying a glass of White Zin for herself and a diet soda for him. Tony rarely drank alcohol. He had seen it destroy too many people, from fellow students at college to victims of car accidents and violent crimes in his news coverage. Lisa didn't seem to mind and never commented about it, which was one more thing he adored about her.

As they cuddled up on the couch, Lisa turned on PBS to watch the latest British drama series, allowing Tony to let his mind wander back to his work.

He ticked through a mental list of the key points of the prosecution's case: Ralph Wells' old .22 rifle was almost certainly the murder weapon. The ballistics expert from the Iowa DCI had been convincing on that point. And there was the clothing. The young girl had seen a jacket and boots identical to those found in Wells' trunk.

And then there was Francie Wells and the bag of meth. Ralph's sister and Sheriff Mackey had provided the key points missing from the pre-trial coverage. Until they took the stand, there had been no indication of what Wells' motive might have been. They had provided the "why" with the introduction of a drug deal gone bad and the growing wrath of a cheated partner. Even though Wells had no criminal record and no other evidence of his involvement in drugs had been offered, Francie had sworn to it. Tony knew that coming from Wells' sister, it would be believed.

Lastly, Wells was known to be around that night and hadn't been seen by anyone during the apparent time of the killings. While the defense hadn't presented its case yet, the testimony of the sheriff was that Wells had no alibi.

So there it was: means, motive, and opportunity. Convincing evidence in all elements required to prove Wells' guilt. Tony knew these three elements were more factors of popular culture than a technical aspect of criminal law in Iowa, but he also knew this was how some jurors thought. Tony felt himself react physically, sighing and slumping back against the couch.

Lisa didn't comment. She just hugged him closer until eventually his head slid down and found an adequate pillow on the flesh of her leg. He pulled his legs up onto the couch and fell asleep.

Town Crier

Daughter of Murder Victims Describes Intruder's Jacket

Description Matches Jacket Found in Accused Man's Car

Tony Harrington, Staff Writer

ORNEY, Iowa – Ten-year-old Alissa Ennis, daughter of Jerry and Anne Ennis who were found dead in their rural Orney home last January, provided tearful testimony Thursday in the trial of Ralph Adam Wells, 29, who is accused of killing the girl's parents.

Ennis described to an emotional courtroom being awakened from her sleep on the first floor of the farmhouse on the night of the murders.

She testified that she saw a man exit from the stairway to the upstairs bedroom, where the two bodies were found. The man walked through the first floor of the house to the kitchen and turned on a light. The girl said the man's face was obscured by what appeared to be a ski mask. However, she said she clearly saw the man's bright yellow jacket with bold lettering on the back...

Chapter 10

The next morning was overcast and cool, as if winter was making an early grab for a day or two of what otherwise had been a great September. Tony was sorry Lisa had left before he awoke. A note on the fridge told him she had an early breakfast with her dad. She wished him a good day and signed it, simply, "Love."

"Jesus," Tony gasped. He then glanced upward and addressed the heavens. "Sorry, Lord, but is that really possible?"

He arrived at the courthouse in plenty of time and, miracle of miracles, found Doug Tenney there ahead of him.

"Holy cow," Tony said as he walked down the marble corridor. "Did your landlord finally discover your pot farm in the basement and throw you out?"

"Jeez..." Doug said, grimacing and backing away. "That's not funny when you're standing in a hallway surrounded by law enforcement officers."

"Oops, sorry," Tony smiled, then spoke loudly to the walls. "Just kidding, folks!"

Doug reached into his shoulder bag and pulled out a convenience store donut bag, passing it to Tony, who looked inside and chose one without frosting.

"So seriously," he said, "what brings you here early?"

Doug made a face and said, "My boss decided it would be a good idea for the Big K to do a live remote from the courthouse this morning. If you ever listened to us, you would have heard me eloquently describing yesterday's events and speculating about the excitement to come."

"Really?" Tony deadpanned. "Excitement? If you can make today exciting, I will start listening to your 5-watt ham radio station or whatever that thing is."

"Hey," Doug shot back. "Don't make fun of us. Since I started reading your stories on the air and pretending they were accurate, the Big K is up to twenty-four or twenty-five listeners. We even sold an ad last week."

The two men grinned and finished their donuts, then entered the courtroom and took their seats.

***

Pike called several witnesses who had known Ralph Wells all their lives and who testified they had never known him to be violent and had never known him to be involved in using or selling illegal drugs.

After each round of direct questioning, Nelson's cross-examination was equally predictable.

"So you've known Ralph Wells all your life?"

"Yes, since grade school anyway."

"So you consider Mr. Wells to be a friend?"

"Yes, I guess so. We still play pool together and sometimes

meet to watch football or just hang out."

"Do you consider yourself a good person, I mean the kind of person who looks out for and supports his friends and neighbors?

"Yes, but..."

"And you're hoping your testimony today will help Ralph, is that right?"

"Yes, of course, but..."

"No further questions, Your Honor."

The point was clear. No matter how many friends Pike paraded through the courtroom, their testimony on behalf of someone they wanted to help just wasn't very compelling.

Pike then called a couple of expert witnesses. One testified regarding his review of the crime scene investigation and autopsy record, attempting to call into question the time of the murders. Tony knew if Pike could succeed in establishing that the killings occurred earlier in the evening, when Wells was still being seen by people in the bar, then he would have an alibi.

The expert testified the body temperatures were lower than expected when first examined on the scene. He said the cooler temperatures indicated the events could not have had occurred as presented, with no delay between the gunshots that awoke Alissa Ennis and the killer's departure from the house, followed by Alissa's call to 9-1-1 and the first deputy's arrival at the house. However, the discrepancy wasn't big enough, in Tony's opinion, to be convincing. It was an old farmhouse and the upstairs was cold, heated only by vents in the floor that allowed first-floor heat to rise. *Cold room, cold bodies,* Tony thought.

This, in fact, was the exact point Nelson made in his cross-examination.

The second expert actually testified about clothing. Pike used him to make the point about the thousands of yellow jackets in the world. He even testified about the number of yellow jackets distributed by NAPA. This, Tony knew, was grasping at straws.

Nelson didn't bother to cross examine him at all.

After a brief recess, the defense resumed with Pike calling Wells' wife, Amber, to the stand. As she took the stand, she looked even paler and more frail than the night Tony had seen her at the trailer house. She looked like a sickly teenager, but testified that she was twenty-two and had a two-year Associate of Arts degree from the community college in Fort Dodge. She worked as a secretary at the local grain elevator.

She wore a modest white dress, gathered at the middle by a wide blue belt and accented with a blue and white scarf around her neck. The billowy scarf made Amber look tiny, as if her head was about to disappear into its folds.

After establishing the basic facts about herself and her marriage, Pike went right into asking Amber about Wells' interest, or not, in firearms. She seemed sincere as she described Wells' distaste for guns and was adamant the .22 rifle hadn't been out of his trunk even once in the three years they had been married.

When Pike asked Amber about the night of the murders, she described how she had become concerned because her husband was out even later than usual. When it was nearly 2 a.m., she got out of bed, she said, and decided to walk out to the road to see if he had driven into the ditch. She said she worried that he had tried to drive home while intoxicated and had an accident.

"I know it was silly to think he would be right there, but I couldn't just lie in bed any longer. I had to do something."

"So let me ask you, Amber. Did you get dressed?"

"Not really," she replied. "I just put my robe on over my pajamas, and then put my winter coat on over that."

"Did you put on shoes?"

"No, I just pulled Ralph's work boots on over my slippers. That just seemed simpler and warmer than putting on my shoes."

Pike walked over to the evidence table and picked up the plastic evidence bag with the boots the deputies had confiscated. Tony smiled, realizing where Pike was going.

"Amber, would you please examine the boots in this bag and then tell the court if these are the boots you wore that night?"

"Yes. Yes I'm sure they are because Ralph had two different shoe laces in his boots. He had the original red laces on the left boot, but he had tied together a couple of ordinary black shoelaces for the right boot after he broke the original one. You can see it right here."

"Thank you." Pike smiled and then grew somber. "Amber, I'm going to shift gears now. You weren't in the courtroom, but a previous witness said your husband was angry with Jerry Ennis because he cheated him out of money in a drug deal. Do you believe that to be true?"

"Absolutely not." Amber's voice grew louder and more pointed. "Ralph isn't exactly a coward," she glanced at her husband apologetically, "but he hates confrontations and he wouldn't have the courage, or the ambition, to get involved in illegal drugs. In fact, I've never seen him angry at another person. He's just this harmless guy who tries to get along."

At Pike's urging, Amber testified quietly but without hesitation about her husband's good points, as well as his not-so-good points. Tony once again found himself admiring Pike's tactics. *Get it out on direct,* Tony thought, *so you don't let the opposition do it.* The bottom line of Amber's testimony was that her husband was lazy and spent too much time with his friends in the bar and too little time with her.

"But," she said, "he wouldn't hurt a fly."

"Mrs. Wells," Pike said, "this may or may not be directly relevant to the case, but your testimony has made me wonder, and so perhaps others are wondering, about your marriage to Ralph. Your description of Ralph doesn't exactly paint a picture of an ideal husband, does it?"

"No," she said, almost in a whisper while looking down at her feet.

Judge Schroeder interjected, "Mrs. Wells, please be sure to answer in a manner that the jury and the court reporter can hear."

"Sorry, Your Honor," she said, looking up and turning to the jury. "No, Ralph isn't the perfect husband."

"So why," Pike asked, "may I ask, did you marry him?"

Nelson rose quickly, saying, "Your Honor, please. Is this relevant in any way to the case?"

Schroeder answered, "I have no way to know at this point and neither do you, Mr. Nelson. However, the question seems harmless enough, so I'm going to allow it. Mrs. Wells, please know in the State of Iowa you can't be required to testify for or against your husband, so it's completely up to you which questions you answer."

"I don't mind, Your Honor," Amber Wells said, turning to Pike. "I married Ralph *because* he's harmless. You see, I grew up in a household with an abusive father. My mother, my sister, and I lived in fear of my dad every day for nearly twenty years. It was a horrible situation. Intimidation and actual physical abuse were common. In the end, my dad put my mother in intensive care, and the authorities finally put him behind bars. I vowed I would never live like that again. When I met Ralph, I could see he had his flaws. But I also could see he loved me, and I knew I would never have to be afraid of him. And I was right," she added, wanting to get in one last thought as tears began to trickle down her cheeks. "I have lived a peaceful, happy life with Ralph, right up until the night the deputies dragged him out of our home."

"Thank you, Amber," Pike said, patting the railing in front of the witness stand and letting the grandfather in him shine through. "I have no further questions."

Nelson once again declined cross-examination.

Score one for the defense, Tony thought, as Judge Schroeder gaveled the recess for lunch.

***

After lunch, Pike called Ralph Wells to the stand. This, of course, should have been one of the highlights of the defense but it simply wasn't. Whether because of his IQ, his nervousness, or his lack of good answers, Wells was completely ineffective in defending himself. He was wearing a dark suit with a plain maroon tie. The suit seemed to be the right size, yet his chubby frame didn't seem to belong in it. His curly hair was clean and combed, but somehow still looked unruly. Tony couldn't help it. As he studied Wells, everything about the man shouted "loser" back at him.

Pike had to have debated about putting him on the stand at all. However, the state's strong case made it essential. Pike knew Iowa juries wanted to hear from defendants. He had zero chance of convincing them Wells was innocent if Wells was unwilling to take the stand and say so.

In fact, Wells said all the correct things about his growing reluctance to hunt, his lack of criminal behavior, his lack of knowledge about the Ennises or their deaths, but Pike had to lead him through it every step of the way. Wells never offered one fact or thought on his own. He answered each question as briefly as possible, and squirmed in the witness chair as he did it.

Even when Pike asked him directly, "Mr. Wells, please tell the court, did you kill Jerry Ennis?"

"No."

"Did you kill Anne Ennis?"

"No."

"Did you have any involvement, in any way, with their deaths?"

"No."

That was it.

Jesus, Tony sighed. *Even a person with half a brain knows when the key question of guilt or innocence comes around, you have to look each juror in the eye as you say loudly and with conviction, "I did not do this!" This poor bastard is clueless.*

On cross-examination, Nelson was brutal, taking full advantage of Wells' demeanor and inability to explain what happened. Claiming he passed out in the bar and then not being able to explain why no one saw him there was the epitome of a weak testimony. Saying these things with a quiet voice and averted eyes compounded the problem. Wells looked and sounded like a very bad liar.

Nelson pounded on him to admit he was a murderer. Wells continued to say no, but as the prosecutor's accusations grew louder, the defendant seemed to withdraw even further into himself.

Pike objected regularly throughout Nelson's badgering, and eventually Judge Schroeder said that enough was enough.

"I'm sorry, Your Honor, if I get overly emotional. Just one more question to clarify what we've been hearing from the defendant." Turning back to the witness stand, Nelson asked, "So Mr. Wells, let me ask you about your testimony this way. If you didn't kill this young couple in their home, can you explain how your gun came to be the murder weapon, how your jacket and boots came to be seen in their house, why you don't have an alibi for your whereabouts at the time of the murder, and why your own sister testified that you wanted to kill Jerry Ennis?"

Nelson's voice had grown steadily louder as his question dragged on, but by the end Pike was on his feet and shouting, "Your

honor! Please! That question violates so many rules of trial procedure
I don't even know where to begin with my objection!"

Schroeder slammed his gavel on the sounding block and both
men instantly were silent. "You don't need to, Mr. Pike. The court
reporter is ordered to strike the question and the jury is admonished
to ignore it. Are you finished, Mr. Nelson?"

"I'm sorry, Your Honor, yes, the state has no further questions
of this witness."

"No." A meek voice spoke from the witness stand.

All eyes turned back to Wells, who had just answered the question the judge had ordered the jury to ignore. Then, Wells spoke
again, "No, I guess I can't."

Unbelievable, Tony thought, as murmurs from spectators swept
through the courtroom and the red-faced judge told Wells he was
finished and could step down.

The judge then gaveled for silence once again.

"Mr. Pike?" The judge stared at the defense counsel.

"The defense rests, Your Honor," Pike said, straining not to
sound as stricken as he looked.

The judge then announced the trial was in recess for the day.
"We will reconvene at 9 a.m. Friday." A bang of the gavel, a swish
of robes, and the judge was gone. As the last people filed out of the
courtroom Lawrence Pike was still sitting in his chair at the defense
table, staring at the witness stand.

Chapter 11

Lawrence Pike leaned into the full-length mirror mounted on his closet door as he removed his tie. He peered closely at his own face, drawn and deeply lined. Where was the face of the young man he used to see? He wasn't angry. He wasn't surprised. He wasn't embarrassed. He was exhausted. After nearly forty years of practicing law, he couldn't remember ever having been so utterly spent, physically and emotionally. As he contemplated his image in the mirror, he realized he looked as old as he felt. At age 66, his hair shouldn't be quite so white or quite so thin. His stomach should be smaller and his muscles bigger. He was five feet, seven inches and just shy of two hundred pounds. Pike knew his doctor was being kind when he referred to Pike as "out of shape." The fact was, Pike had lived a bookish life. He loved the law. When he wasn't buried in books and papers working on a case, he was studying legal journals and law reviews and even the criminal code itself. For Pike, the law was like a masterpiece of art. The more he examined it, the more the nuances and complexities, the textures and colors, revealed themselves.

Throughout those four decades, Pike had been content to let others play rounds of golf or go to the Y to work out while he sat in his favorite chair and read.

"And look where it got you, you old fart," he said aloud, shaking his head. He moved slowly as he hung his suit and tie, pushed his dress shirt into the clothes hamper and pulled on an old Drake University sweatshirt. He slipped his feet into a pair of deck shoes and headed downstairs to the kitchen.

It was times like these he most missed Ginny. His wife of thirty years had been taken by breast cancer five years previously. If she had been here, she would have fixed his drink, rubbed his shoulders, and encouraged him to relax while she cooked dinner. They wouldn't have talked about his work, but knowing she was there and sharing his struggles would have been a huge help.

Pike's ancestry was a mix of French and German, which Ginny used to say explained how he could be both charming and stubborn. Pike preferred to think of himself as "ornery." He also was proud of the fact he had spent many more hours of his life laughing than complaining or crying. Pike loved to tell stories and enjoyed a good yarn more than anyone he knew. But these were traits only Ginny and his closest friends ever saw. Now Ginny was gone and his friends too few in number and too far away.

As a result, he now found himself in the familiar routine of pouring his own scotch into a tumbler of ice and digging through the refrigerator for something edible. As he was debating the merits of cold leftover pizza versus a cold leftover hoagie sandwich, he was interrupted by the sound of the doorbell.

It wasn't Pike's nature to be grumpy, but he wasn't happy about being bothered at home in the evening after a difficult day in court. He opened the door fully expecting to tell whoever was there to go away and leave him alone.

The face that greeted him was that of Tony Harrington from the *Crier*.

"Good evening," Pike said, trying to sound less worn down than he felt. "Tony, isn't it?"

"That's right, sir. I was wondering if we could visit for a few minutes."

"Well, Tony, I'm just fixing myself some dinner. And besides, I don't think it's appropriate for me to be talking about the trial, assuming that's why you're here, at this crucial juncture. If I were to say something I shouldn't and cause a mistrial at this point, Judge Schroeder would nail my hide to the courthouse door."

"I understand and I'm sorry to bother you at home. But please understand, I'm not here to interview you for the paper. I'd just like to talk, completely off the record."

Against his better judgment, Pike decided some company, even a reporter's, was better than sitting in his kitchen alone. He pulled the door open to its full width. "Come on in."

Tony declined Pike's offer of scotch but did accept a Coke before following Pike out to the deck on the back of the house. The evening was cool, but the lack of any breeze made it perfectly pleasant to relax in the well-padded deck chairs with cold drinks.

Pike studied his young guest closely, deciding to keep quiet and let Tony decide when and how to open the conversation. Tony's Coke was half finished before he finally broke the silence.

"I assume you're wondering why I'm here." Another long pause. Pike waited and Tony finally continued, "It may surprise you to learn I'm wondering the same thing. Maybe I just need to hear it from you, from the person who knows him best at this point." Another long pause, this time broken by Pike.

"What is it you need to hear?"

"Is he innocent?" Tony blurted the question and then said, even more awkwardly, "I think he is." He paused before continuing, "You probably know, having seen the law enforcement reports, that I was there the night he was arrested. After seeing him in that setting, so utterly confused and...and...harmless, I don't know, I just never believed he did it."

Pike leaned back in his chair and looked up at the cloudless sky as he absently tipped his glass back and forth, causing the ice to churn in the scotch. He wasn't surprised. Somehow he had sensed Tony's support in his reporting of the case. Pike was, however, completely baffled regarding how he should respond. After a few moments hesitation, he chose to be open.

"Yes, Tony. I believe Ralph Wells really is innocent of these horrendous crimes. However, I'm sure you realize that no one ever can be completely certain. Only Ralph and the Ennises, God bless their souls, know for sure if he was involved. But you're right. I feel I know him and I can't imagine him killing two people in cold blood while their young daughters slept nearby. The circumstances just seem to exist in a universe completely different than the one in which Ralph lives."

"So what's going to happen?"

This question caught Pike completely off guard and actually caused him to laugh out loud. "Are you really asking me to predict the outcome of the trial?"

"I don't know, but I'm worried Wells is going to be convicted. Sorry, no offense, Mr. Pike, you've been terrific. It's just..."

"No offense taken. I understand better than anyone that the facts are the facts, and I'm excruciatingly aware of the real risk that the jury is going to make the wrong decision." Saying this out loud caused Pike's anxiety to spike. His stomach felt like he had swallowed the tumbler instead of its contents. Perhaps inviting Tony in had been a mistake after all.

Tony was oblivious to Pike's reaction and stared at his Coke as he continued, "I feel like I should have *done* something. It's so frustrating to report the facts of the case when I have all these feelings that I have to keep to myself."

"Tony, stop. In the first place, it's not your job to help Mr. Wells. It's mine. And in the second place, you have no idea what frustration is. Imagine my angst about not being able to do more for Ralph. This is just the way it is. We all do our jobs to the best of our abilities and hope for the best. It's all I can do and it's all you can do."

"I appreciate your counsel, Mr. Pike. Really I do. But it doesn't help much."

Pike chuckled again. "Of course not. No one who supports Ralph is happy about having to live with the situation, least of all Ralph. But we do."

"Does he talk to you about it? I mean, he seems so quiet and disconnected from what's happening in the courtroom."

"I'm sorry, Tony, but now you've wandered into an area that clearly is off limits. I cannot and will not even hint at what transpires between me and my client."

"Of course," Tony nodded. "I should have known better than to ask." Another long silence and then, "When this is all done, regardless of the outcome, could you do me a favor?"

Pike's brow wrinkled in curiosity as he waited for Tony to explain.

"Could you arrange for me to interview Ralph? I'm embarrassed that I haven't done a more in-depth article about him before now."

"I certainly will be happy to ask him, but it will be entirely up to him whether he says yes or no. As you've noted, he's a pretty quiet person."

Tony nodded again, "I understand completely. All I can ask is

that you communicate my request to him. I just think that will be better than having him hear from me directly."

Tony stood. "Thanks for the Coke. I can see myself out." He
started to go, but turned and spoke to the back of Pike's chair. "I'm
sorry I bothered you, Mr. Pike. I should have realized you have a lot
bigger things to think about than my frustrations. I appreciate your
time."

"Tony." Pike spoke but didn't move from his chair.

"Sir?"

"I'm glad you came. I'm glad to know there are people who
see this case the way I do, and I'm glad Ralph has your support."

"Well I..."

"I'm not finished. I don't know the answer to your question
about what's going to happen. Here's what I do know: I promise you
I will do everything in my power to give Ralph Wells a chance."

"I know you will, Mr. Pike. I never doubted that for a minute."

As Tony stepped off the deck and around the house to the front,
Pike remained in his chair, swirling his ice and staring at the darken-
ing sky.

How did I end up with this mess? It wasn't a real question. Pike
knew exactly how it had happened. He remembered getting the call
months ago from the clerk of court's office, saying Judge Schroeder
wanted to see him. It wasn't common to be summoned to a judge's
office, but it wasn't unheard of either. Pike told his secretary he would
be gone for an hour or so and left immediately for the courthouse.

Once there, Schroeder had waved him right in.

"I suppose you've guessed why you're here," Schroeder had
opened.

"Actually, Your Honor, I don't have a clue," Pike had responded
honestly.

"You're here, Mr. Pike, because I'm going to appoint you to

represent Ralph Adam Wells in his defense of the two murder charges."

"But, Your Honor," Pike had protested, "I checked the pro-bono list and Steve Tylerman's name was at the top for the next felony case. Steve's a perfectly capable attorney and in a law firm a lot bigger than mine. He would be a perfectly acceptable choice for Wells' defense."

Pike wasn't used to debating such matters with a judge, especially a hard-nosed, stubborn judge like Schroeder. On the other hand, if he accepted the Wells case, it would completely dominate his small practice for most of a year, maybe more. Even worse, Pike had read the news stories about the case. The police had the murder weapon and other evidence that would be hard to dispute. Whoever took this case was likely to lose. *Ahh,* Pike thought, just as the judge confirmed what he was thinking.

"Larry, I'm not giving this case to Steve Tylerman because he's in the prime of his career. Whoever defends Wells runs the risk of alienating a big part of the community, and then is likely to lose. These are not exactly outcomes that help an attorney maintain a successful practice."

"Well, judge, I appreciate your honesty, but for those same reasons I am reluctant to step in and solve this problem for Steve."

"Come on, Larry, be a little pragmatic here. You have a small practice. A handful of clients a year is all you need to keep bread on the table. More importantly, you're at the tail end of your career. If this goes really badly, you don't have to deal with the fallout if you don't want to. You could retire anytime."

"While that may be true, Your Honor, I'm not really interested in retirement. The law is all I have. More to the point, the fact that Steve is younger than me does not seem to be an appropriate basis on which to ask me to do this."

"Let's be clear, Mr. Pike," Schroeder responded, rising out of his chair and staring right into Pike's eyes. "I'm not asking you to do this. I'm telling you that you will do it."

"And if I refuse?" Pike asked, staring right back without blinking.

"Then the negative fallout of this case begins for you much sooner and much more directly. In short, I'm going to make your life in court as miserable as possible."

"Your Honor, if I may speak openly, that threat is unfair to me and, more importantly, it's unfair to every client I bring into court."

"Life isn't fair, Mr. Pike," Schroeder said, easing himself back into his chair. He looked back at the paperwork on his desk, saying, "The court order will be in your mail tomorrow. You're dismissed."

Pike had left without another word.

Looking back on it now, from the chair of his deck on a cool fall evening, Pike still found the episode upsetting. However, he found some comfort in the fact that he had never let his resentment of the circumstances prevent him from giving his all to Ralph Wells. He had accepted the case and worked it as if Wells was his best friend in need of help. Unfortunately, just as he had told young Tony, the facts were the facts.

Well, Pike thought, *I have a promise to keep. I'm going to do all I can to give Mr. Wells a chance.* He stood, walked over to the deck railing, and poured the remainder of his drink into the bushes. He then walked back into the house to put on a proper shirt and head back to the office to rework his closing argument.

The cold pizza and hoagie still lay on the kitchen table as Pike went out the front door.

Chapter 12

Tony awoke early on Friday morning. *Too early*, he thought, as he rolled over and looked at the clock radio's digital display: 6:45 a.m. "Ugh," he said as he headed for the kitchen to start the coffee pot. He had spent Thursday evening, and even worse Thursday night, alone. He had worked late, struggling with how to describe in his story the defendant's piss-poor performance without saying too bluntly the defendant had put on a piss-poor performance. He was alone because on Thursday evenings Lisa volunteered at the local community theater, helping with everything from set construction to ticket sales. After volunteering, she had gone home to spend the night in her own bed. She preferred to sleep at home most nights, not wanting her father to think she was actually living with Tony. Her dad knew, of course, that Lisa stayed overnight with Tony sometimes. Fortunately, it didn't appear to be a problem. He was still cordial whenever Tony stopped at his home to see Lisa or if they bumped into each other somewhere in town. Her dad was apparently no prude, or at least was a realist about the likely behaviors of a woman of Lisa's age.

Tony was looking forward to the day with a mixture of anticipation and dread. Both stemmed from the fact that today the court
would hear closing arguments in Wells' trial. Closing arguments were
a lot of work for a reporter who wanted to capture the theatrics and
drama of the experience as well as try to summarize all of the facts
in the case as presented from two distinctly different points of view.
Tony wanted to do all of that, so he knew it would be another late
night in the newsroom. Even worse, however, was his anticipation
of how it would go. A slick prosecutor with an airtight case versus
an elderly defense counsel with virtually no case at all.

So, if those are facts, why do they gnaw at me? Tony wondered
for the thousandth time. *Wells did it and I should be glad he's going
to prison.* In his mind, the words sounded empty, as if they weren't
real words at all, just made-up sounds designed to lull him into sub-
mission. As Tony slid his tie up and grabbed his pad and pen, he wondered if Pike would pull some miracle out of his closing remarks.
Some statement so dramatic it would move everyone in the courtroom to feel like Tony did.

Not a chance in hell, he thought, and walked out the back door
to his SUV.

***

"Ladies and gentlemen," W. Rodney Nelson began after getting
the word from Judge Schroeder to proceed. "The State of Iowa has
asked a great deal of each of you. We've asked you to take time away
from your jobs, your hobbies, and your loved ones and to sit attentively in the courtroom each day. We've asked you to look at dozens
of pieces of evidence and listen to thousands of words of testimony,
all while not growing tired as we attorneys got revved up and forgot

when to stop talking."

At this, everyone smiled and a few chuckled.

"Well, ladies and gentlemen," Nelson continued, growing serious once again, "now the great State of Iowa is about to ask you to do the hardest thing of all. It is going to ask you to go into the jury room down the hall and bring to justice this man, Ralph Adam Wells. The State of Iowa knows Mr. Wells is young. The State of Iowa knows Mr. Wells has friends who like him and a wife who loves him. The State of Iowa knows that if you find Mr. Wells guilty of these crimes, as I believe you must and you will, it will be a great tragedy for his wife and his family. We don't expect you to take this lightly; we don't ask you to take it lightly. You have a serious responsibility and we want you to take it seriously."

Nelson paused for effect. "So. Let's talk for a moment about that responsibility. While I've acknowledged that when you find a young man guilty of such horrendous crimes, it is a tragedy, but let me remind you that letting a ruthless, cold-blooded killer remain free on the streets of our community would be the far greater tragedy. You cannot return to this courtroom with anything except two findings of guilty... guilty of murder in the first degree, because if you don't, that is exactly what you will be doing. You will be letting a monster go free.

"Ladies and gentlemen, whether or not Ralph Adam Wells looks like a monster to you, I maintain that is exactly what he is. That is what the evidence says he is. And that is the bottom line regarding what the State of Iowa asks of you today. You are charged with looking at the evidence in this case and determining what the evidence says about Mr. Wells' guilt. And if it isn't obvious to you already, let me assure you the evidence is absolutely, unquestionably clear."

Nelson then walked through a summary of the State's case, moving quickly so as to not irritate the jury, but holding up each exhibit as the item was referenced in his remarks. Tony took only a few notes. He knew the list by heart at this point: Wells' gun killed the victims, the young girl in the house saw a man wearing Wells' clothes leave the house immediately after the killings, Wells had no alibi for the night of the killings, Wells' own sister testified he was in a state of mind to do the killings and had a motive for wanting one of the victims dead.

As Nelson continued, he recapped the photos of the crime scene, the testimony of the experts, and a dozen other pieces of evidence. At the end of all this, he paused once again and then walked to the prosecution's table. From it, he picked up a photograph, blown up to three times the size of a normal portrait. Tony could see it clearly as Nelson turned to face the jury again. In full color, Jerry and Anne Ennis could be seen dressed in a tuxedo and wedding dress, smiling as they held hands while walking down the aisle on their wedding day.

"Ladies and gentlemen," Nelson said, with as grave a voice as he could muster. "As you know, this trial is about more than Ralph Adam Wells. This trial also is about these two young people, these two victims of Mr. Wells' evil deeds. Jerry and Anne were in the early years of what was destined to be a long and happy marriage. They had two beautiful daughters. They too had friends who liked them and family who loved them. They had *lives,* until Ralph Adam Wells drove to their farmhouse, brazenly walked up the stairs to their bedroom, fired four bullets from his rifle into their brains, and left them dead on their marital bed." He strode to the evidence table and slid another photo, this one in a clear plastic evidence bag, into his free hand. He then held up the two photos. The jury was confronted with the stark, cruel contrast of one photo of the smiling couple on their wedding day and one of their two bloody bodies sprawled on the bed soaked in blood. He faced both photos toward the jury.

"As you can plainly see, you cannot save Jerry and Anne Ennis. You cannot ease the grief in their two daughters' hearts. You cannot take our community back to the innocence it enjoyed before these horrible murders. What you *can* do is make sure their killer is brought to justice today.

"Take your job seriously," he said, slamming the two photos onto the table, "and bring back two verdicts of murder in the first degree. Thank you."

Nelson sat down. He had been performing for a little over an hour. It was early for a break, but an obvious point for one. The judge left it up to Pike.

"Mr. Pike, we can take a short recess here, or you can proceed with your argument. Do you have a preference?"

"Your honor, I would prefer to get on with it if you don't mind," Pike said cordially.

"Very well, you may proceed."

Tony assumed Pike was eager to proceed to give him some chance to mitigate Nelson's passionate and effective plea for guilty verdicts. He didn't want the jury to have twenty minutes to think only about what Nelson had said.

Pike picked up a yellow legal pad covered with scribbles and approached the jury. He studied the pad for a moment and then lowered it to his side.

"Ladies and gentlemen, I want to begin by thanking you for your service to the court, to our community, and to my client. As Mr. Nelson said, we know serving on a jury is a tremendous burden and we appreciate you for fulfilling your civic duty. I also want to remind you that you were picked through a long and tedious process of jury selection. We picked you because we trust you to be fair and impartial. We trust you to look at the facts, and the lack of facts, and to do as the law instructs you. To be honest, I trust you with my client's life.

As you know, I'm Larry Pike and I'm just a country lawyer trying to do the right thing, not only for my client but also for the 'great State of Iowa,' as Mr. Nelson likes to call us." He paused, moving his free hand lightly along the highly polished walnut railing. "I have real respect for Mr. Nelson. He is a man who has achieved a high position in our profession. He has a law degree from a top-rated law school out east, and I got mine just down the road in Des Moines. I know his suits are a lot nicer than mine, and he probably drives a better car. I also know he has a big fancy office in Des Moines and a whole team of investigators, agents, deputies, lawyers, and clerks helping him do a great job and I've got...well, me."

Jurors smiled.

"But believe me, just because I respect Mr. Nelson, and just because we all love the great State of Iowa as much as Mr. Nelson, does not mean they are infallible. And I am determined to convince you that they have indeed failed in this case. They have failed Mr. Wells, they have failed Jerry and Anne Ennis, they have failed the people of Iowa, and they have failed the justice we all seek. They have failed because they have charged and brought to trial the wrong man...an innocent man.

"A moment ago I pointed out the difference between Mr. Nelson's situation and mine. Please don't think that difference is a small matter in this case...because it's not!" Pike said sharply. "The great State of Iowa has enormous resources available to accomplish what it wants to accomplish. Mr. Nelson has had those enormous resources at his disposal for more than a year to achieve what he wants to achieve. And, by the way, please understand how this system works. Once my client's name came to their attention, when they thought they had found someone they could arrest and charge with these terrible crimes, the enormous resources of the great State of Iowa were brought to bear on one goal: convict my client.

"And you know what I think? I think despite all those investigators and lawyers and clerks and laboratories and everything else they have, Mr. Nelson still couldn't make a case against my client." Tony looked up from his notetaking. His weren't the only raised eyebrows in the room.

Pike continued, "That's right, ladies and gentlemen. There is no case here against my client. Yes, there are these...*things*...that Mr. Nelson has brought to you as circumstantial evidence." Pike jabbed a finger at the clear plastic evidence bags and grimaced as if they were rotting garbage." In fact, every single thing he brought to you is circumstantial evidence. What that means, ladies and gentlemen, is that Mr. Nelson and the State of Iowa have no direct evidence against my client. I believe he forgot to mention that in his summation.

"So let's talk for a minute about the direct evidence Mr. Nelson *didn't* bring before you. Mr. Nelson didn't have a single witness who saw Mr. Wells at the crime scene, ever. Not on the night of the murders, and not before or after.

"Mr. Nelson did not have evidence of Mr. Wells' fingerprints at the crime scene. Believe me, they lifted plenty of prints from the Ennis house, but none of them matched Mr. Wells. Mr. Nelson did not have a strand of Mr. Wells' hair or any source of Mr. Wells' DNA to place him at the crime scene. Again, believe me, the crime scene investigators collected plenty of hair and flecks of skin and bodily fluids and all that stuff you see on TV. But nothing they collected matched that of the defendant.

"And lastly, Mr. Nelson did not have a credible witness who could testify that Mr. Wells even knew Jerry or Anne Ennis. Wouldn't you think if these two men were involved in selling drugs together that Mr. Nelson and his investigators could have found one person who had seen them together at some point in their lives?

"Oh, but you ask, 'What about his sister?' Well I submit to you,

ladies and gentlemen, that Francie's testimony was, as my grandmother used to say, a crock of hooey. If Francie loved her brother,
she would not have been in court saying these things about him. Or
at the very least, she would have been here under subpoena as what
the state calls a hostile witness. And if she didn't love him, then why
not? What has happened in the past or is happening today in her life
that caused her to come here? What was her true motivation for making up these lies about her brother? I don't know, and you don't
know, and apparently Mr. Nelson and his team of investigators don't
know. At least they didn't tell us.

"Well, believe me, ladies and gentlemen," Pike was speaking
quietly now. He moved closer to the jury box looking each juror in
the face, "If I had the resources Mr. Nelson has, I sure as heck would
have found out, and you wouldn't have to go into that jury room
wondering what really is going on here."

Pike backed away, paused for a long moment and resumed a
normal tone of voice. "So yes, there's circumstantial evidence. But
I ask you to remember there's a reason it is labeled as such. It
means it *could* exist because of the circumstances the State wants
you to believe. It also means it could be there under a lot of other
circumstances.

"Did my client's rifle kill those two people? Apparently, yes.
But...who held the rifle? No one knows. Who fired the rifle? No one
knows. Oh," he added, "I'll tell you one thing we *do* know. One of
the most important facts you heard in this case is the fact that whoever *did* fire the rifle was probably a lot taller than Ralph Wells."

Pike continued, "Did the sheriff find illegal drugs in the Ennis
home? Yes. Did the state make any connection between these drugs
and Mr. Wells? No! Did the state find any evidence of illegal drugs
in Mr. Wells' possession? No! Did the state find any evidence in Mr.
Wells' finances that he was benefitting from involvement in illegal

drug sales? No!

"Did the killer wear a yellow jacket in the Ennis' home that night? Apparently, yes. What yellow jacket was actually worn? No one knows. Who wore a yellow jacket that night? No one knows. And when I say no one knows these things, I mean *no one*. Not the investigators, not Mr. Nelson, not the great State of Iowa and, most importantly, not you.

"Mr. Nelson has made a big issue of the fact these items were in my client's car trunk. But we learned from Amber Wells that the boots were not in the car trunk on the night of the murder. We learned the boots were not on the feet of Ralph Wells on the night of the murder. So, whoever that young girl saw in his house in brown work boots was *not* Ralph Wells."

Pike took a deep breath and continued. "It is true, of course, that the rifle and the jacket were in the trunk. Ralph never has denied that. In fact, he led investigators to them. So, the rifle and jacket were in the trunk...the trunk of an old car that is never locked, that often is parked in an alley downtown, and is known to half the people in Orney. Quite frankly, if I wanted to kill someone, where would I go for a weapon? Hey! I think I'll grab the rifle out of Ralph's car," Pike grabbed the rifle off the evidence table and swung it around, as if to emphasize how easy it was to pick it up. After laying it down again, he continued.

"Please think hard about that rifle. It must be as obvious to you as it is to me that if my client had actually killed someone with that rifle, all he needed to do was get rid of it and he would never have been a suspect in this case, let alone be on trial today for murder. Do you really believe that a man clever enough to plan and commit two premeditated murders, and clever enough to do it without leaving any trace of himself at the scene of the crime, and clever enough to have a history of selling drugs without anyone knowing about it, and clever enough to do business with a man but never be seen with him... Do you really believe this criminal mastermind pulled all this off, then took the murder weapon and the clothes he wore and threw them in the trunk of his car, and left them there for weeks? And then, this criminal mastermind, when asked by investigators if he had a .22 rifle, happily said, 'Sure,' and retrieved it from his trunk for the investigators to test? This scenario the state is trying to make you believe is completely, disgustingly absurd." Pike was red-faced and paused to collect himself.

"Ladies and gentlemen, the judge is going to give you instructions in a little while. In those instructions he's going to talk about the standard of reasonable doubt. You listen to the judge on this point, and not to me, but I believe he will tell you the requirement under Iowa law is, if you find there is reasonable doubt in this case, you must find my client innocent. When you hear the judge's instructions, I would like you to think long and hard about Mr. Nelson's words. He told you to take seriously your job of upholding the law and seeing that justice is done. I would urge the exact same thing. When you look at the evidence and, more importantly, the lack of evidence, and the absurdity of the tale the state has spun here, you're going to see there is reasonable doubt all over this case, and your responsibility to bring back two verdicts of not guilty is clear.

"Lastly, ladies and gentlemen, I too want to talk about Jerry and Anne Ennis." Pike went over to the prosecutor's table and picked up the color photo from their wedding day.

This was a risky move, Tony thought. Usually a defense attorney tried to downplay images of the victims as much as possible. Then Pike made him smile when he looked at Nelson and said, "The prosecution may be surprised that I want to focus attention back on the victims of this crime. Well, I do." Pike held the photo high for all to see.

"I grieve for this couple as much as Mr. Nelson does. I cried right along with the rest of you when that young girl described her ordeal. I'm saddened by the fear and confusion these killings brought to our community. I want the perpetrator of these horrendous crimes arrested, tried, and convicted as much as Mr. Nelson and as much as any person in this room.

"But ladies and gentlemen," Pike said firmly, "convicting an innocent man of these crimes accomplishes none of those things we all want. In fact, it makes the accomplishment of these things impossible.

"So please do what both sides in this trial have urged you to do. Go into that jury room and make sure you uphold the law. Look at the facts, look at this poor young man who has so unjustly had his life turned upside down, look at all the missing pieces in the case, at all the doubt about what really happened, and vote to find Ralph Adam Wells not guilty. Thank you."

***

Friday was taco day at Willie's and Tony, Doug, and Lisa sat together, the two men wolfing down a plate of tacos while Lisa enjoyed a taco salad. Lisa had joined them because she was anxious to hear how the morning had gone. Tony couldn't stop smiling and said, "I thought Pike was brilliant. He brought into the bright sunshine of a cloudless day all those nagging shadows that had been plaguing me for months. I swear, the greatest actor in Hollywood couldn't have outperformed Pike this morning. I think Wells has a real shot."

Because Tony was so happy, Lisa smiled too. She looked at Doug and said, "How about you? What did you think?"

Doug was far more skeptical but reluctant to spoil his best

friend's mood.

"Tony's right. Pike was surprisingly good," Doug nodded. "I might hire him myself when I get caught stealing beer off the loading dock behind the market."

Lisa groaned but was smiling as she kicked him under the table.

"Ow!" Doug exclaimed, "Geez, it was just a joke."

"Yeah, well just remember," Lisa said. "Now when that store manager accuses you of stealing, I'm going to have to go into court and testify that I heard you say it."

"Okay, okay, let's focus, kids," Tony said. "Any thoughts on what's left?"

"You mean the tacos?" Doug asked, smiling as he scooped the last one off the platter.

"No, I mean the trial. Do you think Nelson will do a rebuttal?"

Doug knew Tony wanted to hear him say no, but they both knew the answer was yes.

"I wish he wouldn't but I'm sure he will," Doug replied. "Not only will he feel compelled to respond to such a strong summation, but he never passes up a chance to perform."

"Yeah, you're right," Tony acknowledged, losing his smile for the first time since they left the courthouse. "I can just hear..." His voice trailed off and the three remained uncharacteristically quiet while they finished their last few bites of food, paid the bill, and headed outside into a much cooler, much more fall-like September day.

***

In Iowa, the prosecution always gets the first and last word. The state is afforded the opportunity to respond to the defense's arguments. The remarks in rebuttal, by rule, must be confined to responding to points made by the defense. However, a closing as all-encompassing as Pike's left very few restrictions for the State. Nelson had the added benefit of the lunch recess, which gave him the opportunity to prepare.

Tony knew all this, and so was surprised when Nelson was uncharacteristically brief. Tony speculated that Nelson didn't want to tick off the jury by revisiting a bunch of things that had already been said, and he didn't want to give the jury the impression that Pike's closing worried him in the least.

"Ladies and gentlemen," he began, "I'm going to take a moment to address just three things Mr. Pike said in his summation that I don't think he got quite right." He smiled a wry smile and continued, "Since Mr. Pike talked about me, let me say a few words about him. You see, I have great respect for Mr. Pike as well...and so should you. Do not let his 'I'm a poor country lawyer' routine fool you. Mr. Pike is a highly respected and shrewd attorney. And his law school 'down the road in Des Moines' is Drake University, one of the top-rated colleges of law in the country. So don't be fooled by Mr. Pike's approach. This is not his first rodeo. And while I would love to be flush with all the people and tools and resources Mr. Pike ascribed to me, the fact is, the great State of Iowa has a limited budget and limited resources and we do the best we can with what the taxpayers of Iowa can afford.

"The second point I want to make is, don't buy Mr. Pike's assertion that there's no evidence in this case. I'm not going to bore you by going through it all again, but for Pete's sake, look at the pile of evidence on that table. Every piece of it points at Ralph Wells. Do I wish I had a credible eyewitness standing in the corner of the Ennis' bedroom recording a video of the crime on an iPhone? Sure I do. But we all know, that never happens in real life. We have to convict cold-blooded killers like Ralph Wells with the evidence they leave in their wake. And he left plenty.

"Lastly, I simply want to say that criminals do dumb things. I don't know why and I never sit around and wonder about it, but I see it all the time. I don't know why Ralph Wells was dumb enough to leave the murder weapon in his trunk, and I don't know why he voluntarily handed it over to our investigators. Maybe it was for just this reason, to plant doubt in your minds. But whatever his reasoning, I can tell you this: I'm glad he did it. I'm glad he made mistakes. I'm glad he left the clues that allowed us to identify him, arrest him, and bring him to this court to see justice done.

"The facts are that Mr. Wells did some smart things in committing these crimes, and he did some dumb things in committing these crimes. Ladies and gentlemen, that's called being a human being. We all make mistakes. Don't let Mr. Wells' mistakes become a loophole to get him out of the punishment he deserves. Don't let the fact he is a human being fool you into thinking that he's *human*.

"In closing," Nelson said, lowering his voice, "I just want to repeat my request that you find justice for these two young lives that were cruelly and needlessly snuffed out and for the loving children, parents, and friends they left behind." He once again lifted up the two pictures: the happy couple and the murdered bodies. "Go into that jury room, look at the facts, and come back here with two verdicts of guilty. Unanimously find him guilty of murder in the first degree, and give that monster in the chair behind me what he deserves."

Chapter 13

It was, as they say, all over but the shouting. Judge Schroeder asked if the attorneys had any final motions or other business for the court. Hearing none, the judge read the jury its instructions and discussed with jurors the schedule for the next few hours and for Saturday. Tony knew this was a sensitive issue. The judge needed to manage the process, but he had to do it without implying he expected the jury to take a short or a long time deliberating. The bottom line was, it was not yet 3 p.m. If the jury hadn't reached a verdict by 6 p.m., the judge would dismiss them for the evening and they would reconvene at 9 a.m. Saturday. He polled the jury and no one objected to the plan.

Schroeder then dismissed the two alternates, thanking them for their service. He commented that they had the toughest job of all, sitting through the trial and then having to sit on the outside like everyone else to see what the jury would decide.

After the jury filed out, the judge declared the court was adjourned, and a murmur immediately broke out in the room. Spectators were talking to their seat companions, debating whether to stay or go. To Tony, there was no debate. He was going. Even the shortest deliberations took hours in a trial of this magnitude, he knew.

The judge's admonitions had included urging the jury to take its time, elect a foreman, and refrain from rushing to judgment or stating an absolute position before the evidence was reviewed and the first secret ballot taken. Tony had heard similar jury instructions many times. "...for when a juror begins by stating his or her strong opinion at the outset, personal pride may become involved and the juror's position may become intractable, even if an examination and discussion of the evidence proves the position to be wrong."

For all these reasons, Tony knew the process would take time. He fully expected to be back in the courtroom tomorrow. He was wrong.

***

Tony sat motionless at his computer, staring at the completed article on his screen. It was evening and the newsroom was quiet. Ben was in his office, but Tony hadn't spoken to him since returning from the courthouse. It felt as if everything around him had slowed to a crawl. Tony could feel his heartbeat and was conscious of his own labored breathing. *Why do I hate this so much?*

He was reluctant to push the "send" button on the keyboard, as if moving the story to the copy desk would make it more real some-how – would add to the finality. In truth, it was final when the bailiff read the words, "We the jury find the defendant, Ralph Adam Wells, guilty of murder in the first degree..." It was final in every way that mattered. Ralph Wells would spend the rest of his life in prison. The official sentencing wouldn't happen for weeks, but the outcome was predetermined. There would be appeals, of course, but they would lead nowhere. The Iowa Supreme Court almost never overturned murder convictions.

Tony's heart ached. His mouth was dry. He pushed "send" and walked out the door without a word to anyone.

Town Crier

Wells Found Guilty of Double Homicide

Tony Harrington, Staff Writer

ORNEY, Iowa – After deliberating for just over 70 minutes Friday afternoon, a jury of seven men and five women returned two verdicts of guilty of murder in the first degree in the trial of Ralph Adam Wells.

Wells, 29, of rural Orney, was convicted of shooting to death Jerry and Anne Ennis, also of rural Orney. The couple was found dead of gunshot wounds to the head in the second floor bedroom of their farmhouse. A daughter, who was 9 years old at the time, found the bodies and called 911 on the night of January 12, this year.

Wells was represented at trial by Lawrence Pike, a longtime Orney attorney. After the verdicts were read in open court shortly before 5 p.m. and the jury sent home, Pike stayed in the courtroom long enough to answer a few questions. He was visibly upset by the verdicts and said, "What can I say? I believe with all my heart Mr. Wells is an innocent victim. I did my best to show the jury that the state's case was based on circumstantial evidence and to

show them clear evidence of his innocence. Obviously, it wasn't good enough. I'm disappointed, but more importantly, I'm heartbroken on behalf of Mr. Wells and his family. I'm sorry. That's all I have for you tonight."

A few minutes later, on the front steps of the Quincy County Courthouse, a jubilant prosecutor, Attorney General W. Rodney Nelson, told reporters, "Clearly, justice was done today. The evidence of Mr. Wells' guilt was overwhelming. I want to thank the jury for seeing it clearly and doing the right thing for the victims of this crime and for the people of Iowa."

Wells' sentencing is set for November 23. However, state law gives presiding Judge Arnold Schroeder no leeway in the matter. The first-degree murder convictions carry mandatory sentences of life in prison with no opportunity for parole.

The verdicts followed two weeks of proceedings in which...

Chapter 14

Snow was falling lightly as Tony pulled up the Freeds' drive-way early on a Saturday morning. It was the second weekend in December, and he and Lisa were headed for Des Moines to do some Christmas shopping. Tony left the Explorer running to keep the interior warm for Lisa as he headed up to the breezeway door between the house and garage. As he reached for the bell, the inside door swung open, and Lisa pushed through the storm door. She looked great, wearing a gray Columbia quilted jacket with a red and gray scarf twisted around her neck. She was pulling a small roller bag with one hand as she hugged him with the other.

"You goofball," she said and pulled away, refusing to let him help with the bag. "You didn't need to get out of the car. It's cold."

"What can I say?" Tony asked. "My mommy taught me to be a gentleman." He finally tugged the bag from her grasp and carried it to the back as she got in the passenger seat. He pushed the bag into the gap next to his own and noticed, with some embarrassment, that Lisa's bag was smaller than his. He had never learned to travel lightly.

"I'm glad we're leaving early," Lisa said as Tony tossed his coat in the back seat and slid behind the wheel. "I think the snow is supposed to be a lot heavier this afternoon."

"Maybe we'll get stuck in the hotel in Des Moines for a week or two." Tony smiled as he put the Explorer in gear and slid his hand up the inside of her leg, squeezing the denim of her Levis.

"Down, boy," she laughed. "It's snowing. Eyes on the road."

"It's not my eyes you have to worry about," he replied, sliding his hand further up her leg as she laughed again.

Tony felt good. A full weekend off work; a trip to Des Moines with a beautiful woman; gas in the tank; money in his pocket; Jimmy Buffet on XM Radio. He was smart enough not to take for granted how good he had it.

Ironically, the thought of how good he felt immediately reminded him of what a tough couple of months it had been. The Wells verdict had felt like a sucker punch to the gut. Intellectually, Tony knew he should not have been surprised, but emotionally it had taken a huge toll. He had kept going, doing a thorough job, covering the verdict, the reactions to it from all parties involved, the sentencing, and the imprisonment at "The Fort," as the state penitentiary at Fort Madison was called. He had, of course, written dozens of other stories in the meantime, trying hard to set the "Wells thing" aside and get on with his life. But far too often, when he was doing something fun or romantic or fulfilling, the thought of Ralph Wells sitting in that cold fortress reached out of the depths, gripped his heart, and sent his mood spiraling downward.

Thankfully, Lisa only rarely became irritated at his mood swings. She clearly didn't enjoy seeing him down, but she did seem to appreciate the fact he didn't take lightly the tragedies he covered in his work.

As the SUV sped across the countryside on a mostly empty

Highway 141, Tony glanced at the clock on the dashboard. At 9 a.m. he punched a button on the radio and brought up a Des Moines station. As a CBS affiliate, it had news at the top of the hour. "You can take the boy out of the newsroom, but..." Lisa said, shaking her head.

The news could have been lifted from just about any day of the past decade. Conflicts in third-world developing countries, worries about the latest strain of influenza, record-breaking weather somewhere, and politicians blaming each other for the latest budget problems. As the local news came on, Tony turned the radio up and listened more intently. Lisa understood. She was more interested herself in what was happening in Iowa. The lead story surprised them both.

"At the annual holiday gala and political fundraiser held last night at the downtown Marriott Hotel, Attorney General W. Rodney Nelson announced his intention to run for governor in next fall's general election. Calling Governor Harry Roskins 'A man who cares more about his wealthy friends than the working families of Iowa,' Nelson said it is time for people of conscience from both parties to band together and help the governor learn what it feels like to be out of work."

The radio announcer went on to say the announcement wasn't a huge surprise, as Nelson had formed an exploratory committee months ago and had begun raising money last summer. "Political insiders have said Nelson kept his activities unusually quiet during the summer and fall because he didn't want them to be a distraction as he led the prosecution of Ralph Adam Wells, an Orney, Iowa, man convicted in September of a double homicide. During his speech last night, Nelson described Wells' conviction as 'one more example of my ability to successfully tackle a difficult problem for the benefit of all Iowans.' In fact, Nelson said his campaign slogan will be, 'I won't just serve you, I will protect you.' Aides to the governor said he would have no comment regarding Nelson's decision to run. In other news..."

Tony groaned out loud and punched off the radio. Then, imitating Nelson's voice, "I'm W. Rodney Nelson. Please ignore the Ivy League degree and the Cadillac Escalade as I convince you I'm a man of the people."

"Tony..." Lisa said, with obvious concern in her voice.

"No, no, relax," he responded quickly. "I swear, I am not going to let this bother me. Our weekend is safe. If I start to dwell on it, you can distract me with another romp on top of the TV."

Lisa giggled, obviously relieved. "That could be a little tough. Aren't the TVs at the Marriott mounted inside wooden cabinets?"

"I wouldn't know," Tony said. "Until I met you I only took girls to the Motel 6."

She punched him hard in the shoulder, but then immediately leaned over and placed her head on it, slipping her arm under his and holding tight. "No more Motel 6 for you pal," she said. "Tonight I'm going to show you why you take a woman to a Marriott."

Tony's mouth went dry and he forgot all about Ralph Wells and W. Rodney Nelson... for about ten minutes.

***

Eleven hours later, Tony and Lisa were dining on cavatini at Marco's Ristorante in Des Moines. It had been a long day of shopping and Tony was exhausted. They had debated going to a movie or to one of the bars on Court Avenue to hear a live band, but in the end decided to have a quiet dinner and turn in early. Tony was trying not to think too much about the "turn in early" part.

Des Moines was a city with many outstanding restaurants, including the most expensive upscale chains as well as establishments with renowned professional chefs and the latest "foo-foo" foods.

While Tony appreciated and occasionally dined at these places, he secretly preferred the handful of local restaurants that had been operated by the same families for decades. Marco's was one of these.

Located on the near west edge of downtown Des Moines, Marco's was nice without being fancy. The food was delicious and served without fanfare. If you were lucky, Marco, *the* Marco, would stop by your table and wish you well. Tony had no idea how old Marco was, but the locals said he had to be close to 100. Many people could remember him stopping by their tables when they dined there as children with their parents or grandparents.

In the mode of many shoppers, their chat over dinner included a recap of the day's successes and failures. As always, Tony had struggled to find something for his mother and eventually had settled for a handmade scarf of Italian wool. It wasn't enough, but at least the labels convinced him it was genuine. He was much more excited about the gift he'd found for his dad. While perusing the antique shops in Valley Junction, the historical district of old West Des Moines, Tony had found an autographed copy of *The Hour Before the Dawn,* by W. Somerset Maugham. Tony's dad collected books, and Tony knew he would love this one. It set him back $300, but Tony knew enough about old books to know it wasn't a bad deal.

Lisa responded by saying again how much she had enjoyed the tiny shop owned and operated by the young female artist. Every painting and sculpture in the store was the artist's work, and Lisa had loved it all. She was still debating which piece to buy her father, requiring a return trip to the store tomorrow. As Tony listened, he wound another strand of warm cheese and pasta around his fork and lifted it to his mouth. He began chewing as a door at the side of the main dining room opened and a stream of well-dressed men and women began filing out of a second dining room. It was undoubtedly a room the restaurant used for private parties. Tony could hear all of

the usual chatter of a dinner party breaking up, "Lovely evening...
Thank you so much...Great to see you...Best of luck to you,
Governor..."

Just an expression? Tony wondered, his reporter's "Spidey
sense" beginning to tingle.

Lisa turned her head to see what had grabbed his attention.
Together they saw Governor Harry Roskins stop in the doorway to
shake hands with the last of the well-wishers.

"Good Lord, Lisa," Tony said. "That's the governor."

"Good call, Clark Kent," Lisa said dryly. "I can see why you're
in line for investigative reporter of the year."

Tony smiled, but said with some urgency, "God, what an
opportunity. In light of Nelson's speech last night, I would love to
talk to him. Ben would kiss my butt for a week if I got an exclusive
reaction to Nelson's announcement. Do you think I could just go over
there and introduce myself?"

"Well," Lisa began, and then suddenly from across the room:

"Lisa Freed! My dear girl, how *are* you? You look wonderful."
And suddenly the governor of Iowa was standing next to their table
and Tony was spilling his water as he attempted to scramble out of
his seat.

"Hello, Governor," Lisa said, rising graciously and standing on
her tiptoes to give him a polite hug. "It's good to see you too. Allow
me to introduce you to my boyfriend. This is Tony Harrington."

Tony composed himself and held out his hand as the governor
took it and said, "Of course, of course. I've heard all about you, Tony.
You write for the *Crier*, right?"

"Uh, yes, I mean, it's an honor to meet you," Tony managed to
say. "I'm surprised you've heard about me, sir. Surely you don't read
the *Crier*."

"Well, I'm a politician, so I can't lie to you," the governor said, and then broke into a loud, deep laugh. "Of course I have read it a few times over the years but no, I've heard about you from Lisa's father. We had breakfast together just last week. I'm trying to get him to chair my fundraising committee in Quincy County, but I think he's going to decline. Hard to get the old goat to do any real work when Lisa's around. Some things never change." The governor laughed again, enjoying his own humor and clearly enjoying seeing Lisa.

By then, every other patron in the restaurant's main dining room was focused on the exchange at Tony and Lisa's table. Governor Roskins was a tall, broad-shouldered man with big hands and an even bigger smile. He had silver wavy hair and a rugged complexion accented by laugh lines around the eyes. Except for a nose he had broken as an all-state wrestler in his youth, his appearance was made for the covers of magazines. "Born to be elected to something," a post-election article had said years earlier after his first victory in a statewide contest. The weekly free paper, a typical, low budget "tell-all," didn't like Roskins at all. Despite that, it still named him the "Sexiest Man in Iowa" three years in a row.

The governor continued, clearly accustomed to dominating the conversation, "Lisa, seriously, I want to thank you for your volunteer work on my campaign. I would have sent you a note, but I only just learned about it from your dad. I'm sorry I didn't spot your name sooner on the routine lists of volunteers."

"Don't apologize," Lisa said cheerfully. "I enjoy helping and I certainly wouldn't expect you to take the time to write to every volunteer."

"Well, perhaps," the governor replied, "but you're not every volunteer. You're Lisa Freed for God's sake!"

He turned to Tony and said, "You should know I've known Lisa since she was a baby. Her father and I have been friends since law school. If you ever do anything to hurt her, I'm going to have the

state troopers handcuff you and toss you in the Des Moines River."
He laughed again. "I would do anything for this young woman."

Tony forced a smile. "No need to be concerned, Governor. I
can't imagine anyone wanting to hurt someone as terrific as Lisa."
Lame, lame, lame, he thought, even as he said it.

"Actually, Governor," Lisa said, "if you mean it...I mean, about
doing anything for me, there is one favor that would make my day."

"Well, anything Lisa. Just name it." The governor beamed.

"Would you mind giving Tony a comment about Nelson's
announcement last night? It would mean a lot to both of us if we
could go back to Orney with a comment for the paper that other
reporters weren't able to get."

"Well, well," the governor said, his smile fading a little. "You
know how to hit a politician where it hurts, right in the 'no comment'
zone. Well, what the hell. I wasn't that crazy about the 'no comment'
position we took anyway." He turned to Tony. "You may have noticed
I prefer talking." Then he surprised them both by pulling out a third
chair at the table and plopping down.

"Sit," he said, turning his palms face up and spreading his arms
as if to say, "I'm all yours." He turned to an aide and said, "Paul, get
Mr. Harrington a pen and paper from your briefcase. We're going to
give this fine young reporter an interview."

***

That night in the hotel room, after making love, laughing,
recapping the day's unusual turn of events, and making love again,
Tony lay exhausted with just a sheet pulled up to his chin.

He thought back about his interview with the governor. Something about it nagged at him. The governor had declined to comment
about Nelson's campaign directly, saying only that democracy

required contested elections and he welcomed the opportunity to explain to the people of Iowa why electing Harry Roskins once again would be the people's best choice. *Blah, blah, blah.* Tony was willing to bet he could have written these responses before the interview and come pretty close to creating exact quotes.

When Tony had asked the governor about Nelson's campaign slogan, Roskins again had declined to comment. Again, it was no surprise. However, the look that flashed across the governor's face was intriguing. Tony could swear it was a smirk, a self-satisfied curl of the lips that was there and then gone an instant later. Tony asked the obvious follow-up question, "As Iowans know, you are a lawyer too, Governor. Will you try to respond to Nelson's obvious attempt to position himself as better able to protect Iowans because of his record as a prosecutor?"

Again, the governor declined to comment. The look on his face was...what? The governor then surprised Tony by asking what *he* thought of the Wells case.

"Well," Tony began, "I'm not sure what to say. I thought there was a strong case on both sides. But I, uh, I guess what I would say is that I was surprised the jury came back with two guilty verdicts so quickly. Why do you ask?"

"Oh, no specific reason," Roskins had replied. "Lisa's dad told me you covered it and even mentioned you were bothered by the verdict. Your mention of Nelson just reminded me of it, since that clearly is his most publicized win in the courtroom. I have to admit I tend to agree with you. As an old defense lawyer, I was baffled by some of the unanswered questions raised by the testimony. Of course I also learned during my twenty years at bar that juries rarely get to see all the facts in a case. I guess we shouldn't be surprised if that happened here."

Tony didn't know what to say. There was an uncomfortable lull in the conversation. Then, as Roskins rose to excuse himself, he said, "Lisa's dad also told me that despite your misgivings, you did a great job of giving fair coverage to both the prosecution and the defense. Good for you, Tony. You may end up being the one reporter I don't have to dread hearing from." The governor chuckled once again at his own joke, shook Tony's hand, kissed Lisa on the cheek, and disappeared out the door with his entourage in tow.

***

Later, as Tony stretched out in the king-sized bed, he found himself bothered by the governor's comments, especially the references to the Wells case. *Other facts? What did he mean by that?*

One cardinal rule in Ben's newsroom was that you never wrote an article that asked a question it didn't answer. *Geez, Ben and I both must be losing our touch*, because there were unanswered questions all over the Wells case. Some, such as the fundamental question of whether Wells was dumb enough to hand over the murder weapon or whether someone else had used it were unanswerable unless Wells decided to confess or, by some miracle, a second suspect was arrested.

However, one nagging question could at least be asked of the person who created it. *Francie,* Tony thought, *someone needs to ask you why you testified against your brother.*

At that point, Lisa rolled over and pressed her bare breasts against his back. All thoughts of trials and witnesses melted away as a lovely, pale arm reached over and pulled him tightly to her. Once again, he was dumbfounded at Lisa's obvious affection for him. Was there another woman on the planet who would have risked her life-long relationship with the highest elected official in the state in order to help him get a story? One so beautiful, so smart, so much fun to be with? Tony tried to think of a flaw, any flaw. *There's that one small birthmark on her side, just at the bottom of her ribcage,* he thought, smiling. *And she can't sing a note. But that's about it.*

He lay awake a long time thinking seriously about all the things he loved about Lisa. Then, just as he drifted off to sleep, he finally admitted to himself, *yes, I am in love with her.*

Chapter 15

The drive to Viscount took less than thirty minutes on a good day. Today was just such a day. The earlier December snows had been cleared from the roads long ago and the dry pavement allowed Tony to push the SUV a little faster than might be appreciated by a state trooper, should he have the misfortune to encounter one.

However, the chances were low, and Tony took advantage of the beautiful weather to ignore the highway and take the winding county blacktop through the Raccoon River valley. Not only did Tony appreciate the minimal traffic, he enjoyed getting off the main roads and pushing the limits of the tighter and more numerous turns of the county road. He was *driving*, and he loved it.

Tony was wearing khaki pants and a ski vest over a black sweater with an Iowa Hawkeye logo on the left breast. He had on snow boots and his winter coat was lying in the back seat if he needed it. No tie today. He wasn't sure he would even find his subject and, if he did, he had no idea if she would talk to him. Tony guessed, in any case, if he did find her he had a better chance of getting her to talk to a guy in a ski vest than a guy in a tie.

Tony had done his homework. He got her address from the official court records and he located the property on Google Earth as well as on his GPS system. He knew Francie Wells lived in a modest two-bedroom bungalow across the alley from the laundromat. Her house, in effect, formed the border between the tiny business district of Viscount and the few streets of residences to the east.

Viscount was a town of about 1,500 according to the most recent census. Tony called it a "three town." It had three churches and three bars. In many Iowa towns, the two things were found in equal numbers. A town might have more bars than churches, but he rarely found it the other way around.

Tony had timed his trip to arrive in Viscount in the late afternoon. He knew Francie worked as a clerk for the town, meaning she probably spent her days doing everything from processing payments for water bills, to calculating payroll checks for city employees, to preparing agendas for city council meetings.

City hall consisted of four offices and a meeting room built within the big steel building that also housed the town's two fire trucks – a traditional pumper and a smaller, four-wheel drive fast-response vehicle used for carrying volunteer EMTs or firefighters to traffic accidents and anything else not requiring 1,500 gallons of water.

Tony parked a block away and walked to the city hall/fire department building. Not wanting to approach Francie in front of others, he didn't go in, but walked past as casually as he could. Glancing in the two large windows in the front of the building, Tony could see that the city manager's office and the clerk's office were in the front. The offices were modest, with modular furniture, a few steel file cabinets, and a computer and telephone on each desk. It looked like the front door opened right into the clerk's space, which meant Francie

Wells was most likely cold all winter and hot all summer.

Tony was pleased to note that Francie was there behind her desk. It was after 4 p.m. and the daylight was waning thanks to a winter sun low in the southern sky. The good news was that the office lights painted the activities inside on the windows as if they were movie screens. Similarly, Tony knew, it meant the two women inside couldn't see him, or at least not very well.

Harvey's Grill and Bowling Alley was right across the street, so Tony headed there to wait for the workday to end. When Tony stepped inside, he noticed no one was eating and no one was bowling. About a half-dozen men and two women sat on tall stools at the bar, sipping various brands of beer and chatting as a pair of TVs behind the bar showed out-of-season sports reruns with the sound muted.

He chose the stool closest to the glass front doors so he could see the front of the building across the street, and ordered a diet soda from the heavyset man behind the bar. When it arrived, Tony asked, "You got anything to snack on here, nachos or something?"

The bartender didn't have to move his feet. He reached under the bar and pulled out a cardboard box filled with assorted candy bars, packs of peanuts, packaged pretzels, and other assorted off-the-shelf fare. "Sorry, pal. This is it," the man said. He had a gravelly voice, and his mouth sagged as if used to having a cigarette hanging from it.

"How about later?" Tony inquired, assuming he would be hungry if he spent a couple of hours or more in Viscount.

"Nah. We only cook one night a week here now. We do a steak fry on Friday nights."

"Except during Lent," the older of the two women at the other end of the bar hollered without looking up from her beer. "Then it's a fish fry."

The bartender sneered and said, "That's right, Diane. And if this young man wants to sit here until March, he can have fish on Friday night."

"Up yours," Diane said, eyes still straight ahead.

"Not in your lifetime," the man growled under his breath, rolling his eyes as he returned to his regulars.

Tony didn't risk a response and simply pulled a couple of chocolate bars out of the box, wondering how long he would have to wait and just how he would go about talking to Francie before she shut herself inside her house. Once there, she would have the option of simply ignoring his knocks on the door.

With just the first bite of chocolate in his mouth, the lights in City Hall clicked off and three people came out – the two women and an older man Tony assumed was the mayor. Francie was last. She turned to lock the deadbolt with her key. Tony chewed fast, not wanting to be so obvious as to run out the door with a mouth full of Snickers. He swallowed and was about to call for the check when he noticed Francie coming straight toward him. More to the point, straight toward Harvey's not-so-much-bowling-alley-or-grill.

As she came through the door, the bartender croaked a greeting and asked what she wanted to order. She asked for hot chocolate with a shot of Jack Daniels and then plopped down in a booth at the far end of the room, near the arched opening leading to the bowling lanes. She probably could smell the rental shoes from over there. He wondered about her choice of table but thought it fortuitous. He could approach her there, out of earshot of the others, and she would at least have to say yes or no to him. He decided to finish the candy bar first and took another bite as he received his second big surprise.

Deputy Sheriff Denny Peters slipped off one of the bar stools to his right and walked over to Francie's booth. Without a word, he slid in next to her, sitting close and speaking quietly.

Tony hadn't recognized the deputy out of uniform, and he was pretty sure the deputy hadn't recognized him. So he shifted positions on the stool, pretending to watch the TVs, but observing the couple in the booth. It didn't take long to surmise that was what they were – a couple. Tony could only speculate, of course, but Francie clearly was glad to see Peters. The dramatic differences in their heights caused the deputy to tower over her, but he pulled her so close they could have shared his parka.

Tony suddenly wished he knew a lot more about Peters. He knew many deputy sheriffs were former military who sought the work because they liked the prestige and authority, mostly the authority, that came with a badge and a gun. However, Tony doubted Peters was the hothead type. He was middle-aged and had been a deputy a long time. If he was trouble, surely Tony would have heard about it by now.

Still, if Peters was married and he felt threatened by being seen by the press then...what? Tony asked himself. *Really, what's he going to do? Beat me up in front of a room full of people?* So Tony called for his check, added a far too big tip, and left the money on the counter. He then climbed off the bar stool and walked over to the booth where the deputy and the witness were cuddled together.

"Excuse me," Tony said with as light and friendly a tone as he could muster.

"What?" Deputy Peters swung around, ready to tell whoever it was to get lost. The deputy's words froze in his throat as he recognized the young reporter standing in front of him.

"I'm Tony Harrington from the Orney *Town Crier*. I wrote the local news coverage of the Wells trial and, Ms. Wells, I was hoping I could have a few minutes of your time, you know, to ask you about the experience."

"Francie has nothing to say, do you Francie?" The deputy placed his arm around her as if to protect her from the paparazzi.

"Thank you, Deputy," Tony said, confirming for the man that Tony knew who he was. "I'd like to ask Francie, if you don't mind."

Francie Wells almost buried her face in the folds of Peters' parka as she replied, "Denny's right. I really don't want to talk about it."

"I understand," Tony said sympathetically. "It must have been a very difficult time for you. I thought maybe, now that it's over, you'd just like to share a little more background with people. You know, help everyone know you and your brother a little better."

Now the deputy stood up. A full five inches taller than Tony, he moved close and looked down into Tony's face. This, Tony knew, was his "intimidating cop" move, designed to scare perpetrators, witnesses, and potential troublemakers. *The thing is,* Tony thought wryly as he took two steps back, *it's working.*

"Okay, okay, officer. I'm going. Here's my card in case she changes her mind." As he pulled his business card from his pocket and held it out, Peters just stared at it, not moving a muscle. Tony finally set it on the table next to him, turned on his heels, and headed for the door.

As he climbed into his SUV and started the engine, Tony was tempted to race out of town for home. However, he knew from experience that now, after a news subject had been spooked, was the time to wait and see what happened next. Sure enough, he hadn't been in his car thirty seconds when Deputy Peters rushed out the door of Harvey's and jumped in his cruiser. However, he didn't start the car. As he sat in the dark vehicle Tony could see the tiny flicker of light and then the glow against the side of the deputy's face.

Well, well, Tony thought. *Denny Peters has rushed outside to the privacy of his car to make an urgent cell phone call. I wonder what that's about?* He waited for Peters to go back inside before he turned on his lights and put the SUV in gear. He was careful not to go past Harvey's as he drove out of town.

He thought about the encounter all the way home, exploring it from every angle. It wasn't lost on him that he had gone to Viscount to find answers, and all he had found were more questions.

Chapter 16

Tony had not intended to forego his interview of Francie. As a result of the encounter in Viscount, Tony was eager to ask her about her relationship with Peters in addition to the basic questions about her relationship with her brother. However, over the next several days, his attempts to call her at home went unanswered, and his one attempt to call her at work ended in an abrupt slam down of the city clerk's reception phone. Tony came away rubbing his ear and resigning himself to the obvious fact he would have to approach her again in person and uninvited.

However, the time somehow slipped by him as he engaged in other projects at work. As the time passed, it became easier and easier to push his questions for Francie to the back burner. Suddenly it was ten weeks later. Tony realized how much time had passed when he came out of Willie's after lunch one day and saw melted snow running in the gutters of First Avenue on the north side of the square. The sight stopped him in his tracks and Doug nearly ran into his back. "What the h...?" Doug stopped himself.

"Spring is here," Tony said simply, staring down at the wet concrete.

"Well, maybe not quite," Doug replied, gesturing at the seven-foot-high pile of snow on the town square. The city fathers always piled a good amount of snow on the square's playground as part of the street clearing efforts in the winter. It had begun as a practical matter. Where better to pile snow than an unused park? But over the years it had become a local attraction for kids of all ages. Games such as "King of the Mountain," dares regarding who could burrow the deepest tunnel fort, and bets on who could make the most flips in a dive off the top were commonplace. Many laughs, plenty of tears, and a few bruises emerged from that pile of snow every year, but the people of Orney still flocked to their manmade mountain.

Tony smiled as he acknowledged Doug's point that it wasn't exactly sunbathing weather. "Still," he said, "look at the running water. It's supposed to get up to forty degrees today. We may not lose Mount Orney over there, but I bet we lose most of what's on the ground."

"It's only March, so don't get your hopes up," Doug said. "We both know Mother Nature isn't finished beating us up yet. Don't get me wrong. It's fine by me if winter ends early. I'm tired of drying my sneakers every night."

"You know, Doug, there's a new invention you should try called 'boots.' You'd like it. You just slip these vinyl things over your shoes and you can walk anywhere without ruining the leather or, in your case, the canvas or plastic or whatever is in those things you wear on your feet."

"Yeah, yeah, smartass. I suppose you mean boots like the ones you're wearing?"

Tony, of course, was in his street shoes. He rarely wore boots once the sidewalks and streets were cleared of snow. He was contemplating his next smart remark when Doug brought him back to the point.

"So what's your obsession with spring this year? I've never known you to be one of the winter-haters."

"No, that's not the point at all," Tony replied. "The changing of the seasons just wacked me upside of the head, as our friend Willie would say. It reminded me of how much time has passed since I went to Viscount to talk to Francie. I really have to find the time to get back there and camp in front of her house until she'll talk to me."

"Maybe not," Doug looked over Tony's shoulder and across the square. "Isn't that her coming out of O'Neill's?"

Tony spun around and peered through the trees to the opposite row of storefronts. O'Neill's was an office supply store in the center of the block. Tony couldn't swear to it, but he was pretty sure Doug was right. Walking to his left along the block was a woman who looked very much like Francie Wells.

Tony zipped up his jacket. "Well, I guess I'll see you later," he said, turning to go.

"You want me to come along?" Doug asked.

"Well, you have as much right to interview her as I do," Tony said over his shoulder. "But I'd rather go alone if you don't mind. You can always read my brilliant article to your listeners in the morning...like always."

"Yeah, well up yours too, Mr. Kent. Don't get your cape wet in the melting snow." By now, Doug was nearly shouting at Tony's disappearing back. Tony heard him and turned just long enough to flash his middle finger, then took off in a jog.

***

Tony moved quickly, but not quickly enough. He turned the

corner just in time to see Francie Wells climb into a late model red Toyota Avalon parked at a meter on the next block. She wasted no time in starting the car and pulling away from the curb. Tony stared as the car drove past him, but Francie didn't seem to notice him. Tony watched to see which way she went from the intersection. She turned south in the general direction of the highway. As soon as he was sure of her direction, Tony took off at a full run. His SUV was just down the alley in the *Town Crier's* back lot. He hopped in, turned the key with his right hand while grabbing the seat belt with his left, and spun the tires as he turned down the alley.

Tony's guess was that Francie was headed back to Viscount using the main highways. She had probably been in Orney on her lunch hour to shop and perhaps to enjoy a decent restaurant. Now she would be hurrying back to work. Tony pushed the SUV past the speed limit posted on Skillet Boulevard, a wide, tree-lined thorough-fare that carried most of the traffic in and out of Orney from U.S. 26. In less than two minutes, he spotted the red Toyota up ahead, still headed south and slowing to stop at the intersection with the highway.

Tony was surprised, however, when the Toyota crossed the highway and continued straight south on what became a county blacktop. Tony stayed back as far as he dared. With so few cars on the road outside of town, he didn't want to be spotted following her. However, he felt even stronger that he didn't want to lose her.

But why, he wondered? *What the heck am I doing out here any-way?* He didn't have a good answer. He only knew he wanted a chance to talk to her. It had to be worth his time to see if an oppor-tunity presented itself, didn't it? Tony decided to seek Ben's counsel. With his right hand on the steering wheel, he pulled his cell phone from his pocket with his left and thumbed the buttons to call the newsroom. He was glad to hear Ben answer the phone directly.

After explaining where he was and what he was doing, Tony had to admit his boss sounded less than thrilled about it.

"Tony, you know I admire your dedication and your initiative. I always have. But I have to admit I'm not quite sure what you hope to accomplish." Tony could only grunt an acknowledgement that his boss might be right before Ben continued. "I'm not going to tell you what to do. If you're asking my opinion, then I think you're wasting your time. But," he continued before Tony could respond, "I also don't see any harm in following her for a while longer, just to see if her destination gives you some new insight into her background.

"My advice comes in the form of three cautions I'd like you to take to heart. One, don't get into a position of harassing her. If she doesn't want to talk, you'll have to live with that. Secondly, don't follow her onto private property. My petty cash fund doesn't have a big enough balance to cover bail money. And thirdly, try to remember she has a boyfriend or some kind of relationship with a man who carries a gun and already has demonstrated he's protective of her. He's just as reachable by cell phone as I was."

"Thanks, boss," Tony replied. "It's good advice and I promise I won't ignore it. Talk to you soon."

Tony ended the call and tossed his iPhone on the seat of the Explorer just as the red Toyota braked and turned left into the Quincy County Park and Game Preserve. "What the hell..." Tony wondered aloud. He slowed the SUV to a crawl to put more space between it and the Toyota, and then he made the turn. He knew he wasn't being exactly true to Ben's advice, but it was a public park, so at least an arrest for trespassing was off the table.

Tony wasn't worried about losing Francie now. There was only one paved road in the park. It wound through the trees, around campgrounds, picnic areas, and entrances to hiking trails, ending at the lake. The road had been kept clear of snow, as the park was open to snowmobiles, sleds, and even horses during the winter. Because of the thick stand of trees covering the hills, nearly everything else was still covered with several inches of snow.

Tony slowed the Explorer as he arrived at the large parking lot with a boat access ramp to Lake Oakley. The lake was still white with snow and ice, and Tony could see snowmobile tracks leading out onto the expansive open area. In light of the warming weather, he hoped no one was foolish enough to attempt it now. The sole vehicle parked in the lot was the red Toyota. Francie was nowhere in sight.

Well, in for a dime, in for a dollar, Tony thought, wincing at his use of another of his grandmother's truisms. He pulled the Explorer into the parking stall next to the Toyota. As Tony got out of his vehicle, he pulled on his winter coat and paused to admire the Avalon. It was practically new and very impressive. He was pretty sure it was Toyota's most luxurious and expensive model. He wondered how a worker bee in a small town clerk's office could afford a car like this. Inheritance? No, not based on what he'd seen of both Ralph's and Francie's homes. Jackpot at the casino? Perhaps, but not likely since the *Town Crier* hadn't been contacted. The only thing the nearest casino hated more than giving away money was giving away money without getting a lot of publicity for it. Gift from a boyfriend? If the boyfriend was Denny Peters that seemed unlikely too. Deputy Sheriffs didn't make a lot more than small town office workers. A rental? Stolen? Tony gave up on his speculations and just added it to the list of things he wanted to ask Francie Wells. He also made note of the license plate number and the sticker on the back identifying the dealer who sold it – Quad Cities Toyota. *Huh,* Tony thought, *that's a long way to go to buy a car.*

Tony looked up and gazed out on the frozen lake. Where the hell was Francie? He walked around the car and quickly spotted her footprints in the snow, leading toward the shelter house by the lake. It was a large, permanent structure of hardwood and stone. The building included changing rooms and restrooms for swimmers and other park visitors. It also had a large room for hosting parties – typically picnics in the summer when a wall of windows could be opened to an even larger covered patio. During peak times, county employees would staff a vending area with windows to the outside, selling bait for fishing, snacks, and the requisite oils and lotions to keep away the sun, or the mosquitoes, depending on your activity that day. On a cold late winter weekday afternoon, the building was almost certainly empty except, it appeared, for the presence of Francie Wells.

Tony followed her tracks around the back to where the entrances to the restrooms were located. Francie's tracks clearly led to the door of the men's room. *Curiouser and curiouser,* Tony thought as he walked up to the building, pushed open the door and stepped through.

"Ms. We...?" He started to say her name as something large and heavy crashed into his side, knocking him to the concrete floor. His head just missed the edge of the porcelain sink, but scraped along the drain pipe underneath. "Hey!" Tony screamed, as the object crashed down a second time, this time on his hip. A searing pain shot down his leg. "Stop! Jesus. You're going to kill me! Stop!"

Francie Wells stepped back. She was holding a wooden bench used by people when changing their clothes. It was, essentially, a 2 x 10" plank with legs affixed to the underside. Francie held it above one shoulder and screamed at him: "Don't you move, you sonofabitch, or I swear I'll break both of your legs and leave you here to crawl back to your car."

"Okay, okay, just stop, please," Tony said, the pains in his side, head, and hip now beginning to pound in sync with his racing heart. "All I wanted to do was talk to you."

"Yeah, well, I thought I made it pretty clear, I don't want to talk to you," Francie said, red-faced and breathing hard.

"Please, put that down and help me up," Tony said. "I swear, I won't bother you any further."

"You swear?" Francie asked, clearly wanting him to repeat it.

"I swear," Tony said, rolling to his knees and using the sink to help himself stand.

Francie backed farther into the room, but still held the heavy bench. "You think you're so smart. Jesus, I spotted you following me on Skillet. And now look at you. Who's the smart one now?"

Tony was pretty sure she wasn't expecting an answer, so he held his tongue. His hip and side hurt like hell and he was breathing heavily, the steam coming in puffs from his mouth and nose. Thank God he had worn his coat. She would have broken some ribs for sure if he hadn't had the protection of the goose down padding.

Francie continued, "What's so damn important, anyway? Why can't you just leave me alone?"

As much as he hurt, Tony couldn't help but take a chance. "Francie, I just wanted to understand your relationship with Ralph. You must know that those of us in the courtroom wondered why a sister would provide such damning evidence against her brother so voluntarily."

"Well, if you were there then you know I was asked the same thing in the courtroom that day. I gave my answer then and I'm sticking to it."

In Tony's mind, these words were practically a confession that she had lied, but considering she still held a solid oak weapon and he didn't, he decided to move on.

"Okay, I get that, but then I was curious about your relationship with Denny Peters. Were you seeing him already? I mean, were you two together at the time of the trial?"

Francie screamed, "What business is that of yours? You bastard. You're going to spoil everything! You keep nosing around and pushing people. Something's...someone's going to come apart and you're going to regret you ever heard of Ralph Wells!"

Francie moved forward and Tony quickly pressed himself back against the wall, expecting another blow. However, she dropped the bench with a loud crash and headed for the door. Now that she was barehanded, Tony's courage rose.

"Was that a threat Francie? What are you saying?"

Francie stopped outside the door and turned to face him.

"I'm saying," she barked, as tears inched down her cheeks, "that you are totally clueless. You don't know anything about this and you have no idea what's at stake or who you're up against. Just stay away. Stay away, or a few bruises from a bathroom bench will be the least of your worries."

She turned and fled. She was long gone by the time Tony limped back to his car.

Before climbing in, Tony stopped to examine his face in the large exterior mirror on the driver's door. Blood seeped from a wide scrape running from in front of his right ear to his chin. *Dear Lord,* he thought. *How am I going to explain this to Ben or to Lisa? Outsmarted, ambushed, and injured by an interview subject I would have described as simple-minded. Good grief.*

He strapped himself back into the driver's seat and started the SUV. Once again, he realized his encounter with Francie had generated more questions than answers. The difference, this time, was the questions were more serious. While Tony couldn't imagine he was actually in danger, except from this crazy woman, he had to acknowledge he was pursuing a murder case. If Ralph Wells was innocent, then someone else was guilty, and that someone might go to extremes to hide the truth. What had she meant when she said he had no idea "what was at stake" or who he was "up against?" That sounded like the real perpetrator was more than just some pissed off kid who got burned in a drug deal and knew where Ralph Wells kept his .22.

What's at stake? Who am I up against? Tony shook his head, started the car, and backed out of the parking space as he forced himself to admit Francie Wells was right; he still didn't know anything about what was going on.

***

After a quick stop at home to clean up and change clothes, Tony went directly to Ben's office. As he plopped into the chair across from Ben's desk, his boss looked up. Tony wasn't sure what to expect and wasn't sure how to react when Ben's face clouded and then reddened.

"Please tell me you got that from a barroom brawl and not from Francie Wells," he said, clearly trying to control his anger. *No, not anger.* Ben was trying to control his disappointment.

Tony replied, "Oh I wish I could. And I'm sorry to tell you that what you see on the side of my face isn't the worst of it."

Ben, still red-faced, asked, "Do you need to see a doctor? Anything broken?"

"You mean besides my self-confidence? No, I'll live."

"Okay," Ben said. "You'd better tell me all about it."

After walking Ben through the facts, Tony asked, "So what do you think I should do?"

"About this? Nothing. If you make an issue of it, either in the paper or with the police, it will become your word against hers. Worst case scenario, she'll accuse you of assaulting her or, God forbid, attempted rape. You'll end up fighting this thing for months or years. I say let it go, and hope she does the same."

"But..."

Ben interrupted him, this time in a loud voice. "Tony, stop! You *did* follow her into that park, knowing full well you would find her alone there. How do you think that will look? Face it, she outsmarted you. Learn a lesson and move on."

Tony nodded begrudgingly. He didn't care about not reporting her to the police, but he hated the idea of not writing the story. However, he knew Ben was right, so he made up his mind to let it go and save the story for his grandchildren or his memoirs. As he began to mumble a thank-you and rise from the chair, Ben stopped him.

"Before you go, tell me if you have any other ideas about next steps."

Tony was surprised Ben hadn't exhausted his supply of patience, but welcomed the opportunity to contemplate the question.

He responded, "Well I've thought about interviewing most or all of the other trial witnesses, but I have to be honest, I'm not confident it would yield anything new, so I can't recommend you approve that much investment of time and effort. I think the one person besides Francie who is most likely to know more than he's telling is Denny Peters. But it's really obvious he isn't going to tell me anything. I couldn't even get him to touch my business card."

Ben acknowledged the logic of this with a nod and then asked, "So do you let it go and see what happens with the appeals?"

"No...not exactly," Tony said. "There's a sidebar issue I want to explore, and I'll probably talk to Rich at the DCI and see if he can help."

Ben said, "Okay, you certainly have my support to do that. However, Tony, this is no joke. Do not put yourself or this newspaper at risk again. I'll tolerate a lot, but not that."

Tony looked his boss in the eye. "I promise, no more chasing wild geese or getting beat up. I'll try to stay focused on news I can actually write about for publication."

Ben relaxed, saying, "Well don't go getting all boring on me now. You know I don't mind you following your gut from time to time, as long as the feature story about the flower show still gets written."

It was Tony's turn to relax as he headed out his boss' door.

***

Twenty minutes later, Tony was standing in the Quincy County Courthouse trying to look nonchalant. Because of Ben's obvious support for his continued pursuit of this story, Tony had decided to do one next step immediately, before he even went back to his desk. He didn't want to be distracted by phone messages or overdue assignments.

He was standing in the hallway of the courthouse's basement level, debating whether to go into the County Treasurer's Office or not. It was late afternoon and two of the staff had already left. The treasurer, an elected official, was in his private office, visible through a glass partition at the back of the larger staff workspace. A long hardwood counter separated the work area from a public waiting room. The treasurer's office handled everything from county tax collections to budgeting and managing the county's accounts. However, Tony was here because of one other duty of the office: issuing license plates for motor vehicles.

Tony knew the motor vehicle records, like all public records in Iowa, were legally available for him to review. He also knew from experience that county employees didn't always follow the law, at least not without asking permission of their bosses and, occasionally, of the County Attorney's Office. Making a major issue of a minor request most often happened when the request was unusual, such as a reporter wanting to see the title on someone's private vehicle.

Tony did not want this request to become a major issue. In fact, he wanted it handled as quietly as possible, which is why he smiled broadly when he looked through the door of the Treasurer's Office and saw the lone staffer behind the counter was Edith Perrimore. Tony had made requests of Edith before when working on stories about county government. She had been employed in the office for as long as anyone could remember and she didn't ask permission from anybody for anything. She was more likely to tell the treasurer what to do than to ask him.

Tony walked through the door, greeted Edith warmly, and explained what he needed.

Minutes later, Tony walked out of the courthouse with a copy of the title. The $40,000 car was owned by Francie Wells of Viscount, Iowa. Even more remarkably, there was no lien filed, meaning Francie didn't owe any money on the car, or at least didn't owe it to a lending institution.

***

The following Saturday, Tony made the long drive to the Quad Cities, on the eastern edge of Iowa, to visit the dealership which had sold the Avalon. He didn't expect to learn anything more, but justified the trip by noting he could stop on the way home and spend the night with his parents in Iowa City.

As much as Tony hated getting up early, he was on the road by 7 a.m. and arrived at Quad Cities Toyota nearly four hours later. It was a big, modern dealership with a huge inventory and was bustling on a beautiful winter Saturday. Tony pushed through the glass doors into the show room and stopped at a large oval reception desk.

"Can I help you?" a pretty twenty-something blonde asked him as she placed the handset of a telephone into its cradle.

"Yes," Tony smiled, "I'm thinking about buying a new Avalon. I'd like to speak to whoever sold Francie Wells her car recently. Francie is a friend of mine and she recommended I ask for her salesperson. Unfortunately, she couldn't remember the name."

"Well, all of our sales staff are well trained regarding the full line of new vehicles," the young woman replied. "But let me see if I can figure out who that salesperson was. Did your friend say it was a man or a woman?"

"Oh gosh," Tony said. "I'm embarrassed to say I didn't think to ask her."

"No problem," the woman said. "Let me ask our new car sales manager if he can figure out who it was. We sell a lot of cars, but Jack takes great pride in meeting every buyer before the deal is done."

She picked up the phone, reached the sales manager, and concluded the call surprisingly quickly.

"Good news," she said. "Jack remembered Ms. Wells immediately. He said Billy Thorngood helped her. That's especially good news for you. He's our best."

"Great," said Tony, still smiling, but knowing she would have said that regardless of which name the sales manager had given her. "Let's give him a try."

The young woman picked up the microphone for the overhead paging system, and in less than two minutes, a stocky man with close-cropped gray hair came charging across the showroom with his hand extended.

"I'm Billy Thorngood," he said. "How can I help you, uh..."

"Tony. I'm Tony. I'm interested in a new Avalon."

"Wonderful, wonderful," Thorngood said. "You've come to the right place. Let's go over to my desk. I'll pull our inventory up on my computer and we can see how it matches with what you're looking for. We'll try to narrow it down to just a few cars so we're not dragging you all over the parking lot in the cold."

"I appreciate that," Tony said, happy to finally be speaking the truth about something.

For the next fifteen minutes, Tony painted himself as a picky and somewhat eccentric buyer, setting the stage for the issue he had come to pursue. At the right moment he asked, "Tell me, does it help or hurt my negotiation on the price if you know I'm not going to finance the car?"

Thorngood replied, "I'm not sure I know what you mean."

"Well, I know you or Toyota make money on financing the deals, so I just want to be sure that paying cash won't cost me more in the selling price. Oh, it may help you to understand I'm a friend of Francie Wells. In fact I'm here because of her recommendation. I know she worried about this issue in negotiating her deal."

"Really? That's pretty funny because I didn't think Ms. Wells worried about anything in buying her Avalon."

"Knowing Francie as I do, I'm surprised. Tell me what you mean."

"Well, it was just about the easiest sale I ever made. Ms. Wells walked into the showroom, pointed at the red Avalon and said she wanted to buy it. There wasn't much negotiation about the price. If I remember right, she lived a long way from here. She wouldn't even let us do the dealer preparation on it. She drove it out of here in less than an hour."

"Well," Tony tried to chuckle, "I guess that would explain why she spoke so highly of you and your dealership. She told me dealing with you was really easy. I guess I failed to understand just what she meant. And obviously, she was comfortable that skipping the financing would be no problem."

"Obviously," Thorngood said, leaning back in his chair. "In fact, it's the first cash sale I ever made on a new car."

"Really?" Tony said, surprised. "I would never have guessed that everyone finances with you."

"No, no you don't understand," Thorngood said, shaking his head. "Francis, uh Francie...right? Yeah, Francie paid in cash. I mean *cash*. She literally counted out over $38,000 in cash on my desk – uh, that included taxes and fees you understand. No one here was even sure how to handle a sale that way. But we made it work, by God. You better believe we made it work."

Thorngood laughed out loud and then asked, "You're not going to do that too, are you?"

"No," Tony assured him. "When I pay, there's likely to be a check from my bank involved."

Tony spent the next twenty minutes extricating himself from the salesman's clutches, saying he hadn't made up his mind on which options he wanted and promising to return. Once out the door, he jumped in his Explorer and headed west on I-80. Iowa City was about an hour away.

Curiouser and curiouser, he thought again as he drove, *Francie Wells, you are just full of surprises.*

Chapter 17

Tony hated parades. He especially hated covering them as a reporter. What can you say about a parade that hasn't been said a thousand times before? He mostly hated having to fudge the truth. Parades were like Santa Claus: everyone knew the truth, but everyone preferred the fiction. The truth was that the local high school band wasn't very good, most of the floats were made in someone's garage and looked it, and the county fair queen looked a little wilted riding on top of the back seat of a Corvette convertible in the hot July sun. These were all things Tony wouldn't write. He and his boss knew that the parents of all those kids, the readers of the *Town Crier*, preferred the fudged version.

At least the car is cool, Tony thought, but then it was gone. Not having time to look at the one cool feature of the parade was just another reason to dislike the whole affair. Tony didn't feel as grumpy as he had every right to be. He appreciated the truly beautiful day and was glad to see that many people watching from lawn chairs and blankets along the route genuinely seemed to be having a good time.

And these kids are thrilled to be in the parade, Tony thought as he snapped a photo of an overly adorable troupe of 8-year-olds prancing and spinning through a promotion of Eva's Dance Studio.

Next came the obligatory fire truck, with firefighters sitting on their perches on the back, tossing candy to the kids lining the curbs. As the children scrambled around him to scoop up the goodies, Tony had to step carefully. He typically started at the front and moved toward the back when he photographed a parade. It actually took less time that way, and it ensured he saw everything while in motion on the parade route.

Up ahead he spotted Nelson's campaign banner moving toward him, held aloft by two long poles which were held in turn by two young blonde beauties wearing matching shorts and halter tops in red, white, and blue. "I won't just serve you, I'll protect you!" the banner proclaimed above "Elect Nelson/Fitzgerald." Behind the girls and the banner was a black Hummer. Speakers mounted on the top blared a patriotic march tune. There, behind the Hummer, walking back and forth from curb to curb, shaking hands and handing out flyers, was W. Rodney Nelson.

As Tony lifted his Nikon SLR, Nelson paused, raised his hand in a wave, and broadened his smile. *Good grief,* Tony thought. *He's posing for me.* He snapped the picture anyway, knowing Ben wouldn't use it, favoring a picture of a local cute kid over a politician every time.

Tony turned and matched strides with Nelson as he resumed campaigning.

"Mr. Nelson, Tony Harrington from the local paper. Can I ask you how the campaign is going?"

"I couldn't be more pleased," Nelson responded without hesitation. "The people of Iowa have been wonderfully welcoming of me and my family as we've traveled the state. More importantly, they've been clear in their support of our campaign. The people support our message of good government, supporting the middle class, and ensuring people are safe."

"Thank you, sir," Tony said, turning again to continue his walk into the parade stream. "Thanks for nothing," he muttered when out of earshot.

Tony had of course heard identical comments from Nelson on the news for weeks. Somewhat surprisingly, the fact was the assistant attorney general was right. His message had gotten legs, and he was showing surprisingly strong in the polls. Governor Roskins still led, but it was early in the race and Nelson trailed by just three points. Nelson had been a viable candidate before, but he clearly was using his visibility as a law and order candidate to its best advantage.

Nelson had something else working in his favor. Iowa elects its governors on the midterm cycle, meaning there would be no presidential race on the ballot this fall. In addition, this was the cycle in which neither of the state's U.S. senators was up for re-election. In other words, the turnout for the governor's race would likely be low. Tony knew that somewhere behind closed doors, a campaign strategist had calculated for Nelson exactly how many votes he would need to upset the popular governor. Now, Nelson and his campaign simply had to go out and find that number of people to get out and vote for him. Not an easy task, but not insurmountable either.

Of course, seeing Nelson churned up thoughts of his performance at the Wells trial and all the uncertainty and angst Tony still felt about that entire case. Tony wasn't sure which gave him more sleepless nights, the thought of an innocent man rotting in The Fort, the thought of the guilty party roaming the streets, or the thought of an unfinished story. He knew his top concern should be for justice, both for Wells and the guilty person. He also knew, as a man who tried to be honest with himself, his concern for the unwritten story was at least as great.

After his encounter with Francie and the trip to the Quad Cities, Tony had tried for weeks to take the story further. Every angle he pursued and every attempt he made to find additional facts ended up running into a brick wall. Short of illegal wiretapping or perhaps kidnapping and torture, Tony couldn't think of a way to get below the surface of what he was sure was an ocean of unreported facts.

Ben had been supportive of Tony's efforts as long as he continued to produce other good articles as well. But eventually, even Ben had suggested Tony let it go. It wasn't easy, but it was made easier by the fact that life was filled with plenty of distractions both at work and in his relationship with Lisa. Soon winter had melted away, spring had come and gone, and a hot, dry summer had moved in. Tony marveled that it was already the Fourth of July.

As he reached the end of the parade, he continued walking the twelve blocks to the county fairgrounds where the annual carnival was cheating people out of their hard-earned money with bad rides and unwinnable games. Despite the dirt and noise, the carnival's two biggest attributes, Tony knew it would be good for a couple more photos. He would find an ice cream-covered face on a four-year-old, or the terrorized face of a pre-teen on the Tilt-a-Whirl, or just maybe the joyful face of a dad who managed to win a stuffed bear for his pleading child.

Snap, snap...a few questions of the people whose images he captured...a few signed photo releases (which were more courtesies than legal requirements in a public place), and Tony headed back to the *Crier* to write up the day's events.

***

"Do I bore you?" Lisa asked, rolling back onto her side of

the bed.

"Of course not," Tony replied quickly, raising himself up on one elbow and sliding the palm of his hand up over her stomach, between her breasts and stopping to lightly stroke her cheek. "I was just thinking..."

"You were just ignoring me, which is something you never used to do," Lisa replied in a voice that was trying to be kind but was straining to get there.

"I was just thinking," Tony said, dropping his head back to the pillow and trying to control the frustration in his voice, "about that damn trial. Jeez, Lisa, I covered the biggest story of last year, maybe the biggest story of my life, and I'm not sure I did the job right. The thought has me... has me, I don't know... discombobulated I guess."

"What do you mean?" She warmed to the sound of his voice and slid closer. "You did a great job with the coverage. You were thorough and factual and, like always, your descriptions of the court-room and all the players had me and lots of other people feeling like they were there with you. How can you feel you didn't do the job?"

"I don't know..." Tony hesitated. "Are you sure you want to talk about this?"

"We might as well," Lisa smiled and sat up. "If I can't keep you interested in sex, then I'd better convince you what a good partner I am for other reasons."

Tony also sat up as he made up his mind. "Well, for starters, I hope you've noticed you have no problem keeping me interested in sex. But more to the point, you know I've felt for months there's more to this case than anyone knows... or is telling."

"But we've been through it all before, Tony. You did everything you could. It's not your job to prove him innocent, or guilty for that matter. Your job is to report the facts."

"Don't I know it," Tony pulled his knees up and lowered his

head onto them. "But it was all just too pat. Too simple. Too cut and dried."

Lisa groaned. "You have to stop second-guessing the evidence. You know better than I do that when all the facts point to the accused, he did it."

"I know, I know, but not in this case." Tony always felt his misgivings most when he began venting them. Now he felt as if he was a stallion bursting through the gate. "That ass Nelson had it all: the weapon, the clothes, the shoes, and even that young girl."

"So..."

"I'm not finished. What Nelson didn't have was a motive. Why? Why in the hell would this poor schmuck who's never ever even had a parking ticket suddenly take a rifle and blow the brains out of two people he barely knew?"

"His sister said..."

"I know what she said. I'm the one who had to tell everyone how she sealed her brother's fate. But it's such a crock. She claims she heard him threaten to kill the Ennises over some meth deal. But there's no evidence Wells was involved in dealing meth. And would a man known for his dislike of confrontations and violence suddenly decide to kill two people over a bag of meth?"

Tony plunged on. "What's more important is the part I couldn't report in the newspaper." Lisa looked puzzled and he continued, "I don't get to tell people what I see that can't be captured in a picture... my impressions. As I watched, one of those strong feelings was that Miss Francie was a lying bitch. I'd bet my car... well maybe not my car, but I'd bet a lot that she never heard Ralph say one word about the Ennises."

"Now wait a minute," Lisa said, taking her turn to sound irritated.

Tony knew Lisa disliked it when he jumped to conclusions

about people. He also knew she was right – he was too quick to form opinions and too slow to change them.

"Okay, okay, I know what you're going to say. I don't know her and maybe I'm wrong. But even if I am, I can tell you something I'm not wrong about. I saw her look at her brother, and she feels nothing for him. I also heard what she said in the park that day. Her testimony wasn't about Ralph. It was about something else altogether. Something involving love, or money, or both."

"Back up a minute. Are you trying to say you could tell by sitting in the courtroom that a woman doesn't love her brother?"

"I know how egocentric that sounds," Tony said earnestly, "but you had to see the way she looked at him. She felt none of the things you or I would have felt if we were sending one of our loved ones to prison for life. No love, no sympathy, no guilt. I'm not surprised she volunteered to testify. In fact, I'd bet she approached Nelson and not the other way around."

"Well, that should be something you could find out."

Tony was struck by that thought. His muscles tightened and little peaks of flesh began to form at the base of the hairs on his arms. Lisa was right. As hard as it was to get information from attorneys during a trial, the further it faded into the past, the easier it should be to find out exactly what led to Francie appearing for the prosecution. If she came forward on her own and not because an investigator had identified her and urged her to cooperate, then why? His mind was immediately considering all the possibilities. It made the scene he had observed between her and Peters all the more intriguing, and he said so.

"Oh cripes," Lisa moaned. "I should have kept quiet. I'll never get any of your attention now." Tony turned and looked into her eyes. Her big, soft, hazel eyes. He smiled, "Oh, I think I know some things you can do to get my mind off of Ralph and Francie Wells." His eyes dropped from her face, to her breasts, to the blanket, gathered in a soft pile in her lap. He thought, *Holy shit, this woman has a great body,* but said aloud, "Besides, I need to thank you for your ear and for your wonderful idea."

He then leaned over and whispered, "Now where's that ear I wanted to thank?" He rolled onto her and flicked his tongue across her earlobe. His hands gripped the sides of her rib cage and he kissed her on the side of the neck; then kissed her again, lower; then again, lower...

Later, as they pushed the covers back to cool off, it was Lisa who surprised Tony with thoughts of the trial.

"By the way," she said, "if Ralph Wells didn't kill the Ennises, who did?"

Tony almost paused to ask her if she had been thinking about this while they were making love, but stopped himself knowing he wasn't prepared to answer the same question if she turned it on him. He thought about the question of who did the crime if not Wells. It was a question he had considered many times since the trial, but never too seriously.

Tony groaned aloud. "I'm so sure I'm right on the one hand, and I'm completely clueless on the other. I don't even know how to begin to find out who really killed them. It looks like Francie and maybe even Peters are wrapped up in this somehow, but even their involvement is a mystery."

"It all goes back to motive," Lisa said sleepily. "To know who killed them, you have to know who benefited from it."

"Of course. I've tried to look at that, but I'm still at a loss."

Nothing Tony had learned in the trial or in talking to his friends in the DCI had given him any indication of a potential beneficiary. There was no inheritance involved at all. The house had been rented, and the couple's bank accounts were meager. Even the two daughters had been left with next to nothing and now were foster children being cared for by the state. Without another suspect, it was impossible to investigate potential benefits or motives. Now, with Wells serving prison time for the crime, he knew there would never be another suspect coming from the DCI or the Sheriff's Department.

"You don't need another suspect handed to you," Lisa replied, yawning. "Just dig deeper. As you've said, no one killed two innocent people for no reason. So someone benefitted, at least indirectly. Look past the people directly involved." With that comment, Lisa drifted off to sleep.

But Tony was wide awake. He considered with amazement the insight of the woman beside him who hadn't spent one percent as much time thinking about this case as he had. He lay awake a long time mulling over the possibilities. A crime of this magnitude must have had lots of ramifications beyond those who were dead and the man sitting in prison. He began to relax and drift into sleep, thinking, *don't focus on the crime. Find out who benefitted.* There was a certain comfort in finally having another avenue to pursue. Tony sighed, smiled, and soon joined Lisa in her dreams of happier things.

Chapter 18

Lisa liked being busy. She had to remind herself of that as she briskly walked the two blocks from Purdy's Office Systems, the computer store where she had begun working part time, to party headquarters, where she still volunteered one or two evenings a week. It was just after 5 p.m. and the downtown stores were in various stages of closing for the day as she passed. The July sun was still blazing, and the heat smothered her like sharing a sleeping bag with a first love. She was sweating visibly by the time she passed through the glass door into the air-conditioned surroundings of the makeshift offices. Because it was an election year, the party had rented an old downtown storefront, larger than the office it normally shared with the Extension Service and the Farm Bureau, on the highway at the edge of town. Lisa actually preferred this old building. It had most recently been an antique shop, but originally had been the town's opera house, which meant it had hosted vaudeville acts in the days before movies, television, DVDs, and the Internet. It had later been a movie house, showing the first "talkie" seen in this part of Iowa.

The original stage still existed on the second floor above her head, but Lisa hadn't seen it in years. She ventured to guess that most of Orney's current residents had never seen it.

Her opportunity to explore the mysterious opera house had been as exciting for a young girl as it had been unexpected. Her father had been serving as president of the local Chamber of Commerce that year, and had ventured upstairs to assess whether the facility could be restored enough to host a portion of the town's annual Harvest Festival. Lisa had been lucky enough to be beside him in the car when he had decided to take the time for a look. Her father had quickly determined that the upper floor of the opera house was beyond hope but had waited patiently while Lisa had investigated every room, reading bits of century-old graffiti and marveling at the props and flats that still remained. Memories of that day were pleasant and reminded her how much she still enjoyed her relationship with her father.

Lisa entered the building and threw down her shoulder bag. Because she knew computers and could type faster than Clark Kent on speed, she was a valuable commodity to the party's county office. Even though it was an election year, the office had only three paid staffers. Lyle "The Smile" McCabe was one, and the designated director of the office. People joked that McCabe hadn't stopped smiling since the governor had hand-picked him for the county post seven years before. Lisa didn't know, or much care, if that was true. But she did know McCabe was all smiles for her ever since she had walked into the offices the previous year and told him she wanted to volunteer for the governor's re-election campaign.

Despite his smile, Lisa didn't like McCabe much. He was so obviously full of himself, and for no reason she could understand. Short and slightly overweight, he was far from attractive. Much of his hair had long ago disappeared, but his ego required him to grow long what was left and try to stick it to his scalp with some greasy hair product that obviously wasn't up to the task. By the time Lisa arrived most evenings, McCabe's strands of hair were lying against the side of his face, mingled with sweat from a day on the phone, asking favors and raising money.

It didn't help that Lisa frequently caught McCabe staring at her and finding excuses to stand at her desk or to ask her to his office. His eyes seldom rose to look above her neck, and she found herself uncomfortable and embarrassed in his presence, which only served to irritate her further. Each time she arrived to volunteer, she reminded herself that she wasn't there to serve McCabe. She was there to help Governor Harry Roskins, a man she had known for most of her life and, more importantly, a man her father admired and supported.

Lisa had been a little in awe of Roskins since her senior year in high school when the governor had invited her father and her to dine with him at the governor's mansion in Des Moines. Called Terrace Hill, the governor's mansion was everything the title implied. Sitting atop a hill in a beautiful neighborhood near downtown Des Moines, the 18,000 square foot mansion was built in the style of Second Empire architecture and featured a ninety-foot high tower with a commanding view of the city. Built in the late 1860s by Iowa's first millionaire, Benjamin Franklin Allen, the home featured meeting rooms and space for events on the first floor and the governor's residence on the second floor.

During Lisa's visit there, she had been enchanted by the governor's stories of travels around the world, of hosting foreign dignitaries, and of political maneuverings in the Iowa Statehouse. And she had to admit, she was captivated by his physical presence. The governor was the definition of distinguished. He looked at least a decade younger than his actual age. He worked hard to preserve the body that had captured several track and field titles, in addition to All-American honors in wrestling while an undergraduate at the University of Michigan.

Because of that one evening with Governor Roskins, Lisa never wondered how he had won and kept the support of Iowans for three terms. Tony teased her, when he was willing to risk her ill will, about her attraction to Roskins. He said her politics were dictated by her heart and not her head. She simply shot back that Tony was jealous that he didn't look as good at thirty as Roskins did at sixty-five. It was a tired joke by the second time they exchanged it and a source of tension by the third. They let it drop, knowing the truths that lay behind it and trying to respect each other's varying views of the state's chief executive. In short, Lisa saw Roskins as a skilled and dedicated public servant, occasionally showing his force of will but always in the interests of serving Iowa. Tony saw him as an old-school political boss who maintained his position by maintaining a powerful grip on people in his party at every level and in every corner of the state. Lisa knew Roskins was simply a good politician. He kept supporters in key roles and paid attention to details. He proved how good he was by increasing his margins of victory in each election. Tony always twisted those things into something less than honorable, *or worse,* Lisa thought bleakly. He painted the governor as a man obsessed with his seat and with his popularity in the state.

Lisa was pleased she and Tony were smart enough to avoid the subject, but she wondered how long the truce would last.

"Hey, Lisa, save a little air for breathing." It was Molly Parks, the staffer in the office who coordinated Lisa's weekly assignments.

"I'm sorry, what was that?"

"The sigh. You let out enough air to blow the windows out of the room. What's up?"

Lisa chuckled. She appreciated Molly for her personality as

much as for her help in the office. She looked around to make sure she and Molly were the only ones in the room for the moment, and then replied, "Oh, you know...men." She drew out the word m-m-e-n-n and shook her head, which made Molly laugh in turn.

"I hear you, girl. You and Tony having problems?"

"Actually, no. He's terrific. He's a little distracted and working too hard, but he's made a real effort to make time for me, so I can't complain."

Lisa paused, expecting another question, but it didn't come. Appreciating Molly even more, Lisa continued, "I guess I was thinking about his politics. I'm not sure I can let myself fall for a guy who leans toward the other wing, if you know what I mean. Don't you find it awkward that I'm here, knowing that he's not exactly one of the governor's admirers?"

"I have to admit, I've wondered about it," Molly answered. "I even heard McCabe talking about Tony the other day. But I figure if you two are good together, you'll work it out."

Lisa looked up from the PC. "What was that? McCabe was talking about Tony?"

Molly realized she had inadvertently changed the subject. "Well, yes. Lyle was on one of his marathon telephone calls a couple of days ago. I was in and out of his office several times and overheard Tony's name. You know, probably something like, 'That dumb-ass Harrington.'" Molly laughed. To McCabe, everyone who wasn't a Roskins supporter was a 'dumb-ass.' But Lisa wasn't laughing.

"Who was McCabe talking to? You said one of his marathon calls. You don't mean a call to Des Moines, do you? Why would Des Moines care about Tony? When was this?"

"Whoa, girl. Before you get your pantyhose in a bundle, try to remember this is politics. I hear McCabe talking about 'dumb-ass' media people almost every day. I certainly wasn't surprised to hear

Tony's name. I'm sure it was nothing. But for the record, I don't know who The Smile was talking to, and I don't know what he said. As for the when, let me see. I guess it must have been Tuesday morning."

"But Tony doesn't typically write political stuff. He's written very little about the governor's campaign." The level of Lisa's anxiety surprised even her, but the thought of McCabe talking to anyone about Tony was distasteful; and the thought that it might have been someone important, perhaps even someone close to the governor...She didn't   understand why, but the thought of it caused a tightness in her stomach like a hard, cold fist.

She wasn't sure how, but she had to find out who McCabe had been talking to. For the moment, however, she realized she had to let it drop or risk raising a red flag with Molly. The last thing Lisa wanted was for Molly to say something to McCabe. That would only bring up Tony's name again in a negative light, and this time with her name attached.

Lisa pretended to listen to Molly's sound advice, and then quickly changed the subject to the task at hand. "Are there other flash drives in the trash bin?" she asked, using their favorite term for the basket in which work for the volunteers was thrown. She forced a smile as Molly dug through it and produced two thumb-sized storage devices bearing the "Re-Elect Roskins" campaign logo.

Much of Lisa's volunteer time was spent reconciling mailing lists. Each week, the governor's office sent the local county office one or more flash drives with names and addresses of supporters and potential supporters in the county, including those who had contributed directly to the governor's re-election headquarters in Des Moines. Lisa's job was to match those names with the local county office's mailing lists, adding the names of new supporters, making sure that the addresses of known supporters were up to date, and eliminating any duplicate entries. The database program she was using made the job simple and easy, but very boring.

Early in her volunteer work, Lisa had asked why the party didn't just use one statewide database. Going online to a master database would simplify the whole process and free up a lot of volunteers who were undoubtedly doing identical work in the other 98 counties of Iowa. The answer was not what she expected: "Security," McCabe had said. "If we did all of this online, the risk would be too great that some hacker could tap into our records. We keep this all segmented so we don't have to worry about outside intrusions." It had seemed at the time like the party was going to a lot of extra work over a concern that was pretty farfetched, but considering the labor was free, Lisa had decided it made sense enough. Later, when she had remembered that most campaign records were public under Iowa's campaign disclosure laws, she had reconsidered. She had decided the re-election staff was filled with a lot of McCabe types. That was a scary thought. *Does the governor know what a bunch of paranoid schmucks he has working for him?* she had mused, thinking she would mention it to her father sometime. But the thought had left as quickly as it had come, and she had never bothered to raise it with anyone.

Around 8:45 p.m., Molly announced she was heading home by way of the Dairy Queen. "Want to join me for a double chocolate mint sundae?" she asked as she pushed shut the file drawer in her desk and slipped her heels back on.

"No thanks, Molly," Lisa smiled. "I've got a Diet Coke in the refrigerator and Hershey's Kisses in the desk. What else could I need? Besides, when you only work two nights a week, you have to keep at it."

"Suit yourself, girl. And don't think your efforts go unnoticed. We all appreciate everything you do for us."

"You're welcome. Now leave me alone to fight my battle to the death with List 1-B113, A through J. And by the way, leave your PC on, will you? If mine freezes up again, I'm just going to move to your desk."

"No problem. See you Thursday."

Both women were smiling warmly as Molly went out the door and locked it behind her. As soon as she was gone, Lisa's smile faded and she sat back in her chair. Did she really have the courage to do what she was contemplating?

What the heck, she told herself. *I'm a volunteer. What are they going to do, fire me?*

She stood up, stretched, and walked over to the water cooler. From there, she could look out the front windows of the building. Daylight was fading, but she could see that the street was quiet. No one was approaching the building from either direction. It was simply too hot for people to be out for casual strolls. That suited Lisa just fine. She quickly strode to McCabe's office, a glass enclosure at the opposite side of the room. She did not turn on the lights. She didn't want to be seen and the windows provided adequate light from the ceiling fixtures in the outer office. Without hesitation, she walked through the door and around his desk and began looking for his telephone log. She expected to find it lying on top of the desk but did not. The office was a mess of filing cabinets, bookshelves, and cubbyholes. Lisa knew if McCabe kept the book anywhere but in one of the most obvious places, she wouldn't have the courage to stay long enough to find it.

She sat in his chair and pulled open the middle drawer of the old wooden desk. Pens, campaign buttons, Post-It Notes, the usual junk, but no telephone log. She pushed it shut and turned to the first drawer on the right. *Jackpot.* On top of the miscellaneous papers stuffed into the drawer lay the black leather book that McCabe kept beside the telephone whenever he was in the office. Lisa had seen him use it many times and knew he was meticulous about keeping track of every call made or received.

The book fell open in her hand to today's date. She had to remove a large paper clip to go back one week to the previous Tuesday. She scanned down the page. *No wonder he thinks he's a hot dog,* she thought as she read the list of VIPs in the log. One in particular caught her eye. It said simply: "HR." That could mean "Human Resources" at the statehouse or it could mean "hour" or it could mean "home run," but Lisa knew what it did mean: Harry Roskins. McCabe had talked for forty minutes with the governor on Tuesday morning. Lisa was beyond impressed. She was astonished, and more than a little agitated. Could that have been *the* call? Lisa felt the cold fist returning to her belly. What could McCabe have told the governor about Tony? This made no sense, and the thought of the governor hearing anything negative about Tony from a slimeball like McCabe infuriated her.

Lisa's hands were sweaty and shaking as she closed the book to replace it in the drawer. In her haste, she dropped it. She pushed the chair back and bent over to retrieve it, noticing that it had fallen open to a new page, near the back. There, taped to the page and glittering in the dim light, was a key. Lisa raised the book slowly and stared at the key. Every ounce of her being was telling her to put the book back in its place and leave now, but she couldn't.

Her dislike for McCabe, her fears about the telephone call, and the unlikely hiding place for the key combined to overwhelm her inhibitions and her good sense. She was compelled to pursue the mystery one more step. Lisa peeled the key from the page and peeled the transparent tape from the key. She carefully wadded the tape into a ball and slid it into the pocket of her slacks. She turned the key over in her hands. The word "Steelcase" was imprinted on it. Lisa knew from experience that this was a key to a filing cabinet or desk. So she knew what she was looking for, and the brand. With a little luck, she would get a look at McCabe's secrets. She made one turn around his office, stopping to face the north wall. Along it, covered with books, boxes and dust, was a row of six typical office file cabinets, each with four drawers designed to hold hanging files. Only one cabinet was locked. She smiled, thinking, *I hope McCabe is dumb enough to make it this easy.*

Three steps across the office and one turn of the key confirmed her suspicions. Her excitement and self-satisfaction faded quickly, however, as she opened the top drawer. It was filled with files of financial records for the party's operations in Quincy County. If McCabe's secrets were financial, it would take her and a dozen accountants a month to find them. She closed the drawer and opened the second. More of the same. She glanced over the labels, but nothing caught her eye, and she pushed the drawer shut.

The third drawer contained personnel records – a slim file on each of the volunteers in the office. She wanted very badly to pull her own file and read it. She wondered if McCabe had anything meaningful to say about her or any of the women. She wouldn't be surprised if he used the files only to rate them sexually: legs - nine; breasts - six. Lisa realized it was a sick thought and she pushed the drawer shut. She refused to consider that she had taken the key and was ransacking another person's private files just so she could see her own records. This had to be more important than that. *Three down and one to go,* she thought as she slid it closed and knelt to open the bottom drawer. As she pulled it open, her heart leaped once again. Filling the bottom drawer was a leather zipper bag. It looked new, and Lisa knew she had found the reason for the locked cabinet.

She pulled back the zipper and audibly squealed. The bag was filled with money. Bundles of one hundred dollar bills. She was breathless, but still her mind raced. Ten thousand, fifty, one hundred. *My God,* she wanted to scream. *There must be $150,000 in here.* She had seen enough. She had to get out of there. She tried to pull the zipper closed, but the bag had opened too widely and the zipper was stuck at the far end. Lisa grabbed the side of the bag opposite her and pulled it toward the center, to ease the zipper's path. As she did, she could feel something hard under the leather. "Oh please, nothing more," she whispered, but she couldn't resist reaching under and pulling out the black, portable computer hard drive. She stared at it a long time. If she took it out to her computer, she really increased the odds of being caught. She considered the risk. This much cash, stored in a place like this... She knew it had to be something illegal. Campaign payoffs? Dirty tricks? Those kinds of things didn't happen in Iowa unless...unless you had a sleaze like McCabe working for you.

Lisa was appalled and quickly made up her mind. She had to know more so she could tell her father. He could get word to Governor Roskins before McCabe did something stupid and ruined everything. Lisa jumped to her feet and practically ran to the nearest computer – Molly's. It was now dark outside, so anyone passing by would be able to see her through the storefront windows. She turned the PC screen away from the front of the building and pushed the drive into the USB port. The disk appeared to contain one word processing file and one spreadsheet file. She decided to look at the word processing document first, assuming it would be more understandable than a bunch of numbers, at least to begin with.

As the words came up on the screen, Lisa read: "CONFIDENTIAL TO: L.M. FROM: T. RE: OPERATION DUPE." As she continued reading, Lisa began to shake her head. This had to be a joke. This couldn't be. Her eyes widened and she began to mutter: "Oh no, no, no..." She practically chanted as she absorbed the contents of the document. Her face reddened and her temples thumped harder and faster. Then she pounded the keyboard tray: "No, goddammit no!" She realized she was crying and struggled to calm herself. This was no longer a game and was no longer a dirty little secret of Lyle McCabe's. Suddenly she was terrified. Trying to keep her hands under control, Lisa copied the document onto the hard drive. *What to call it?* Lisa strained for a moment and fear welled up again. *Come on, come on!* Then she typed: MOL-XMAS.LST, hoping that if anyone else ever spotted the file, he or she would think it was Molly's personal Christmas list. She saved it in the generic documents folder, closed the file, unplugged the drive from the PC, and raced back to McCabe's office. She tucked the disk back into the side of the bag where she had found it, and tugged at the zipper. She was crying again as it finally moved and slid shut. She pushed the file drawer closed, pulled the key from the lock, and pushed the lock into place. She turned and faced the desk and thought: "Tape." She needed a piece of transparent tape. Rather than search for it, she ran out into the office, grabbed a strip from the dispenser on Molly's desk, and ran back to McCabe's office. As she sat down to affix the key to the logbook, she realized she hadn't paid enough attention to exactly how it was positioned on the page. At this point, she didn't care. She was scared, shaking, and fighting back more tears. She just wanted to get out of there.

She stuck the key to the page, dropped the book in the desk drawer, slid it shut and stood up, just in time to see Lyle McCabe walk through the back door into the outer office. Her first instinct was to hide, but she immediately ruled it out. Even if a hiding place could be found, she couldn't bear to stay another minute. She leaned down and quickly brushed the floor dust from her navy slacks, and then simply walked out of his office to face him.

"Excuse me, Lisa, but what were you doing in there?" McCabe

asked pointedly, still smiling.

"I'm sorry, Mr. McCabe. I'm a mess. I... I just had some bad news from home, and I was looking for a Kleenex."

"I see," McCabe was clearly at a loss. "Why don't you wait a minute and I'll try to find you one."

"No...thanks, really," Lisa stammered. "I'll be okay. I'll just go home for tonight. I know you won't mind if I finish my work later."

"Of course," McCabe said, staring at her for a long moment, unblinking. This time he was looking her right in the eye. Then he turned and walked slowly to his office.

Lisa couldn't frame into words what had just passed between them as their eyes met, but she knew that McCabe knew. Soon he would see that his book and the bag had been disturbed, removing any doubts about what she had seen. She fought the urge to run out the door, walked deliberately to her PC, and shut it off. She desperately wanted to transfer the file to another diskette, but knew she had to steer clear of Molly's machine. She slipped on her shoes, grabbed her purse, called, "Good-night," over her shoulder, and walked out the door. As the door closed behind her, she stole a glance back through the plate glass window. What she saw sent a wave of fear through her, like a physical pain that rolled from the soles of her feet to the top of her skull. Lyle McCabe was seated at his desk, dialing the telephone, but was staring at her through the windows. It was a focused, icy stare. He wasn't smiling.

***

"City desk." Tony jammed the receiver between his ear and his shoulder and returned to typing the short accident story he had received from the Quincy County Sheriff's Office. Two serious injuries was a page three story here, or page one if Jeff got good art to go with it. He still marveled on occasion at what was considered news to the *Crier* compared to the *Chicago Tribune* where he had interned prior to returning to Iowa.

He was expecting to hear the voice of the nursing supervisor at St. Vincent's, the local hospital where the two accident victims had been taken. He had paged her ten minutes earlier to get condition reports on the two victims. Instead, he heard Lisa's voice, "Oh Tony... you were right."

"Well, it's about time," he quipped, not noticing the tone of her voice.

"Uh, I...Tony, I have to see you."

Tony stopped typing and straightened in his chair. Lisa was crying. "Honey, what's wrong?"

"I have to see you. *Now.*"

Tony glanced at the newsroom clock. It was just shy of 9:50 p.m. and he was scheduled to work until 11 p.m., when tomorrow's paper would be put to bed, meaning the newsroom would hand the final pages over to the production crew.

"I can't get away quite yet. Why don't you come here?" he offered.

"No," Lisa said quickly, then sniffling. "I...we...we have to *talk.*" She obviously meant they had to talk about something private. Tony found himself wondering if she was pregnant. He pushed the thought from his mind.

"Well, Lisa, I don't know what to say. I can't just walk out on Ben." Only one reporter worked the late shift at the *Crier,* and tonight Tony was it. Because of the paper's small staff, Ben often said there were only three valid excuses for not accepting your scheduled evening: if you were getting married, if you were in jail, or if you were dead, and only then if you had a note from the coroner.

"Tony, you don't understand," Lisa was sobbing again. "I have to see you."

"Where are you?"

"I'm at home, but I can't stay here."

"Why not?"

"Because I'm scared!" Lisa practically yelled into the phone.

"Hey, Lisa, take it easy," Tony said softly, looking at the stack of notes on his desk, and glancing over at Dave, who also had a telephone receiver propped so he could type the caller's information. "I'll tell you what. I'll churn this stuff out in record time, and I'm sure Dave will let me out of here by 10:30 or so. Can you get by until then?"

"I don't know. I suppose so. But I'm not staying here. Can I stay with you tonight?"

"Of course," Tony responded without hesitation, and was immediately ashamed of the thoughts that came to mind. "You can let yourself in and I'll get there as quick as I can."

"No, I can't. I can't go to your place until you're with me," she said. "I know I sound...I know I...Oh Tony, it's terrible."

"Hang in there, sweetheart. Is there somewhere you can go? Somewhere you can wait a few minutes until I can meet you?"

Lisa was quiet for moment. "Yes," she brightened. "Meet me where we started, at the crib."

"The crib?" Tony had to think. He knew he should know what she meant. The crib? "Oh, you mean *the* cr..." Tony started to smile.

"Don't say it," she said. "You know where I mean. Come as quickly as you can."

The phone went dead, and Tony slowly replaced the receiver. He was completely baffled by the call. What could be so terrible, and why didn't she want him to confirm what she meant by her reference to Uncle Harvey's corncrib? Tony knew it wasn't modesty, although it might have been with some women. Then his mind quickly shifted to admiration.

Clever girl, Tony thought. But he still couldn't understand the secrecy, the urgency, or the fear that Lisa conveyed in her call. Tony was finishing the accident story as he thought about all of these things. He was just about to get up to talk to Dave when the radio scanner crackled to life: "Car three." A fainter voice: "Three." Then: "Car three, we have a reported ten-fifty P.I. at the intersection of Highway 26 and Hoover Street." The response: "Ten-four, I'm on my way." That would be Harriet at Central Dispatch, what the public called 9-1-1. She was talking to Tom Sullivan, one of the new young officers in the Orney Police Department.

Tony took a deep breath. Lisa wouldn't be happy, but he had to follow up. A ten-fifty P.I. was a personal injury accident. Tony knew from experience that the call could mean anything from a bloody nose to multiple fatalities. He also knew from experience that because the location was the intersection of one of Orney's busiest streets and the highway, there was a good chance it was serious. More importantly, he knew there was no way Ben would let him go now that they had heard the call. It was a breaking news story and he was the only reporter on duty. Tony's only comfort was knowing that Lisa was safe while she waited.

***

Lisa found the heavy, stale aroma of the old corn bin comforting. It brought back memories of playing on Uncle Harvey's farm when she was a child. She remembered sunny days when the neighbors and farm hands were shelling corn while the wives and daughters fixed a spread on folding tables under the shade trees. It was a meal that would put a cruise ship buffet to shame. The women were proud of their work, as the men were of theirs. Old fashioned, yes, but she ached for those days. Uncle Harvey's rough hands lifting her up onto the John Deere, Aunt Doris' pumpkin pie, showing off the baby kittens to anyone who would look. Lisa was crying again.

The surroundings also reminded her vividly of her first night with Tony. God, how she wished he would hurry. She was parked inside the bin with her engine and lights off, the windows up, and the doors locked. The heat was stifling, but she was too frightened to leave herself vulnerable to the outside. She had backed into the bin leaving the big sliding barn door behind her closed, but the one in front of the car open. This gave her a view of the lane leading out to the gravel road in front of the acreage. Although the view was narrowed by the tunnel effect of the bin, she would have adequate warning if anyone but Tony approached. The keys were in the ignition and she knew she could start the car and race out of harm's way before anyone could reach her.

Headlights popped into view on the road. "Oh please, Tony, let it be you," she pleaded. Her heart sank as she realized the lights were too low and too far apart to be Tony's Explorer. The lights turned into the lane and her heart began to race. The lights flashed in her eyes and she reached for the keys. Just as quickly, the car made a full 180-degree turn in the farmyard and stopped. As Lisa's eyes readjusted to the dark, she recognized the car. It was a big, late model, four-door sedan with a star on the door and a light bar on top. It was a deputy sheriff's cruiser. Knowing Deputy Peters worked the day shift, Lisa relaxed a little. Explaining her presence in the corncrib to a young deputy on patrol would be awkward, but it wouldn't be all bad to have a deputy's company until Tony arrived. She reached over and unlocked the door as the silhouette climbed out of the police cruiser and walked toward her.

***

Tony glanced at the clock in the dashboard stereo. It glowed a green 11:40. "Jeez," he said aloud. He pushed the accelerator even further, knowing as he watched the speedometer slide past 60 mph that he was past the safety margin on a gravel road at night. A ridge of loose gravel, an excited deer, or any number of other obstacles could put an end to his speeding, permanently. On the other hand, a beautiful blonde was waiting for him. *A beautiful frightened blonde,* he reminded himself.

He had tried to call Lisa on her cell twice. First, as he had headed to the accident scene, he had called to let her know he would be late. He wasn't surprised she didn't answer. Lisa always left her cell zipped in her purse when she drove, and she had probably been headed out to Harvey's. Tony had called again a few minutes ago to let her know he was on his way. She still hadn't answered, which had caused his anxiety to rise significantly.

Now he gripped the wheel tightly with both hands and pushed the Explorer even faster. He knew he didn't have to worry about a ticket. The state troopers never patrolled the gravel roads, and he had passed a deputy sheriff going the other direction. Tony thought about how lucky he was to have passed the deputy before he had brought the Explorer up to full speed. Every patrol officer Tony had ever known considered nailing a news reporter a special bonus. And if it happened to be Deputy Peters...well, Tony didn't want to know how that would have gone.

Those thoughts quickly dissipated as the Explorer cleared the next small hill and Tony saw the blackness of Uncle Harvey's grove rise against the purple sky. He eased off the accelerator and braked into a skid as the lane approached. He hoped Lisa would see how fast he was driving, so she would know he had hurried. In his heart,

Tony knew a display of macho driving would not ease her disappointment at him for being over an hour late.

As he drove up the lane, he could see the door of the corncrib
was closed. His anxiety increased again. Either Lisa had left already,
or she was so frightened she had shut herself inside the bin. He didn't
like to contemplate either scenario.

The Explorer slid to a stop a few feet short of the bin. Tony
switched off the ignition and hopped out in one motion. He jogged
to the door and was about to call out her name when he realized he
could hear her car running. *What the...?* "Lisa!" he yelled, grabbing
the door and pulling hard. The door was heavy and rusty, but it
moved. A cloud of exhaust billowed out of the opening. Tony stepped
back coughing. "Lisa!" He turned his head, took a deep breath, and
ran into the fog inside the bin. Even in the pitch-blackness, he had
no trouble finding the driver's door. He pulled hard but the door
didn't move and the handle snapped back into place. Locked. He
quickly felt his way around the car to the passenger side. Also locked.
His eyes began to sting and against his will, his lungs sucked a gulp
of exhaust. He started to cough and ran back out. Two deep breaths
of fresh air, and he started back in. Somewhere deep in his left brain,
reason stopped him. He turned to the door and pushed it the rest of
the way open. Immediately, more of the cloud rolled out, which
meant more fresh air was rolling in. Tony ran to his Explorer,
punched on his headlights, and leaned around the bucket seat to grab
the tire iron out of the back. For once, he was glad he hated storing
it and the jack in the spare tire compartment.

He ran back into the crib to the passenger side of the car, and
smashed out the window with one blow. He didn't even notice the
pain as he reached through and pulled the inside door handle. He
reached across the passenger seat and felt Lisa's hair in his fingers.
She was seated in the driver's seat, but was folded over with her head

and shoulders lying across the center console. She was motionless. "Oh God, no." Tony frantically reached in further, grabbing under her arms and dragging her out of the car. He didn't stop until he was beside the Explorer. He then eased her to the ground and turned her over on her back.

"Lisa! Please Lisa! Wake up!" Tony was shouting and crying as he fell to his knees and put his ear to her chest. Nothing. "Please, Lisa, please..." He pulled her head back, pinched her nose and put his mouth to hers, blowing hard. One, two, three. He knelt beside her and pushed on her chest. "Oh God." He couldn't remember exactly how to give chest compressions. "Lisa, God please..." More mouth to mouth, more compressions against her chest. Nothing. More mouth to mouth, more compressions.

Tony knew she was dead. He also knew his efforts were wasted long before exhaustion overtook him, and he collapsed sobbing on the ground beside her.

Chapter 19

Doug didn't wait for Tony to answer the door. He rapped twice on the glass and walked briskly through the door from the front porch to the living room of Tony's modest two-bedroom bungalow.

"Tone?" he called.

"Huh," Tony's soft voice came from the overstuffed chair facing a blank television screen.

Doug dropped into the couch on Tony's right and placed a brown paper sack on the coffee table. "I thought you could use a cold beer." He didn't wait for an answer, popping the top and holding it out for Tony's grasp.

As he waited he examined his friend closely. Tony was curled up in the chair, arms pressed together at the wrists and tucked between his knees. He was in jogging shorts and an old Nitty Gritty Dirt Band T-shirt. His hair was greasy and his face was red. The sockets around his eyes were almost black. Doug stared at the stark contrast between the rings and the whites of Tony's eyes; not the bright, sparkling white he was used to seeing, but a cold, empty white that sent a chill through him.

Tony lifted his chin and pulled one hand free to take the beer. He didn't seem to notice that some of it ran out on the arm of the chair as he tried to sip it from his awkward position.

"Hey, pal, I gotta be honest. You look like shit."

"Yeah, well, I feel like shit, so I guess it's okay."

Tony pushed his head back and legs out to assume a more natural sitting position. Doug was encouraged by his response, so he plunged forward.

"I guess you know how sorry I am about Lisa."

"Don't start, Doug. I've done all the crying in the past 24 hours that I can stand for a while."

Doug didn't know what to say, so he sat quietly sipping his beer, watching the profile of Tony staring into the wall above the TV. After a long time, Tony started talking. Doug was surprised at how familiar all the emotions sounded. He hadn't suffered much tragedy in his life, but he recognized everything Tony said as if he had heard it all in a bad movie – the disbelief, the longing, the self-doubt, the anger.

"I should have been there!" Tony practically shouted, and then retracted into his chair stuttering through his sobs. "I should have been there on time."

"Hey, hey." Doug leaned in close to his friend, laid his hand on his shoulder, and spoke softly. "Don't you start down that road. This was not your fault. Lisa screwed up and now she's dead. It's as simple as that. It doesn't make it easy, or right, or even understandable. But it is simple and it's not your fault. You have to remember that."

Tony wiped his face on his T-shirt and turned slowly toward Doug. "Nice words," he said in an almost icy tone. "But whether you like it or not, the fact is that I was late and that may have made the difference."

Again Doug was without words, and the silence hung between them like a dark curtain. By the time Tony spoke again, Doug had to retrace the conversation in his mind to remember the context of his question.

"You don't really believe that, do you?" Tony asked.

"Believe what?" Doug was struggling to remember.

"That this was simple," Tony said pointedly. He stared into Doug's eyes as he continued. "You really believe that a girl as bright as Lisa just pulled her car into a corncrib, closed all the doors, and left the motor running. Then as the car filled with fumes she just allowed herself to pass out and die."

"Tony, it happens," Doug said a little too strenuously, worried about where his friend was headed with this. Maybe she thought since the bin was empty, enough air would flow through it to carry away the fumes.

"Well, just so you know, Sherlock, I don't see it that way and neither do the DCI boys."

Doug was taken aback. "The DCI? Really? You've talked to Rich or someone?"

"Talked to them?" A smile actually crossed Tony's face briefly. "You obviously haven't had a girlfriend die recently. Those guys put a rod up my ass and roasted me over the fire for about three hours this morning."

"You gotta be shittin' me," Doug responded. "They can't think you had something to do with this."

Tony was back to a blank stare. "Oh they can, they can. Don't you know, my friend, when a young woman buys it, the boyfriend is always the first suspect. Of course it didn't help that I was the one who found her and called it in."

"But these guys know you. Hell, they *owe* you."

"Yeah, that may save my ass, but they still have to go through the motions."

"So they've got nothing, right?"

"You asking as a friend or a competitor?"

Doug was hurt by the question, but as he glanced at Tony, he saw the glimmer of a smile. Tony went on, confirming that it was a feeble attempt at humor.

"Apparently Lisa had a nasty bruise on the side of her head. She could have gotten it when she passed out and fell forward onto the shift lever, but it also could indicate something more."

Once again, Doug didn't know what to say, and once again Tony rescued him by going on. "That's probably my best indication that they don't really think me a suspect. As close as Davis and I are, he would never have told me about the bruise if he was planning to charge me with something. I think he could tell how I felt about her."

Another pause and the sobs welled up again as Tony cried, "What a fucking stupid thing to say."

Tony almost never used the 'F' word. It surprised Doug but he kept his silence.

"How could my friends in the DCI discern, through all of this crap even I don't understand, how I felt about Lisa?" Tony was on his feet now, bumping the coffee table as he walked around to the back of the chair. He started to wipe his face again with his t-shirt and then came completely unglued. As Tony sunk to his knees, pressed against the back of the chair and bawling like a baby, Doug could just make out his words.

"Even Lisa didn't know how I felt about Lisa. She didn't understand what she meant to me. I never told her I...how I felt. And now it's too late."

Doug set his beer on the arm of the couch and lowered himself to the floor. He put his arms around his friend and held him for a very long time.

***

Much later, as the two men sat, somewhat embarrassed, back on their respective pieces of furniture, Doug was startled when Tony suddenly said in a clear voice, "There's more."

"What do you mean, more?"

"There's more to the story. Haven't you wondered why Lisa was out there, out at Harvey's place?"

"Sure, but I figured you'd tell me when you were ready. And besides, I just figured it was somewhere the two of you went to meet. I don't want to offend you or your memory of Lisa, but my take was that she was the adventurous type. I wouldn't put it past her to meet you in a corncrib for a little...shall we say, dance? Just for the fun of it."

"You surprise me, Sherlock. That's quite perceptive about Lisa. As a matter of fact, we *had* been there before. But before you go apply for one of those DCI jobs, I might as well tell you, you're dead wrong about last night."

Tony then told Doug all about Lisa's telephone call and her extreme agitation. The fact was, she was scared shitless, and he had let her down. Tony was crying again, but this time Doug better understood the overwhelming sense of guilt his friend was feeling.

"So what did the DCI have to say about all of this?" Doug asked.

"I didn't tell them," Tony replied, almost off-handedly.

"You what! Are you nuts?"

Tony spoke very deliberately, again looking right into Doug's eyes. "Think about it, Doug. In a situation like this, if I tell the DCI about the frantic phone call and Lisa's plea for help, what does it sound like?"

Doug had to admit it. "It sounds like you're one of those idiots who does something stupid like loses his head, kills his girlfriend, and then makes up a story to cover his ass."

"Exactly. And I'm not planning to tell the DCI something that makes me look guilty, even if it is the truth. At least I'm not telling while they're still investigating. If they try to close the case, I might come forward to spark a little interest. Not too many murderers go out of their way to keep a case open. And another thing, how the hell do you think it would make Lisa's dad feel if everyone knew she was frightened but didn't go to *him*?" What went unspoken was the obvious: how *Tony* would feel if everyone knew Lisa had called for help and he hadn't responded right away.

Doug could see the logic in Tony's approach, but it still made him uneasy to hold back information from the DCI.

"One other thing I didn't tell them," Tony abruptly added.

"Oh?"

"The time Lisa and I went to Harvey's to park?"

"Yes?"

"Lisa wouldn't let me shut the doors to the corncrib while I had the engine running. She said it was too dangerous."

***

Hours later, as Tony was rinsing out their eight or ten empty beer cans, he thought about what a good friend he had. He would have refused to talk to anyone this afternoon if Doug hadn't forced his way in. And Doug had just the right...how could he phrase it? The word *karma* came to mind, but Tony dismissed it as too ridiculous. He didn't know what it was, but he was glad his friend had it.

Tony was still numb with grief, but thanks to Doug, he had learned quickly that life wasn't just going to end for everyone else the way it had for Lisa. He still had to interact with the world.

As he climbed into bed, Tony was almost ashamed that his thoughts were of the incident itself. He realized he was analyzing it as he would any crime he was assigned to cover. Of course, he wouldn't be assigned to cover it. Even at a paper as small as the *Crier,* they didn't assign a reporter to a story in which the reporter's name was all over the police reports. He would be interested to see how Ben handled it in the morning edition. *That's sick,* he thought, *to even be thinking about this as a news story.*

He began to cry softly into his pillow, thinking about their laughs together, their spats, their lovemaking. He could hear her soft voice in his ear, talking silly, talking sexy, and even giving him advice. He tried to fight it, but he couldn't help thinking about the night they had talked about the Wells case, and the advice she had given. What motive could someone possibly have? Who could benefit from the death of such a lovely, warm, engaging...

Goddammit. He was sobbing again. He thought about her father and then remembered a piece of his conversation with Doug earlier. Why *hadn't* Lisa called her father? She practically worshipped him and he would have mobilized the National Guard to protect her. And considering the number of friends he had in the county, he could have done it too.

Sleep overcame him before he could attempt to answer any of the questions.

***

The funeral was mostly a nuisance in Tony's mind. Doug was kind enough to take another day off work to accompany him, but it wasn't necessary. It was another hot day, and the Lutheran pastor was too stingy to adequately cool the church, even for the standing room only crowd. Tony went through the motions with limited actual involvement. It was almost as if he was an android, programmed to play the role but not really be there.

Tony had always believed in God. *But now...now if there is a God*, Tony feared he had harmed Lisa somehow in His eyes by having sex with her outside of marriage. Surely, a just God would reward her for her kindness and love and not punish her for the things she had done for him.

He had no idea how Lisa's dad would treat him at the funeral. Even after all these months, Tony had not made any real attempt to be close to him. Despite Lisa's assurances that her dad liked him, it had always felt awkward. Tony had been welcome in their home, but seldom had taken advantage of their invitations. In light of Tony's role in her death or because Tony had failed her, he was prepared to accept that her father would resent him, even hate him.

In the church, Tony selected the fourth pew, close enough to demonstrate he was more than an idle spectator, but respectful of her actual family's place at the front.

However, Mr. Freed surprised him. When he saw Tony in the fourth pew, he came out of his own front row seat, and with a simple gesture insisted that Tony join the family. It was the kindest thing anyone had ever done for him, Tony realized, crying as he took his new seat.

Not a word passed between them until later, after the graveside service was finished. As he walked to his car, he heard Freed's voice at his right, soft and very close. He looked over and saw that Lisa's father was looking straight ahead, so Tony did likewise.

"Two things, Tony."

"Yes sir?"

"Well, make it three things. First of all, don't call me sir. My name is Nathan and my friends call me Nate. For you it always will be Nate. Secondly, the DCI came to see me today."

Tony immediately tensed and hoped Lisa's dad wouldn't sense it to no avail.

"Relax, son. I told them the same thing I'm going to tell you. I know you would not and did not hurt Lisa, and I in no way hold you responsible."

Tony was genuinely moved. He said, "That means a great deal to me, sir...uh, Nate. But just so you know, I don't just feel responsible, I am responsible. I should have been there sooner. I let her down and I never will forgive myself for that."

Freed waived a hand, attempting to cut him off. Through clenched teeth he said, "I do not want to talk about it. Absolutely nothing good can come from you or I or anyone else second guessing what happened or wishing someone had done something differently."

"That's what everyone keeps saying but..."

"Then listen to them," he said forcefully, turning to face Tony. "Don't let a second young life be ruined over this."

He turned and resumed his walk up the grassy hill to the white crushed rock cemetery road. Tony had to scurry a couple of steps to resume his place at his side.

A few more steps and Tony asked, "You said there was a third thing, sir?"

"Well...yes. I'm not a man who likes to ask favors. I'm not ashamed to tell you I've spent most of my life doing favors for others."

"Well, it has paid off, sir. I've never met anyone who didn't like and respect you."

"You really must stop calling me sir," Freed replied, almost smiling. "The point is, I have a favor to ask of you."

"Anything."

"I want you to write about her."

"Sir?"

"You're a fine writer, Tony. I would like people to know her the way you and I knew her, bright and funny and thoughtful and full of life. I know it's a cardinal sin to try to tell a reporter what to put into his paper, but I would very much appreciate it if you would find a way to pay tribute to her there, where everyone could see it."

"Well, I, uh..."

Freed interjected, "Also, Tony, you must be aware that some are trying to call Lisa's death a suicide. You and I know that's simply not possible. I want everyone else to know that too."

Tony didn't know what to say. This was too sudden. He hadn't even been back to work yet. He hadn't even sorted out his feelings. He felt exhausted from the emotional battle that had been raging for the past three days. How could he? How could he not?

"Of course, sir. I would be honored to try. But you must understand at this point, it's just a try. I honestly don't know if I can do it."

Freed stopped and again turned to face Tony. This time he was smiling. "I know," he said simply, and walked off toward the hearse at the front of the long line of cars.

My God, Tony thought. *No wonder she was extraordinary.* As he dropped into the seat of his car, another wave of grief washed over him. Doug was already waiting in the passenger seat.

"You okay?"

"No," Tony said, burying his face and crying into his arms which were folded over the steering wheel in front of him.

Town Crier

Governor Assures Supporters of Victory

Claims "No Worries" Over Nelson's Rise in Polls

Ben Smalley, Editor

ORNEY, Iowa – Governor Harris "Harry" Roskins spoke confidently of his re-election in November as he addressed an enthusiastic crowd of supporters in the Orney town square Sunday evening. He discussed his opponent's recent rise in the polls as nothing more than the "natural bump" that occurs after Labor Day, when the political ads and activities go into "full gear."

The governor said he was certain Iowans would return him to office for a fourth term.

"We've worked hard for you," the governor told the crowd of about 2,000 people gathered for an old-fashioned potluck dinner in his honor. "We've cut taxes, increased our investments in alternative fuels production, and attracted an unprecedented number of high quality jobs to Iowa. Now is not the time to change direction."

It was the ninth night in a row of major events around the state for the governor, who insiders say loves to campaign.

Longtime aide Jimmy Freestone commented, "The man is tireless. He seems to gather energy throughout the day rather than expend it. I've never seen him work harder than he is right now."

A small crowd of protesters gathered across the street from the park as the governor spoke. Most held signs decrying his tax cuts for the rich and claiming the poor and middle class were suffering under his administration's policies.

One young woman held a sign saying "No More Dirty Harry." Asked if she was surprised the governor was campaigning in Orney, the woman said, "No. You've seen the polls. Despite his fancy words, he's afraid he's going to lose. And he needs to be afraid. He can speak in every town in Iowa and it won't get him past the facts."

Governor Roskins first was elected...

Chapter 20

Tony read through Ben's article and the rest of the *Crier* without much interest. It was late, almost midnight, and everyone from the newsroom had gone home except him. He was tipped back in his desk chair reading, primarily to avoid going home to an empty house.

It was nearly two months since Lisa's death, but it still felt like yesterday. He had been working nearly every night since returning to his job, finding it was easier to stay occupied at night and to be alone during the day. At least during the day he could take a hike through the river valley, jog, go to the library, or talk his way into the high school to borrow a piano in a practice room and spend some time at the keys. Ben and the other newsroom staff certainly didn't mind the extra help in the evenings, and Tony was still happy to take daytime assignments as needed. The little respite he ever found from his grief came when he became absorbed in a good story.

Ben had been amazingly tolerant of his moodiness and had even urged him to return to work at whatever pace he liked. Because Tony had been jogging more and eating very little, he found he was in the best physical shape he'd ever been. He found no consolation in it.

Tony's parents and sister had been to Orney to visit him almost every weekend since the funeral. He knew his parents were worried he was falling into a true clinical depression and concerned he might do something unspeakable. On their third visit, Tony spoke about it.

"Hey guys, you know I love you and I really appreciate the company, but I don't want you to worry about me. I have no interest in joining Lisa in heaven, at least not for a very long time. I'll be fine. Just give me some time."

"Well of course, of course," his parents had said, almost in unison. But Tony could see the relief in their faces.

The truth was, it did help when they were there. It helped just to know they were coming. He was especially impressed that Rita made the effort to join them on several weekends. Tony knew she had a full plate now that she had left her first job and was back in school, pursuing a PhD in music at the University of Chicago. It couldn't have been easy for her to make the trip to Orney. In any case, Tony was grateful. His family's visits gave him something to anticipate and plan for nearly every week. He tried hard to find interesting things for them to do as a family, primarily for his sister's sake.

Tony assumed Rita found most of his excursions lame. Visits to the nature center, a tour of the railroad museum, and shopping at the antique mall were not activities high on a young woman's bucket list. However, Tony had managed to wow her on the most recent visit, the week before last. Without any advance notice, Tony had driven them to the racetrack east of Orney. It was a quarter-mile dirt track used for stock car racing. The Orney Races had been a feature of Friday nights for many summers.

When they arrived, a large, heavyset man in coveralls was there waiting for them. More importantly, Number 24 was there. Sponsored in part by Ben and the *Town Crier*, Number 24 was a late-model Dodge, deconstructed and rebuilt as a bona-fide racecar. Tony knew nothing about the engine, or suspension, or fuel, or even its top speed. He only knew three things: it was loud, it was equipped with roll bars and all the latest safety gear, and it was available for his family members to drive.

The fact that the paper was a sponsor undoubtedly helped, but the man in coveralls, Del Peterson, was the key. He was the chief mechanic on the car's team. Del's day job was working to maintain heavy equipment for the county road crew, such as road graders and dump trucks. However, his passion was building and tuning this car's racing engine and every other piece of its performance equipment. He had the car positioned on the track and held a helmet in his hand when the Harringtons arrived. When Del handed the helmet to Rita and asked if she would like to drive it, she squealed with delight. For the next two hours the family had oohed and aahed and laughed and high-fived as each of them drove the car in turn. Rita was still talking about it as the three of them parted to return to their respective destinations the next day.

***

Of course the most important person in Tony's life during the difficult days was Doug. Like a loyal puppy, Doug was there, full of energy and determination, and pulling on the leash, saying "Let's go. Let's go." Several times throughout the week, Doug would show up in the newsroom at dinnertime and take him for pizza or call him at lunchtime to see if he was nearby, asking if they could meet at Willie's for lunch. Doug never lectured him, never questioned him, and never pulled him beyond where he was ready to go. Doug was just there. The perfect friend, Tony had to admit.

Tony folded the paper and dropped it in the recycle basket next to his desk. Despite his dread of the empty house, he decided to call it a night.

***

The harsh sound of his cell phone once again woke him from a deep sleep. *I absolutely have to take the time to change the ring tone*, Tony thought as he fumbled for it in the dark.

"Harrington?"

"Rich? Is that you? Again? You do realize there are *two* 3 o'clocks in a day, right?"

"Sorry pal, but trust me. You're going to want to see this. Ten minutes." The phone went dead.

Once again, Tony was ready and waiting in front of his house when Rich Davis pulled up in his state-owned sedan. Tony had gulped down a glass of milk and had a bagel in one pocket, a diet soda in the other. As he climbed in the passenger door, he didn't wait to ask, "What's up?"

Davis didn't hesitate. "Denny Peters is dead."

Tony was stunned. After a long pause, he asked, "Deputy Sheriff Denny Peters?"

"Yep. An apparent suicide."

"Suicide? Jesus Lord. Suicide. Really?"

"Well, I've been around the block a few times and that's what it looks like to me," Davis said.

"Rich, you know I appreciate the call, but I have to ask. Why would you take time out to call me and bring me in on this if you're convinced it's a suicide? Usually those things are treated very privately. In fact, why are you involved at all?"

"Well, Tony, let's just say the suicide is only part of the news. Uh-uh...hold your questions," Davis said, holding up his right hand. "Let's just say we've learned some things about Deputy Peters this morning that surprised us. It turns out we may have made a mistake, a colossal mistake, and we're going to need as fair of coverage from the press as possible. My bosses and I agreed that if we brought you in early, and gave you the breaking story exclusively, maybe it would help keep the focus on the real crime and not have this turn into a roasting of the DCI."

"What does *that* mean?" Tony asked, with a bit more exasperation in his voice than he intended.

"You're about to find out," Davis said, as he turned the sedan down the street on which Denny Peters had lived.

As they pulled up to the curb and scrambled out of the car, Tony first noticed how serene the scene was. No flashing lights, very few cars. Only a couple of uniformed officers were in the front yard of the modest ranch home which mirrored dozens of others in the neighborhood. Built in the '50s, it was the kind of place you could buy for less than $100,000 in Orney, which made it affordable for people on the public payroll. The lack of commotion typically found around a death scene was evidence of how hard they were trying to control the publicity.

Tony then saw the director of the DCI standing on the front porch. Even with Davis' comments fresh in his ears, the director's presence shocked him. Unless by some strange coincidence the director had been nearby already, it meant officers had been working this scene for at least two hours. More to the point, it meant someone early on the scene had realized immediately some magnitude of crisis and had called the DCI without waiting for approvals from up the command chain. Normally, getting the DCI on the scene took hours, and the director would be the last to be called. In fact, Tony realized he couldn't remember a case where the director had ever been called to the scene of a violent death. Suddenly Tony couldn't wait to get inside. He was very glad his Nikon was slung over his shoulder and his pad and pen were in his pocket.

As Tony and Davis approached the house, DCI Director William Vandergaard stepped down from the porch and met them in the front yard. He didn't look like the state's leading crime official. He was about Tony's height and had a head full of bushy red hair and pale skin typical of people of Dutch heritage. There were several communities in Iowa founded by Dutch immigrants and were fiercely proud of being Dutch. Many families in those communities stretched back several generations. Tony couldn't remember from which one of these towns Vandergaard hailed, but he remembered it was one of them. Vandergaard looked, Tony realized, a little like the funny uncle you looked forward to seeing entertain everyone at your birthday party. He shook Tony's hand, introducing himself and saying, "We appreciate you getting out of bed for us, Mr. Harrington."

"It's no trouble," Tony said. "Please, call me Tony, and no thank-yous are necessary. Rich knows I appreciate the opportunity to get the story early and get it right" (which they both knew meant "get it first and get it exclusively").

"So what's going on?"

"In a moment," Vandergaard said. "First, let's talk about some ground rules. Can we begin with a conversation off the record?"

Uh-oh, Tony thought, but tried to be patient and agreed to hear him out. Vandergaard must have sensed Tony's uneasiness. He said, "Let's think of this more as a negotiation."

Davis suddenly interjected, "Would you like me to step away, director?"

"No, Mr. Davis, please stay," Vandergaard said. "It's a good idea to have a witness to what Mr. Harrington, uh, Tony, and I agree."

Davis nodded and Vandergaard continued, "Tony, I'm willing to take you into the crime scene. I call it that only because, as you probably know, suicide is classified as a crime in Iowa. You'll have a chance to see everything we found, just as we found it, except the body of course. The deputy has been removed, and I have the suicide note in an evidence bag in my briefcase, but everything else is exactly how we found it. We will allow you to take pictures and afterward we will follow you down to your office and allow you to photocopy the suicide note. I want to assure you what you're about to see is going to be a very big story, and it's going to answer some questions that I'm told you've been asking."

Tony was nearly coming unglued from curiosity, but managed to say, "And for all this you want what?"

"Let me finish with what I'm offering first. Lastly, I'm willing to do everything in my power to embargo this story until noon today, giving you a chance to get it on the *Crier's* website before the other media has it."

Tony nodded, but said, "I know that's a generous offer, but the *Crier's* website is read by about a dozen people, and that includes four guys who live in their moms' basements. I really need an embargo until after the 6 p.m. news. The broadcast media will still beat us at 10, but at least the morning paper won't be eighteen hours behind the story."

Looking thoughtful, Vandergaard said, "Five p.m. is the very latest I can promise. We're trying to manage the media here and I can't have them all hating me before we even get started."

"Okay, I'll have to live with that. Now what else did you want?"

"First the obvious. You must promise not to touch anything inside. There's going to be enough criticism of this case without problems associated with contaminating the scene." Tony nodded and Vandergaard continued, "Equally important, and I want you to know I'm sincere in this, what I want most is fair treatment. The DCI was another victim here and not a perpetrator. You'll see that clearly. I just want your assurances you'll look at the facts and focus the story on what was done to us, and not what we did unwittingly." Vandergaard's voice rose almost to pleading as he said, "We were fooled by a very clever criminal. While I'll regret that for the rest of my career, I don't want anyone to blame the fine men and women of the DCI who work hard every day to see that justice is done."

"Well," Tony said, "If I can get a quote like that from you for my story, it will go a long way toward creating some sympathy for your position, whatever the he...heck that is. But to get to the point, I'm assuming I'm here because Rich has told you that you can count on me to get the facts straight and to treat you fairly without having to bargain for it. So why don't we go inside and let me get started?"

"Tony, please," Vandergaard held out his hand. "This was a negotiation and I want your answer regarding the terms."

Tony shook his hand once, uttered a terse, "Yes," and headed for the front door. He was thinking the theatrics unnecessary, but he knew enough psychology to understand why Vandergaard had put him through it. After that formal handshake, Vandergaard knew, as Tony knew, that Tony would move Heaven and Earth to make sure he got this story right.

At the front door, a uniformed Orney police officer and a plain-clothes DCI agent blocked his entry. Vandergaard came up behind him and with a simple nod, the guards stepped aside and let them enter. The front door led directly into the living room, with the dining room to the right and kitchen behind it. A hallway straight ahead led to the bedrooms at the back on the left. Tony paused to look around, but Vandergaard nudged him and pointed over his shoulder at the hallway. "In there," he said.

Tony walked through the arched doorway and turned left into

the first bedroom. It looked like a scene from a bad movie about a serial killer. There was no bed. A small table was in the center of the room with an older personal computer and not much else. On the floor beside the table was what appeared to be a photo album lying on its spine with the pages open. Dangling behind the table was the loose end of what looked like electrical cord. Tony quickly followed the cord up to the ceiling where it had been tied to a light fixture.

He pieced it together in an instant. He assumed the deputy had stepped on the table, tied the cord around his neck and jumped off, kicking the photo album to the floor as he did so. Later, someone, presumably the police or the medical examiner, had cut down the body.

Tony knew these were all assumptions he would have to ask about later, but for the moment his attention moved past all of that and focused on the walls...walls which were covered by large photographs of women.

No, wait. Tony realized every one of the photos papering the walls of this room was of the same woman. All appeared to have been taken without the woman's knowledge. Photos of her on downtown sidewalks, shopping in stores, hanging her laundry on an outdoor clothesline on what appeared to be a farm, walking her two girls across the street...her two girls.

"Holy Mother of God," Tony said aloud as the blood drained from his face. Every photograph was of Anne Ennis.

Town Crier

Deputy Sheriff Confesses to Murders in Suicide Note

Dennis Peters Found Dead in his Orney Home Friday Morning

Tony Harrington, Staff Writer

ORNEY, Iowa – In a suicide note found on a computer at the scene of his apparent suicide, Quincy County Deputy Sheriff Dennis "Denny" Peters described in detail how he stalked and murdered Anne Ennis and her husband Jerry in their rural Orney farmhouse 20 months ago. The deputy also described how he meticulously planned and carried out the crime in order to frame Ralph Adam Wells of Orney as the perpetrator.

Wells was convicted of the double murder in a District Court trial held in Orney a year ago. He is currently serving two life sentences at the State Penitentiary at Fort Madison.

In the suicide note, Peters said he loved Anne Ennis and had stalked her for months prior to killing her. "I couldn't bear the thought of her living with another man," the note states. Peters does not say how his obsession with Anne Ennis began or if he even knew her personally.

Peters' home was filled with more than 100 photographs of Anne Ennis as she went through her normal daily routines. A digital camera, with the photographs still stored in its memory, was found in a desk drawer near Peters' body.

The confession apparently was written on a personal computer on a desk in the room where Peters killed himself. While the note was printed and left on the computer printer on Peters' desk, it was also left on the computer screen.

DCI Agent Richard Davis said Peters apparently died of asphyxiation late Thursday night as the result of hanging himself in his home on Polk Avenue in Orney. However, Davis said that is a preliminary finding and the official cause of death will come later from the county medical examiner.

Peters' body was discovered by a neighbor around midnight when the man got out of bed to get a drink of water and spotted the shadow on the window shade of Peters' home. While asking not to be named, the neighbor said, "It was just obvious what I was seeing. I didn't even go over there. I just called 911 right away."

Davis led the original murder investigation for the DCI and was one of several investigators who testified against Ralph Wells in his murder trial. When asked about the contents of Peters' suicide note and home, Davis commented, "Let me say first of all, every piece of evidence and every word of testimony given at Mr. Wells' trial was factual. The DCI prides itself in bringing facts, not opinions, to the court. Likewise, make no mistake, the DCI will investigate just as thoroughly everything we have found related to Deputy Peters' apparent suicide. If the evidence and the facts bear out the claims in the suicide note and demonstrate that Mr. Wells indeed was framed by the deputy, we will not hesitate to support Mr. Wells' attorney in asking the court for relief for his client."

Defense attorney Lawrence Pike, upon learning of the contents of the suicide note, said, "As I've said publicly for more than a year, I've always believed Ralph was innocent of this terrible crime. I will be praying for the investigators to finish their work quickly so Mr. Wells can be returned to his family where he belongs."

In the suicide note, Peters apologized to Wells for framing him. He said he no longer could live with himself, thinking of a man serving life in prison for a crime he (Peters) had committed. He then apologized to his parents and siblings for any pain he caused them and for being "...too much of a coward to face the music in this life." Peters was not married and lived alone.

A clerk at the County Sheriff's Department said Sheriff George Mackey would have no comments at this time about the deputy's suicide or about any aspect of the Wells case.

Attorney General W. Rodney Nelson, the lead prosecutor of the case for the state, also declined to comment. Nelson currently is running for governor of Iowa on a platform that features a law and order theme.

The note described how Peters had gone to an Orney tavern where Wells was playing pool on the night of the murders. "His car was parked in the alley parking lot, so I knew he was in there," Peters wrote. He went on to say he entered the back door of the tavern, waited until Wells was between pool games, and then motioned for him to join him in a small party room at the back of the establishment. Peters then engaged Wells in conversation, he wrote, and slipped sleeping pills in Wells' drink. Once Wells passed out, he pushed him under a table in a row of booths in the unused room.

Peters said he then drove Wells' car to the acreage rented by the Ennis couple. After parking in a grove of trees near the home, he took the yellow jacket and .22 caliber rifle from the trunk of Wells' car. He wore the jacket and used the rifle to kill the couple.

Peters wrote that he then drove Wells' car back to the alley parking lot, entered the back door of the tavern, and pulled Wells to a sitting position near the door to the party room, assuming that when Wells awoke, he would stumble into the bar and not realize where he had been. Wells had testified at his trial he had passed out in a booth at the bar but had no explanation for why no one had seen him.

Other evidence at trial also appears to be explained by...

Chapter 21

Tony was exhausted. He had worked all day on his article and then had stayed in the newsroom until late to see the first copies come off the presses. Two full pages of the *Crier* were devoted to the article, its sidebars, the reprinting of the suicide note, and photographs from the scene. Now it was midnight, and he and Ben were staring at each other over a pair of beers at the Iron Range.

Ben had been nearly as excited as Tony and had pitched in to help with telephone calls to solicit comments and to make suggestions for what to include in the article and what to leave to the reprinted suicide note and the photographs. In true Ben fashion, regardless of all his help, he insisted Tony have the byline solely. Ben knew the *Crier* had the news first because of Tony's relationship with the DCI. He wanted credit to go where it was due.

"Savor it, Tony," Ben was saying. "News like this doesn't come to you every day no matter where you live. You did a hell of a job on this one, just a hell of a job. I couldn't be more proud."

Tony managed a smile and a thanks and lifted the beer to his lips. He was half afraid to drink it, worrying he would fall asleep right where he sat.

"Of course it won't end here," Ben added. "There will be follow up stories about the court proceedings and I hope some additional interviews. The sheriff and the prosecutor can't stay silent forever."

Ben paused and said, "By the way, does the lack of a signed note bother you at all? Any chance there's something hinky going on here?"

"Like what?" Tony replied.

"Hell, I don't know," Ben said. "Maybe some over-zealous friend of Wells set this up to shift the blame?"

Tony nodded, seeing his point. "Well, it doesn't look like it. Rich Davis told me the electronic note and unsigned printout sent up a red flag for the DCI too, but the fingerprints on the keyboard were Peters'. His preliminary read is that it's a legitimate suicide. Besides, you've seen Wells in the Iron Range a few times. You ever see him with anyone that smart or that ambitious, or that close a friend for that matter?"

Ben shook his head as he smiled.

Then Tony asked, "How long?"

"How long what?

"How long do you think it will take before Wells is released?"

"Well, that's hard to say, but it will be longer than you think. It helps that the DCI immediately rolled over on this and didn't try to cover it up. But even with all this evidence it could take weeks, even months, for the investigation to wrap up, for the courts to rule, and for things to actually get finalized."

"Months? Jeez. That poor sap," Tony said, not having to explain about whom he was talking. Then shifting gears again, he said, "And what about Nelson? He kinda hung his hat on Wells' conviction. Do you think the governor will make an issue of this in the campaign?"

"You're joking, right?" Ben laughed. "I can all but promise you the governor is going to take this false conviction and shove it right up W. Rodney's ass."

Tony grinned but found no real pleasure in it. The truth was, he didn't like either one of these guys very much. Since Lisa's death, he had decided to vote for Roskins just to honor her, but it saddened him to think Iowans' two choices for governor were equally self-centered and self-righteous asses whose only distinguishing characteristics were the breeds of animals on their lapel buttons.

When Ben got up to leave, Tony stood as well but left his coat lying in the booth. Ben raised an eyebrow and Tony nodded at the old upright piano in the corner. Ben nodded back and Tony headed for the piano stool. Other patrons in the bar noticed but said nothing when the bartender shut down the country music playing over the loudspeakers and Tony began pounding out "Mr. Bojangles" on the keys. He played a few more songs, including a couple of less popular but far better Dirt Band tunes. He played Delbert McClinton's "Why Me," but at a slower pace than the original recording. He was just too tired to work that hard. He ended with "New York State of Mind." As he took his foot from the sustain pedal on the last note, he wiped the tears from his eyes, trying to smile as the bar crowd set down their glasses and pool cues and erupted into applause. Tony didn't notice Ben applauding in the back before quietly slipping out the door.

***

When his head finally hit the pillow, it was nearly 3 a.m. on Saturday. While he should have gone right to sleep, he found himself thinking about the suicide note Peters had written, or allegedly written. The investigation was just starting. He had to guard against assuming too much.

He wasn't obsessing about the circumstances of the note. He was thinking about the contents. If this was someone who was able to plan and commit the cold-blooded double murder of two innocent people, and then frame an equally innocent young man for the crime, could that heartless bastard really write a note like Peters wrote? A note that talked about love and an overwhelming sense of guilt? Tony knew it was possible and knew it looked like it had happened just that way in this case.

However, he couldn't stop himself from thinking, *I met Denny Peters. I saw Denny Peters up close, much closer than I would have liked. It's hard to believe the man I saw wrote the note he wrote. Especially the apology.*

As soon as that word occurred to him, Tony knew that was the crux of what was bothering him. Yes, Lisa would tell him he was too quick to judge people. "I'm sorry, honey," Tony said to the empty room," but I find it hard to believe Denny Peters would apologize to anyone for anything."

And just like that, the dreaded question surfaced again. *Just what in the hell is going on here?*

Chapter 22

The resolution of Wells' situation didn't take months.

When Tony walked into the newsroom at 11 a.m. Monday morning, Ben hollered at him from his office at the back. "Harrington! Hop to it."

Ben sounded cranky, but Tony had learned this was just his voice when news was breaking and he wanted people to move quickly.

"What's up, Chief?" Tony asked as he scooted through the doorway.

"The governor's called a press conference for noon."

"And..." Tony prompted, surprised that Ben would get revved up over what was likely a political event. "Is it here in town or something? What's the angle?"

Ben was twirling an editor's pencil through his fingers. As curious as Tony was, he almost missed Ben's response as he suddenly wondered where Ben had gotten a red editor's pencil, since the newsroom had been fully computerized for more than three decades.

"What was that?" Tony asked.

"I said no, it's not here. It's in *Fort Madison*."

"Fort Madison? What could he...Oh, Holy Mother, he's going to pardon Ralph Wells." The words came out of his mouth as a certainty.

"Gold star, Mr. Harrington," Ben beamed. "I'll bet you the BMW I'll never own that's exactly what he's doing. I told you he was going to ram this Wells case up Nelson's ass. I just didn't know he would do it this fast or this deep."

Tony couldn't help smiling. "I've never heard of a governor going to the prison to issue a pardon. In fact, I can't remember a governor ever going to a prison at all."

"You're so right. Governors hate being associated with The Fort. However, in this case, I'd say Roskins is brilliant. He will escort Wells right out the door into the sunshine of a new life, demonstrating his deep compassion and his determination to help Wells escape the clutches of that evil over-zealous prosecutor, who just happens to be his opponent in the race. Goddamn political genius, I'd call it."

Tony nodded his agreement as he contemplated the logistics.

"Well, chief, obviously I can't get to Fort Madison in less than an hour, even if you've charted me a private jet. So how do we work this one?"

"The Des Moines media is going to cover it live on the noon news. That's why I didn't call and roust you out of bed. I figured we can see the live event from here as well as from a folding chair in the front lawn of The Fort. However, I want you to be posed over your phone with Nelson's number pre-dialed. I want you to be the first person to get to him after the announcement. By the time four or five reporters have called him, he'll clam up like a Dick Cheney hunting buddy. Start thinking about what you'll ask him, and give some thought to who else we should call for reactions."

Tony was out the door and headed for his desk before Ben finished talking.

***

It all unfolded exactly as the two of them had envisioned. As they and others from the paper's staff gathered around the flat screen TV on the newsroom wall, the local TV news anchor called on his colleague in Fort Madison. A young woman appeared on the screen holding a microphone. In the background was the imposing structure of the prison, and directly behind and slightly left of the reporter was a temporary platform with a podium and a microphone. The female reporter commented about the uniqueness of the occasion and said no one on the governor's staff had been willing to say in advance what the topic was. She said speculation was it had something to do with the problems the state had been having with the computerized heating, cooling, and security systems in the relatively new prison.

"Bzzzz," Tony made a weak attempt at a game show buzzer. "Sorry, Miss, that's incorrect. Over to you, Mr. Greenjeans."

Appreciative chuckles came from Tony's co-workers. Then suddenly everyone was quiet as Governor Roskins took the stage.

Town Crier

Governor Pardons Ralph Wells

Travels to Fort Madison to Correct a 'Serious Miscarriage of Justice'

Tony Harrington, Staff Writer

FORT MADISON, Iowa – Speaking from a hastily-assembled platform in front of the Iowa State Penitentiary at Fort Madison at noon Monday, Governor Harris "Harry" Roskins announced he had pardoned Ralph Adam Wells of Orney for "any and all crimes and misdemeanors." The governor then stepped off the platform long enough to personally escort Wells through the prison doors into freedom, explaining that he had arranged for the normal pre-release processes to be waived and for Wells to be set free immediately.

Wells had been convicted in Quincy County District Court a year ago of the double murder of Jerry and Anne Ennis in their rural Orney home.

On Friday, the Iowa Division of Criminal Investigation (DCI) revealed evidence indicating the Ennises actually may have been killed by Quincy County Deputy Dennis Peters, who was found dead

in his home of an apparent suicide. Peters had more than 100 photos of Anne Ennis in his home. In a suicide note found at the scene believed to have been written by Peters, he said he killed the couple because he couldn't live with the thought of Anne Ennis being with another man.

In his speech Monday, the governor called Wells' conviction a "serious miscarriage of justice," saying the evidence that Peters committed the crime is "overwhelming."

The governor then laid the incident, what he called a "travesty," firmly at the feet of the prosecutor in the case, Attorney General W. Rodney Nelson.

Nelson is the governor's opponent in next month's gubernatorial election. He has been running on a platform focused, in part, on a law and order theme.

Roskins said Monday, "Anyone who knows the facts of Mr. Wells' case knows he was convicted on a few pieces of circumstantial evidence and on the emotional testimony of one of the unfortunate girls who lost her parents in the killings.

"Mr. Nelson used this meager evidence, cloaked in the emotions of a young girl, to convince a jury of good and true Iowans that Mr. Wells was guilty of this most horrendous of crimes. A crime which we now know, thank the good Lord, Mr. Wells did not commit. Mr. Nelson claims he wants to protect Iowans. Well, I say being overzealous and seeking to put an innocent man in prison just so you can boost your win-loss record in court, all for the sole purpose of seeking the governor's office, is anything but the definition of protecting the public. In the language of most hard-working Iowans, it's just plain shameful.

"Mr. Wells, I'm pleased I have the power as Iowa's governor to right this injustice, and I'm proud to be the first person to welcome you back to freedom."

Wells shook the governor's hand and posed for pictures, but spoke only briefly after the formal presentation was completed. As reporters gathered around him, Wells said only, "I'm grateful to the governor. I'm grateful to Deputy Peters for finally revealing the truth, and I'm grateful to my wife and friends who never stopped believing in me. Now I just want to go home."

In a bit of irony, the governor then directed a state trooper at the scene to give Mr. Wells a ride back to Orney.

When reached for comment in his Des Moines office, W. Rodney Nelson replied in a raised voice to questions about the governor's remarks saying, "His accusations that I somehow railroaded an innocent man for political gain are outrageous and beyond the boundaries of acceptable political discourse. I took the facts as gathered by investigators and presented them to the jury to the best of my ability. I was proud of the job I did for the people of Iowa then, and I'm still proud of it today.

"If these new facts, which I assure you were unknown to me until today, prove Mr. Wells was wrongly convicted, then I will join the governor and all Iowans in celebrating his release from prison."

DCI officials declined to comment beyond a simple written statement issued Monday afternoon saying the investigation into Peters' suicide and other facts of the case would continue in order to confirm or not the governor's interpretation of the new evidence.

Deputy Peters' body has been turned over the Quincy County medical examiner. An official ruling on cause of death is expected...

The article continued and was accompanied by two sidebar articles – one recapping the original case and another about the role the case had played in the political campaign for the governor's office. The articles also were accompanied by Tony's crowning achievement, a front-page photograph of Ralph and Amber Wells hugging in the front yard of their trailer home.

Tony had seen the news coverage of Wells climbing into the trooper's cruiser. It was simple to calculate the exact time Wells would arrive home. He was pretty sure the trooper wouldn't be stopping along the way to treat Wells to a Starbucks or a Dairy Queen.

When the cruiser pulled into the gravel drive in front of Wells' trailer, Tony was there waiting with a signed photo release from Amber and his Nikon at the ready. His only disappointment was that Wells declined to comment any further. Before Wells disappeared inside the trailer, Tony did manage to tell him, "Mr. Wells, I want you to know I'm really glad you're free. I never believed the prosecution's case. If you change your mind and want to talk about it, you know where to find me."

***

W. Rodney Nelson's anger was erupting into pure rage. He stood behind the desk in his office, teeth clenched and red-faced. His breathing was shallow and fast and his temples throbbed. He realized his hand was gripping the paperweight from his desk, a crystal disk with the image of the Iowa State Capitol etched on its surface. He desperately wanted to throw it, but refused to give the news media, or even his staff, more fodder for gossip about him.

Someone tapped on the door, but instead of his usual welcome Nelson said just a bit too loudly, "Don't even think about it."

Realizing he couldn't stay in the office without making a scene, he dropped the paperweight, grabbed his suit coat off the valet stand in his office closet, and headed out the back door.

As he pulled into his Tudor-style home in the plush near-west neighborhood of Des Moines, he realized he couldn't remember driving to his house from the Iowa Justice Center downtown. His mind was filled with fury and disbelief at the turn of events and not much else. As the garage door dropped behind the Cadillac, he knew he was truly alone and finally succumbed to what he was feeling. Pounding the dash, he screamed, "Son of a bitch! Son of a bitch! Son of a bitch!" He pushed open the door, climbed out, and slammed it so hard the windows in the garage rattled.

As he walked from the breezeway into the back foyer of the house, he ran into a wide-eyed Lillian. "Oh! You scared me," she said, brushing a strand of hair from her face with a hand wearing a gardener's glove. "I was just re-potting some flowers when I thought I heard the garage door. Are you okay?" Her concern grew when she saw his face.

"No," he barked, causing her to rear back. "Of course I'm not okay. How could I possibly be okay? This is an unmitigated disaster."

"But Rod," Lillian replied, "I saw you on TV, and I thought you handled the news perfectly."

"Lillian, please don't be such a naive ass," Nelson growled. "This could mean the end of everything."

Lillian started to respond but stopped abruptly as Nelson put up his hand. "You know I was using this case to fuel my campaign. All my great speeches about protecting the people of Iowa from killers like Wells. Didn't you hear how that fucking Roskins used this against me in his speech? Don't you understand how he will continue to use this against me every day until the election? That ass will roast me with this. What I thought was the perfect case to carry me to the governor's office turns out to be exactly what Roskins needed to bury me. Do not think for one minute, Lillian, that this is no big deal. This is the biggest damn deal in our lives." He pushed past her, kicking open the door to the house, and headed for the bar.

Lillian stood, dumbfounded, watching him go. For the first time in memory, she didn't know what to say or do. Rod never cursed, and he had never treated her rudely. She swallowed hard, determined not to cry. She then headed out the breezeway door to the backyard to return to the garden. This, of course, was why she had a garden in the first place and why she worked it herself. If she was going to cry, she would do it here, alone. Her azaleas and day lilies would be the only ones to witness her anguish over a fuming husband and his failing political career.

***

Late that evening, Tony and Ben were back in the bar, debriefing about the case. Tony pointed out that Rich Davis, Sheriff Mackey, and a whole lot of other people were undoubtedly angry at the governor's pardon. They certainly were smart enough to understand the governor had moved quickly in order to take full advantage of the situation through the final weeks of campaigning. Tony also knew that now, no matter what the investigators found, this case was over.

"Yeah, so what?" Ben said, playing the curmudgeon role of the stereotypical editor. "They'll get over it. Politically motivated or not, the governor did the right thing to get that kid out of prison as fast as possible."

Tony couldn't argue with that, so he took another sip of diet cola and popped a fried mushroom in his mouth.

Ben preferred the onion rings on the platter they had ordered. After chewing through a few, he looked up and said, "Tony, let me ask you something."

"Sure, Chief, anything."

"You were right all along about the evidence, correct?"

"Well yes, I guess so."

"And now you've been proven right about the whole case, correct?"

"Yes-s-s-s."

"And the man you agonized over is free from his unjust sentence, correct?"

"Yes...what's this..."

"Hang on. So in a nutshell, this is the fairytale scenario, in which everybody lives happily ever after, that you only dared to dream about."

Tony held his tongue and nodded.

"So what the hell is still eating you?"

Tony could have argued he was fine, but knew he couldn't sell it. It took him a long beat to assemble a response. Ben grabbed a nacho off of the plate between them, but didn't take his eyes from Tony. Finally he said, "Oh, I don't know. I think it's just Lisa. After all, not *everybody* lived happily ever after."

"Well, of course that's true, and I apologize that I didn't choose my words more carefully. I'm sure it's on your mind every minute. But that's not what has you so distracted. You know it and I know it," Ben said, leaning forward. "There's something else about the Ennis-Wells-Peters case...jeez, we're going to have to find a better name for this thing. There's something about it still buzzing around in your head. I can see it in your face."

Tony didn't respond right away, debating. "C'mon, you know me. I get these feelings and I obsess about them. I don't want to bother you with my nonsense every time I think I'm smarter than the people who do this stuff professionally."

"By 'this stuff' I presume you mean investigating," Ben said. "Tony, let me be honest. You have great instincts. Maybe the best I've ever seen next to my own. You should never hesitate to tell me when something doesn't feel right to you. Besides, I have to admit that it bugs me a little that this got all tied up in a neat little package so easily. But I figure sometimes life works out. Not often, but when it does you should only look that gift horse in the mouth once or twice. If everything looks good, move on." He paused. "Good God, did I really say that? Anyway, I can tell you're bothered by something more than what I just said, and I want you to be honest with me."

"Okay, okay," Tony said, holding up his hands in surrender. Then, trying to add a note of sarcasm, "Here are the two great insights I bring to the latest developments in the case. Sadly, the first is based on my prejudices about people. Lisa always said I was too quick to judge someone."

"Well, she was right, but that doesn't mean you're wrong."

"So, here's the deal. I met Denny Peters and he was an ass. I find it hard to believe he was overwhelmed with remorse and stooped to apologize to a lowly soul like Ralph Wells."

"Hmm, you're right. I mean you're right that you've made a big leap based on the fact you met Denny Peters a couple of times. Hard to say what a man thinks or feels in that situation."

"I know, I know. But it just feels so wrong. The second thing is a little more problematic." He paused, debating if he really wanted to go down this path. "You see, I noticed something at Peters' house."

"Something like what?" Ben asked, leaning in even closer.

"I noticed the thumb tacks and photographs were clean."

Ben looked puzzled but waited for Tony to continue.

"You see, in the room where Peters had his 'shrine' to Anne Ennis, there must have been sixty or more of those one hundred photos pinned to the walls. As I was taking pictures of my own and examining the pictures of Anne, I noticed the thumb tacks looked new. They were those wide, flat, shiny kind of chrome or polished steel or something. There were four stuck into each picture. It seemed odd that all of the thumbtacks were identical and gleaming bright. It was a small thing, but it caused me to look more closely. I inspected every single thumb tack and, as far as I could tell, there were no fingerprints on any of the tacks."

Ben was careful not to comment or react, wanting Tony to finish his thoughts.

"Now obviously, I didn't have a fingerprint kit. But the crime scene guys had spotlights in the room and I had a zoom lens on the Nikon. I'm telling you, there were maybe 240 bright silver thumb tacks and not one thumb print. Also, it seemed odd to me that all the photos looked new. Not the content, but the prints themselves. No fading, no dust, identical borders and physical appearances. If this was a longstanding obsession, wouldn't the prints have been hung over a long period of time? Wouldn't they have had some variation in appearance?"

Tony wanted a reaction but Ben was determined to remain mute, so Tony continued. "So my mind – I warned you about this part – my mind immediately raced down the path of asking, why would a man hanging pictures of the woman he loved in his own home wear gloves or wipe all the thumb tacks clean? Would he take photos over a period of months or years and then wait to print and hang them all at once, apparently within days of his suicide? I say he wouldn't. So who would? Well, it's obvious. Okay, it's obvious to a cynical and perhaps delusional person like me that the person who would do this is a person who wanted it to look like Denny Peters was obsessed with a woman we have no evidence he ever even met. There, now you've heard it all."

They both sat silently for a long time. Ben finally asked, "So have you asked your pals at the DCI about this?"

"No," Tony admitted. "But think about it. Wells was framed, and the likely perpetrator was on the inside. A member of the Sheriff's Department. Now here I am I wondering if Peters was framed or... or who knows what, and who's to say the perpetrator of *this* isn't on the inside? I don't know if I should talk to anybody. I don't know if I *dare* to talk to anybody."

"You know," Ben said slowly. "When I started this conversation I intended to advise you to be careful; that if you weren't careful you were going to drive yourself crazy. Now I see the real problem." Tony raised his eyebrows quizzically.

"Now I know you're going to drive me crazy." Ben took the last swallow of his beer and stood up to leave. Looking down at Tony in the booth, he said, "My advice is to tell everyone who will listen exactly what you observed. If you're the only one who knows it, you're in a lot more danger than if you've shared it with all the agencies involved. And don't forget, there's a hell of a news story in this if it turns out you're right."

"Uh, thanks, Chief," Tony said numbly, not thinking about a news story or his boss standing at his elbow. He was thinking about the "danger" comment. He had been carrying a notion in the back of his mind that he might personally be at risk, but hearing Ben say it out loud brought it to life in an entirely new way. It was like the difference between knowing a bear was sleeping in the cave and hearing it roar as it chased you through the forest. He felt a growing, hollow sensation in his stomach he didn't like at all.

As Ben zipped up his jacket, he said, "I say again, be careful, Tony."

Before Ben could turn to go, Tony jumped up and grabbed his boss' sleeve.

"Sit down, please," he said.

Ben looked puzzled but eased himself back into the booth and waited patiently.

Tony chose his words carefully. "If I'm in danger, then you could be too. If there really are people out there trying to cover up a murder...no, multiple murders, then they might be worried that I've given you information or evidence that could hurt them."

"Perhaps," Ben began, "but..."

"No, listen," Tony interrupted forcefully. "I've already lost the woman I love. If something happened to you or anyone else because of me, I couldn't bear it. I think we should talk about whether I really do walk away from this completely. Use the 'tidy package' as an excuse to let it go, and make sure everyone knows that's what I'm doing."

"Tony, if you want to walk away, that's your call. You know me well enough to know I would never force you to pursue something dangerous. But do not do it for me or for anyone else at the paper. In fact, if you walk away, I probably will take it up myself."

Tony looked up in surprise.

"Don't be shocked," Ben said. "As I said, if you're right this will be a huge story. This is the kind of stuff we live for in newspaper work."

Tony began to protest but Ben cut him off.

"Perhaps," he said, "it's time to explain to you why I left the East Coast."

***

After waving at the bartender for another round of drinks and snacks, Ben recounted for Tony in great detail what had happened to him in Baltimore. In a nutshell, Ben had been pursuing an article about an embezzlement at a local car dealership. What appeared at first to be a simple case of a bookkeeper taking advantage of his boss turned out to be something more. Being the thorough professional he was, Ben had dug into the thief's background and had quickly realized he wasn't working alone. Two other names in other dealerships were shared with him by an anonymous source.

After months of digging, Ben had assembled an astonishing story involving organized crime and money laundering. It was a complex scheme and Tony didn't understand it all, but the crux of it was the mob was using the car dealerships to turn illegal profits from drugs and prostitution into funds that could be accounted for and used. As Tony understood it, the car dealers would sell a car legitimately to a customer at a typical discount. On a new car purchase, customers always negotiated a price less than the sticker price. If the customer's discount was $4,000, for example, the bookkeeper would record a discount of $2,000. The balance would be "paid" by bringing in cash that needed to be laundered. The excess funds went straight to the dealerships' net profits. These profits then were paid back to the silent partners in the businesses or as bonuses to people listed on the dealerships' payrolls.

By the time he had finished, Ben had hard evidence of involvement in the scheme by people in seventeen dealerships scattered across four eastern states. Millions of dollars had passed through their books and back into the mob's pockets in this way. He had been very excited the day he brought his investigative work to the editorial conference at the paper and presented the facts to his bosses. The editors were pleased and excited, but they said that because it named names and accused people of mob connections, the publisher and the attorneys would have to get involved.

"To make a long story short," Ben said, staring down at his bottle of Sam Adams, "they killed my article."

"What? Why?"

"Well, they said all the things a reporter fears. They were worried about the risks of taking on organized crime. They were worried about the liability of naming people who were working for the mob. They thought the risks were too great for a story that didn't really hurt the people buying cars or the 'average person.' Blah, blah, blah."

Tony was contemplating how to respond when Ben continued.

"Understand, that wasn't the worst of it." Tony raised his brow and Ben continued, "The worst part was that everything they told me was total B.S. What they really feared was losing advertising revenue. You see, the car dealers were the single biggest advertising segment the paper had. They were unwilling to piss them off. That's when I decided I needed to be my own boss. I walked out that night and never went back."

"I'm sorry," was all Tony could think to say.

Ben looked at him sharply. "Don't be sorry, Tony. I love what I'm doing now. I wouldn't trade my life today for any other journalism job in the world. But understand the impact the experience had on me. I have vowed that fear, and I mean fear of any kind, is not going to drive my decisions at the *Crier*. I'll take afraid and free over safe and hog-tied every time."

He chugged the last of the beer and stood up once more. "So, to hell with whoever or whatever is behind all of this. I say we move forward, and if it turns out you're right, we put these bastards behind bars where they belong."

Ben turned and was gone before Tony could formulate a response.

He sat alone in the booth for a long time thinking about everything he had heard and everything he had said. Ben's story had only made Tony admire him more, if that was possible. While taking on the mob took a level of courage Tony couldn't imagine, he also knew that walking away from a successful career; from everything you knew, took another kind of courage. Ben had demonstrated both.

Tony ached to be more like him, but in fact, contemplating Ben's courage only made Tony feel inadequate. The truth was, Tony was numb with fear. He didn't want to be the next "suicide" found in his house with who knows what elaborate setup to make him look crazy. The thought gnawed at him. He realized that tonight, and maybe for many nights into the future, returning home late at night to a dark house would be a very stressful experience. He wondered if he could handle it.

Chapter 23

Tony sat in blue jeans and a T-shirt in his favorite leather chair. Wide and soft, and positioned near the front windows of his house, the chair was his favorite reading spot. He wasn't reading. It was just after 1 a.m. and he couldn't sleep. He sat in the chair in the dark, staring out the big plate glass window into the moonless night. Joe Cocker's gravelly voice was singing rhythm and blues out of his computer's speakers in the other room. He had the volume down low, just something to keep the house from feeling so empty. It occurred to him he needed to buy a piano. It was times like this that knocking out a few tunes would be perfect.

It wasn't fear keeping him up. At least he didn't want to think it was. He was awake and his mind was still racing because of an overwhelming sensation that his life had been out of control for the past two years. Ever since the Ennis couple had been found dead and Lisa had entered his life, he had felt like a surfer clinging to his board as a tsunami hurtled him toward the shore.

As he replayed all the events of the past two years, he just couldn't make sense of it all. That nagging sixth sense told him that somehow it all tied together, but how...or why? He thought about Lisa's advice, given so off-handedly. *Figure out who benefits.*

"Sure, honey, easy to say, hard to do," Tony said aloud to the empty room. The irony in all this was that the man who was clearly going to benefit the most was Governor Roskins. Today's events would put Nelson's campaign in the dumpster and Roskins was headed for another four years in office.

Speaking out loud once again Tony said, "See, honey, it's simple. The governor did it."

Wait...See, honey, it's simple. The governor...

Suddenly Tony couldn't breathe. The thought stopped him cold. He could feel goose bumps on his arms and the clammy sensation of blood draining from his upper body.

"The governor did it," he repeated aloud. It was as if speaking the unspeakable had ripped a giant hole in the curtain of confusion.

Was it possible Roskins was somehow involved in all this? Tony thought back to the beginning. If the governor had known Nelson was going to run against him, could he have arranged to have the Ennises killed? Could he have made sure the evidence looked convincing; could he have positioned the case to be irresistible to a prosecutor wanting a big win before the race? He would have had to arrange for Francie Wells' testimony. Holy sh... did that explain her windfall of cash and the relationship with Peters? Peters. Good God. Could he then...?

No, no, no. This was insanity. Over the course of two years, there were hundreds of things that could go wrong with a plot as involved as Tony was now imagining. Roskins would have to be a cold-blooded SOB to kill an innocent young couple on the chance this crazy idea *might* work. So was the governor a cold-blooded SOB? Tony had no idea, but had to admit he wouldn't put it past him.

His thoughts were interrupted as a car's headlights flicked against the glass of the window. Tony wouldn't have noticed a car going by, but it was late, and so it was one of the few interruptions to his solitude. Then, more curiously, a car *didn't* go by. Tony was sure he had seen the reflection. So why had no car passed by on the street?

Tony pushed his bare feet into his jogging shoes by the front door and stepped out into the darkness on the front porch. The street was quiet. Tony busied himself bringing a few things into the house from the porch to give the appearance of having business there while he glanced quickly down the street in both directions. There, to his left, past two of his neighbor's homes, he could see a large sedan parked on the street. The streetlight further down the street shone partly through the car's windows and displayed a silhouette in the front seat. From this distance in the dark, Tony couldn't tell if it was a person or a headrest. But now he was just paranoid enough to want to know for certain.

He picked up another potted plant from the porch and went back into the house. He closed the door and locked it. He then sped to the rear of the house, grabbed his black Hawkeye sweatshirt off the peg by the side door and exited into the makeshift carport beside the house. Tony never parked there, but used the cover to protect his barbecue grill and lawn furniture. Because the neighbor's house was close, Tony knew it was unlikely he would be seen from the street unless from a position directly across from his home.

Now he was glad he was in good shape because he ran swiftly through the neighbors' back yards in seconds. Less than a minute after he'd left his front porch, he was crouched behind the air conditioning compressor unit beside the second house, staring directly into the passenger window of the car parked on the street. It was a big, late-model sedan, dark in color, with standard wheels and two antennae on the back. In other words, a government car.

Tony plopped back onto his butt and leaned against the side of the house. What did this mean? Was this someone sent by the governor? Had Tony just confirmed his crazy, wild-ass idea? Or was this an agent keeping him under surveillance because he was still a suspect in Lisa's death? Or was this just some cop who stopped to eat his donuts in peace?

Mustering more courage than he ever dreamed he had, Tony decided there was only one way to find out. He stood up and marched down the neighbor's driveway to the side of the car and yanked open the passenger door. Sitting behind the steering wheel, whirling in surprise to face Tony, was Rich Davis.

"What the hell?" Both men spoke in near unison.

Tony jumped into the passenger seat and slammed the door shut. Paranoid or not, he couldn't imagine Davis doing anything to harm him. Or at least couldn't imagine him doing it in a government vehicle on a public street.

"Hey, I..." Davis began.

"Shut up," Tony snapped. "No, don't shut up. Tell me what the hell you're doing here, night."

"What? Wait, you know I can't tell you..."

"Damn it, Rich. You *are* going to tell me. This is my life you're messing with. So tell me. Now. What are you doing here?"

"Okay, okay. You won't believe me but here's the truth: I honestly don't know."

"What's that supposed to mean?"

"It means I received orders to watch you and to report everything you do. No explanations. Nothing further."

"Orders from whom?"

"From my boss of course, but before you go after him, I'm not sure he knows either."

"You're not sure..."

"I'm serious. When he told me to do this, I could tell he hated the idea. It's coming from somewhere else. I thought maybe it had to do with Lisa's death, but no one seems to be looking at you for that. You in trouble with the FBI or the IRS or something?" Davis attempted a smile but Tony wasn't in the mood for it.

Tony stared straight ahead for a long while. Finally, he said, "I have to know." He turned and looked directly into the agent's eyes. "Even if it means you haul me off to a gravel pit and put a bullet between my eyes, I have to know."

"Whoa there. Easy. I'm just watching your house. You're supposed to feel safer when the DCI is watching over you."

"I'm serious. I have to know if you were in on all this from the beginning."

"In on all what? What are you talking about?"

So Tony told him. He spelled out his entire crazy, wild-ass idea.

***

Davis shook his head and showed a wide array of negative facial expressions as Tony walked him through it but, to his credit, he kept quiet and listened attentively. When Tony finished, Davis said, "Okay, my turn. First of all, I think you're out of your damn mind. No. No, wait. I did not and would never have any part in a crime. Good God, the series of crimes you're talking about are horrendous beyond my comprehension, and I have to say I'm offended as hell you would even ask me that. But getting back to the main point, what you've described is beyond imagination. Politicians don't kill people for political gain. Especially not popular politicians. He's a three-term governor for God's sake, and he's an Iowa governor. We don't elect criminals to public office in Iowa. You've found a cute theory that happens to fit some of the facts of these cases, but that's all."

"Rich, I swear I hope you're right. But Roskins has just gone from potentially losing to winning re-election, all because of this series of events. The more I contemplate it, the more I think it's possible."

"Well, you're wrong. Now get out of my car and go to bed before we both get in a lot of trouble."

"Not yet. Tell me about the thumb tacks."

"Oh shit," Davis replied glumly. "You noticed that, did you? I wondered if you had. The guys in the room with you reported that you'd examined every single picture up close."

"Yeah, I noticed the tacks with no prints and the photos with no fading or dust. What do you guys make of that?"

"Well, we don't know. Wait...before you say anything. We're not stupid. We're off the record here, right?"

Tony nodded, but secretly wished he hadn't thought to ask.

Davis continued, "We know the implications could be that this obsession thing was a setup, and maybe the whole suicide was faked. But it doesn't necessarily make it so. It could simply be that Peters wore gloves when he hung the pictures in order to keep them pristine. Lots of people wear gloves when working with photographs. It also could be that he polished the tacks as part of his adoration of the pictures."

Tony looked skeptical and Davis acknowledged it. "I know, it sounds like we're grasping at straws, but there *are* other explanations than the one you apparently are choosing to believe."

"I'll give you that, but when you consider..."

"One more thing, and again this is strictly off the record. After we found Peters' body, we did a rush job on his DNA. It was a perfect match with the DNA of hair found at the scene of the original double homicide. So now we know Peters was there when they were killed; or he was in the Ennis' bed sometime previous to that. Either way, it supports the current theory of the crimes. Hopefully that puts your mind at ease and gets you off this crazy idea about political conspiracies."

Tony sincerely appreciated knowing this latest piece of the puzzle, and told Davis so.

Davis looked at him expectantly, assuming they were done. They weren't.

"Rich, tell me this," Tony continued. "Where is Peters' cruiser?"

"You mean his deputy sheriff's patrol vehicle?" Davis was baffled at the turn in the conversation.

"Yeah, his car. Has it been reassigned or is it in custody or what?"

"Well, I'm not sure, but the last I knew we still had it impounded. It would be unusual to let anything go before the case was completely closed. Why in the world would it matter?"

Tony looked hard at Davis and took a deep breath. "I have another itch I need to scratch."

"Well, scratch away," Davis said. "Nothing you say now can top what you've already thrown at me tonight."

Tony swallowed hard. "It has to do with Lisa's death. I'm pretty certain it was no accident."

"Tony..." Davis began.

"No. Hear me out. I was with her once, in my Explorer, in that same corncrib. Parking."

"You mean..."

"Yes, but please, just listen. When we were there, Lisa would not let me close the crib doors because of her fear of carbon monoxide poisoning."

Davis' eyes widened, but he held his tongue.

"If I'm right, and she was killed, then who's the likely perpetrator? Well, we have to hope it was Denny Peters, right?"

Davis nodded, understanding the logic.

Tony continued. "If it wasn't Peters, then we have to admit we have two homicidal maniacs running around Orney. That's pretty tough to swallow. So, if we assume it was Peters, then why? And just as importantly, if he did it, then why didn't he confess to it in his supposed suicide note? Where was his remorse and apology for his third murder?"

Davis was at a loss for words. Again, he simply nodded and waited for Tony to continue.

"So here's what I think. I think Denny Peters did kill Lisa. It occurred to me later that I may have seen him near the scene. At least a car like his drove past me as I headed out to the farm that night. I think he didn't confess to Lisa's murder because he didn't kill himself. Someone else staged the suicide to cover up the bigger conspiracy. Whoever killed him didn't put it in the suicide note because they didn't want Lisa's death linked to him. And it doesn't take a genius to figure out why."

"It may not take a genius," Davis said, "but it takes someone smarter than me. You're going to have to finish the story for me."

"Think about it. Where was Lisa working the night she was killed? She was at party headquarters working for Roskins." Tony paused to take a breath and get his emotions under control. "Connecting Peters to Lisa would significantly increase the risk of someone making the connection between the politics and the murders." Tony turned to face the windshield, fell back in the seat, and closed his eyes.

"Tony, you must know how farfetched all of this sounds," Davis said quietly. Tony nodded but could tell he had sparked at least a smoldering interest from Davis.

"Do you have any evidence at all, other than seeing a Sheriff's Department car on a rural road; which, by the way, is where those cars are supposed to be at night?"

Tony turned back to face his friend and opened his eyes. "That," he said, "is why I asked about the car. I'm hoping we'll find something in it that links Peters to Lisa's murder. I know you've been through his house with a fine-toothed comb and I'm sure whoever killed him did the same before you got there. But maybe there's something somewhere else."

"I doubt it's in the car," Davis said. "I don't even know what we would look for, but if it's incriminating he's too smart to have left it there."

"Then where?" Tony asked, with a note of pleading in his voice.

"Probably nowhere," Davis said, not meaning to sound as abrupt as he did. To fend off Tony's reaction, he quickly added, "but there is one place we could look."

Tony's eyes widened and his brow furled as he waited for Davis to finish the thought.

"Peters' aunt owns a farm not far from Orney. No one lives there and Peters was pretty much the designated caretaker for the place. Dan and I were going to give it a once-over at some point, just so we could say we did if anyone asked. We never expected to actually be looking for something."

"So you'll let me join you. Tomorrow." Tony spoke in statements, not questions.

"Well, I guess my boss couldn't complain about me keeping an eye on you if you're riding with me," Davis said wryly. "So sure. Why not?"

"I need some sleep," Tony said. "If you don't mind, let's head out at ten in the morning. I'll be ready if you don't mind picking me up again."

"It's a date," Davis said, trying to sound lighthearted but failing.

Tony grabbed the door handle and pushed open the door. He could see Davis' face, his friend's face, pale and strained in the stark light from the car's dome.

"I'm sorry I had to ask you about being in on all this," Tony said. "I just had to know."

"It's okay. We're both tired and we've both been consumed by a series of unspeakable events. Tomorrow will be a better day for both of us."

Tony closed the car door and turned for home, hoping Davis was right but fearing he wasn't.

Chapter 24

It was a spectacular fall morning. Despite his desire to sleep in, the bright sunshine leaking past his bedroom blinds rousted Tony at dawn. He decided he could use the extra time to eat a decent breakfast for a change and get a few chores done before Davis arrived. He groaned as he climbed out of bed and headed for the shower.

Once scrubbed, brushed, and shaved, Tony headed for the kitchen to scramble some eggs. Standing at the stove, he could look out the back of the house. A wooden birdfeeder hung from the branch of a huge and ugly ash tree. The tree was a major feature of the small, well-kept yard, but it was a pain in the ass. At the slightest breeze, it rained sticks and small branches like confetti at an astronaut's parade. Tony had always said he didn't need to do stretching exercises because he was in the yard picking up sticks every other day.

Keeping the birdfeeder filled was also a hassle, but Tony didn't mind that chore. He enjoyed watching the cardinals, finches, and occasional hummingbirds flitting on and off the perch. On a good day, Tony would catch the woodpecker as it came in for a snack. The woodpecker had beautiful shades of red and orange and was twice the size of any other bird in the yard. He clearly scared the stuffing out of every other avian creature on the property.

Tony wasn't quite smiling, but he was glad to be thinking about something other than Lisa, or murders, or conspiracies, or work. *Ah yes, work.* He pulled the cell phone from his pocket and gave Ben a quick call. After explaining he would be with the DCI for at least a couple of hours and promising to be careful and check in when he was done, Tony ended the call and sat down to his plate of eggs and toast and gulps of orange juice right out of the Minute Maid carton.

Davis and Rooney were right on time and Tony climbed in the back of the DCI sedan. As they drove, Tony thought for the hundredth time how different Davis and his partner were. While Davis was tall and dark, Rooney was short and had red curly hair. He didn't look at all like an agent, which probably explained why the DCI liked him. He was perfect for undercover work.

Rooney also was different from Davis in that he was quiet and had a very subtle sense of humor. Tony had rarely heard him speak, and when he did, it always seemed Rooney was primarily talking to himself. That was fine with Tony. He didn't think his biorhythms could survive two agents who liked to call him in the middle of the night.

True to form, Rooney remained quiet as Tony and Davis chatted in the car. It was mostly small talk, a feeble attempt to ease the tension and avoid topics such as Lisa's death. Davis mentioned he had re-taken his physical tests recently to keep his DCI badge, as well as re-qualified on the shooting range. "I don't mind saying I score pretty well on my targets, but I have to admit I nearly miss the reload deadline every time." Tony must have looked puzzled because Davis continued, "In addition to demonstrating your ability to hit a bad guy under pressure, you have to show them you can reload your weapon quickly. I'm always fumbling the magazines and dragging my score into the 'pathetic amateur' range by taking too long."

Tony had no doubt Davis had scored just fine. "Speaking of physical activity," he said. "I've finally decided to actually put some miles on my bicycle."

"This is the time of year for it, when it's not too hot or too cold."

Tony nodded his agreement. "So far I haven't done much but ride to the store, but if the weather is like this tomorrow morning, I think I'll take the bike path down to the Raccoon River. It's just far enough and hilly enough to give me a decent workout without doing me in. If I'm still able to move by the time I get to the river, I may even keep going."

"I'd join you if I could. I could use a good ride myself, but I have to work."

Tony didn't reply. He thought about extending an invitation to Rooney, but realized Rooney didn't expect it and would only have to think up an excuse of his own. They finished the trip in silence.

A few minutes later, they pulled into the farmstead owned by Peters' aunt. Rooney had a warrant signed by Judge Schroeder, which they left on the dashboard before climbing out and locking the car. Each man was wearing blue jeans, work boots, and a sweater or long-sleeved T-shirt. All wore light jackets only because a breeze made the morning seem more chilly than it actually was.

As Tony zipped up his windbreaker and looked around, his heart sank. There was almost nothing here but weeds. There was a small grove of trees to the left and, to the right, a small shed that appeared ready to collapse on itself at any moment. The gravel driveway onto the property ended in a small circular patch of gravel in front of the remains of a brick foundation, undoubtedly that of the now destroyed farmhouse. The rest of the property was just unmowed brush. The property totaled perhaps ten acres. The weeds were matted down in two parallel rows – the obvious tracks of a modern four-wheel drive tractor that used the farmstead as an access path to the cornfield beyond.

With no house, garage, or barn to search, Tony feared they would be done and empty-handed in very short order.

"Where do we begin?" he asked.

Davis said, "Dan, if you don't mind, why don't you take the shed? I don't want our civilian guest going in there. With our luck, the roof would fall on his head. He'd get rich suing the state, and you and I would be working traffic stops for the next decade."

"No problem," Rooney said, sounding almost like he meant it. He quickly headed toward the shed.

Davis then voiced what Tony was thinking. "If Peters did bring anything out here, he could have just heaved it into the weeds and the three of us might never find it. I won't have any luck pulling together a larger team to search the grounds without some idea of what we're seeking."

"I know, I know," Tony said. "And if he buried it, a team of a hundred people might not find it."

"Actually," Davis said, "if he buried it that would be good. We should be able to spot signs of a fresh dig, *If* we spent enough time looking."

Tony looked at the grove. "Maybe we could spot something if we got up above it."

Davis glanced at the trees. "Are you thinking what I think you're thinking?"

"Yep," Tony began jogging toward the nearest tree.

As he arrived, he noted the tree appeared to be an old maple. It had obviously never been pruned, so large branches reached out from the trunk low to the ground. The first was no higher than Tony's chest. He easily pulled himself up onto it. From there he found purchase again and then again. Soon he was twenty feet up with a clear view of the property. *Thank goodness for fall,* Tony thought, realizing this was working only because most of the tree's leaves had finished their work for the year and were now resting comfortably among the weeds on the ground.

The bad news was that the clear view still didn't afford Tony a very good look at the ground. Once his eyes moved more than a few feet from the tree, the weeds still provided a veil of secrecy for anything lying below their outstretched stems. He wrapped his right arm tightly around the branch of the tree, which stood beside him, and used his left hand to shade his eyes from the sun. He silently scoured the property for several minutes.

Finally, Davis called up to him. "See anything at all?"

"No, dammit," Tony shouted back, louder than necessary. He hated giving up but couldn't see much use in staying in the tree.

Davis encouraged him to take another look.

"Try it once more," he said. "This time, forget about digs and just look for anything that looks out of place. Anything at all that catches your eye."

The shift in perspective was all it took.

"Holy shit," Tony barked.

"What?"

"I can see a trail through the weeds. Someone has walked from the tractor's path to a spot behind and to the left of the shed." Tony quickly scrambled back down the tree, brushed himself off, and said, "Let's go."

"Okay," Davis said, clearly happy to have something to investigate. Then, as experience caught up to him, he added, "Be careful not to get your hopes up. It's probably the route the farmer uses to take a leak in the weeds before taking the tractor into the field."

"Yeah, maybe," Tony said, "but maybe not." He broke into a run.

While finding the path through the weeds was trickier from the ground, knowing its approximate location made it possible to spot the disturbed brush on their second pass. Moments later Tony and Rich Davis were staring at a sheet of rusted metal lying nearly flat on the ground. Its slight elevation indicated something was below it. Tony bent and reached for a corner of the metal, but Davis grabbed his arm.

"Hang on there, Joe Hardy," he said. "This may be nothing but it also may be something. Something, for example, like a crime scene. We don't just grab. First, we get tools...and backup."

Tony was dying to see what lurked beneath the metal sheet, but he backed off. Davis used his cell phone to contact Rooney and give him instructions to join them, after getting the camera and the toolbox from the trunk of the car.

While Tony stood not very still in the background, the two agents put on their latex gloves and safety glasses. They then took photographs from multiple angles and used a mirror to ensure nothing under the lip of the metal indicated it had been booby-trapped.

Finally, after what seemed an eternity, Davis said, "Okay, we're ready." He and Rooney then carefully lifted the sheet metal and set it to the side. Below was a well. Its wide diameter, brick sides, and poor condition indicated it was probably the original water well dating back to when the property was settled in the 1800s.

"Flashlight," Davis commanded.

"Careful," Rooney replied as he handed him the light and Davis leaned over the opening in the ground.

Tony knew Davis would soon speak, so he fought the urge to ask. Then Rooney did it for him.

"Well, what do you see, Rich? Jesus, don't leave us here with our thumbs up our butts."

"Okay, okay," Davis replied. "I see something but I'm not

sure what. Get a rope so I can be secured before I try to reach down in there."

Rooney ran back to the car and this time drove it up the tractor path until it was just a stone's throw from the well. He pulled a yellow nylon rope from the trunk and jogged back to Davis. Soon the two men were tethered, and Tony stood behind gripping the rope's tail. Davis dropped to his knees and leaned over the well. As the rope tightened, he leaned down as far as he could with his right hand, keeping his left on the top edge of the bricks on the opposite side of the well.

"We got lucky. Whatever it is got hung up on a rough patch where the bricks of the well are sagging in. I think I can just reach it. Give me a few more inches," he said, his voice obviously straining as it reverberated out of the well.

Rooney and Tony took a baby step forward and heard Davis cry out, "Got it!"

They tugged on the rope as Davis raised his torso and then leaned back on his haunches. Following his arm out of the well was a long, flexible, black tube about three inches in diameter. By the time Davis pulled it all from the well, they could see it was nearly twelve feet long. Dangling from the end of it, apparently caught on an edge of the hose that had been roughly cut, was a black woolen ski mask.

"Well I'll be a frog on fire," Rooney said. "I bet that's the mask he wore at the Ennis place the night he killed them."

"You could be right," Davis replied. "But what's the black tubing?" It looked like rubber, similar to a radiator hose only much longer.

"I don't have a clue," Rooney said.

"I do." They turned to look at Tony.

Tony could feel his stomach clench and a wave of dizziness as he said quietly, "It's the smoking gun." Davis and Rooney stared open-mouthed as he continued, "It's obvious to me this is the hose that Peters used to connect Lisa's tailpipe to the interior of her car."

Tony could see from the stricken look on Davis' face that he realized Tony was probably right, and then, just as quickly, realized the ramifications of what that meant.

Rooney, of course, had no clue. Not being privy to Tony's theories, he could only fumble out the obvious questions. "Lisa? What's this have to do with her? What are you talking about?"

Davis was the one to respond. "Dan, please hold your questions. Trust me, I'll fill you in later."

Tony continued as if neither man had spoken. "He probably held a gun on her, making her sit there, helpless, while he hooked up the hose and ran it through an opening in the window." Tony was crying now, his voice shaking. "Once he was sure she was dead, he removed the hose, shut the crib doors, and left the car running so it would appear the fumes got her as a result of being in the enclosed building. That's how I found...that's how I found her when I was too late. When I was late."

Davis made a move to console him, but Tony turned away and fled to the back seat of the car.

"Well I'll be a frog on fire," Rooney mumbled to himself.

***

On the trip back to Orney, Davis forced Tony to talk about practical, and necessary, things, such as how the news coverage of the discoveries would be handled. They agreed Tony would write about the discovery of the ski mask but would leave out any mention of the hose. Once it had been tested for exhaust residue and fingerprints, they could decide the appropriate time and way to publicize it or not.

Tony used his cell phone to call Ben. He told him the whole story and related what he and the agents had struck as a deal. Ben's only response was that he appreciated knowing all the facts, and it was up to Tony to decide how to handle it.

While the telephone conversation was underway, Davis and Rooney were discussing next steps in the investigation. They decided they needed to call in a DCI team with the training and equipment to explore the well further. If Peters threw in those two items, which possibly represented evidence from two different episodes of murder, what else might be down that well?

By the time they dropped him at home, Tony had pulled himself together enough to ask Rooney to email him a couple of pictures from the scene. As Tony stepped onto and across the porch, entering the house to get a change of clothing, he realized how glad he was to have a job to do and how glad he was to have a boss like Ben. Despite Tony's obvious emotional state, Ben trusted him completely to do what was best for the newspaper and the investigation. Support like that was worth more than any salary paid by any paper anywhere.

When Tony arrived at the paper, he didn't go to Ben's office but headed straight for his own desk. He logged onto the computer and began typing the story. He didn't stop until he was finished. When he finally looked up, he could see Ben watching him from inside his office. Tony pushed the code that sent the story to the copy desk for editing. He then stood, stretched, and took two big gulps of a diet soda which someone had thoughtfully placed on his desk while he had been writing. He was debating what to do next when Ben waived him in.

"It's only 3 o'clock and you've already had a full day," Ben said with a smile.

"Can't argue with that." Tony smiled back, hoping the fact he was on the verge of tears again wasn't obvious.

"I was going to be my usual lovable self and give you the rest of the day off, but the school superintendent just called to say they have an announcement to make, probably related to the bond issue they're going after in the election. Since everybody else is tied up, would you mind heading over there? It shouldn't be any big deal. A couple hundred words is all we'll need."

"No problem at all," Tony was genuinely relieved again to have something specific to do.

"That's great, thanks. In return, I'll give you tomorrow morning off if you like. You can sleep in or whatever."

"Thanks. I actually had been thinking about asking you for a couple of extra hours of free time in the morning. The weather has been perfect so I think I'll get on the bike in the morning and take a ride. It's been too long since I've had a decent workout."

With that settled, Tony headed out for the public high school where the district's administrative offices were housed. *Maybe some controversy about a bond issue will take my mind off Lisa...Lisa, sitting helplessly while that bastard stole her life,* Tony thought. *Yeah, maybe not.*

Chapter 25

The following morning was cool, clear, and just as spectacular as the day before. Tony slept in. When he arose at 8:30, the sun was shining through the east and south windows, warming the hardwood underfoot wherever it found a clear path to the floor. The events of the previous two days seemed surreal, like a bad dream sequence in an old movie. Here, with the sun shining through the windows and neighbors raking leaves across the street, it wasn't possible to conceive of conspiracies and murder and fear. This was Orney, Iowa, and the beautiful fall colors were beckoning him to get out of the house.

Tony brushed his teeth, shaved, and pulled on sweat clothes and sneakers. He then grabbed his ten-speed bicycle in the front room where he had pulled it from the porch the previous morning, rolled it down the front steps to the sidewalk, and hopped on. Ten minutes later, he was on the public bike trail headed for the Raccoon River. Warm coffee from the corner convenience store sloshed in his water bottle strapped to the frame as he peddled faster, trying to get his heart rate up.

He had remembered sunglasses, but quickly realized he should have thought to bring gloves. The October air was chilling his hands to the bone. *Oh well,* Tony thought, pulling the sleeves of his sweatshirt down over his fingers. He wasn't going back. It was just too perfect here.

Tony had been on only a few of Iowa's two thousand miles of bicycle trails. He enjoyed riding but somehow failed to make it a priority in his outdoor activities. However, he had been on this particular trail several times and loved it. The trail was wide and hard-surfaced. It was built on a former railroad line, as many of the trails were. This one, however, went right into the timberland between Orney and the river, providing its riders with protection from the wind, solitude, and, best of all, spectacular scenery. Where the trees thinned, he had views of the wide river valley practically shouting, "Look at me," as thousands of trees proudly displayed the reds, yellows, and golds of fall. As it reached the river, the trail crossed over on the former railroad trestle, having now been rebuilt with a concrete surface, protective guardrails, and even lighting for those riding after dusk.

Tony had two options. He could ride to the river bridge, turn around, and then ride back – a trip of about eighteen miles – or he could cross the river, catch the trail north to the state park, cross back over the river on the highway, and return on the blacktop. This was a trek of nearly forty miles. He still hadn't decided which to take when he reached the end of the first leg.

Tony glided to a stop on the river bridge. He paused to admire the view up and down the valley. The maple, ash, oak, and other trees were in their full glory. Tony realized he regretted not bringing his camera even more than the gloves.

Then, reluctantly, he turned the bike around to ride back to Orney. Forty miles would make him late for work and, while Ben would never say anything, Tony felt like he had imposed on his generosity enough over the past three months. Before beginning the more difficult ride back up the hill and out of the valley, Tony bent over to grab his insulated container of coffee out of its cradle on the frame, just as he heard a loud "ping" ring out from the metal bridge strut next to him, followed immediately by a crack in the distance.

He began to straighten his back, turning to see what had caused the noise, when the realization struck him like a two-by-four. That was a gunshot. Tony dove to the pavement, his bike crashing down beside him. *What the hell...?* Tony lay flat on his stomach, turning his head from side to side, straining to see every patch of woods he could from the cold surface of the bridge deck. He quickly realized how ridiculous he was being. The woods could be filled with a whole division of Marines and he wouldn't be able to see them among the trees, grass, and leaves that filled the hillsides in every direction. *Dear God, I'm a sitting duck up here,* he thought.

He was terrified to move but knew he had no choice. If someone truly was shooting at him, lying still on the bridge would only protect him until the shooter shifted positions to get the required angle for a clear shot. *Stay calm, Tony. Okay, okay,* he thought, forcing himself to breathe normally. There hadn't yet been a second shot, so he must be right. The shooter couldn't get a clear angle from where he was originally. So, he probably was moving. Because of the delay between the ping on the bridge and audible crack of the gunshot, Tony knew the shooter wasn't nearby. He was back in the hills. It was equally likely the shooter couldn't just swing his weapon up and take a quick shot. Even with the best long-range weapon and scope, he'd need time to find a firing position and aim.

In other words, Tony, get your ass out of here! He crawled up on his knees, then pulled his feet under him and stooped over as low as he could. If he was wrong and the shooter was waiting him out from the original sniper position, he didn't want to give him a target. He grabbed the bike and dragged it along the bridge deck. As he waddled and dragged, it seemed to take forever to cover the forty yards to the end of the bridge and the additional twenty or so up the hill to where the trail curved into the woods. Tony's back ached and he was covered with sweat when he reached a spot where he felt safe enough to mount. He scrambled onto the bike as fast as his shaking hands would allow and began peddling furiously through the trees toward Orney.

***

He rode straight to the *Crier* offices, never slowing down until his bike reached the rear parking lot. He tossed it off to the side against the aging brick and practically jogged into the office. There, he suddenly realized, he had no idea what to do next. He knew he should call the police, but who could he trust, really? While catching his breath he glanced around the room and noticed three different colleagues staring at him. Then he looked down and realized his sweat suit was smudged with dirt and oil from the bike and the bridge, his hands were red from the cold, and he was shaking. He tried to compose himself as he headed straight for the men's room to clean up.

When he came out, two people were in the hallway waiting for him. Ben was one. The other was the young woman Ben employed to take advertising orders, primarily classified ads, over the telephone. Both tried to talk at once. Ben decided to be a gentleman and stepped back, encouraging Laurie to speak first.

Between chews of what smelled like bubble gum, Laurie said, "Well, I'm sorry to bother you, Tony, but there was a message for you on the answering machine when I got to work this morning.

Somebody named Molly asked you to call her right away. She said it was, like, you know, super important." Chew, chew.

"Molly?" Did Tony know a Molly? There was Molly Parks, Lisa's co-worker at the party headquarters. The governor's party headquarters..."Do you mean Molly Parks?"

"Dunno," Laurie said. Chew, chew. "She said you would know. But here's the funny part, she said not to call her from any of your 'regular' telephones. I wonder what that means?" Chew, chew.

"Did she leave a number?" Tony hadn't realized his heart could race even faster than it had already been.

Chew, chew. "Well, sorta. She said she has Lisa's old phone. She said when Lisa moved back to Iowa she got a new iPhone and wanted a new number with an Iowa area code, so she gave her old phone to Molly." Chew, chew. "I know, I don't quite get it, but she, this Molly person, said she couldn't afford a cell phone, so Lisa just kept paying the bill and let her have it. Can you figure that? I don't have nobody in my life paying my bills." Chew, chew. "You wanna hear the message? I saved it."

"That's good, Laurie," Tony said. "Good thinking. Hang onto it, but for right now I'll just give her a call and see what she needs. Thanks."

"No prob, Bob," Laurie said, chewing as she walked back to the office.

Ben was still standing against the hallway wall and Tony turned to face him.

"Care to explain any of that?" Ben asked.

"Oh, I would if I could. I barely know Molly Parks, but she works for the Roskins campaign at the party's county office, so who knows? Maybe she's got a scoop for us?"

"And this?" Ben asked, gesturing to the sweat suit which Tony had failed to make presentable through his efforts in the men's room.

Tony knew Ben wasn't criticizing his dress, but was wondering what had happened to him. "I'm anxious to tell you all about it, Ben. I swear. But let me make this call first. Molly said it was urgent, and if she left the message before office hours this morning, it's at least four hours old."

"I agree. Come see me when you're done."

Tony looked on his smart phone, then rummaged through his desk and finally realized he didn't have Lisa's old cell phone number at work. If he had it at all, it was at home, where he jotted it on the desk planner after he and Lisa first met. So he decided just to call her at work, hoping she wouldn't mind too much.

Honoring her bizarre request, he went to the Bat Phone and called party headquarters. The Bat Phone was what reporters labeled an old-fashioned desk phone, which sat in a niche at the side of the newsroom. It was a phone on a separate line from the *Crier's* regular phone system. It served as a backup phone in case the computer system that ran the modern phones crashed or lightning or some natural disaster knocked out the service. Tony had actually heard of this happening, so the idea of a backup made sense to him. However, as far as he could remember, this would be the first call he had ever seen made on the phone.

"Re-elect Governor Roskins!" A very perky and young-sounding voice spoke in his ear. "How can I help you? Will you be making a contribution today?"

"Sorry, no," Tony said, smiling to himself as he thought: *you don't sound anything like Commissioner Gordon.* "I would like to speak to Molly Parks please."

"I'm sorry, sir, but Ms. Parks isn't here at the moment. Can someone else help you?"

"No. I'm returning her call, so I need to speak to her."

"Really? Did she call you today?"

"Well, yes. I think so. Why do you ask?"

"Oh, well, it's just that she didn't show up to work yesterday or today. She's usually so reliable and everyone's been a little worried about her. We've tried calling her but haven't had any success."

Tony could hear some noise in the background on the other end of the phone line, and then a male voice: "Cynthia, who's that you're talking to? Did I hear you talking about Molly?"

"Oh jeez, uh, sir, who did you say was calling?"

Tony realized he didn't want to say and simply hung up the phone.

He made a beeline for Ben's office. Ben motioned for him to sit, but Tony stayed in the doorway.

"I'm sorry, Chief, but I need to run home. I don't seem to have that phone number for Molly here at the office, and I just learned from one of her co-workers that she's been AWOL from work for the past couple days. With everything else that's happened around here, I'm a little anxious to reach her."

"Of course," Ben said. "Go rescue the girl and then get your butt back here and write about it."

It was Ben's stab at a humorous comment, but it landed with a thud in Tony's ears. He said, "Thanks," and turned to go. Then spun back into the office. "By the way, can I borrow your pick-up? I rode my bike here."

Ben smiled and without further comment pulled the keys to the truck out of his pocket and tossed them across the desk to Tony's outstretched hand.

Ben owned a beautiful Chrysler 300. Tony had seen it once or twice. But Ben's normal ride to work was a 1963 Chevrolet Fleetside pickup truck. It was in nice, if not pristine, condition, and it was one of the things Tony loved about Ben.

He tossed his bike in the back of the truck, jumped in the

driver's seat and spun the tires on the gravel lot as he headed home.

***

After taking ten minutes to shower and change and another ten minutes to find the faded telephone number on a long-outdated desk calendar, Tony raced back to the pickup and drove to the Emergency entrance of the Quincy County Medical Center. The hallway near the ER lobby was the only place in town that Tony could think of that still had a pay telephone. He parked outside and rushed through the glass doors. The waiting room was busy, as usual, but not jammed, and as Tony headed down the hall, he was pleased to see the phone nook was unoccupied. He slipped onto the stool below the phone, pulled out some quarters, and dialed the number.

"Hello?" The voice was quiet, small somehow, and hoarse. Had she been crying?

"Is this Molly? It's Tony, Molly."

"Oh, Tony. Oh thank you. God, I'm so glad you called. What are we going to do? Oh, Tony, I'm so sorry."

"Hey, hey...slow down." Tony tried to sound soothing, even confident, but it was difficult as his anxiety rose again. "What's this all about?"

"Tony, we have to talk fast. They could have this number and I can't let them find me."

"Who? What are you talking about, Molly?"

"I have something I must show you. Oh, Tony, it explains everything...*everything*. They did it. These bastards and the governor, they did it."

"Did what, Molly?" Tony asked, straining to keep his voice under control and dreading what he knew the answer was going to be.

"We have to meet, so listen carefully. You know of course that Lisa went to Northwestern. But do you remember where she almost went to college, but didn't?"

Tony hesitated only for a moment. "Oh sure, of course I do. It was..."

"Stop! Don't say it. I'm trying to prevent them from finding us."

Tony realized Molly was assuming someone was listening in, even with the precautions they'd taken. "Okay, I got it. What about it?"

"Now listen closely. There's an Italian woman who lives in that town. She has a nice family and I'm going to take a chance that she'll understand and allow us to meet at her house. Please get there as fast as you can."

"Okay, I promise I'll leave right away. But I'm not sure I know who..." He stopped, suddenly realizing what Molly was saying. Lisa had almost gone to college in Iowa City. Molly was headed there. "I get it," he said. "I know where you're going and I'm sure you'll be welcome there."

"And Tony..."

"Yes?"

"I said I'm sorry because I meant it when I said this explains everything. And God help us both, what I mean is...Lisa too."

The line went dead. Tony sat stone-faced staring at the receiver until it started beeping at him to hang up. He dropped the receiver and slid off the stool onto his knees. He curled forward as the tears started flowing again.

Three different people in various hospital garb stopped to ask if they could help him, but he shrugged them all away. Regaining a measure of composure, he stumbled into the restroom and washed his face with cold water. He slowly raised his head and stared into the mirror. "You fuckers!" he said fiercely, and then was off.

Tony made the three-hour drive to Iowa City in two hours and forty minutes. He was still driving Ben's old pickup, figuring if the DCI or anyone else was still looking for him, he'd be less likely to be spotted in Ben's vehicle. He also knew that in a '63 pickup he didn't have to worry about being tracked by some fancy GPS or LoJack or other electronic system connected to the grid. Ben would be pissed at first when Tony failed to return with the truck. Then he would be worried. But Tony was pretty sure Ben would keep quiet for a while at least, buying him some time do what he needed to do.

Tony hoped he had guessed right about Molly's disguised directions. He was pretty sure he had. He and Lisa used to rib each other a lot about the Big Ten rivalry between their universities and, early on, Lisa had admitted she came "this close" to attending the University of Iowa. Tony often had wondered what might have happened if she had. Would she have found someone and been married before he ever met her? As much as he hated the thought of it, Tony had to consider that she might still be alive if her life had taken that alternative path.

Tears welled up in his eyes again, and he forced himself to set those thoughts aside. There's no going back. Now there was only making sure the bastards didn't get away with it.

It was late afternoon when Tony arrived at the Iowa City exits on Interstate 80. He took Dubuque Street south along the Iowa River. He continued through Campus Town to the southeast side of the city and pulled into the driveway of the stately old home where he had grown up. He entered the back door and climbed the four stairs into the kitchen. There, he saw Molly Parks seated at the butcher-block table, sipping a cup of tea and talking quietly with his mother.

***

Carla Harrington smiled and jumped up to embrace her son. "Tony! Welcome home," she said, finally releasing him from her grip.

"Hi, Mom. It's good to see you too. Is Dad here?"

"No, he has workshop this evening, so he's staying on campus as usual and working until it starts."

Tony nodded and said, "You should call him and ask him to slip home now. While I'm grateful to you for helping Molly and, I must say, I'm impressed with Molly's inventiveness to think of this as a meeting place, I'm afraid she may have put you in danger."

"Well, she warned me of that when she first arrived, but of course I couldn't turn her away."

"Of course not, Mom. What you did is great, but I'm serious about the danger. Molly's here to tell me about some terrible crimes some important people have committed. If those people think she told you or Dad or Rita, then they could come after you."

"Really, Tony, I know you've seen some terrible things recently, but isn't that being a little overly dramatic?"

Tony took his mother by her shoulders and looked right into her eyes. "Mom, I'm not fooling around here. Someone tried to shoot me this morning and..."

"They what?" Tony's mom shrieked.

"Easy Mom, I'm fine. But I'm serious. Call Dad and tell him to come home, now. While you do that, Molly and I are going into his study to talk."

Tony avoided his dad's desk and opted for the two chairs in front of the window. Before he could speak, Molly began, "Tony, I'm sorry. I should have thought about..."

"Forget it," Tony said. "My Dad will know how to take care of the family and, besides, he's gonna love this crap. Remember, he used to write books with plots like this."

Molly almost smiled and then pulled onto her lap the purse that had been hanging from her shoulder. She reached in and pulled out a flash drive.

"It's all there," she said, handing it to Tony.

He held it gingerly, as if it was as fragile as a snowflake and just as likely to melt away.

"Before I look at this, tell me about it," he said, settling back into the chair.

Molly then explained how, with just three weeks left in the campaign, McCabe had directed everyone in the office to do a thorough review of what they had stored on their computers. "He wanted to be sure we didn't have any potential donors listed in our contacts who hadn't been solicited, or unfinished work hiding in a documents folder, or things like that. So, I did what I was told and spent the day before yesterday going through my computer folders and files."

"And?"

"I came across a file with a name indicating it was my 'Christmas list.' The thing is, I was sure I never put a Christmas list on my computer or a file with that name. McCabe was a stickler about paid staff using their time or office tools for personal stuff. Naturally, I opened the file to have a look. I almost fainted, literally. You won't believe what was in that file; what's now on that flash drive."

"Actually, I think I will believe it. So then you copied it onto the flash drive and left the office?"

"Exactly. Well, I waited for the end of the day. I didn't want to attract any attention before I had the chance to get a long way from there. *I was so scared.* I was sure someone would see my hands shaking as I tried to type. Tony, it seems obvious to me that Lisa found this file somewhere in the office and copied it to my hard drive before she died. I'm not sure why she did that – maybe she had to hurry and didn't have a flash drive handy; maybe this was a second copy she made for insurance; who knows? But if McCabe found out she had taken it, then there's no doubt in my mind her death wasn't an accident. And there's no doubt in my mind I'll...I'll...be next."

Molly was shaking and wringing her hands. Tears dripped from her cheeks. Tony reached over to the desk, grabbed a tissue, and passed it to her. She continued, "I didn't know what to do or where to go. I was headed for Chicago but didn't know what I would do when I got there. As I passed Iowa City, I decided to find a room where I could hide for a few days. I figured a college town has plenty of motels that are used to young people getting rooms without reservations and paying cash. This morning when I got up, I remembered you were from here and thought maybe I could ask you and your family for help."

Tony reached out and gripped her hand. "Thank you for bringing this to me. You could have just erased it and pretended to never have seen it and no one would have been the wiser, but you..."

"No, I could not have done that," Molly said forcefully. "Lisa probably died for this, and you'll see other people died too. How could I have lived with myself if I just ignored all that?" The tears flowed more heavily and Tony could tell he was on the verge of joining her.

He stood up. "Well," he said, "I guess it's time I had a look at it."

He walked over to his dad's PC, plugged in the flash drive, pulled up the file, and began to read. It was all there, in a proposal to the governor from Lyle McCabe, dated more than two years ago. It was *all* there.

Chapter 26

Tony stared at his hands. They looked small grasping the steering wheel as he sat quietly in the dark. Clean, well-manicured, free of calluses, they made him feel soft. *Inadequate* was the word that formed in his mind. One of those four-syllable words that Ben Smalley discouraged. "Remember your audience," he would say. Tony made a face. His audience tonight would understand the words all too well. The only question was whether Tony had the courage to tell the story.

He glanced up through the windshield and felt even smaller. He was parked on a street he knew well but only because Lisa had lived here, in that house, the one he was looking at now, at the end of a very long lane. It was a neighborhood where newspaper people only came to cover the occasional tragedy or to attend a Christmas party thrown by someone with political ambitions...or to date a rich man's daughter. Despite his privileged youth, Tony felt out of place here and always would. It was simple. Tony loved his work, and his work paid for rented two-bedroom bungalows with one-stall garages

– not stately mansions with tree-lined drives and multiple fireplaces.

Tony had been sitting in his darkened car on this street for a long time. It was nearly 10 p.m. and he was exhausted. He had driven straight here from Iowa City after receiving his dad's assurances that he and the family and Molly would leave immediately for Chicago and would stay there until it was safe to return. Nearly every minute of the drive back had been consumed by Tony's anguish regarding what to do with the evidence in his pocket. Go to Ben and convince him to put it all in the paper? Call Rich Davis? Confront the governor himself? Run away? *Get serious,* he thought.

Throughout the debate with himself, there was only one certainty. The very next step had to be talking to Lisa's dad. Nathan Freed had a right to hear the whole story; to hear it first; and to hear it from Tony personally. Next to letting the EMTs take Lisa's lifeless body from his arms, this was the hardest thing Tony had ever had to do. Freed was not only an adoring father, but he was friends with the man who had sanctioned her death. Tony had no idea what to expect when he went inside, but he had no doubt it was what he must do.

Tony had expected to find Lisa's father at home and by himself. Unfortunately, when Tony arrived, the lane had been lined with cars. He didn't know if the gathering at Freed's was social or business. It could easily have been both, and he didn't much care. He simply knew he had to talk to Mr. Freed alone, and that meant he would have to wait.

The waiting was hard, exacerbated by the dropping temperature and thoughts of the task ahead of him. After more than an hour, the last car pulled out. As Tony stared at the house, he could feel his stomach churning. His mouth was dry. He found it hard to make himself move. He realized how tightly he was gripping the wheel. Slowly he released the fingers from each hand. *Too soft to handle the evils of reality,* Tony mused again. He flexed them to reduce the discomfort. *Well, here goes,* he thought, swallowing hard but coming up dry. He reached down, started the car, and drove up the lane.

As Tony stood in front of the double oak doors at the front of the house, he ached with the memories of times he had stood there in anticipation of seeing Lisa. Sometimes dressed to kill for a dinner date or party, sometimes in blue jeans and an old college sweatshirt, she always flung open the door as if she couldn't wait for him to get up the portico stairs. She reminded him of a puppy with boundless enthusiasm and energy and unquestioning affection. *My God, it was wonderful.* Now it hurt to stand here and know she was not on the other side of these doors. The pain was nearly crippling, but Tony wanted to savor it, wallow in it.

The pain, however, also served to strengthen his resolve, and he reached out to touch the doorbell. Before his finger found the button, the door swung open and a startled Tony looked up into the warm smile of Nathan Freed.

"Good evening, Tony. I'm sorry if I startled you. I saw you on the security monitor. Come in, come in." Freed was dressed in khaki slacks, a navy golf shirt, and deck shoes. He held the door and Tony walked in, mumbling his thanks.

"I'm not sure if I've seen you since…since the funeral," Freed said carefully. Tony was already sorry he had made Mr. Freed revisit his pain. He was barely into the house, and he knew how much worse it was likely to get.

"Can I get you something?"

Lisa's father was trying hard to smile and keep the mood light. Tony admired and appreciated him for it.

"That would be nice. I have to admit I'm a little dry."

Without another word, Freed led the way to the great room at the back of the house. The room had vaulted ceilings, a wall of glass windows overlooking a deck and pond on the left, and a huge fireplace at the back. It reminded Tony of the lodge at the nearby Boy Scout camp.

Freed went to the refrigerator behind the bar. There were a few glasses around, but it was obvious to Tony that the cars hadn't been here for a party.

"Sorry about the mess," Freed said, "I had a few guests here tonight."

"Yes, I saw the cars leaving," said Tony, purposely setting his curiosity aside.

Freed offered, "Just a few of the party faithful planning some final campaign strategy for our friends in the statehouse. Everyone's nervous and pulling out all the stops now that the election is less than a month away. Unfortunately, they're also pulling out the money, *my* money in too many cases."

Tony hated the thought of Freed's money supporting the governor's campaign, especially in light of what they were about to discuss. He couldn't believe Freed would support anyone he knew to be a criminal. How would Lisa's dad react? Disbelief? Anger?

Suddenly Freed was in front of Tony, smiling and handing him his favorite, a diet Dr. Pepper. Tony instantly remembered that Lisa had kept some here just for him. Her dad probably would be glad to be rid of it. Freed mixed a scotch and water for himself and smiled again, "I don't like to drink when we're talking money, so I hope you won't mind if I have one now." He sank into a deep leather chair and motioned toward the couch in the middle of the room. As Tony sat on the edge, elbows on his knees, Freed lifted his glass and spoke into it, "But I doubt you're here to talk about politics…or money. So what can I do for you tonight?" Then before Tony could respond, Freed added quietly but intensely, "If you're here to profess your love for Lisa or, God forbid, confess something to me, just be aware you don't have to do it for my sake. I know how she felt about you, and

I'm glad she had a chance to be that happy during the final months of her life."

Freed's last word caught in his throat and Tony could see his eyes glisten and his knuckles turning white as they gripped the glass. Suddenly Tony realized Freed was as tired, heartbroken, and angry as Tony.

"Mr. Freed...Nate, you are amazingly kind to say that to me and I can tell you honestly that I did love your daughter. The only regret I have to confess is that I never told her how I felt." Saying it out loud sent a shiver through Tony. He repeated it through a sob, "I never told her I loved her. How could I be such an ass?"

Freed spoke firmly in a manner that commanded Tony to look up. "Forget about all that. Lisa knew. She never doubted it from the first night you two were together. You can't agonize about not telling her in words. You told her in plenty of other ways."

Then, more quietly, but still staring into Tony's eyes, he said, "Besides, let me assure you, I told Lisa I loved her nearly every day for twenty-six years, and it doesn't help ease the pain one bit." Suddenly Freed threw his glass into the fireplace hearth where it shattered. Tony jerked in surprise but stayed in his seat.

The two men stared at each other, both looking red-eyed and defeated. Tony knew he had to get to the point before he broke down altogether and lost his courage. Freed started to speak, "Well, that was rather embarrassing..."

"Thank you again, sir, for sharing. I have to tell you, I wish with all my heart that I was here to reminisce about Lisa," Tony sensed he now had Freed's undivided attention. "Sadly, in a way, I guess I am here to talk about politics."

"Well, don't be mysterious about it, Tony. I think you know me well enough to know I like to hear it straight. What's this about?" He leaned back in his chair and gripped the arms.

"Yes sir," Tony took a big swig of soda and set the bottle on the glass table in front of him. Looking directly into Freed's eyes, he said, "I came to tell you a story." Freed's eyes narrowed and looked hard at Tony, who quickly said, "It's a story I believe to be true and have some evidence to prove but, perhaps, don't have the courage to write."

"And what's this story about?"

"Well, sir, it's about Lisa. I think I know what happened to her."

"You *think* you know?" Freed sat up straight and leaned forward in the chair.

"Yes sir. I don't have all the evidence to prove what I'm about to tell you, but I have enough to be confident in my own mind regarding what happened. If you'll hear me out, I'm guessing you'll agree with me. But I want to warn you, you're not going to like where this leads."

"Tony," Freed said, "I do want to hear everything. I think you may be the only person who understands just how much I want to know what happened to my baby. But before you continue, do you mind if I ask why you're telling me? I know you have friends in law enforcement. If you know something they don't, shouldn't you be talking to them?"

"Actually, sir, I'm not sure who my friends are anymore, and I'm talking to you for three reasons. First, I'm not sure who I can trust; secondly, I know how much Lisa loved you, so I can only guess at how much you must have loved her; and third, I need your advice."

Freed closed his eyes and spoke carefully. "Okay. You talk and I'll listen. And then I'll do whatever I can for you."

So Tony talked. He started at the beginning with his concerns about the trial, his deep-seated belief in the innocence of Ralph Wells, and his role in discovering the truth. Freed, of course, knew all of this but, despite his desperate desire to get to the heart of the matter, he allowed Tony to continue.

"It's fun to be right, I'll grant you that," Tony said, shaking his head. "God help me, I felt like a hero when I wrote the story about Wells' rightful release from prison and exposing the 'true' evil-doers. But despite that, I knew something still wasn't right."

Freed finally broke his silence. "Like what, Tony?"

"There were lots of things," Tony felt his face redden. "I know that sounds silly but think about it. Wells went free, which is what I believed was right from the beginning. And Rod Nelson was shamed into what I'm willing to bet will be political Siberia for the next twenty years, which should have made me ecstatic because I saw firsthand what an egocentric ass he was. But something still wasn't right and as I thought about it, I remembered what Lisa had told me."

"Lisa…?"

"Yes. When I was trying to sort out the truth about the double homicide from the beginning, Lisa always told me to look for the person who benefitted. She would say, 'Find the person who gains the most and that's your prime suspect.' Sounds simple enough, but who gained from these murders? Wells does jail time he doesn't deserve, Denny Peters is dead, and Nelson is washed up. Therefore, no suspect. I found myself smiling at her naivety.

"I wanted so much to be able to hold her and laugh and say, 'Silly girl. In this case the only person who benefited was your friend, the governor.' And then it hit me." Tony paused as Freed leaned forward, taut, and unblinking. "Dear God in Heaven it suddenly was clear what had happened."

"Are you saying the governor, our Governor Roskins, was somehow involved in this? I'm sorry, Tony, but you've lost me."

Tony wasn't surprised. He *was* surprised at how unconvincing Lisa's father sounded. This just added another brick to the wall as Nathan Freed's tone made it obvious that he, who knew the governor so well, had no trouble believing the governor *could* be involved. Freed's face got red and his hands began an almost imperceptible quiver. Tony could see Freed knew the governor capable of exactly what Tony was about to describe.

"For the sake of getting to the point, sir, let me skip the details about evidence I have and simply tell you what happened. I know it sounds outrageous, but hear me out. It started two years ago. Governor Roskins learned Rod Nelson was going to make a run for governor. He and his political hacks decided somehow that Nelson, as a popular attorney general, was a real threat and they resolved to end his political ambitions. The best way to do that was to give Nelson enough rope to hang himself. So, the governor needed Nelson to make a colossal public mistake, and the best way to ensure that was to hand him a sensational criminal trial that he was certain to get wrong."

"So," Freed spoke in a whisper, as though he couldn't get enough air into his lungs, "the governor has two innocent people killed, frames an innocent man for the crime, waits for Nelson to pounce, which he had every right to assume he would, and then exposes the bungle, shaming Nelson right before the election."

"Bingo," Tony said, sounding far more somber than the word implied. Very quietly, he added, "And of course the governor didn't expose it directly. With the help of the DCI, I did. Which means if you buy my theory, I have to accept that I've been manipulated throughout this mess. The same probably is true of others, although one of the problems I have is that the written description of this horrendous crime, which I have on a thumb drive in my pocket right now, doesn't make it clear who's on the governor's payroll and who is an innocent dupe like me."

"Such as Rich Davis, you mean," Freed said.

"Exactly," Tony said. "It was Rich Davis who called me to the

Wells arrest scene, which made sure I saw Wells' face when he was arrested, which is what planted the original seed of doubt in my mind. It was Rich Davis who called me to the scene of Peters' suicide…to make sure I made a huge and immediate story out of the fact Wells was likely innocent. Then, last night, it was Rich Davis parked outside my house, watching me, he said, on orders from his boss."

"Well, Tony, I have no facts to help you sort out the demon-versus-dupe issue. I hardly know Davis. But the little I know about him tells me he's a good man. I'd be surprised if he's involved beyond taking orders."

"I desperately want to agree with you, but the worst part is, I told Rich yesterday that I was going to take a bike ride down to the river this morning."

"Uh, sorry, Tony. You've lost me again."

"This morning when I rode out onto the bike bridge across the river, someone took a shot at me from the woods. My brains would be splattered all over the bridge railing if I hadn't bent down to grab my coffee."

Freed looked stunned.

Tony continued, "I've never been so scared, or so lucky. But worst of all, I can't get around the fact Rich was the only person who could have set that up. Well, Rich or his partner, I suppose; but they're both DCI. Now you understand why I need advice on how to proceed."

"I don't know what to say to that, Tony, except that I'm glad you're okay. And I still find it hard to believe Rich Davis or another DCI agent would arrange for the cold-blooded murder of anyone, let alone a friend. Is it possible it was a stray bullet from a hunter or some sick stranger trying to scare the cyclist on the bridge?"

"Anything is possible, I suppose. But it seems far more likely, in light of everything else that's happened, that this was a legitimate attempt on my life. Jesus, what a mess."

Freed sat quietly for a few moments. "I'm sorry to sound so self-serving, but I still want to hear how Lisa fits into this nightmare. And I want to understand if Peters did indeed kill the Ennis couple in the first place."

"Yes, I'm pretty sure about that. It looks like Lyle McCabe cooked up this whole scheme. The plan he outlined for the governor is in the document I mentioned that's on the thumb drive in my pocket. McCabe and the governor apparently had used Peters for years to do various dirty jobs as needed. McCabe suggested him as someone they could hire to kill two people. They knew Peters to be someone who wouldn't give it a second thought. I'm guessing the original crime all happened pretty much the way it was described in the suicide note except, of course, Peters didn't give a rip about Anne Ennis. He was just a hired gun."

Freed seemed content to listen, so Tony kept going, "In addition to using Wells' gun and jacket, Peters used money supplied by McCabe to bribe Francie Wells to testify against her brother. Based on what I observed in Viscount...oh, you may not know I saw Peters and Francie together in the bar there. Anyway, I'm guessing Peters kept some kind of relationship going with her, either to ensure her silence or keep an eye on her, or both. The young girl waking up and seeing the man in the jacket was also part of the plan. If the girls hadn't awakened on their own, Peters was instructed to make sure he did something to wake them up."

"So then," Freed said, "when they wanted to expose the Wells conviction as a, quote, 'travesty,' they had to reveal Peters as the real killer. That meant they had to kill him too and make it look like a suicide so they wouldn't have to worry about him telling the truth about the original crime."

"Once again, sir, you've nailed it. Believe it or not, all of that was planned in advance. They just failed to mention that last part to their hired hit man."

"And Lisa?" Freed's voice suddenly dropped to a near whisper.

"Well, Lisa clearly wasn't part of the original plan, because it's not spelled out anywhere. I can only speculate, but once I found out Lisa was the source of this document..." Tony patted his pocket, "it all suddenly made sense."

"Tell me what you mean when you say Lisa was the source." Freed stood up and walked to the windows which covered one entire wall of the cathedral-ceilinged great room. He stared out into the dark as Tony shifted his position on the couch and continued.

"Molly Parks gave me this flash drive right after she showed me its contents late this afternoon. She said the file, which spells out in detail what the governor and McCabe were planning to do, was in a folder on her computer desktop. Molly said she didn't put it there. She believes Lisa found the file while working at party headquarters and copied the file to Molly's machine.

"Probably that was the same night...the night Lisa died. You'll recall Lisa had been working at the party headquarters as a volunteer. She called me at the *Crier* wanting to talk. She was very upset. She wanted to meet. She even talked in riddles as if she was worried someone was listening. She was frightened...Despite all that, I didn't go to her right away. I took care of my needs first. I was late. I didn't know..." Suddenly Tony was crying and Freed was standing by his side.

"Tony." His voice was firm, even as his hands shook more obviously. "This was not your fault. Now that you're learning the whole truth it should be more obvious than ever that you did not kill Lisa. If you had shown up immediately, they just would have waited and killed her later, or maybe would have killed you both."

"In any case," Tony stuttered through his tears, "I have to

believe she found this incredibly damning document while working that night and fled from the offices in a panic. McCabe was there. It would have been an easy thing for him to know or suspect what had happened and to call in the hired gun."

It looked as though Freed might speak, but Tony held up his hand, "Sorry, but one more thing. As I was desperately trying to revive Lisa that night at Harvey's farm...guess who arrived first at the scene? Yes sir, Deputy Sheriff Denny Peters. I never thought about it at the time, but obviously he was nearby because he had just left there. He had been at the scene just moments before where...where he had just forced her to sit in her car while the exhaust fumes killed her. No one knows this, but we have found the tubing that Peters used to gas Lisa in her car." More tears flowed and Tony nearly wailed, "I actually saw his car headed the other way on the gravel as I arrived there."

Tony saw the anguish on Freed's face and quickly said, "I'm so sorry. I didn't need to share that. I didn't come here to hurt you further."

"No. I want to know everything."

"Well then," Tony took a deep breath, "know this. I'm speculating, but I have to believe McCabe would have made sure he had the governor's approval before doing something so drastic. He knew about the governor's relationship with you and Lisa, so he would have felt compelled to get permission to..." Tony couldn't bring himself to say it again.

Freed turned from the windows and stared at Tony, then suddenly strode back to the bar. Sounding like he was trying to put up a brave front, he said, "Well, Tony, you're right. You've put all the pieces together and it makes perfect sense. Now we need to figure out what to do next. I need another drink, and I think it's time you let me put something stronger in that soda you're drinking."

Quickly, Freed was back with a bottle of Scotch in his hand. As he came up beside Tony, the bottle suddenly jerked forward and Tony's head exploded in pain. He fell onto the glass table and rolled onto the floor as everything went black.

Chapter 27

Tony's consciousness crept out of a very dark place. He slowly opened his eyes. It was still dark. He blinked to make sure his eyes were open. It was pitch black. It was cold. The pain in his head was excruciating. He instinctively reached up to rub it...and realized he couldn't. As his consciousness grew so did his panic. He was on his side, in a fetal position. He tried to move. No. Something was...Suddenly he was wide awake and, just as suddenly, he was in more pain than he realized a person could feel. His head throbbed, but so did his legs and his shoulder and...

He tried to move again. *Shit!* His ribs. It hurt to breathe. When he did, the smell was not pleasant. Oil? Charcoal? No... rubber. He could smell rubber, like when he had changed the blown tire on his SUV. He continued to squirm and take stock of all his senses, and then it was obvious. He was in the trunk of a car. A car that wasn't moving. There was no road noise; no sound of an engine; no sound of any kind, in fact, except Tony's labored breathing through his nose. His mouth was sealed. Duct tape? Probably. His hands were secured behind his back and...Tony grunted...yes. His feet were pulled back and affixed to whatever was secured around his hands. Rope? Wire? He didn't think it was either.

As Tony struggled against the bindings, he fought to control the fear that threatened to consume him. He hadn't ever considered himself claustrophobic, but he desperately needed to get out. As he pulled, the pain increased and he was forced to stop. Breathing heavily through his nose, he forced himself to lie still. *Think. Think!*

How in the hell had he gotten here?

He had been with Lisa's dad and...and then what? He had passed out? No, Nathan Freed had hit him with something. *I think he bashed my head with the bottle,* Tony thought. *Why would he do that? We had been talking about...*

Oh no, the thoughts continued to churn. Is it possible Mr. Freed was in on this? Tony refused to believe that. But then why? Tony thought about Freed's anger and grief, his shaking hands and red face. Another thought occurred to Tony, a terrible, frightening thought. Tony had been cold-cocked because Lisa's dad had made up his mind to do something about what he had learned. Even as he formed the thought in his mind, Tony became convinced that was exactly what was happening. Now Tony had to stop him. Nathan Freed was no match for cold-blooded killers, and even if he was, any success he had would just result in another life destroyed by these asses. He must stop him.

He squirmed again and the pain in his head and his shoulder and his ribs screamed at him.

First things first, Tony thought, as he fought to ignore the pain. *I have to get out of here.*

Tony knew he was most likely in the trunk of the Cadillac. Freed owned three vehicles that Tony knew about, plus Lisa's Mustang which Freed had not been able to bring himself to sell. This trunk was too big to be the Mustang or the BMW convertible, which Tony always had assumed was Freed's classy response to a middle age crisis. He obviously wasn't in the Lincoln Navigator SUV, so this must be the Cadillac. Tony felt a spark of hope. He knew about Cadillacs. Tony's dad had owned a couple of Cadillacs when Tony and Rita were young, wanting a big comfortable family car. *Bless you, Dad,* Tony thought, *for teaching me about Cadillac trunks and their emergency release handles.*

With any luck, Freed didn't know about it or had forgotten about it when he shut Tony in the trunk. Tony prayed Freed hadn't somehow disabled it.

Tony forced himself to ignore the pain as he twisted around to get his hands closer to the rear of the trunk where the small, T-shaped handle protruded. Sweating and cursing, he raised his back up and pushed it, and therefore his hands, into the cramped space. *Ow, ow... there!* He grasped the handle and allowed himself to roll forward, face down on the floor of the trunk. His forward movement pulled the handle and the lid popped open. Cold air rushed in as a small light in the lid came on. Probably all of four watts, it still blinded Tony until his eyes adjusted. It didn't matter all that much. He still couldn't see anything except a better-illuminated car trunk.

With the trunk open, however, Tony was able to wrangle himself up onto his knees and look out. The Cadillac was in a small paved parking lot. At the end of the row of vehicles was a big brick building that appeared to be a multi-stall garage. Behind the garage and across the parking lot were many large, old trees surrounded by well-manicured grass and the occasional flowerbed.

Everything he saw spoke of pride and attention to detail. *Okay,* Tony thought. *Freed has driven me to the estate of one of his rich friends.* Tony couldn't think of anyone in Orney, or near Orney for that matter, who had an estate as large as this appeared to be. He needed to see more, and once again gritted his teeth through the pain as he twisted around and succeeded in getting his body facing in the opposite direction.

As he did, there it was. Terrace Hill. He was sitting in the parking lot on the grounds of the Iowa Governor's Mansion. As cold and sore as he was, he was still taken aback by the sight of the giant old house, lit from the outside, sitting atop the hill in front of him. Nearly instantly, however, the pain in his head, side, shoulder, and wrists dragged him back to the problem at hand. He had to get free, and he had to get inside that house before Nathan Freed did something he would regret forever.

He could see his bindings now and realized it all was duct tape. His wrists, ankles, and mouth had all been taped and then something...it appeared to be an ordinary leather belt...was threaded through the gaps in his arms and legs, to pull his wrists and ankles together. It made sense that Freed would have bound him quickly with whatever he could find close at hand. Tony was pretty sure this hadn't been planned in advance. Freed couldn't have known what Tony was going to tell him when he showed up at the front door.

Tony knew the multiple wraps of tape would be too strong to pull free, but he also knew duct tape was designed to tear across the grain. He just had to find something with an edge sharp enough. Of course Cadillacs' trunks are well designed and insulated, so this proved fruitless at first. Tony debated trying to kick through the back seat into the passenger compartment, but worried it would take too long and he would get stuck trying to squirm through or, if he made it, would find himself stuck in the back seat which was far more plush than the trunk. He thought about the tail light assemblies, but they were recessed too far into the corners.

He first tried the trunk latch itself. The lower part of the latch, affixed to the main body of the car, wasn't much more than a

U-shaped piece of rounded steel. Tony turned and leaned back to it, but between its round shape and the grease from the latch, Tony was unable to get any purchase. The tape slid off. Tony tried more than a dozen more times. Realizing he had made no progress, he gave up.

Drooping his head and breathing hard, Tony looked at the floor of the trunk and got another idea. He hooked the heel of his right shoe on one of the side braces of the trunk and pulled off his shoe. He then allowed himself to flop back down to the fetal position – *my God that hurts* – and pushed himself as far into the front of the trunk as possible. He then curled his toes around the carpet at the open end of the trunk and squirmed around ninety degrees, peeling back the heavy material as he turned. The carpet pulled free and fell back into place twice, but on the third try, Tony succeeded in getting enough of it turned back that it stayed, as he rolled over it onto the bare floor of the trunk.

Just as he remembered, the surface under the carpet was a false floor covering the spare tire. Holding the false floor in place was a single recessed bolt – the same bolt and hand-sized wing nut that held the tire in place. The end of the bolt didn't protrude very far above the nut. It was designed, of course, to make sure it didn't. But when Tony rolled onto his back with his hands under him, he was just able to get the tape to catch on the end of the bolt. Rocking back and forth, he could hear, and then feel, the tape tear away bit by bit. Five minutes later, his hands were free. One minute after that he was completely free and standing beside the car rubbing his wrists and ankles, and pulling on his shoe.

***

Tony checked the pocket where he always kept his phone. Of course, Freed was smart enough to remove his cell. So, what to do?

It seemed to Tony he had three options, and in considering those options it occurred to him he had to be very careful. Standing where he was, he was an intruder on the grounds of the Governor's Mansion in the middle of the night. If he wasn't smart, he could trade the trunk of the car for a hospital bed, or worse, the stainless-steel table at the morgue. The state troopers and security personnel who guarded the governor took their jobs very seriously.

So, option one: start screaming or smash a car window and wait for the guards to respond to the alarm. Option two: run down the driveway to the guard shack at the street and ask for help. Option three: go the rest of the way up the hill to the house, quietly and carefully, and try to understand what's going on before raising any hell.

Tony contemplated the fact the governor was clearly the bad guy in all of this. Considering he had at least one deputy sheriff on his payroll as an assassin, it wasn't too much of a stretch to worry that the guards at Terrace Hill might be the governor's hand-picked henchmen as well. Tony also considered that, whether good guys or bad guys, the guards might arrest him, hurt him, or shoot him first and ask questions later.

So, it's option three, Tony thought, and slowly began limping up the hill, moving from tree to tree as he skulked through the cold, wet grass.

***

Ben Smalley looked up from his desk and saw a tall, slender man striding across the newsroom in his direction. Looks like a cop, he thought, and then realized it was Tony's friend from the DCI. He didn't know him personally, but had read about him plenty of times and had seen pictures.

Ben held out his hand. "Ben Smalley. It's Rich, isn't it?"

"Yes sir," Davis replied with a quick shake of Ben's hand. "I'm looking for Tony. Do you know where he is?"

"No, I don't," Ben answered truthfully, noticing how tense the agent looked and the urgency in his voice. "Is there some sort of problem?"

"I hope not but I have to confess I'm getting nervous."

Ben raised an eyebrow but remained quiet.

"Has Tony told you about what he calls his 'wild-ass idea' regarding the murders we've seen over the past two years?"

"I'm sorry, Agent Davis, but you must know I'm not at liberty to discuss what information one of my reporters may or may not have."

"Please, call me Rich. And please understand I'm only here for Tony's benefit. He shared with me his suspicions about the political conspiracy behind the murders and even the possibility of the governor's involvement. I thought he was completely insane at first, but the more I thought about it, the more I began to wonder if it was possible. So, I went to see my boss, Director Vandergaard, to discuss it."

Ben moved discreetly around Davis to pull closed the door to his fishbowl office and then moved back around to his desk. "Please sit down...Rich."

"I'm sorry, Mr. Smalley, but I need to go off the record here." Ben didn't reply except to tell Davis to call him Ben.

Davis continued, "To my complete surprise, Vandergaard didn't think Tony was crazy. He actually described his own curiosity regarding the governor's unusual interest in the events in Orney. He said from the first report of the double homicide, the governor had been hovering in the background, wanting to know everything about the investigation. The governor had demanded personal 'Eyes Only' reports and had even made suggestions along the way for Vandergaard to carry back to his agents. Then, the governor himself had ordered the surveillance on Tony and had insisted on knowing everything Tony told me."

Davis went on to say that when he heard this, he realized Tony may have been right in his suspicions. "I hate the thought of this. The possibility the governor of Iowa could even contemplate something as horrendous as this is beyond the imagination, but I can't ignore the possibility. So, after meeting with my boss, I called Tony to tell him what I'd heard and warn him to watch his back in case the governor or his people got wind of the fact we were looking at him."

"And..." Ben prompted.

"And my calls went to voice mail. Now I've tried to call him six or eight times and have been to his house. I didn't find him there but his Explorer is sitting in the driveway. He had talked about taking a bike ride today, but surely he would have been back from that hours ago. So, I decided to stop here to see what you know."

Ben smiled grimly, deciding it was time to share what little he knew. "Well, I know one thing. Tony's bike is in the back of my pickup truck, or at least that's where Tony threw it when he left here this morning. He said he would come right back, but obviously he didn't. So, trust me, I'm more worried about him than you are."

Ben then shared everything with Davis: Tony's arrival on his bike, his condition, the phone message he received, his unusual use of the "bat phone," and his quick departure.

"I don't suppose you have any idea how to reach this Molly Parks?" Davis asked. Ben confirmed he didn't with a shake of his head. Davis then launched into full agent mode. He got a description of Ben's old truck and called it in to the state patrol dispatcher, asking for distribution of an all-points bulletin. He then called the local police and asked them to send a couple of detectives to Tony's house, to see if they could find any clues as to where he might have gone.

Ben said he would go to Willie's and some of Tony's other

regular spots to see if anyone had seen him. Davis thanked him and said he was going to visit the only other person he could think of who might have a clue about Tony's whereabouts. He headed out the door to pay a visit to Nate Freed.

***

It was dark, but Rich Davis immediately spotted the Chevy pickup parked in the illuminated circle driveway just short of Freed's front door. However, when he rang the bell, he got no answer. He waited and pushed the button again, followed by loud raps on the door. Nothing. Davis then called the phone number. He could hear the phone ringing inside the house, but no one answered. He peeked through the narrow windows beside the door but couldn't see much, so he walked around the back. He barely noticed the large swimming pool and deck or the well-manicured lawn as he sought a decent view into the house. He did notice the rose bushes that poked at him as he pushed up next to the huge windows that reached from floor to ceiling of the great room. Pressing his nose to the glass, Davis could see inside. It was a beautiful room with a fireplace, comfortable furniture, and a wet bar. The lights over the bar were on and the room appeared to be empty. Davis almost moved on when his eye caught sight of a crystal stoppered whiskey decanter lying on its side on the floor near the couch.

Probable cause? Perhaps not, but Davis made up his mind it was all he needed tonight. He strode over to the deck doors and smashed in the glass with the butt of his service revolver. He checked the house quickly, turning on lights as he went, and confirmed it was empty. Then he examined the decanter of whiskey and the corner of the nearby coffee table. Dried blood was evident on both. He took out his cell once more, calling for local police to secure the house and calling for a state crime scene van to be dispatched.

"Okay, Tony and Mr. Freed, where are you?" Davis headed for the garage and immediately saw the empty stall. The phone came out again. "Dispatch, this is Agent Davis once again, DCI number 02-47345. I need you to run the name Nathan Freed of Orney through the state license database and tell me what vehicles he owns." Less than a minute later, Davis knew that Freed owned three cars and a 24-foot sailboat. Two of the cars were sitting in front of him but the third, a large late-model Cadillac, was missing.

"Dispatch, it appears the Cadillac is missing. Please contact GM Onstar and request a GPS location on that car. Yes," Davis said, trying to keep a measure of calm in his voice, "I'll wait."

When the dispatcher returned to the phone, Davis listened intently and then felt the blood drain from his face. Freed and Tony were missing and Freed's car was parked at Terrace Hill, the Iowa governor's mansion in Des Moines.

He ended the call and then moaned, "Dear God, Tony. What have you gotten yourself into?"

***

When Tony reached the top of the hill on the grounds of the mansion, he saw he was facing the business entrance to the building. It was at ground level and on the west side, facing away from the streets that bordered the grounds on two sides. Most likely designed originally as a servant's entrance, this now was the entrance used for the daily routines at the mansion. The grand front entrance was reserved for official receptions and events, and the family used the entrance at the back which had a staircase and elevator directly to the living quarters on the second floor.

The business entrance had been modernized to be disabled-accessible and had a metal detector and security booth discreetly built into a small structure at the side of the house. Tony peeked out from behind the nearest tree, expecting to see a guard in the booth. He did not. He strained to hear any sounds. It was as quiet as a tomb except for the occasional car passing by on Grand Avenue at the bottom of the hill. Tony took a deep breath and walked up to the door.

When he reached the guard booth, he looked inside, expecting to see the guard sitting on a stool sipping coffee or perhaps even asleep on the job. What he saw was a uniformed man crumpled in the corner with a bruise on the side of his head and duct tape wrapped around his arms, legs, and mouth.

It was obvious to Tony that he was right. Nathan Freed had come to Terrace Hill to confront the governor or, God forbid, had come here to kill him.

Tony stepped into the guard's booth just long enough to check the man's pulse and then stepped out again. The pulse was strong, and Tony didn't want to get caught there and be accused of having done this. So, ironically, to avoid a charge of assault, Tony quickly stepped through the door into the house, making himself guilty of illegal entry and, because it was *this* house, probably a host of other crimes.

Tony stepped through a small reception area and into an anteroom with waiting room furniture. He was so frightened he almost forgot how much he hurt and in how many places. Moving as quietly as he could, he passed through and entered the hallway beyond. Clearly a recent renovation, the hallway was lined with a series of offices on each side. At the end was a pair of large wooden doors. Tony put his ear to the doors, heard nothing, and pulled open the one on the right.

He stepped into a large, formal office in what appeared to be the former parlor or sitting room of the mansion. This clearly wasn't a working office. The governor undoubtedly used it for meetings with dignitaries, other elected officials, and business leaders. There was a small ornate desk on the left, bay windows on the right, and a large fireplace at the back of the room. Between the desk and the fireplace on the left wall was another door, so Tony kept going.

His exploration of the first floor took twenty minutes and gave him nothing but growing bewilderment. *Where is everybody?* he wondered. *Surely they have a surveillance system in here. Someone must have seen me by now.*

"Right this way, Mr. Harrington."

Tony nearly jumped out of his shoes. He spun around and began to say, "Holy crap, you..." He stopped when he saw a beast of a man standing five feet behind him in the dark. Illuminated only by the glow of a couple of computer screens in nearby offices, Tony could still see the man stood at least six feet, four inches tall. He had a big fleshy face and closely cropped hair. He wore a dark suit with a less dark turtleneck under the coat. Of more interest to Tony was what the man held in his right hand, a large chrome-plated handgun. It looked like a cannon.

"I...I...can explain," Tony said, his heart sinking at the thought of being arrested.

"Don't bother," the man said in a deep, booming voice. "Just come with me. And please do something stupid." Tony wondered if he had heard him right until the man continued, "I would love to blow your damn head off. I hate reporters. So please, give me an excuse."

Tony then knew what people meant when they used the expression "his blood ran cold." Tony felt like his veins had turned to ice.

He went through the doorway the beast indicated and followed the hallway to the end.

"Through the door and down the stairs," the man said.

As Tony descended a long, dimly lit staircase into the basement, it occurred to him he was in very serious trouble. Option one or two might have been the better choice.

The basement didn't look like a 150-year-old basement. At some point in the past, it obviously had been excavated and converted to business uses. It had high ceilings, office cubicles, and even a flat screen TV on one wall. Unlike the first floor and stairway, it was well-lit by florescent ceiling fixtures. At the back of the room was a wall with a wide glass window and a door with an electronic security lock. The man motioned toward a cubicle off to the side. "Sit."

Tony sat.

The man punched in a code, pulled a card from his shirt pocket and slid it through a card reader, and the door swung open. Inside was the security station for the mansion. TV monitors glowed above two desk stations with small computers and some type of second keypad built into each desk. The wall to the right of the desks was filled with electronic gear of some type. *Radios?* Tony wondered, his mind racing to consider whether he could figure out how to use one to call for help.

The beast didn't allow him to loiter and consider the question. He gave Tony a shove toward the back and through one more doorway. There a short hallway provided access to two small rooms with beds. Obviously these were sleeping quarters for guards, and perhaps other staff, who might have reason to need to stay overnight. The first room was empty, but in the second, lying on the bed and handcuffed to the metal headboard, was Nathan Freed.

Lisa's dad looked like he was a hundred years old. His hair was in disarray, there was blood on his cheek and on the sheets, and his chin hung down to his chest.

"Nate?" Tony said, "Are you okay?"

At the sound of Tony's voice, Freed looked up, moaned, and then sagged even further. He tried to speak but simply gurgled as blood seeped out from between his lips.

"Dear God, what have you done?" Tony seethed. "What are you doing?"

From the corner of the room behind him, a familiar voice spoke.

"Welcome, Tony. I can't tell you how glad I am you're here."

Governor Harris Roskins took two steps forward as Tony turned to his voice. The governor was holding a Louisville Slugger baseball bat in his right hand. He smiled his famous wide smile and said, "I believe you know my good friend here, Mr. Nathan Freed. He came here tonight to kill me. He told me so himself. He brought a gun and everything. Show him, Taurus."

The beast pulled a second gun from his side suit pocket.

"Can you believe that? For all these years, I thought Nathan was a friend and a stand-up citizen, and it turns out he's a violent criminal. Well, you just never know, do you?" The governor laughed long and hard, and then continued.

"Well, Tony, we've been trying to get my good friend here to tell me how he learned all about my excellent, and may I say successful, campaign strategy. He has been reluctant...no, to be fair, I should say, he has been completely unwilling to tell us who told him. I was about to trade my bat for a more gruesome instrument of persuasion when Taurus here noticed you on the monitors.

"Would I be right in guessing you're the source of Mr. Freed's information, Tony?" The governor didn't wait for an answer. He suddenly swung the bat fiercely into Tony's mid-section. With a scream of pain, Tony crumpled to the floor.

Gasping for air and writhing on the floor, Tony heard Lisa's dad stir. "No, no," he pleaded. "Please stop." The words were slurred, but understandable enough.

Taurus grabbed the front of Tony's sweater, lifted him up in the air, and tossed him onto the foot of the bed like an oversized Raggedy Andy. Tony's head hit the wall and once again exploded in pain. He saw stars and began to sink down onto the mattress.

"No, you don't," the governor said, gesturing to Taurus, who grabbed Tony and sat him up straight. "We are running out of time here. It's nearly 3 a.m. I have very ambitious staff members, some of whom will start showing up for work shortly after six. You are going to tell me everything you know and who knows it. And you're going to tell me quickly so we can get you out of here."

"You mean so you can kill us too," Tony coughed out. Then, as the governor took a backswing with the bat, Tony said, "Wait, wait. That's not necessary. I'm happy to tell you what I know. Just put that thing down. Where do you want me to begin?"

The governor began asking questions, first about how Tony knew so much. Tony explained about Lisa stealing the file from the office, but left Molly out of the story completely. He also went into great detail about how he had detected inconsistencies and why he had suspicions about Wells' guilt and Peters' suicide. Tony was, in fact, trying to think of everything he could to keep talking, assuming that once he was done, he would be done forever. And worse, so would Lisa's dad.

Finally, the governor cut him off and got to the crux of the matter. "So now, Tony, tell me who you have told. Every name, every person who knows anything about this, and where every copy of that file is. If you hold back one single fact, Taurus is going to put an ice pick in my good friend Nathan's eye. And then he's going to start in on you. And trust me, Tony. I know you think Denny Peters was, shall we say, a ruthless murderer. Let me assure you, Denny was a kitten compared to Taurus."

The beast spoke, "If you don't believe the governor, perhaps I should mention I would have killed you already with a bullet through the brain as you sat on that river bridge...if you hadn't been so damn lucky."

Tony's fear was beginning to overwhelm him. Despite the pain, he was clear-headed enough to know the beast would not have shared this confession if he expected Tony or Nathan to leave Terrace Hill alive. Tony was shaking but tried to muster as much sincerity in his voice as possible as he said, "Governor Roskins, I swear to you. My only regret in all this is I failed to tell someone."

Roskins stepped closer, slapping the barrel of the bat into his left hand.

Tony held up his palms. "Wait, I know it seems unlikely, but let me explain to you how it happened. When I found the file, which Lisa had left on the PC at my house, I copied it onto a flash drive and decided to go see Mr. Freed. I thought he had a right to hear first and directly from me what had happened. I assumed I would go from his home to the newspaper and then to the police, but he knocked me out cold before I could do anything."

Freed began weeping openly but Tony continued. "I woke up in the trunk of his car in your parking lot. You can check that by the way. The tape he bound me with is still out there next to the car."

"Well, that explains how you got past the gate tonight, I have to admit," Roskins said. "But if you don't mind, I think I will check it out." He nodded at Taurus, who handed the governor the extra gun and headed out the door. "Make it quick," Roskins called after him, and then, to Tony, "So let's have it, the copy you put on the thumb drive."

Tony stretched his legs out enough to get at the pocket of his slacks. He reached deep into the pocket, and it was empty. *Oh no,* he thought.

Roskins knew he had come up empty. "Mr. Harrington, please

don't make me do this," he said, swinging the gun to the right and pointing it at Freed's forehead.

"Just wait! I had it. Maybe it fell out in the trunk."

Then Lisa's dad spoke. "Gluff bochs," he said.

"What?" Roskins and Tony asked in unison.

"Gluff bochs," Freed said.

"Well, well," Roskins smiled. "I believe he's telling us it's in his glove box. How convenient. Since Taurus already is outside, I think we'll just all go out and join him, what do you say?" Roskins chuckled, dropped the bat to the floor, shifted the revolver to his other hand, and pulled a key from his right pocket. He tossed the key to Tony, telling him to uncuff his good friend. Once the two prisoners were standing, the governor gestured for them to lead the way out the door.

Tony's mind was working overtime, trying to think of a way to escape before they were back in Taurus' clutches. There was no doubt in Tony's mind how this all had to end, from the governor's perspective. Unfortunately, no brilliant James Bondian escape plan came to mind. The governor stayed back far enough that trying to wrestle the gun away from him was not an option. Tony had zero confidence in his ability to do that anyway, especially in his current condition. And while Tony might be able to take off running, Lisa's dad was in no shape to move beyond a slow shuffle. Tony couldn't just abandon him. So like sheep to the slaughter, they quietly mounted the stairs and plodded down the hall, through the anteroom, and out the side door.

Freed was first and as he went through the door, he seemed to stumble and fall, disappearing from sight. Tony rushed forward to see if he was okay. As soon as he cleared the doorway, he was yanked forcefully to the side by a pair of large hands attached to long, burly arms. Roskins' angry voice called out from behind them, "Stop, wait!

What..."

As the governor bounded through the door, another pair of arms reaching out from the guard booth grabbed him, shoved something black and oblong up against his throat, and shot 20,000 volts of electricity through his body.

Roskins dropped like a rock, the gun clattering to the brick walkway. A smiling Rich Davis stepped out of the shadows and kicked the gun out of reach.

"Harris Roskins," Davis said, "It is my duty to inform you that you are under arrest on charges of conspiring to commit murder, accessory to murder, false imprisonment, and assault. You have the right to remain silent. You have the right..."

As Davis finished reading the governor his Miranda rights, Tony recovered from his astonishment and realized all of his questions would have to wait. He then made a sweeping scan of the grounds, looking for Lisa's dad. He spotted him with two EMTs in front of the mansion. An ambulance was parked in the circle drive. Nathan Freed was being helped onto a stretcher near the ambulance doors. Despite his pain, Tony moved fast and was at Freed's side in an instant. Before he could utter a sound, Freed reached out and grabbed his arm. The grip was firm.

"I'm fine, Tony. Those SOBs hurt me, but it's nothing that won't heal. Really. I'm okay. I tried to make it look worse than it was, thinking they would go a little easier on me if they were worried about me passing out or dying."

Tony once again marveled at the man's intellect.

Freed continued, "I've asked these nice young people to take me to Mercy downtown. I probably don't need it, but why not get a little tender loving care after a night like this? You can visit me there later."

Freed squeezed Tony's arm even tighter and leaned forward as he said, "I'm so sorry I hit you so hard. And I'm sorry I locked you in the trunk. I'm sorry for all of this. I just couldn't *not* do something. This pathetic bastard killed my baby. I was determined to get him and I knew you would try to stop me. Once you were unconscious I realized I had to take you with me or I risked you waking up and getting to the police first." Tears rolled from Freed's eyes as he once again said he was sorry. "I was selfish. I so desperately wanted Roskins, I just became blind to everything else. I still can't believe I hurt you like that. I didn't know I was capable..."

A part of Tony's mind wanted to scream at him. *You could have killed me!* But it was a lesser part, and Tony had no trouble pushing it into the background. Out loud he said, "Stop it, Mr...Nate. Don't say a word. You didn't do a thing. Not to me, not to that guard in the shack, and not to the governor. I don't even know what you're talking about. You must be delirious from your ordeal."

"Fair enough," Freed smiled, letting his head fall back on the stretcher's pillow and releasing Tony's arm. "But let's be clear about the guard. I actually didn't do anything to him."

Tony's face showed his real surprise as he leaned closer and whispered, "So just what did happen?"

"I found him like that when I walked up to the mansion. My best guess is the governor had Taurus put the guard out of commission after learning I was coming up to the house. When I first arrived at the entrance gate on the street, I had no choice but to tell the guard there I was here to see the governor. That guard recognized me from my previous visits, so he called the house and then waved me through. I was hoping the governor would think it a social call or a bit of campaign business, but obviously he quickly realized I was here about Lisa. When I walked through the door with a gun in my hand, it took Taurus all of three seconds to disarm me. Not my finest hour..."

"I would say you have a lot to be proud of," Tony said sincerely. "It took a lot of courage to walk into the devil's lair and confront him. And if you hadn't, we would still be sitting in a room in Orney trying to figure out how to convince people the governor of Iowa is a murdering bastard."

"Perhaps," Freed said quietly as the EMTs' pain killers allowed him to slip away into the bliss of grogginess.

Tony smiled, nodded, and limped back up to the house as fast as his battered frame would take him. In the distance, Roskins was standing next to a state trooper's cruiser about to be taken away. Taurus was already locked in the car behind it.

Davis came up beside Tony, nudging him in the side. "Ow!"

"Here," Davis said.

Tony looked down and saw Davis had both hands held out to him. In one was a gun and in the other a smart phone.

"What's this?"

"The gun is Freed's I think. I'm taking it out of here discreetly. I wanted you to know so you can back me up in whatever you tell these guys. As far as you know, Freed had never a gun and just came here to talk to the governor. I don't want to lose my job, or worse, because I tried to keep Lisa's dad from having to face felony charges."

"That won't be a problem, since I really don't know anything, assuming you exclude the governor's ranting and the fact you just showed that thing to me."

Davis smiled and slipped the revolver into his suit coat pocket. Tony added quietly, "You're a good man, Agent Davis."

"The second," Davis continued, "is a smart phone...my smart phone. However, at the moment, you may want to think of it as a high definition camera with the ability to email photos to say, um-m-m, a newspaper editor? I assume you and Ben will want pictures of this. I can't let you use the DCI camera in my trunk, but you're welcome to use my personal phone until you get yours back."

"Thank you, Rich, really. But tell me, how in the hell did you guys end up here?"

"Later," Davis said as he handed over the phone and headed back to lead the team of agents and troopers swarming over the mansion's grounds. Tony smiled broadly, ignoring his pain. He limped back to the center of the action and began snapping pictures.

Chapter 28

It was the biggest story ever to come out of the State of Iowa, and Tony was right in the middle of it. He and Ben divided up the coverage to avoid Tony writing about himself. Later, Ben said, Tony could write a first-person piece about the experience. The *Crier* carried multiple stories the next day, telling the full story of the crimes with additional articles on Lisa's death, the details of the events at Terrace Hill, and the potential political ramifications of the entire affair. Tony or Ben or both also authored at least one article every day for weeks afterward as the governor of the state worked his way through the criminal justice system. Seven articles in all, which originated at the *Crier*, made the national AP wire service.

In addition to covering the story, Tony was enough a part of it that he almost immediately began getting requests for interviews. To competitors like the *Des Moines Register*, Tony was polite but brief in his comments. On the other hand, when *Rolling Stone Magazine* called, Tony agreed to a lengthy interview with the young woman assigned to the story. He didn't particularly like being the focus of so much attention, but he knew it would help the *Crier*, and that would help Ben, and so he said yes to as much of it as he could stand.

When the *Today* show called, however, Tony begged off, suggesting Rich Davis was the hero of the story and they really should invite him to be a guest.

***

Davis was indeed the hero. When they finally had a chance to talk, Tony was all over him about how he happened to be there, ready to rescue Tony and Freed as they came out of the mansion.

Davis explained how he had gone looking for Tony and how he had found him. He admitted that without Tony's "wild-ass idea" firmly in his head, it would never have occurred to him to approach Terrace Hill from the perspective that the governor and others in the mansion might be the criminals rather than the victims. However, because he did, he had immediately called the DCI's SWAT team after learning Freed's car was at the governor's mansion.

"I wasn't sure what was happening, but I knew it couldn't be good," Davis explained. "And because the governor was involved, good or bad, no one questioned the necessity of calling in the pros. I told SWAT to get set up around the mansion and wait for me." Davis then had driven to Des Moines with lights and siren going full bore. Traveling at nearly a hundred miles per hour, he arrived in time to participate in the takedown.

Tony asked, "How could you be sure enough about the governor's guilt to use the stun gun on him?"

To which Davis replied with a wry smile, "Despite my deep respect for the local press, I wasn't *really* sure until I saw Nathan Freed come out that door. He obviously had just been through hell. And then when the governor emerged from the door carrying a handgun, I didn't hesitate for an instant. You don't get second chances when the perp has his finger on a trigger."

"Well, God bless you, Rich Davis. I am so sorry I ever doubted you," Tony said, meaning every word.

***

The election, of course, was a circus. Iowans were now faced with choosing a disgraced prosecutor or a governor in jail without bail on charges of multiple felonies. Nearly everyone wanted to postpone the election, but no one knew how to do it. The Election Commission said it didn't have the authority. The attorney general was reluctant to take action without specific authority, fearing whatever he did would be challenged later in court because of his obvious conflict of interest.

Both houses of the Legislature and the leaders of both major political parties agreed they wanted to meet. It was perhaps the first time in a century they all had agreed on anything, but only the governor had the authority to call them into session outside of the statutory legislative session, which ran from January to April.

The governor's party petitioned the Iowa Supreme Court asking it to delay the election, which now was just five days away. The Court took just ninety minutes to rule. There was nothing in the constitution nor statute nor case law on which to base a stay, so the election would proceed as planned.

W. Rodney Nelson won, but by a narrow margin. This left a lot of Iowans shaking their heads and provided a lot of late-night talk show hosts with great comedic material. Nelson was in for a rough four years, as he became known as the man who almost lost to a murderer.

Tony's favorite part of the entire story occurred on January 2, when the Legislature rushed to convene the new session. The House voted impeachment seventeen minutes after the opening prayer was concluded. The Senate voted to convict and remove Roskins from office less than three hours later. All this, despite the fact the inauguration of the new governor was just ten days away. Every elected official in Iowa wanted to be on the record as having voted Roskins out of office.

The action created an unintended consequence that also made national news. Iowa had its second female governor. Upon Roskins' removal from office, Lt. Governor Cindy Francois took the oath, swearing to uphold the constitution and serve the people of Iowa to the best of her ability...for 240 hours. No formal inaugural ball was held.

Chapter 29

Tony was once again sitting in Willie's, watching the kids in the park. It was another sunny, warm morning in June, and he and Doug were having giant sweet rolls and coffee before heading back to the courthouse.

"Okay 'Mr. Hotshot I've been in *Rolling Stone*'," Doug began, as Tony rolled his eyes at the now tired reference. "What's your prediction today? Will Judge Schroeder cut him any slack because of who he is?"

Doug was referencing the fact that Harry Roskins was going to be sentenced in District Court that morning for the five felonies for which he had been convicted the previous month. Tony and all the players – Molly, Davis, Freed, and even Ben – had been called to testify for the prosecution. Roskins had hired a team of first-rate Boston attorneys, including two he had known since law school, but he had no real defense. On the kidnapping charge, Roskins had tried to claim self-defense saying Freed had showed up at Terrace Hill unexpectedly, and then when the governor agreed to see him, had pulled a gun on him. However, crime scene investigators said no unexplained gun was found, and no one was willing to corroborate the former governor's story.

The stake through his heart came when Lyle McCabe testified against his former boss. It had taken the jury more than two hours to reach its verdicts, but Tony assumed that was just because there were so many counts to work through.

Taking a sip of Willie's homemade root beer, Tony looked at Doug over the rim of the glass. "I think just the opposite," he said. "You know a judge sees case after case where some kid who never had anything falls in with a bad crowd and grows up to become a criminal. The judge frequently has to send people to prison who never had a fair shot at a decent life. But here," Tony paused to take another bite of roll, "here is a guy who literally had everything. He had a great education, money, influence, and the love and support of more than half the people in Iowa. Despite all that, he chose a path of unconscionable evil. He directly caused the deaths of four people, three of whom were completely innocent young people, just beginning what should have been full lives.

"I think if Iowa had the death penalty, Schroeder would fry his ass...four times," Tony declared.

Town Crier

Roskins Sentenced to 150 Years

Former Iowa Governor Ordered to Serve Five Consecutive Sentences for "Heinous" Crimes

Ben Smalley, Editor, and **Tony Harrington**, Staff Writer

ORNEY, Iowa – Calling the defendant a "disgrace to his office," District Court Judge Arnold Schroeder sentenced former Iowa Governor Harris "Harry" Roskins to five consecutive 30-year terms in prison for his roles in the murders of four people and the kidnapping and assault of a fifth.

Roskins was present in the courtroom as the sentence was pronounced. He was unshaven and appeared to have lost a great deal of weight since his arrest last October. He made no comments during the sentencing procedure.

At its conclusion, state troopers escorted the former governor from the courtroom and immediately transported him to the State Penitentiary at Fort Madison.

Speaking for Roskins in the sentencing hearing was a single member of the legal team that had represented Roskins at trial. Adamson Delacourt pleaded with the judge for leniency, citing Roskins' age and lack of any prior criminal history.

Judge Schroeder had a four-word reply before issuing the sentence. "Don't make me laugh," the judge said.

Roskins' arrest and conviction ended a long legal and political career in which he...

***

The following Sunday, Nathan Freed invited everyone touched by the incidents of the past two years to his home for a barbecue. It was a long list. In addition to the people from Orney, he included Tony's parents. They brought Molly, who had become like a member of the family when she had stayed with them in Chicago waiting until they all knew it was safe to return. Other guests included members of the DCI and Iowa State Patrol who had helped with the rescue at Terrace Hill.

The steaks, fried potatoes, steamed vegetables, and homemade ice cream were wonderful. Many people left by early evening, but as the sun set, Tony, Ben, Molly, Doug, and Freed still were sitting on the patio. As the air cooled, Freed re-kindled the fire in the barbeque pit. Everyone pulled their chairs closer to enjoy the warmth of the flames. They tried to avoid talking about the cases, as it seemed they'd talked of nothing else for an eternity. But somehow the conversation kept coming back to what had happened, or what might have happened if...

One of the big "ifs" was the governor's attempt, while in jail awaiting trial, to pardon himself. He had written the document in long hand with a pencil and a piece of ordinary lined notebook paper provided by the county. When handed to the guard and passed up the chain of command, it had caused quite a stir. The county had refused to honor it and left the governor right where he was. The following day, Roskins' legal team arrived back in Orney and petitioned the District Court to release their client. The county prosecutor filed a brief in opposition and the three documents promptly landed on Judge Schroeder's desk. The judge was no fool. He declined to rule and sent the question to the Iowa Supreme Court.

Once again, the High Court responded in record time. The very next day the court issued a unanimous ruling stating that the Iowa Constitution "was not written with the intent to allow a person legally charged with multiple felonies to escape prosecution by using the power of the pardon for himself." The court denied the defense attorneys' petition for release and declared the pardon null and void. A large part of Iowa breathed a sigh of relief, no one louder or longer than Tony and the others who now were assembled for the Sunday barbecue.

They had a brief but lively debate about Lyle McCabe. He had taken a plea bargain and leniency in exchange for his testimony. As a result, he had received one 20-year sentence. If he behaved himself in prison, he could be free again in less than ten years. Tony hated the thought of that, but others thought it was good they all didn't have to go through another trial.

Taurus' fate was even simpler but was debated by the group nonetheless. Taurus, whose real name was Thomas Monroe, had already been on probation for two felony convictions. The fact he had been involved in a crime in which he was carrying a deadly weapon put him on the express lane back to prison, no passing "Go." The debate came when Tony was asked if he would press charges against Monroe for taking a shot at him while on the river bridge. Tony had thought about it but, in the end, decided he would not. Doug pushed him, saying it wasn't right to let someone get away with attempted murder. However, Tony's reasoning was simple.

"First," he said, ticking the answers off on his fingers, "it's my word against his. Beyond his claim to me, there's no evidence I know of that he had anything to do with it. Secondly, he's in prison for a long time anyway, so I wouldn't be doing society any particular good. Thirdly, and most importantly, I don't want to waste one more minute of my life thinking about that creep. Governor Roskins and his band of thugs have taken all from me that I'm going to allow them to take."

In the manner of a true reporter, Doug posed the final question. "So, any loose ends? Any other articles to write before we move on to covering the scandal brewing in the local quilting bee?"

"Well," Tony responded, "I never did get Ralph Wells to give me an interview. I guess I can understand his desire to put this all behind him, but I sure would like to have heard this story from his perspective."

"I think we can live without it," Ben said, taking a sip of his beer. "Three Iowa Press Awards, a Pulitzer Prize, and the highest readership in the paper's history should be enough to satisfy all of us for a while." He hoisted his beer. "Here's to Tony, the reporter of the year... perhaps of the decade."

Tony tried to protest but was drowned out by a round of "Hear, hear," followed by the sound of glasses and bottles clinking.

As 11 p.m. neared, Tony decided he too needed to call it a night. As he stood, he heard Nathan Freed get up from his chair and say, "Tony, hang on. One more thing."

Curious, Tony turned and saw Freed was headed for the house. He followed.

"What's up?" Tony asked. "Need help with cleaning up?"

"No," Freed laughed out loud. "I haven't done any of my own cleaning in a very long time. Don't you know they have services that do that for you?"

Tony smiled as Freed continued, "No, I want to give you this."

Tony looked down as Freed pulled a key ring from his pocket. Tony knew immediately what he was holding, the keys to Lisa's Mustang.

He took a step back as if repelled by some hidden force field. "I couldn't..."

"Oh yes, Tony," Freed said firmly, stepping forward and

pressing the keys into Tony's hand. "You can and you will. I've known for a while that this is what I want to do. If it makes you feel better, I hate driving it. Of course I can't bring myself to sell it. So what better home could it have than with the man she loved? Just promise me you'll take good care of it, and the title will be delivered to your office tomorrow."

"Mr. Freed... Nate, you know I will treasure this as much as you." Tony paused. "I don't know what else to say."

"Don't say anything," Freed smiled. "I noticed you've been drinking that damn diet soda all day, so you're in perfect shape to drive her home. Sleep well, my friend."

"Wait," Tony said suddenly. "I do know what to say. I have something for you as well."

Freed's brow wrinkled and his head shook. "You don't need to give me anything," he said, holding up a hand in protest.

"Yes, I do," Tony smiled. "It's just this. The article you asked me to write about Lisa...it will be in the 'My Turn' column of Tuesday's paper."

"Oh Tony, thank you." Tears welled in Freed's eyes.

"Don't thank me until you read it," Tony said honestly. "It was much easier to write than I dreamed possible, but I am still praying every minute that I've done her justice."

Freed didn't respond verbally, but reached out and pulled Tony to him in a tight, tearful embrace. Then he turned and was gone.

Now it really was time to go, so Tony did just that. He backed the Mustang out of Freed's garage and drove it home, taking a slightly out-of-the-way route miles through the river valley and a couple of neighboring towns. It was a beautiful night, so he only cried a little.

***

Tony climbed into bed at 1:45 a.m. He was more exhausted than he could ever remember being. Despite that, he could find some positive things to contemplate as he stretched out on his mattress. He knew he had done good work. He knew he had built lifelong relationships with people he loved. He knew he had played a role in putting a despicable excuse for a man in prison for the rest of his life. And as much as Lisa's death still weighed on him, he was learning to cope. He now believed he would be okay. Closing his eyes, he thought about how good it would feel to sleep late in the morning, then maybe take the Mustang for another spin before work. Or maybe just play some old tunes on the new piano, a Yamaha digital Clavinova, sitting in his living room. *Thank you, Dad, for the annual trust money,* Tony thought.

As he drifted toward sleep, the most positive thought he carried with him was that the nagging questions that had filled his nightmares for the past two years were gone. He finally could rest easy.

At 3 a.m. his cell phone rang...

Afterword

I have been privileged to personally know five Iowa governors. If you know anything about Iowa, this tells you I've been around a long time, because Iowans keep most governors in office for multiple terms. In nearly five decades leading up to 2018, Iowa had a total of just five governors: Robert Ray, Terry Branstad, Tom Vilsack, Chet Culver, and Kim Reynolds.

The fact I met these five elected officials says absolutely nothing about me. A lifelong Iowan who has talked with each governor in turn is nothing special. Iowa is the kind of state where, if you want to be active in public policy, you can get to know as many elected officials and policy leaders as you want, including the governor. Iowa also is the kind of state that elects good people to serve in the statehouse. These five governors were and are the kind of elected officials who want to engage with their constituents.

Years ago Governor Ray called me at home on a Saturday morning to say thank you. Whatever I had done for him was so trivial I can't even remember what it was, but I sure do remember getting the phone call. I'm certain, of course, I wasn't Governor Ray's only call that morning. He simply was the kind of person who wanted to be sure to thank everyone who pitched in to help, no matter how minor the effort.

Similarly, I remember Governor Culver inviting me to Terrace Hill on a Saturday morning to have coffee and discuss health care policy. Again, this was no credit to me. A mutual friend set it up and my position as a health care executive gave me some credibility on the topic. Nevertheless, it was a great privilege to have more than an hour with the state's elected leader. It also gave me a chance to see the inside of one of Iowa's most remarkable buildings. As an aside, the interior doesn't look much like I described it in this book, and I never saw the basement, which may be a dirt cellar for all I know.

The point of all this is that no one similar to Harris "Harry" Roskins ever has served as governor of Iowa.

On a related note, I want to emphasize that all of this book is a work of fiction. While the story was inspired by two different actual crimes I covered as a newspaper reporter many years ago, all of the characters and facts and places in this book are fiction. The only exceptions are some larger cities, a few Iowa landmarks such as Terrace Hill, the Raccoon River, and the numbers of a few high-ways. Even the Raccoon River is depicted as larger and in a slightly different locale than you will find it in real life.

As someone who loves Iowa and appreciates the opportunities I've had to know its governors, I found myself surprisingly reluctant to depict the chief executive as someone as purely evil as the char-acter in this book. Alas, that is where the story took me. All I can do is hope you enjoyed its telling.

– Joe LeValley

Acknowledgements

I want to gratefully acknowledge all of the wonderful people who played roles in the creation of this novel. High on this list are two published authors who read and shared their ideas and expertise with me. John Shors, the *New York Times* best-selling author of *Beneath a Marble Sky* and several other wonderful novels, read a manuscript and made extremely valuable suggestions. Similarly helpful comments were made by Dr. Ronald Weber, author of several very entertaining crime novels and former chair of the Graduate Program in Communication Arts at Notre Dame University. These men were very generous with their time and very encouraging to a first-time novelist.

Of course, any ability I have to tell a story clearly is the result of the help I received long ago from editors in the newspaper world. To them I owe everything, and not just in my newspaper career. Helping to hone my writing skills made possible my management career as well, and certainly was important in writing this novel. The two most important were leaders at the *Globe-Gazette* in Mason City, Iowa, when I was there: Editor Bill Brissee and City Editor Dick Sullivan. Sadly, both have since passed away. I thought of them often when constructing the newspaper articles and newsroom scenes in the book.

I also want to thank the leaders at Mercy Health Network in Iowa. Their tolerance and support of extra-curricular activities made it possible to undertake and complete projects such as this.

Dr. Anthony Paustian and also the wonderful people at Bookpress Publishing have my sincere gratitude. It has been wonderful to work with people who are so knowledgeable and supportive. Their interest in this book and encouragement to write a sequel are greatly appreciated.

I want to conclude by thanking my family. Not only did my loved ones tolerate my hours at the keyboard, avoiding household chores and other responsibilities, but some also played an active role in helping with the book. Daughter Beth's editing is especially appreciated, as she somehow found time to do it while studying journalism and business at Drake University and working two jobs.

There are others, of course. It's hard to know where to draw the line. I only can hope that everyone who has helped me, from my earliest teachers to college professors to the law enforcement officials who let me watch them work to the members of my family, knows that I am forever grateful. Completing this book has long been a dream, and you made it possible. Thank you.